The Girl in the Jitterbug Dress

Tam Francis

Plum Creek Publishing
Lockhart, Texas USA

THE GIRL IN THE JITTERBUG DRESS

Copyright © 2016 by Tam Francis

www.girlinthejitterbugdress.com

All rights reserved.

A Plum Creek Publishing Book
P.O. Box 29
Lockhart, TX 78644

ISBN-13: 978-0692662724
ISBN-10: 0692662723

Printed in the United States of America

1. She Walk Right In
(The Big Six)

The girl's red hair flamed like the tip of a freshly lit match, a whirl of blue, green, and black, fluttered around her bare legs. She spun clockwise, in old-timey shoes stamping out tiny rotations. Her thin partner sported a loose fitting button-down shirt. The fabric moved with his body. His elbow pointed up, as he expertly twirled her, switching hands not missing a beat. He brought his arm down and stepped side, side, and back. His black and white shoes tapped out the beat. He twirled her again and wrapped back to back. Her feet left the ground as she arced through the air braced by his strong horizontal back and landed effortlessly in front of him. They resumed their footwork, miraculous, like magic, or the closest thing to real magic June had ever seen.

June watched, envious. *I want to be the girl in the Jitterbug dress.*

The band behind them thumped loudly. The female bass player, an incarnation of a cat, drove the solid rhythm. The men were 1950s hot with sideburns, slicked back hair, plaid shirts, rolled up jeans, and black combs poking out of their back pockets.

What would my mom and dad think about me being in a bar, drinking a beer?

She was nearly eighteen but years away from the legal drinking age. They hadn't carded her, and Ed had bought the beers.

What the hell, I'm graduating a semester early — one foot in high school and the other in college. Not a complete goody, but she knew what she wanted. And right now, she wanted to dance like them. Desire burned through her, bright and new.

"Looks like fun don't ya think?" She leaned over to Ed.

"What? Dancing or playing in a band? I'd like to learn to play something. The bass looks cool."

"Dancing." She scowled. "I'm gonna talk to her."

"Really? You're gonna walk up to a stranger and say, teach me how to dance?" He smiled his pretty, sexy smile, and she thought again about kissing him.

"You could go talk to the guy. Look, they're taking a break."

"No thanks. But, I'll ask my friend Jay. I don't want to get up in front of everyone. I'm really not that outgoing, I'm the shy artist type, remember." He laughed. "Anyway, look. It was a short break. They're dancing again."

They danced. And danced. And danced. And drank a coke. And danced.

With each twirl and stomp, June's swing fever rose. The dancer girl finally headed to the ladies room. June stood.

"What're you gonna to do? Accost her in the bathroom?"

"Yup, that's exactly what I'm going to do."

June raced toward the ladies room. Her heart pounded. Anticipation curled in her stomach. She didn't know why she was so nervous. Then the memory of watching Fred Astaire and Ginger Rogers in old black and white movies with Julian almost stopped her. The pain was sharp and usually triggered an episode. She wouldn't let it. She'd learn how to dance for both of them.

June checked her hair and make-up while she waited for the dancer girl to come out of the stall. Her dark blonde curls were still bouncy and her dress flattering, but trendy and...un-inventive. *The dancer girl looks so...original. I'd like to have more originality.*

"Wow, I really like your skirt," June blurted when the dancer emerged. Some people got quiet when they were nervous. June got loud.

"Thanks. It's vintage from the 50s," the girl replied as if it

2

should mean something.

Should it?

The dancer washed her hands and then wiped her damp face with a clean paper towel, fluffing her hair in the self-conscious way women do when someone is watching. She smoothed her creased eye make-up, patting the crinkled skin, revealing age that wasn't noticeable on the dance floor. It didn't matter if the woman was older. June wanted to dance like her.

"Your dancing's incredible. How'd you learn to do that? You were so fun to watch."

"Thanks. I've been taking private lessons." June thought she detected a subtle air of condescension in the dancer's voice. "The guy who's teaching me and my boyfriend is starting a group class. You should check it out."

"Yeah. That sounds cool. Where?"

"Camelback and Third Street, in this little rundown strip mall. There's a small studio in the corner. Ballroom Dance Academy. Friday, 7 o'clock. Oh, by the way, I'm Nancy."

"Hi. I'm June. Thanks. I'll try to make it. Hope to see you there."

June skipped back to her seat, buoyed with expectation and promise. Would Ed go with her to the dance class if she asked? Would he be her Fred Astaire? She found their table empty, but spied him at the edge of the stage talking to one of the guys in the band. Nancy and her boyfriend slipped out the back door. *Had Nancy looked her way and smiled?* June wasn't sure, but she was still disappointed. The band wouldn't be nearly as interesting without the dancers.

June glanced at the other people who'd come for the band. Cat-girl sat in a booth with a group who looked like they were from the same clan as the band. But there were more men, a lot more men than women. The bar suddenly seemed tacky and stupid. The smell of cigarettes and stale beer made her sick. A prickle of sweat coated her palms. Her purse bounced nervously against the back of her legs as she walked over to Ed.

"Hey June, this is my friend Jay. He's the one who put us on the list."

"Thanks. Nice to meet you. You guys were..." June couldn't figure out the right word to use, "...cool."

"Cool," Jay replied. She wasn't sure if he was being cool or making fun of her.

"Hey, I'm gonna get some air. Okay?" She looked toward the door.

"Oh, you wanna go?" Ed replied.

"Yes, please."

Ed turned to his musician friend. "Well hey, we're gonna take off. It was good to see ya, man. You guys rocked. Thanks for the invite."

June nodded and smiled. The guys exchanged a look that equated to Jay approving. June was flattered, but also annoyed. It was a fine line between admiration and objectification, and she hadn't worked out where her line was yet. She wanted to be thought of as attractive, but didn't want to be objectified. *Can I have it both ways?*

They walked out into the balmy night and headed toward Ed's car.

"Did you ask Jay about the dancers?"

"Yeah, he said they've been to a lot of their shows, lately. Nancy's been around the scene a little, but Jay's never seen the guy before."

"What scene are you talking about?"

"The car scene. The Rockabilly scene. The guys are really into recreating 50s hot rods, listening to Rockabilly, and hanging out at car shows." Ed shrugged, clearly not into it.

June mulled over the term Rockabilly. It was one she hadn't heard.

4

"Sooo, where do you wanna go? We could hang out at my place. I could show you some of the paintings I'm working on."

No way was she going to his apartment. "Maybe we could go for a walk? It's really nice here."

Imitation gaslights cast soft, yellow light through Scottsdale's faux western village, fading the night into an artist's palette. The overpriced Kachina dolls, t-shirts, and scorpions—preserved as paperweights—watched silently from behind their glass cages.

How do we get where we are?

If she hadn't opted for early graduation and taken the Art Appreciation at Glendale Community College, she wouldn't have met Ed and wouldn't be wondering if he was going to kiss her. And if she hadn't met Ed, she wouldn't have seen the amazing dancers. *Would dance have found me?*

"What are you thinking about?" Ed's hair fell across his forehead when he turned his head.

"Oh." She looked at him sideways. "About kissing you."

He flashed a smile, bent down, and put his lips on hers. She wove her fingers through his auburn hair. Her lips pressed back, parting. He wrapped his arms around her waist and pulled her closer, mashing her against him awkwardly, but sweetly. She closed her eyes and leaned in. Warm sensations washed over her. They kissed with increasing enthusiasm, their breathing accelerated. The world blurred and grew hazy along the edges. His hands and body groped for more.

She realized it was time to go.

The brown and tan strip-mall squatted in an ugly corner of Phoenix. Encroaching oleanders rimmed the lot, lending a secretive sway to the forgotten pocket of the city.

June's stomach fluttered and palms sweated. She cursed Ed for refusing her invite, then cursed herself for her fears. Tendrils of dread crept up her limbs. Her heart beat fast and irrational fears of heart attack or aneurysm took over her thoughts while a subtle disconnection permeated everything around her. She'd had the episodes since the accident, but had become adept at hiding them. With Grandma Gigi's death, she was all raw and remembrance.

She'd never told anyone about the panicky episodes. She didn't want her mom or dad to know she still remembered. They never talked about the accident, and her mom was still reeling from Grandma Gigi's death. June's deep breathing exercise wasn't working. Her brain continued to ooze out her ears, and spiders crawled through her veins.

I need a physical distraction. She stepped out her of truck and flopped the seat forward, re-organizing the miscellaneous items: tire jack, blanket, sweater, water jug, and jumper cables. The exertion helped her feel real and grounded. She gained on the panic and continued, pulling out car-clean wipes.

You're not crazy. You're not going to die. No one is going to die. She continued to scrub the steering wheel, dashboard, window casings, and door panels. *Calm down. You've always wanted to dance. You can do this.* Finally, the panicky sensations began to fade.

I will learn how to dance.

The door scraped and squeaked when she edged into the Ballroom Dance Academy. Mirrors lined the long narrow room. A cubicle wall—*Strictly Ballroom* poster thumbtacked to one side—was flanked by metal office chairs, creating a makeshift lobby. Sterile Fluorescent lights and acoustic ceiling panels topped off the disappointing aesthetics.

A compact, dark-haired man, who looked nothing like a ballroom dancer and nothing—much to her chagrin—like the guys in the band, was taking money and names. June hung back and contemplated leaving. She didn't see the red-haired dancer or a Rockabilly anywhere.

A cute guy, slicked hair and rolled jeans, scooted in behind her. The blood rushed to her face, and a new wave of sweat broke across her back. *This might not be so bad after all.* But then a pretty girl ran up to him and wrapped her arms around him.

"You made it." The girl lightly brushed his cheek with her crimson lips.

"Yeah." He ducked his head.

Envy burned through June, and tears threatened to undo her. She turned to leave, but the guy behind the desk looked up and spotted her. Too late. If she left now, she'd look like an even bigger idiot. She inhaled slowly, walked over, signed in, and waived her right to sue the studio should she injure herself while dancing.

Other girls had left their handbags, backpacks, and random pairs of shoes under the chairs. June did the same, tucking her purse into a corner between the desk and front window.

Students clumped in groups of three or four, self-segregating into ages and types. She wasn't sure what type she was or where she fit. She'd tried to be more original with her red A-line skirt and striped shirt and thought she looked dancerly when she left the house. Now she wasn't so sure.

With the exception of the cute couple, most of the guys seemed older, or nerdy—glasses, dorky polo shirt, pleated pants, pocket protector nerdy. She hated when she thought that way.

I'm sure they're all very nice guys, but this is not my vision of meeting my Fred.

"Hi. Hi. If I could have everyone's attention." The dark haired man moved to the center of the room. "Welcome to Ballroom Dance Academy. My name is Saul, and I'll be your instructor for tonight. And this is my assistant Janet. Okay, if I could have all the guys line up on this side of the room behind me, and all the girls on the other behind Janet."

June and the other students quickly shuffled into lines.

"We're going to teach you the Lindy Hop. Sometimes called Swing, sometimes called Jitterbug. This dance comes from the

1930s and is a direct descendent of the Charleston, the dance made famous by the flappers of the 20s. It's also rumored to have gotten its name when Charles Lindbergh hopped the Atlantic. This is how it looks."

Saul turned on music, and he and Janet demonstrated. They started opposite each other, changed places, and whirled in a continuous rotation, flying but with their feet on the floor.

June's heart lit up and a strong desire pulsed across her body. *I want to dance like that.* She continued to watch. Saul repeated the move, then scooped up Janet and tossed her over his arm into a back flip. Everyone applauded. Janet took a quick bow and scampered over to turn off the song.

"Now." Saul pulled at his dark eyebrow. "You're not going to learn all that tonight. In fact, it's going to take you several weeks before you feel comfortable doing the basic swing-out, but I wanted to show you how fun the Lindy Hop can be. So now, I'm going to show the leads their footwork, and Janet will show the follows theirs."

With her warm brown eyes and honey-wheat hair, the elfin Janet exuded happiness and youth. Her authority rose above her diminutive stature as she demonstrated the eight-count pattern. June had always been fairly coordinated, but when she tried the footwork she twisted and stepped in the wrong direction.

After several run-throughs, Saul drew the students' attention back. "Okay, now it's time to partner up. If you came with someone, you can start with them. If not introduce yourself. We'll be rotating. For those of you new to group classes, that means everyone will get to dance with everyone. All follows will rotate clockwise." He paused and smiled.

"Don't look so scared. The reason we do this is so you're not dependent on your partner. This also makes you a better lead and follow by being able to react to different styles."

June drifted toward a smiling Asian kid with glasses. He

looked her age, seventeen, maybe older.

"Hi, I'm June."

"I'm Andy. Have you done this before?"

"Nope. Virgin dancer."

"Me too." He blushed, and she didn't think he was just talking about dancing.

"Okay." Saul studied the room and continued barking. "Now, some important information about partner dancing. Lindy Hop is not a ballroom dance, but some ballroom skills apply. First, is body position. Leads take your partner's right hand in your left."

June wiped her damp hand on her skirt, placing it in Andy's. Uncomfortable moments ticked by. He beamed at her. She gave him a conservative smile, friendly, but not flirty.

"Now, I want you to take your basic steps: one, two, and freeze. Leads, firmly plant your right hand on the girl's shoulder blade. Follows, your left hand comes up to the lead's shoulder or bicep if he's really tall."

Andy's face stopped inches from June's with his hand on her back. Small beads of sweat stood out on his upper lip. She hadn't realized dancing would be so intimate. If she'd wanted, she could've leaned over and kissed him. Of course, she didn't want to.

Saul jabbered on about compression, tension, and balance. "Also, I know you're thinking about your feet," he added. "Try not to look at them."

What? Try not to look at my feet? Is he crazy?

"Okay, now continue with your first triple step, three AND four, trading places."

Andy and June struggled through the moves with stiff arms, robot legs, and no rhythm. One girl ended up on the floor, one couple let go completely, and the rest finished with varying degrees of success. She and Andy grinned at each other.

"We did okay," she said.

"Yeah. Good job. This is really your first time?"

"Yeah." She smiled again.

"Okay, not too bad," Saul said. "Let's back it up and try it again. I promise you this gets easier."

The rookie dancers continued the combo for an hour. True to Saul's word, they danced with everyone in the room. And truer to his word, it did get easier. But when June thought about her hands and body, she screwed up her feet. When she thought about her feet, she forgot her torso.

Janet ran around and lowered the lights for open dance, practice time. Several students filtered out, but Andy, the cute boy and his girlfriend, and other random students, stayed. June partnered with Andy and tried the Lindy footwork to music. Slow as the music was, it seemed impossibly fast for them.

Janet came over and adjusted June's arms and frame. She was grateful for the fix, but crushed. She thought she was getting it. It didn't feel like dancing, yet, but it did feel like something. June would do whatever it took until she mastered it.

Was it this hard for girls in the 40s?

2. Swinging on a Star
(Bing Crosby)

Violet's sewing machine droned as she labored over Mr. Miller's cuffs. Sunlight streamed through the large plate-glass windows warming her employer, Mrs. Peplinski, known affectionately as Mrs. Peppy. The old dressmaker's proud forehead and smooth cheeks contrasted the deep creases of her eyes and her stern puppet grin. Silver hair waved in matching arches of steel wool, gracefully pulled back into a French knot. Her keen gray eyes twinkled when she spoke, and her outdated clothing gave her a decidedly Victorian appearance.

Behind them, a curtain opened into the back room where they cut, measured, and fitted. Violet's eyes repeatedly flicked up to the clock, an audible sigh escaping with every look.

Mrs. Peppy frowned at her. The thick Polish accent strained Violet's ears.

"Violet, it's almost time to close up. Why don't you go home and get yourself ready for that dance tonight?" She shook her head and muttered, "By byc młodym znowu."

"What was that?"

"Eh, old Polish saying. To be so young again."

Violet blushed, embarrassed, but mostly nervous about the night's possibilities. She counted herself lucky to have found such a good job when she'd had to quit school to take care of her dad. It beat the factory, but wasn't what she'd pictured for herself. She loved to read and had received high marks, might've even gotten a scholarship. Still, it wasn't bad, and Mrs. Peppy always let her go early to meet friends at the malt shop.

She hung up Mr. Miller's suit coat and pants to finish tomorrow, but then remembered it was Saturday. They were closed on Sunday. Violet had spied Mrs. Peppy in the shop after Mass and her heart ached for the old dear.

The Peplinskis had come from the old country at the turn of the century and started their tailoring business, shop downstairs, apartment upstairs. They'd had no children, and Mr. Peplinski died early in the Spanish flu epidemic. Mrs. Peppy offered Violet her spare room, but Violet couldn't leave her Pop. Besides, Violet knew she could never replace Mr. Peplinski.

After last night's dance, Violet couldn't stop thinking about love, real love, different from the infatuations she'd had on boys from school. She wanted to believe in it. She wanted to believe in something, again. Whenever she thought about his hand in hers, his smile, that dance, she tingled all over.

She'd danced with dozens of boys at school, the malt shop, and dance halls, but never felt anything like dancing with the US Navy sailor. Love at first sight was silly. Preposterous. Ridiculous. She was a practical girl and didn't really believe in love. Besides, she'd only had one dance with him. One dance.

How could I tell that much about a fella from ONE dance?

At the end of the night, the band beat a swinging version of Chick Webb's, *Who ya Hunchin*. A man walked toward her, looking quite the man compared to the boys she'd been dancing with all night. His sailor jumper fitted tightly across his chest and arms, accentuating his toned body, dark hair, and smiling eyes.

She'd just finished dancing with Johnny O'Shea, his hand still on her back after walking her off the dance floor, when her eyes were caught by the sailor striding toward her. An involuntary shudder rolled through her body, and although Johnny was saying something, she couldn't hear a word of it.

Everything around her moved in slow motion, except the

steady progress of the beautiful man walking up to her, taking her hand, and asking her if he could have the next dance. Johnny's body went rigid as his hand slipped away. He mumbled a protest, but Violet was already gliding onto the dance floor with the mysterious sailor.

As soon as they leaned forward in unison, everything sped up again. The drumbeat sent hot rhythms coursing through her blood. He wasn't close, yet she felt a heat between them, and something else, a strange connection she'd never felt before. He kept his lead nice and tight. She gave herself over to his will.

She found herself whipping her head to catch his eye with every spin. They hit the music as if they'd choreographed their dance. She planted her foot, arms held behind, chest forward, and rubber-banded into a straight-legged Boogie-drop. Her bottom inches from the floor, but she knew there was no way he was going to drop her.

Somehow, I knew I could trust him.

She popped up for the turn. Her gabardine skirt wrapped around her thighs like a million fireflies alighting on her legs. She'd never noticed the sensation before, but noticed it then, in all its deliciousness. He kept the rhythm, sending her out into solid switches—he the center, she a rotating satellite. They reveled in a cocoon enveloped in the dance. Other people were in the room, but she focused mind, body, and soul on the man at the end of her arm and their joint connection to the music.

I'd never felt the Lindy like that before.

For a brief moment, their bodies would nearly touch when a hip and leg would connect, but it was too fast, barely time to register his muscled leg before twirling away again. But she did register it and wanted to be closer. She wanted to feel his leg pressed to hers.

He wrapped his arm around her forearm and pulled her across his body in an unusual pass-by. She liked it, smiled, and asked for it again. He grinned from ear to ear with devastatingly white perfect teeth. He gave it to her again, and she liked it even more the second time.

She became aware of his overheated body. His smell was soft and sweet, piney and fresh. His right leg expertly moved between hers, delicately pushing out, intricately guiding her into steps. Over and over he threw and caught. His hand firmly planted on her back. Safe.

I'd never felt so safe in my life.

His bicep tensed and released under her fingers as he led the moves. She breathed heavily. Another triple-step and his hand met hers, bodies pressed into a swirling, spinning, waltzy-turn, which she never, ever tired of.

I was Cinderella at the ball.

They transitioned into a dip. His arms cradled her body, her head tilted toward the floor. His face moved forward. His breath on her neck. Their eyes fluttered closed. She leaned in for the kiss.

The overhead lights flickered on. Violet's eyes shot open. He pulled back, and then a face with a wide lopsided grin loomed next to his. She blushed pink in the brightly lit hall. He righted her body and nodded to his friend. Lopsided Grin took a step back and stared at the ceiling.

"Thanks for the dance," the sailor said. "Best first dance I ever had. Are you going to be here tomorrow?"

She looked at him, unable to open her mouth. *The best first dance he'd ever had? The best dance I've ever had in my life. The best anything I've ever had in my life.*

"Um, my name's Charles. I didn't get a chance to introduce myself before. It was too loud, and then we were busy knockin' it out."

After several awkward moments, she realized it was her turn to speak.

"Hi. I'm Violet. Violet Woe."

His friend thumped him on the back of the arm. "Cheesy, we've gotta go. The transport's here, and everyone else is on the bus. Our liberty expires at midnight."

"So, will you save me a dance or two tomorrow night, Miss Woe?"

She'd nodded as he jogged out of the hall.

Violet tidied up her sewing machine, bumping Mr. Miller's unfinished suit, then scurried out of the shop to catch her bus.

Tonight, I am not the least bit depressed going back to my little one-bedroom apartment. I do hope Pop is out though. I don't want to see him tonight.

They'd been a normal family. Her pop was a handsome, Cary Grant look-alike, with a good job. All the girls' heads would turn when he and Mama came to school. But in two short years, his dark hair had streaked gray, and his clothes, once tailored to his muscular frame, now hung haphazardly. She loved him, but wasn't sure she could respect him anymore.

She was anxious to get home and confirm with Jeannie that the boys were still taking them to the dance tonight. She hated the fact that she—or any other girl—couldn't go unescorted.

I won't think about it. I'll think about smoky eyes, a white uniform, the smell of pine. The way he danced, never losing his hold. The way his body felt every time he brushed by.

Is he stationed here? How many times will he ask me to dance? What's his favorite ice cream flavor? What's his middle name? Does he like me or my dancing?

Lost in thought, she missed her stop and had to hoof it a mile home to the apartment she shared with her dad. It might've been nice when it was built in the 1920s, but the faded yellow paint and plaster trim had chipped and discolored over time. She ran up the pitted, interior steps of the two lowers, two walk-ups.

Her neighbor sat on his stoop, smoking a short butt, talking to his skinny mewing cats. She hated cats. She didn't really, but she didn't like his smelly, mangy ones. They left hair everywhere, and he never cleaned it.

She gave Smokey-Joe a curt nod and jiggled her doorknob. It was locked which meant Pop was out, both good and bad. Only one place he could be this time of day, but she was determined not to think about that either.

As she raced through the living room—her makeshift bedroom—she contemplated what dress would dazzle the sailor. Her dresses hung between Pop's rain slicker and wool overcoat. The dark blue rayon with the flounced skirt and rhinestone buttons might be just the ticket.

In the last year, she'd filled out and the fabric hugged her hips giving her an older, curvier look. At least she thought she looked older, and that's how she wanted to look for Charles. He had to be at least eighteen. They had to be eighteen to join up.

The phone rang, and she made a dash for it, sliding to a stop as she grabbed the receiver. The neighbor picked up the party line at the same time. The slow exhale of his smoky breath hissed in her ear.

"Hello. I got it. It's for me." It took a minute before the click and silence let her know she had the line to herself.

"Hiya Vee Vee," Jeannie gushed. Violet pulled the phone away from her ear.

Jeannie had her private names for people, and although Violet preferred Vi, Vee Vee from Jeannie was okay. She wouldn't have it any other way. Violet liked to pretend Jeannie was her sister, even though they looked nothing alike. Violet's dark hair and slim figure contrasted Jeannie's frizzy blonde and stocky frame.

Violet could barely say hello before Jeannie attacked her with questions. "I didn't think it was nice for me to ask about the jive bomber in front of Johnny. Seeing how he's been carrying a torch for you since the eighth grade, but he was murder. Tell me everything about him."

"There's really not much to tell." Violet sighed. "His name is Charles, and he's in the Navy."

"Obviously he's an anchor-clanker. Any chucklehead could see that. What did he sound like? What did he say? Does he have a dreamy voice? Was he a good dancer? Did he ask for your exchange?"

Violet suddenly panicked and felt deflated. He'd not asked for her telephone exchange. *What did that mean?* It meant she'd made too much out of one little dance with a sailor she'd probably never see again. She twirled the phone cord around her fingers.

"No, but he did ask if I was going to be there tonight and to save him a dance or two."

"Ooh yes. That's good. He's definitely interested. If the dance was crummy, well, he wouldn't have asked for more. Or asked if you'd be there tonight. Right? Not that you would ever give anyone a bad dance. You're simply a Ginger on the dance floor. I think we should take this as a good sign. Yes, a very good sign. Well what do you think? Will he be there tonight?"

Violet tried to answer, but Jeannie's mouth moved too fast.

"Ooh, this is going to be tricky with Johnny and Patrick. And don't you blow things for me with Paddy. I really like him, and he's Johnny's best friend."

"I know, I know, but if he's there, I have to dance with him. I have to dance with him as much as possible. I want to dance every dance with him. You can't imagine..." She trailed off, her mind drifted back to his intensity, the ferocity of his swing-out, the security she felt in his arms. *What would it be like to slow dance with him?* An involuntary shudder ran up her spine.

"What, what can't I imagine? Vee Vee, are you still there?"

"Yeah. It's just that...I've never danced with a fella I had such an instant connection with. It was so...different."

"Different how? Did he do some new fancy tricks? Did he try to flip you? That would be so rude of him, since he just met you and could drop you. Who do these fellas think they are? Coming in here from gosh knows where, trying to show up our boys and drop us on our heads."

"No, Listen. You've got it all wrong. He was a perfect gentleman. He did do a boogie-drop, but I didn't bounce my keister. I've never felt so...safe before. It was like I'd danced with him my whole life." She pictured his dimpled grin. "Does that sound crazy?"

"No, that sounds dreamy. You sound like Cinderella."

Violet laughed. "That's what I thought. I felt like Cinderella, like a dream. Maybe it was a dream. Maybe he won't even be there tonight, and he'll be a nice dream I had one night."

"Don't say that, Vee Vee. You've never been slack happy, and you haven't been this excited and happy since..." Jeannie let the end of her sentence hang in the air. "Um, so what are you wearing, anyway? Not one of your malt shop outfits. You couldn't. It'd be murder."

"Of course not. I was thinking of my navy blue. It actually fits a little better than the last time I wore it."

"Oooo, yes. You look older in that." Jeannie's voice smiled, but Violet detected an undercurrent of something else.

"Thanks. That's exactly how I wanna look."

"Well," Jeannie said with mock suffering. "I'll try to take both boys off your hands, but I intend to get a smooch from Paddy tonight. I'm just crazy about that boy, and he's going to be crazy about me. Only he doesn't know it yet."

Violet and Jeannie giggled.

"Seriously, Vi, how are you going to dance with your dream boat with Johnny trailing you?"

"I don't know."

June ~ 1990s
3. Meet me in Uptown
(Mighty Blue Kings)

June arrived early to Amy's apartment for movie night. Amy lounged comfortably, waiting for the rest of the swing gang to come over. Gang was the most apt description of the fast friends June had made at dance class. June jiggled her legs, unable to relax. Before she left school that day, she'd received a note from Mrs. Juarez, her high school counselor. Mrs. Juarez wanted to talk to June about a couple of her classes. Worries pre-occupied her thoughts.

That doesn't make any sense. I don't think I said or did anything. I was late to history the other day. Is it something to do with one of my college courses?

June wanted to talk to Amy about it, but Amy wasn't that kind of friend. Amy was her dance friend and not interested in her high school problems. At least, she didn't think Amy would be interested. She didn't want to remind Amy that she was still in high school. They talked about footwork, old movies, and swing music, but not their lives outside of dance.

They also talked a lot about fashion. June noticed Amy'd begun to reinvent herself into a swing-dancer girl, restyling her classic bob into 40s rolls, but keeping the pink streak down the side of her black hair.

June took another sip of the strong, bitter beer and made a face. "So, who's coming over tonight?"

"Most everyone from class. Do you think it's weird that I invited our teachers? Saul seems so much older than us. Do you think he's banging Janet?"

June didn't know or want to think about that kind of stuff. Her mind turned over what Mrs. Juarez's note meant. She couldn't get it out of her head. Mrs. Juarez had been instrumental in setting her up with the college classes and the dual credits she needed to graduate early. June needed a couple electives to round out her credits for her high school diploma, and Mrs. Juarez had suggested Art History/Art Appreciation, not offered at the high school, but the community college credit would apply toward her high school credits.

It'd been a good fit for June. None of the other high school electives were interesting to her. Plus, the college class was weighted more than a high school course and boosted her GPA.

June was grateful for all the help. She had a hard time fitting in with the high school kids and knew the early graduation was for her. She hated to leave her swing gang, but she was ready to start her adult life. *Please don't let anything stand in my way.*

"I said, do you think he's banging Janet?"

June snapped to attention. "I don't know. I don't think so. They seem all business. Tell me about these movies we're going to watch. Oh, wait, that reminds me, did you get the new Swing-out variation with the Kick-ball-change?" June jumped off the couch. *Moving was good. Action. Dance.* It would take her mind of the note.

"Sort of. It's screwing with my timing, though. I totally need to practice. I tried to get Chad to go over it with me, but he only wants to throw me around."

"You're so lucky."

"I know." They both giggled. "Come to the kitchen, and we'll work on it. The tile floor's easier to dance on."

"What are the movies, again?" June swiveled, triple-stepped, and practiced the new footwork.

"The first one is *Swing Kids*. It's about these German kids during WWII. They couldn't listen to and dance to American music, totally illegal, but the kids can't get enough swing. So, they go to these underground clubs and dance Jitterbug. The story's a little melodramatic, but the dancing and costumes are to die for. I've been getting lots of style ideas from it. Ooh, maybe we can steal some dance moves, too."

Amy stopped dancing and stirred a pitcher of perfumey cocktails. "The other one is *Swingers*. It's about these swing dancers in L.A. There's a huge sub-culture there, you know."

"Do you think we'll get through two movies?"

"Why not, and if we get bored, we can fast forward to the dancing bits. Oooo, that's the doorbell."

Amy sashayed to the door and greeted Andy. Molly and Jack, the young married couple, arrived next. They'd been together since their sophomore year in high school. June couldn't believe anyone actually married their high school sweetheart. They weren't even devout Christians or Mormons. June was convinced those guys got married young just so they could have biblically condoned sex.

Her own motivations for not being promiscuous were complicated. Besides the fact that she was waiting for her Fred Astaire and wanted to be hopelessly in love, the biggest factor was her panicky episodes and trust issues. If only she could erase the memories of her brother's accident. *Maybe if I could conquer dance, I could conquer the panic. But would the hole in my heart ever heal?*

"Hold this." Amy handed June a big bowl of popcorn.

"Got it." June took the bowl and squeezed in between her friends on the couch. The old-fashioned stove-popped popcorn was passed around, while Amy handed out cocktails and beers. June looked at the faces of her new friends and felt a pang of regret. She wished she could take them all to San Diego with her.

"Oh good, you're home." June's mother turned off the burner, setting down her spatula. "Your father just told me. He said you talked to Mrs. Juarez. What are you going to do?" June's mom drew her into a hug.

June burst into tears. "I don't know. I thought I was all set. One credit. One stinking credit. This can't be right. There's no time to take another class. Mrs. Juarez said the GCC class was a dual credit class. I could take it at the college, and it would count at the high school. The apartment. My cute little apartment. What about the deposit?" June's body shook with sobs.

"What about...my scholarship," she continued through her tears. "What will happen? Will the college hold it? They won't make me re-take the S.A.T. will they? Early graduation? Oh god, oh god, oh god. It's all falling apart." Her mom rubbed her back in small circles like she used to do when June was little and woke up from one of her nightmares. June let herself be a little girl again, pretending her mom could fix it all.

Finally, her cries subsided, and she came up for air, taking hitched breaths with shudders. "What am I going to do?"

"You'll take another class you need for your graduation credits, and we'll make sure it's approved."

"I thought this one was." June wiped her wet cheeks on her sleeve.

"I know. I did, too. It'll be okay. You can go a semester to the community college and stay at home another four months. It won't be so bad. Honestly honey, I wasn't ready for you to go." Her mom brushed her hair back and handed her a tissue.

"You know I love you, Mom. And Dad. And I know you're not ready for me to go, but I am. I worked hard for this. I've gotta fight this. It's their screw-up." She took a deep breath and poured herself a glass of water, dropping in two ice cubes. The cold water helped calm her down.

"This doesn't have anything to do with the swing dancing or anything? You didn't overlook something, did you?"

"No." June shook her head. "For the first time I feel like I really fit in. I've met some cool people who get me. Dancing takes me away from my worries. I need it."

Her mother gave her a care-worn smile, worry and love curled at the corners.

"Maybe you'd like to have your new friends over. I'd love to meet them."

"Maybe." June smiled a tight smile. "Speaking of friends..." She needed to get away and clear her head, come up with a plan. "There's a swing dance workshop in Pasadena tomorrow and Sunday. A whole bunch of the swing dancers are going, even the teachers. What do you think?"

June's mother folded her hands in fronts of her. "I think, um. I think under the circumstances, maybe you should skip this one. Do you need that added stress?"

"You don't understand. Dancing will help. It's what I need."

"I know you're growing up, but it's so hard to let you go." Her mother paused and gave her the motherly-look-of-love. "How long of a drive is it?"

"Five hours."

"Well...any of these kids do drugs? Drink? Smoke?"

June didn't want to lie, yet she didn't want her mother biased against her new friends. *If I want to be treated like an adult, I need to act like one.* "No, Mom, no one does drugs. There's one smoker, and everybody drinks."

"What about drinking and driving? You see any of them get behind the wheel that shouldn't? I'll have to run it by your father."

"Mom, it's not like that. Everyone's really responsible. Any alcohol consumed is danced out way before driving. I really need this weekend. Especially now."

Her mother took a deep breath, resignation in the sigh. June knew she'd won, but at what cost? She hated the worry on her mom's face.

"I want all the details. Where you're staying? Address to the workshop? Whose car you're in, make, model, and license number. And who's driving? You have to call me every morning." Her mother shook her head. "It's so hard for me to let you go."

"I know."

The old hall in Pasadena stretched into a long rectangle, a proscenium arch stage—replete with red velvet curtains— anchored the far end. People of all ages and types milled around in small groups. An elite handful of dancers, who looked like they stepped out an old movie, congregated in one corner. The guys wore stripy tees or wide-collared shirts, dress pants, with short slicked-back hair. The girls donned knee-length flowy skirts and sweater tops, their hair tied in satin pig-tails, held back by combs, or pulled into place with bright ribbon headbands. They all had an air of intimidating coolness. June couldn't take her eyes off them. It was just the distraction she needed.

"Hey, Amy, what's up with those guys?" The last few weeks Amy had begun to look more like them.

"They're dancers from LA. It's a huge subculture here. Don't you remember the movie *Swingers*? They totally live the lifestyle. I hear even their apartments are decked out in 40s and 50s." Amy smiled appreciatively, yearning in her eyes.

The lights flickered on and off, and a woman with an old-world, Italian face scampered to the front of the stage. All chattering quieted. People began to sit on the floor and grab the few chairs that lined the perimeter. June's swing gang pulled up some floor.

"Good morning dancers. I want to welcome you to the Frankie Manning Living Legend Workshop." Murmurs rippled around the room. June had heard Saul, their teacher, mention him, but hadn't realized how famous the old guy was.

"It is our great pleasure to bring you this presentation of old film footage and the man himself to narrate and answer your questions…Mr. Frankie Manning."

The hall shuddered with applause. The curtains parted. A big white screen loomed beside an old black man. A petite perky woman sat on one side, a vacant chair on the other. The speaker took the empty chair and mooned over Mr. Manning with obvious affection.

Grainy film clips flashed across the screen with dark figures dancing in a blur, distinct in style, but none more than the man who flew parallel to the floor, unique in his style of Lindy. June was mesmerized. *Could it really be the old guy sitting on stage?* She couldn't reconcile his youth and age. In the old footage, Frankie stretched long, fast, and lean. His swing-outs looked nothing like the ones she'd been taught. The basic footwork was there, but his style was incomparable, a comet streaking across the screen. Her heart ached. *Will I ever be able to dance like that?*

"I remember this one time…" Frankie drew them in with candid—sometimes painful—but mostly funny stories of dancing with Whitey's Lindy Hoppers. "…We were performing at a show with Ella Fitzgerald, and after the dance performance was over, Ella invited us to stay and sit in the audience and watch her sing. The management wouldn't give us a table because we were colored. Blacks could perform for the whites, but they couldn't sit together." A shadow crossed his face, but was gone in an instant. "Ella refused to sing unless her friends were allowed a nice table up front."

He told other stories about Hollywood and Harlem, traveling the world, and sharing the joy of dance. By the end of his presentation, Frankie had the entire room in love with him. He jumped to his feet with surprising agility. June tried to do the math in her head.

When did he say he was born? 1914? That would put him in his eighties. I so want to be him when I'm eighty.

"Okay now, I'm going to warm you up with a line dance we

used to do back in my day." He chuckled and gave the crowd a wide, sincere smile.

He wants to teach a line dance? June didn't want to learn a line dance even if it was from the 40s. If she wanted to learn a line dance she'd have gone country dancing, but everyone was on their feet, faces turned up to the grinning man on the stage.

"We're gonna learn the Shim Sham," Frankie invited. "This dance was originally the national anthem for tap dancers. It's a fun and easy way to learn classic jazz steps you can use in your Lindy Hop. Okay, here we go and a one and a..."

He popped his consonants when he talked with a subtle accent that hinted of Harlem. By the end of the hour, June loved the Shim Sham. Most dancers repeated the moves taught, but the Los Angeles kids switched up the footwork with different variations. Envy prickled June's confidence. *How long had they been dancing? How long had this swing thing been going on? How far do I want to go with it?*

Christmas lights twinkled around the dark perimeter. Dancers flaunted fancy attire and the hall magically transformed into a ballroom for the evening dance.

June's mall dress fit in okay. But, she wanted do more than fit in. She wanted to look like Amy and the L.A. dancers. She felt underwhelming and deflated in her department store dress. *Maybe I could pull my hair back with a ribbon like the vintage girls? Vintage, a new word to add to my vocabulary and my wardrobe.*

Her feet throbbed, but she was determined to try out the new footwork and venture outside her group. How to do it, though? How to ask a stranger to dance? *Hey, would you like to dance? Was that too casual? Would you like to dance with me? Was that better, be specific? Was there dance etiquette?* She didn't know the rules and her anxiety was rising.

She spotted Jake, a guy she'd practiced with in class. She

recognized his apple pie face and crooked smile, but he looked different in his dressy clothes, older and cuter. She noted how clothing could make a man more attractive. She'd have to get over her nerves of asking guys to dance, though. There were two girls for every one guy.

Was it like this for the girls in the 1940s?

While June gave herself a pep talk, Jake walked up and asked her to dance.

Thank god.

She recognized the new footwork and followed it, only kicking his shin once. He was sweet and patient and didn't make her feel stupid. He joked and steered her into another dance move. She relaxed and found herself feeling flirty and pretty, not thinking about her un-vintage dress.

Her skirt swished around her legs, tickling her thighs. She scooted past Jake, aware of his muscled body and warmed another degree, marveling at the new sensations. Before she could contemplate this, the room began to stutter like an invisible game of freeze tag. One by one, dancing couples stopped and formed a large circle. Much to her confusion, Jake dropped his lead and ushered her over to the inner ring, indicating they should sit.

In the center, a guy with jet slicked-back hair, a two-tone, pullover shirt, dark pants, and Ked-like tennis shoes led a tiny girl unlike anyone she'd seen before. Her arched eyebrows and bright red lips framed a dainty heart-shaped face. Her hair swooped up in barrel rolls. The hem of her dress fluttered around her seamed stocking legs, which June quickly realized were not seamed stocking but tattoos, drawn from heel to mid-thigh. The etched lines flashed every time he sent her into a series of spins.

Their dance was dynamic, yet controlled. It looked different than the clips that Frankie showed. Yet, it was all the same moves, only a little less jumpy. Smoother. Sexier? Her movements were undeniably sensual, the way her hips shook as she scooted around him, the way her legs were tighter and straighter than Whitey's Lindy Hoppers.

The guy looked totally cool, no hint of feminine. June thought debonair might be the right word. No, she thought again. He looks forbidden. Tattoos poked out his sleeves at his wrist. *Yeah, he looks like one of those guys your mother warned you about.*

Everyone had stopped dancing and either sat or stood in a big circle clapping, their faces bright, eyes glowing, living vicariously through the shining couple. June ached with desire to feel what the dancer was feeling.

June leaned over to Jake. "What's going on?"

"It's a swing jam."

"What's a swing jam?"

He cocked his head, amusement in his tone. "When some cats…" *Did he just call them cats?* "…are dancing some really cool steps that are out of sight and tight with the music, you stop, watch, and cheer them on. It's an old tradition going back to the 30s."

Everyone did seem to be in on it. The bandleader picked up on it and synced with the couple. The clarinetist took a solo and another couple entered the swing jam. They dropped their handhold and executed choreographed side-by-side footwork, rejoining to do rapid-fire swing-outs, one after another.

June could tell they were winding up for something and then BAM, the guy did the splits as the girl flipped over his head. She popped up, and towed him out of the circle. As they melted into the audience, another couple took the spotlight. The bandleader cued the drummer, his drumsticks thumped like pelting rain.

The new couple busted out the back Charleston, but with stylish variations. They echoed the drummer beat for beat. Then, in perfect rhythm her feet flew, flipping head over heels, not letting go of his hands, she landed and returned to the shadowed footwork. The crowd went wild.

The collective energy vibrated through everyone in the room. June was exhilarated, full of yearning. She wanted to dance like that. At the same time, she was completely intimidated, instantly sobered by the fact that she had a lot to learn.

Violet ~1940s
4. T'aint What You Do It's the Way that You Do It (Jimmie Lunceford)

Hot burning metal, melted hair, and setting tonic mixed with the faint smell of gas as the curling iron heated on the stove. Her electric one had disappeared with her mother. She painted crimson red lipstick across her lips with a tiny brush, imagining Charles's lips on hers. Her skin warmed a few degrees. *He probably won't even be there.* She sabotaged herself with doubt, but continued to get ready, anyway.

She rolled her stockings to the foot, slipped her toes in, and gently slid the silk over her bare legs. The hook slot of her garter gave her a little trouble, but she pushed the thick stocking top into place. The cool metal clips and silk stockings created curious, competing sensations she'd never noticed before. The dress hugged her hips, giving the effect she hoped for. Ankle-strap pumps completed the outfit.

She pulled her hair away from her face with combs, letting her curls bounce around her shoulders. No victory rolls or snoods tonight. She didn't want to look like an able-grable, but didn't want to look like a kid either. From outside, Johnny tooted his horn.

"Move your keister up there," Jeannie yelled through the opened French doors.

Violet said a quick prayer as her heels clicked down the stairs. *Please, please let him be there tonight and look for me at the dance.*

"Hi Doll." Johnny eyes popped and traveled from her hair to her toes and back up again.

It was a good sign, but she didn't want any more attention

from him. He hopped over the car door, raced around to the passenger side, and opened the door for her. Paddy and Jeannie snuggled in the back seat.

"Wow. You look, um, wow, Vi. What's with the duds?" Johnny asked.

"I thought I'd dress up a little tonight."

Jeannie gave Violet a wink, and Johnny caught her out of the corner of his eye.

"Oh, I get it. It's for that swabbie who took my last dance." He narrowed his eyes and scowled.

"It's your dance is it Johnny? Humph. I didn't realize I was indebted to you. Well, forget it. If you don't want to take me, I'll go back up and read a book. I just got a new one from the library. And it's a good one, a Pulitzer."

Violet pinched her eyebrows together and glared at Johnny, embarrassed by her own petulance, but unable to control her emotions. She'd only let Johnny kiss her once and told him it wasn't like that for her. But he didn't listen and then acted like the jealous boyfriend. Johnny didn't own her, not even close. She'd almost rather stay home. But she really wouldn't.

"Hey simmer down buckaroos," Jeanie said. "We're all friends going to a dance. Come on, Vee Vee, come out with us. You can read your stinky old, high-brow book some other night." She turned to Johnny. "Don't you guys want Vee Vee to come hit the jive? Look at her. She looks like a movie star."

"Yeah, Vi, come on," Paddy said. "I've got this killer-diller new step. I wanna see if you can hit it."

Jeannie giggled. "Yeah, I goofed it pretty good last night. Paddy sprung it on me, and I almost landed on my rusty-dusty."

"Hey," Paddy said with mock indignation. "I caught you in time."

They all laughed, and Johnny backed down. "Okay, okay, come on enchantress, but I'm still your escort, right?" Johnny's smile didn't quite reach his eyes.

Violet felt a twinge of guilt and worried she was using Johnny, but wasn't he using her until he found some other dish to moon over? She didn't know. Sometimes it was hard to see what was right.

Bright colors bent and whipped as they made their way across the crowded floor. The band hadn't begun, but the dance floor jumped with swinging limbs dancing to recorded tunes. They nabbed a spot by the French doors, a small breeze drafted across their perch. This early, smokers and guys trying to look tough filled the patio. *Does Charles smoke? Would it make him less attractive if he does?*

"I said, do you want a coke?" Johnny repeated.

"No coke, thanks. Lemonade, please." The fellas walked off to get the drinks.

"Do you see any squids?" Violet asked.

"No boys in white, but we're here early. Don't worry he'll show. They usually come in busloads." Jeannie laughed.

Violet wrung her hands and rubbed her temples.

"Snap out of it, Vee Vee. Here come the boys with our quenchers."

"They are sweet aren't they? I should just enjoy hitting the jive with them."

"A bird in the hand is worth two in the bush." Jeannie winked.

"Hey, guess who I saw?" Johnny handed Violet her lemonade. "Jane and Dick, and a couple other seniors from school are entering the dance contest. Did you hear about it?" He raised his eyebrows.

"Let's do it, Jeannie," Paddy said. "What do you say? See if I can land that new move?"

"I don't know, maybe. You know I can get a little klutzy

under pressure." Jeannie swirled the ice in her coke.

"So, um Vi, what do you say?" Johnny's asked. "Think we oughtta swing a wing?"

"I don't know. When are the semi-finals and the finals? I don't have a lot of free time to practice."

"Vee Vee, you could kill 'em with your eyes closed, what a buncha squares. You and Johnny burn up the leather out there."

Violet shot Jeannie a look. After dancing with Charles, she couldn't bring herself to get excited about dancing with Johnny or anyone else.

"These contests are full of floy floy, anyway." Jeannie took a quick sip of her drink and stood. "Let's go have some fun. The band's about to start."

"What are you doing in the powder room? Johnny's looking all over for you, and I've been busy with Paddy. Lucky for you, Sue and Ronald are here. Some clodhopper kicked Ronnie in the calf. It's pretty bad. He's icing it while Johnny takes Sue for a spin. But Johnny's keeping his eyes out for you."

"I'm tired of dancing with Johnny. I'm tired of dancing with everyone. I think I'll go home. I'm clobbered anyway. I'll catch a bus." Violet was almost in tears.

"Look sweetie, you gotta snap out of it. The dance contest is going start. If you hit the bricks now, the boys will insist on taking you home. And where does that leave me? Can't you hang in there a little longer? I hope to be squished up against Paddy to watch the contest."

"I'm sorry Jeannie. You're right. Enough laying eggs. There are other fish in the sea." Violet forced a smile. "See, I can make a joke."

"That's the spirit, kid. Let's go get 'em."

On the way out of the powder-room Violet was asked to dance by a pimply faced teen. She was so surprised by his request, she hadn't the time or wits to say No. He handled her roughly with clomping steps and crazy pretzel arms, turning her at odd angles. He twisted and bounced to music that must be have been in his head and not what everyone else was hearing.

She wisely let her arms go limp to prevent them from being pulled from their sockets. When the song mercifully ended, she muttered a quick thanks and ran the other direction. Right into Johnny. And after that disastrous dance, Johnny looked like a cool glass of water in a hot desert. It wasn't what she expected for the night, but halfway through the dance with Johnny, it hit her. I need to find the joy.

The music filled her up. She looked at Johnny's earnest face and opened her heart. Her preconceived expectations melted away. She found the joy of dance in his unique rhythm and delighted in the moment. By the end of the song, she was smiling and laughing with him, rethinking swinging a wing in the contest.

"Thanks for the swell dance." Violet grinned then leaned down to adjust her shoe.

"You're welcome how 'bout . . . " The laugh died on Johnny's lips and he froze.

Violet looked up. Her heart swelled, skipped three beats, and momentarily stopped.

"May I have the next dance, Miss Woe?" Charles asked.

She nodded, a thousand birds took flight in her stomach. Her body vibrated from the touch of his hands. They hit the dance floor, and his connection, form, and timing were perfect. He sent her out into rotating Switches with counter balance. She dug in and piked at the waist then kick-ball-chained, bomp-pa-domp, orbiting his body as he tapped out the rhythm. Her body hummed to his tune.

He led a swing-out and wound her up with her hand behind her back, helpless. She felt the heat between them. He smiled, gave a tug, and unwound her body. Her hand floated in air and landed back in his. She felt a zing. They rock-stepped into facing Charleston, mirroring each other's crosses and kicks. Her skin prickled with a light sweat. The song ended with a trumpet blast.

How could the song be over already?

Charles raised an eyebrow. "Woo-wee, you are cooking with helium, Miss Woe. Can I get you a refreshment or would you like some air?"

She eyed the patio. "I would love some fresh air, but I don't think we'll get any out there. Or do you smoke?"

"Me?" He chuckled. "Funny thing, no. Seems darn near everyone else in the Navy does. I reckon it's not good for your health. Plus it smells something awful. Wouldn't you agree, Miss Woe?"

"Yes. My father smokes, and our neighbor has the most disgusting yellow fingernails where he holds his cigarettes." She caught herself making an unattractive face and re-arranged her expression. "And please call me Violet or Vi. That's what my friends call me."

"So, we're friends then?"

He smiled, stuck out his hand, and shook hers. His hands were warm and strong, subtly damp, but not sticky. She didn't want to let go, but one more second, and she knew she'd look like a dope. She dropped her hand and smoothed down her dress. He guided her out the French doors away from the smokers to an unoccupied wrought iron bench.

"Well, Miss Woe, I mean Violet." He pronounced her name with three syllables instead of two. "You are one killer diller little jitterbug."

"You're not whistling Dixie yourself. Where're you from? Where're you stationed? Where'd you learn to dance? How long have you been jitterbugging?" She had to bite her tongue not to ask more.

"Thanks. We seem to work pretty well together." His eyes

twinkled, the side of his mouth curved into a one-dimpled grin. "What do you say we enter that dance contest tonight?"

Not what Violet was expecting to come out of his really pretty, soft, inviting, movie star mouth. "I don't know what to say."

"Say yes." He smiled big and looked into her eyes.

"What the hay. Let's do it." She grimaced, before the last word was out. She remembered Johnny.

Charles's full lips pressed together and he studied her face. "Hmmm, there's a problem? Yep, I can't imagine a pretty thing like you is hurting for dance partners."

"Thanks." She suppressed a giggle.

What's wrong with me? I'm never this girly.

"There's a problem. See, my friend..." She made sure to stress the word friend. "Asked me to do the contest, and I said no, because I...I don't love dancing with him as much as..." She paused. "As much as...Well, enough to do the contest. So, it might be a little hurtful if I ended up on the dance floor with you." She clenched her jaw and began picking the chipped paint on the bench.

"Oh." He smiled. "That's not so bad, but I see what you mean. That wouldn't be friendly now would it?" He scratched the back of his neck and gazed into the distance.

They sat in silence. Violet continued to flick paint pieces onto the ground. She was sure that at any minute he was going to excuse himself and go find some other pretty little thing to enter the dance contest with.

"Well then, if not tonight, let's see if we can work it out for next Saturday. That is, if you'd like to dance with me." He stressed the *me* like there was some doubt that she would.

"Yes," she almost yelled. She tried to calm down, but not only did he want to compete in a dance contest with her, but he wanted to see her again.

"Whaddaya say we hit the hardwood, again. But first, would you like to give me your exchange? I wish I had one to give you, but we don't have an ameche in the barracks. So, it's a little easier if I ring you." He hesitated for a second. "Do you have plans tomorrow? Maybe you'd like to come with us to the beach? Some of the fellas and their gals are having a picnic and bonfire. Whaddaya say?" He drummed his fingers on the bench. "You wanna Jitterbug at the beach?"

"Thank you. That'd be swell. MArket 968. Do you need to write it down? I may have something in my pocket book."

"Nope, I got it." He tapped his head. "I won't forget." He rose and started to go. "So, how 'bout that dance?" He grinned again and held out his hand.

Violet placed her hand in his. His skin was cool and light. She wanted to twine her fingers in his and trace the tendons up his arm to his bicep, but instead she smiled and stepped lightly onto the dance floor.

June ~ 1990s
5. Good Enough for Grandad
(Squirrel Nut Zippers)

The morning sun illuminated the kitchen in a wash of bright light. June noticed for the first time her mom beginning to look old. The skin around her mom's eyes thinner, the lines deeper. June rarely thought about her mom being older than most of her friend's moms, but this morning reminded her.

"So, how was the trip to Pasadena, honey? I didn't hear you get in last night. Give hugs."

June embraced her mom. *She feels like Gramma Gigi. Fragile.* June hugged her mother tighter.

"That's quite a hug kiddo. What'd I do to deserve that?"

"Nothing, Mom. Just thanks for trusting me this weekend."

"Honey, you have no idea how hard it is for me and your dad to let you go. Whenever you're not in my house, it's like half my limbs are missing. It's very hard to watch you grow further and further away."

June did know what it was like. Ever since they'd lost Julian, June felt like half her limbs were missing, too. It'd been twelve years, and she still ached.

"So let's talk about this school thing. Even though I'm really proud of you, and I applaud your efforts to fight for your credit, maybe you should consider it a blessing." Tears perched on her mom's doughy lids. "The idea of you going to San Diego so soon, tears me apart."

June gave her mom another squeeze and sat down at the breakfast counter.

"I know. Thanks for letting me go and believing in me, even

when you're not ready to. Mom, you should've seen the dancers this weekend. It's like if you took pure music and turned it into something visible and tangible. The result would be them dancing."

"You sound like you're in love," her mom teased.

"You know I think I am. I'm in love with swing dancing."

"If you're really determined to fight the power, as they say, and get your credit, don't let this dancing thing distract you." Her mom sighed and looked even older.

"Hey Mom, what's our heritage?"

"Where'd that come from?"

"Talking about school. Not letting dance distract me." June teased and smiled good-naturedly at her mom. "An assignment in World History."

"Your mind is all over the place."

"Yup. So anyway, we're supposed to trace our roots as far back as we can. Ideally to the continent and region. So, we're white or Caucasian, and from central Europe, right?" June grabbed a banana and continued talking between bites. "I want to be something besides white. I mean, where is this Caucasia I'm supposed to be from?"

"I know you're joking about Caucasia, but that's a very intriguing question. Let me go check the encyclopedia." Her mom strolled toward the den.

"You know," June hollered, "there's a thing called the internet now, Mom."

But her mom returned with a worn tome. Dust particles swirled in a shaft of sunlight. June's head filled with images of twirling couples and sparkling lights. Her mother read aloud:

"Of or being a major human racial classification traditionally distinguished by physical characteristics such as very light to brown skin pigmentation and straight to wavy or curly hair, and including peoples indigenous to Europe,

northern Africa, western Asia, and India. No longer in scientific use."

Did Mom say, *no longer in scientific use?* And people from Africa? June's head whirled. *What the hell is the term Caucasian doing on all the questionnaires? And why does it apply to me?*

"That's food for thought, isn't it?" Her mother closed the book.

"To say the least. It illustrates how close we all are, ethnically. Don't you think? Scientists like Bill Nye, the Science Guy, say there's no such thing as race."

"You remember that show?"

"Yeah, our science teachers always leave Bill Nye videos when we have subs. That doesn't help my assignment, though. I still need to know where our people come from, and I don't think Caucasia is going to cut it. Where are Grandma and Grandad and their parents from?"

Her mother hesitated. "Well, Grandad is mostly German and I believe your Grandmother was English and Irish." Her eyes tightened into a look between pain and worry. She sat down and took June's hands in hers. "I guess I can tell you now. I was adopted. Both your uncle and I were."

"What?" June's palms began to sweat. She felt dizzy. "What do you mean you were adopted? You never told me that."

This is too much.

"I know. I wanted to wait until you were older and then . . . Well, you're older now. It's a big thing for some people." Her mother inhaled sharply. "I didn't want to talk about it."

June shook her head. "You and Dad never want to talk about any big stuff."

"I thought the truth would upset you and it has. Me being adopted is not really that important is it? It doesn't affect you at all."

No. Yes. No. Maybe. I don't know. It wasn't really important or was it? It didn't change who she was. Yet somehow, it did. She felt like she'd been lied to. An uncomfortable fear rose inside her.

"Were we...I mean, am I adopted?" June was petrified of the answer, still not understanding why she should feel this way, but knew it had something to do with her self-identity and Julian's accident.

Her mother put her arms around June. "No darling, you were my babies—baby—that I carried in my belly. I'm all yours. And you're all mine, honey."

"Do you ever...Does it bother you being adopted?" She pictured her mom as an abandoned baby. Her heart ached.

"No. Your grandparents always made me feel very loved and secure. Plus, it wasn't until I was about your age that I found out your uncle and I were adopted."

My grandparents aren't really my grandparents? Shouldn't this ease the pain of Gramma Gigi's death? It doesn't. June felt the sorrow fresh and raw. Images of the Julian's accident flashed before her eyes. A creepy dread began to climb through her veins. She rubbed her hands on her face, scrubbing the images away. *I am fine.*

"Can I ask you a question?"

Her mom hesitated. "Sure."

"Weren't you curious who your biological parents were?"

"No, if they didn't want me then, why would they want me now?

But what if they want me, now. Want a granddaughter?

June knelt at Grandma Gigi's grave. The bright winter sun warmed the afternoon to a perfect fifty-seven degrees, just cool enough for a sweater. Rows of marble rectangles rested flush with the grass, a massive matrix of the dead. June could find no way to romanticize the modern cemetery. Although she felt a connection to Grandma Gigi at the graveside, she'd never felt a presence or believed, still the open expanse lent a freedom and anonymity she didn't feel at home.

"Hi Gramma Gigi. Well, my early graduation might not happen. But I'm going to fight it. I know you would've supported me. I wish…"

"Anyway, that's not the only thing. Mom told me. About you and Grampie D. I mean, Mom being adopted. I don't want to hurt you or Grampie D, or Mom. I love you so much."

The tears began to build behind her eyes. She wished she could really talk to Gramma Gigi.

"I just…I need answers. I feel like I've lost my place in the world. You were the only one I could talk to about Julian. I know you're together and he's beating you at Connect Four, like he always did me." She wasn't sure she really believed that, but she wanted to.

"So, I guess I'm here to tell you I'm going looking. For them, or for her, my other grandmother. It doesn't mean I don't love you, but I need to fill this hole in my life."

June shoved the flowers in the cone vase next to the marker. She couldn't bring herself to look at Julian's grave. It hurt more than Gramma Gigi. Her mom had described it best: A person she loved not under her roof felt like half her limbs were missing.

Violet ~ 1940s
6. Elmer's Tune
(Glenn Miller)

"Tell me EVERTHING," Jeannie twittered through the phone line.

"He said I was pretty." Violet twirled a dark curl around her index finger and thought back to her conversation with Charles. "Sort of."

"Okay, tell me EXACTLY what he said."

"He said, *a pretty little thing like me probably doesn't have a hard time getting a dance partner.*"

"True. I always said you could be in pictures."

"I blushed when he said it. Nothing makes me blush anymore." Violet took a breath and sighed. "It was right after he asked me to do the dance contest with him."

"What!" Jeannie screamed. "You didn't tell me that."

"I didn't have a chance. It's not like I could talk about him in front of Johnny and Paddy. It was near killing me, Jean. You have no idea. I wish I could've called you last night, but it was too late. Oh, oh, oh, and guess what else? I'm going to the beach for a picnic and bonfire."

"Oh." Jeannie paused. "I was gonna see if you wanted to go to the Sugar Bowl today. Some of the seniors are getting together to practice for the contest. It's all anyone's talking about, but looks like you've got your own practicing to do." She giggled. "I didn't tell you what else. You're off the hook with Johnny. He's doing the contest with Sue on account of Ronald's leg being bashed in last night. He was afraid to tell you, since he asked you first, and all. I don't think he saw you dancing with your sailor, either."

"That's good." Violet knew Johnny had seen her, but if he wanted to play it that way, it was fine with her. "What should I wear today? Everything I have is awful."

"Don't go into a decline. He's goofy for you. Wear a cute gab skirt, blouse, sweater, and your multi-colored Kedettes. They go with everything."

"Maybe he likes me. Or maybe he only likes my dancing." Violet tried to stretch the phone cord to the built in drawers at the end of the hall. It didn't quite reach. She sighed.

"Stop sighing, you've got a date with a sailor. Paddy says he's going to join up after graduation. He doesn't want to wait to be drafted. He thinks it's un-American. He says it's our civic duty to vote and serve the country. Isn't he high-minded? I think he wants to join the Army, though. Boats make him seasick. Isn't that cute?"

"The thought of it twists my guts. Military service seems exciting and romantic when they run off to England or France to fight for our country, but a lot of them don't come back, Jeannie. It's not a game." Violet's eyes stung with tears. "I don't want to think or talk about war."

"No, you're right, but I know it couldn't happen to my Paddy-cakes."

Violet burst out laughing. "You're not seriously calling him Paddy-cakes? To his face? Please tell me you're joshing."

"No, I just thought of it this minute. I think it's perfect. My very own Paddy-cakes."

"So, is he yours?"

"No, but I'm not giving up. He and Johnny were gonna come get me. Then you, if you were going, but maybe. Maybe..." Jeannie's voice rose. "I'll tell Paddy I want to walk, and he can pick me up at my house and walk me to the malt shop. What do you think of that?"

"It's worth a shot. I'd say don't leave the malt shop 'till it's good and dark."

"Well, I do have a nine o' clock curfew on Sundays."

They giggled and said good-bye. Violet began to get ready for her date, if it really was a date. She couldn't remember the last real date she'd gone on. She didn't count Johnny, but she supposed he'd been the last. *Had it been that long since my life had fallen apart?*

Mrs. Peppy sat at her machine, pulling out stitches with the seam ripper. Violet waited for Charles at the tailor shop. She didn't want him to see where she lived. If only he could've seen her old house. Tears rushed to her eyes before she could quash them down. She took a deep breath, looked up, and fanned her eyes.

She didn't know why her emotions were so near the surface. She'd been successfully ambivalent the last year. Maybe it was the lack of sleep from replaying her evening with Charles and fantasizing about the picnic. Reality never matched up to her dreams, but she couldn't stop herself from hoping.

She spied him on the street and jumped up, almost toppling the dress dummy. The bell twinkled when he opened the door. He was just as handsome in his gray rayon gab shirt as he'd been in his uniform. The outline of his A-shirt held tortoise-shell cheaters and his sleeves were rolled up, showing his muscled forearms, one hand gripping a picnic basket. His blue gab slacks were also rolled up enough to glimpse stripy socks. *Ah, he is a Jitterbug.* He caught her looking at his feet, smiled, and gave her a wink.

"Uhhh..." She stood but was unsteady on her feet. "Mrs. Peppy, Mrs. Peplinksi, this is Charles."

He stepped toward Mrs. Peppy and extended his hand. "Charles Mangino, at your service, Ma'am, but you can call me Chas."

He winked again and Mrs. Peppy smiled coyly. In that moment, Violet could see what a beauty Mrs. Peppy must have been in her youth. His radiance washed away her years.

"We best be off." He tipped his straw boater hat. "Nice to meet you Ma'am."

He guided Violet out the door. His palm brushed the small of her back, and she was pretty sure her feet never touched the ground all the way to the bus stop.

Each time the bus hit a bump a different part of her thigh touched his with a tingly shock. She tried not to stare at him, but he was so easy to look at. He caught her starring and met her eyes. She bubbled over inside, nervous and vulnerable. She looked away.

"So." They both started to speak at once, then laughed.

"You go first." She tilted her head.

"So, what do you think about this dance contest? Can I throw you around on the beach?" He played with the hat on his lap. "How do you feel about aerials?"

"Oh, I love them. If they're done right." She hoped she hadn't insulted him and quickly added, "Not that you'd lay an egg. I wasn't implying...."

He cut her off with a burbling, soft laugh.

"How could anyone go wrong with you? You're tiny and perfect." He crunched up his face and looked away. "Perfectly suited, to...being tossed around, since your timing and connection are so good."

Again with the dancing. "So, you thought we had good connection, too. I thought maybe it was just me."

Unrecognizable emotions slipped across his face. "Nope, you're the jitterinest jitterbug I've ever come across."

"So do you have any other hobbies besides dancing?"

"Not much anymore. They don't give you a lot of free time in the Navy and none in boot camp and training school. I like to go to the picture shows, and I play guitar, but lately I've been goofing around with the ukulele. It's smaller than a guitar and more portable. Can I tell you a secret?" He leaned in close, his warm breath at her ear. "I've got one in the picnic basket."

Violet pressed her lips together, afraid a sigh would escape. She took slow calming breaths through her nose, smelling his pine and fresh baked biscuit scent. She hoped he didn't notice.

He laughed a throaty laugh and she joined him.

"I'll play you a little song I've been working on."

"That'd be killer diller. Um, don't take this the wrong way. I have every respect for our boys in blue, but how come you didn't stay in school? Finish college, before you enlisted?"

A serious look crossed his face, no hint of smile. He looked older, all trace of the gregarious boy gone. "I thought it was the right thing to do. If you see someone beating an innocent dog or a child, you've gotta step in and do something. And those Japs beat the hell out of us in Hawaii. Pardon my French. Not to mention what that greeby idiot Hitler is doing over there. How can any of us have a future with a madman like him in power? Frankly, I don't know how anyone can't join up, now. They'll be plenty of time for college later."

Violet didn't know what to say. She knew he was right, and it made him even more attractive. She wanted to kiss him right now, on the bus, in front of the old lady wearing the babushka. She wanted to feel his lips on hers.

As if reading her mind, he leaned toward her, his eyes intent on hers. Then his focus shifted, and he reached across, smashing into her shoulder.

"Oops, sorry. Didn't mean to squish ya, but this is our stop. We'll have to hop the train from here." He pulled the rope to signal the driver.

Shivers mixed with disappointment coiled down her spine.

The cool water contrasted with the warmth of the sand. Their bare feet melted into misshapen footprints. The tiny grains slowly buried Violet's feet when she stopped walking. *A metaphor for my life? If I stay in one place too long I'll get buried?* She didn't want to think about what to do with her life. She didn't want to think past today.

"So, Miss Woe, tell me a little something about yourself." He smiled and tugged her ponytail.

She flicked her leg and tried to give him a playful kick, but he was too fast and ran down the beach. Violet ran after him, but he dodged until they were both laughing, and she finally managed to splash a little water on him.

"Hey now, you wanna make something out of it?" He taunted. "You'll lose that battle. I'll toss you into the frosty waves. Let the old man of the sea have 'atcha."

"What waves?" She laughed. "Those little things. I'm not afraid of you."

He scooped her up as if she weighed nothing more than an empty milk bottle. He pretended to throw her in, but she clung to his neck, kicked her feet in mock terror, and buried her head in his lovely chest.

Her body tingled with desire. She was surprised and a little embarrassed by the thoughts that flashed through her head. It was impossible not to think about kissing him.

"Okay, if I put you down are you going to behave?" He released her legs and gently guided her down.

"No." She laughed and ran down the beach. He followed like she hoped he would. He caught her around the waist and pressed her against his chest, swinging her around. Her legs flew out in front of her. She laughed and squirmed, turning her body so they were facing. She looked up. Their heads and bodies bent toward a kiss. He picked her up and swung her again, her legs and arms went flying.

"Hey Vi, let's do that again. I've got an idea for a new aerial." He put her down and turned her so her back was to his chest.

"Okay." She smiled tightly and took a deep breath. "What do you want me to do?"

"When I turn you, I want you to put your legs out straight, like you're sitting on the floor. Then I'm going to rotate your lower body and lift my legs, one after the other until you've made a full rotation. Do you get it?"

"I don't get it, but let's give it a try anyway." It wasn't the contact she was hoping for, but it was better than nothing.

"You're such a good sport. Think of your legs as a rag cleaning a plate."

He grasped her more securely under the arms, pinned her to his abdomen, and started the spin. She lifted her legs straight, but then as she rotated to clear his first leg she didn't understand how to bend her body. They crashed and almost fell over.

"Oh, I'm so sorry," she said. "Are you okay?"

"Me? I'm fine. Are you okay? I didn't bruise you did I? How are your arms and shoulders?"

"I'm perfect." She looked up at him with moony eyes. It was obvious. He was all about the dancing. She liked him more than he liked her.

"Killer diller, doll. Let's go again."

They did it over and over until her stomach muscles barely wanted to hold her up. They eventually nailed the move.

"Hey, I've got an idea." She clapped her hands. "What if we go around twice and on the second time I do the splits? Then you scoop me up for a dip or a Boogie-drop? Whaddya think?"

"I think you're brilliant."

He picked her up by the waist and flung her into a spin hug. His face was at her neck. His breath warm and so close it tickled. She was going nuts. It couldn't be her imagination that every time they started getting close, he drew away.

"Woo-wee." He reset her for the move. "Let's do the move again with your variation."

49

After several tries, they executed it like pros.

"Do you mind if we take a breather? I'm a little tired." She exhaled loudly.

"Yeah, sorry. Would you like to go sit down with everyone? They're just down the beach."

"No, not yet." Even though all of his friends were very nice, she didn't want to share him yet. "I need to walk out my tight muscles."

They walked side by side down the beach. She wanted him to reach over and grab her hand, but he continued to pick up rocks and skip them across the water.

"So, where were we before inspiration struck? Ah, yes, I remember. You were going to tell me a little about yourself."

"Was I? I think you were going to tell me about yourself." She smiled slyly.

He frowned then pursed his lips. "How about a trade-off?"

"Okay, what do you want to know?"

"Tell me about your family." He threw another rock.

"Umm, next question?"

"Okay, tell me about working for Mrs. Peppy? How'd you learn to sew?"

Violet's six-year-old self stared at the mole on her mother's bare leg. The twitching muscles made it play jump rope on her skin as her foot rocked the pedal.

"Watch out Violet. You don't want to get your fingers pinched down there."

Small Violet crawled out from under the sewing machine and stood by her mother's side. Mrs. Woe deftly maneuvered the tiny dress, adding delicate lace trim. Her fingers moved fast toward the piercing needle. Violet was certain she would slip, and the pointy metal would stab her elegant finger.

"Come here Vi, let me show you. You want to help make

Dolly a new dress, don't you?"

Violet scooted shyly between her mother's legs and the sewing machine. Her mother caged her between her knees gently guiding Violet's small hands to the fabric. Her foot rocked, moving treadle, moving needle. Violet jerked her hands away. Her mother laughed and Violet thought it sounded like fairy bells.

"Come on sweetheart, don't be afraid. Try again."

Violet placed her hands on the thin cotton fabric. Her mother laid her hands over Violet's and slowly, carefully pushed the edge under the chomping machine.

"I did it, Mama, I did it."

The memory caught Violet off guard. She'd forgotten how sweet her mother could be, but didn't want to talk or think about her right now. Violet smiled and tried to figure out what to tell him about her life.

"I needed a job and Jeannie's, mother's cousin told her about Mrs. Peppy wanting to take on an apprentice. Jeannie thought of me. She knew I was on the look-out for some way to make dough that didn't involve a factory. I took Mrs. Peppy a dress I'd made in Home Ec, and she was impressed enough to hire me."

She wasn't sure what else to say. "See, I told you it was boring." He looked at her for a long minute. Her stomach fluttered. "Okay, my turn. Where are you from?"

"Tucson, Arizona." He threw another rock into the ocean.

"Wow. It's pretty hot there I guess?"

"Sometimes, a little more than here, but it's gorgeous in the winter, and we even get snow on Mount Lemmon. Have you ever been skiing?"

"No, I've never even felt snow. It doesn't exactly snow here, you know."

"What? You've never seen snow? You get snow in the mountains outside of San Diego, don't you?" He looked at her with a puzzled expression. "I'd love to be the one to show you snow for the first time."

"That'd be swell," she replied and knew by the time that it snowed again, he would be far, far away, on a boat in a big, big sea.

"Cheeeeesse, Cheeeeeesy," Marvin yelled and waved his arms for Violet and Charles to join them.

"Looks like we better see what he wants, huh?" Charles asked. "It's a bit of a walk. How 'bout I give my tired jitterbug a piggy back?"

Before Violet could say no, he scooped her onto his back. She squeezed her legs around his warm middle and held on. She wanted to kiss the back of his neck but couldn't bring herself to do it. Her body jostled against his, tickling her in funny ways, building a fire inside. Her breath became shallow and erratic.

She wobbled, unsteady when he set her down by the fire pit. She was both relieved and disappointed.

"Hey, do you think we could make a move out of that?" Charles asked.

"Cheesy, is that all you ever think about? Dance moves?" Marvin flicked Charles's arm.

Violet shook her head and smiled, wondering the same thing.

"Lee and Clyde are working on setting up the horseshoes while I work on the fire. Here, make yourself useful." Marvin tossed Charles the ukulele. "I told Mary and Trudy you knew how to play this thing."

The three girls sat on the blanket and sang along with Charles as he played silly songs. Charles's long fingers scuttled over the ukulele body. Violet envisioned other places for his hands.

He sung unabashedly at the top of his lungs, putting on goofy accents. Violet starred at his full lips. She didn't know what was wrong with her. She couldn't stop thinking about his mouth, and what it would feel like on hers. *Put it out of your head and stop torturing yourself. Nothing but dancing is going to happen between us.*

One of the other squids yelled to Charles, "Do you want to play doubles with us?"

"Sure." Charles put down the uke and offered his hand to Violet.

Violet stretched her toes toward the fire, tired from the day's exertions, happy to be resting. Charles jabbed the fire with a stick. The glow played across his tanned skin while the shadows danced around his handsome face. It seemed impossible, but Violet knew she was falling in love with him. She didn't want to say it, admit it, or feel it, but couldn't help it. She'd hoped a little moonlight would help him fall for her, but every time he seemed about to kiss her, he pulled away, changed direction, or asked if she wanted to try a dance move.

Maybe she was too serious, not light and giggly enough like Trudy and Mary. She could kiss him, but wouldn't. She didn't want him to think she was easy or loose. She was not like her mother.

His feet, crusted with salt and sand, poked out of his sea-stained trousers, toes wiggling toward the fire. Violet didn't know where she felt more heat, from his lean warm body next to hers, or the sparkling fire in front of her.

He traded his uke for Lee's guitar and strummed a sweet tune, one of her favorites, one her mother used to sing. *Elmer's Tune.* She should hate it, but she didn't. The sound of her mother's beautiful voice floated on a memory. The remembrance tangled her up inside. She wanted to run away and cry but Charles's voice anchored her to his side. Even though he sang for everyone, his *Elmer's Tune* seemed just for her.

June ~1990s
7. After You've Gone
(8 ½ Souvenirs)

Why does it all have to happen now? It'd been a very long couple of weeks. June started her battle by comparing class courses at all the high schools in her district, then poring over state education governing laws to make her case. She'd gone to the principal, the counselor, even her GCC professor—although he sympathized, he couldn't help.

She didn't give up and roll over. She'd earned her credits. She was due her credits. She refused to lose her San Diego apartment and postpone her university enrollment. Today would decide her fate. Literally. After speaking to the school board, she gained a meeting with her school district's Superintendent, the Assessment Director, and the Arizona Department of Education's Superintendent—the big boss of everything education.

It was either going to ruin her birthday or make it the best ever. Her stomach hurt. She felt the hot, cold, spidery feeling creep into her veins. She paced back and forth down the hall in front of the state office. Her mom offered to meet her, but June wanted to do it on her own. After all, today she was eighteen. He would've been eighteen, too. The thought almost undid her, but she'd fought hard to get this far and would confront this injustice, head on.

The door opened. "June Andersen, you may come in now and present your case."

"Thank you Ms. Neyman." June nodded to her district's superintendent.

"May I introduce you to State Superintendent Jamal Warring,

and State Curriculum Assessment Director, Delores Sanchez, and also joining us is State Education Secretary, Kathy Wielding."

June took a deep breath, nodded and smiled. *I feel like I'm on trial. I guess I am.* She stepped up to the microphone at the lectern and adjusted the height.

"Very nice to meet you all. I'm June Andersen. Thank you for seeing me today and taking time out of your busy schedules." June undid the clasps of her newly-bought briefcase. "I've brought a packet for you that supports my claim to approve the GCC Art History Class as a credited high school class. If I can draw your attention to…"

The door behind June burst open. The trustees in front of her looked as startled as she was.

"I'm sorry to interrupt." A petite, attractive lady crossed the room with a note and placed it in front of State Superintendent Warring. He nodded and pinched the bridge of his nose.

"Um, Ms. Andersen, I know we allotted you thirty minutes, but I'm sorry, we're going to have to speed this meeting up. The governor is on his way to meet with me about an urgent matter. You have fifteen minutes."

Fifteen minutes? June had practiced her speech, her points, gathered quotes, and research. They timed out at twenty-five minutes, leaving five minutes for questions or clarification. *How can I shave off ten minutes? Or more, if I want to leave time for clarification?* The pit in her stomach churned, her palms sweated. *Stay calm.*

She shuffled her notes and began her fight. After what seemed like seconds, but turned out to be fourteen minutes, the secretary held up her finger, giving June a one-minute warning.

"To wrap up my claim, I think it's clear that we were not the only district that had been told the GCC Art Appreciation class would be accepted for dual credit and applicable to our high school standings." June nodded at Ms. Neyman.

"Not only does the oversight come from the state level, but if you turn to article thirty-five, section eight, I believe it says the State Superintendent and governing officers can approve or give variance in special cases. I fight not only for my particular special case, but for those other students who don't have a voice. Thank you for your consideration." She smiled a confident smile and looked each trustee in the eyes.

"Thank you, Ms. Andersen. If you could now wait outside. We will discuss this, and one of my colleagues will invite you back in to hear our verdict on this issue." Mr. Warring looked at his watch and turned to his colleagues, speaking in a low voice. June gathered her notes and went to wait in the hall.

Two minutes later, Mr. Warring walked briskly out of the room and down the hall. He didn't even look her direction. She took it as a bad sign.

After what seemed like hours, but was actually only another fifteen minutes, Ms. Neyman, opened the door and invited June back in, each took their previous positions—Neyman at the u-shaped table, June behind the lectern.

"Unfortunately, Mrs. Juarez, had made a mistake with the dual credit class. You're not the only one affected. It seems that the Art Appreciation Class should not have been listed as a dual credit in our schedule."

I know that, already. I want to scream. I am beginning to hate that woman's voice.

"But..."

She said but!

"But, since you brought to our attention the new curriculum guideline was passed after you were advised to sign up for that class. And since you've presented us with the documentation. And you've pointed out that the A.D.E. has the ability to grant variances in special cases. We believe this case falls under a grandfather clause. You will be awarded your class credit and your diploma. Congratulations June Andersen. We wish you the best of luck. I know you will make Washington High School proud."

It's over. I did it.

The trustees smiled tight smiles and quickly left the room. Ms. Neyman shook June's hand and said something that went right through June's head.

I have to call my mom and dad. Her mom didn't even cry like she thought she would, at least not over the phone. I feel like crying, laughing, and dancing. Yeah, mostly I feel like dancing.

Everyone June had come to love packed the dance studio. Saul whipped her around the dance floor in her very own good-bye/birthday jam. She thought she'd be more nervous in the spotlight, but she'd been dancing for months, and today's victory swirled happy inside her.

Saul whirled her around in Frankie style swing-outs, brought her in for a turn, and then flipped her over his arm backwards, landing her solidly on the wood floor. She'd finally learned to trust him. Her friends and newbies clapped, oohed, and aahed.

Saul spun her into her next lead, Chad. His swing-out was rowdier than Saul's but as familiar as her drive home. Her body soared at his lead, one with the music, though the heartache of leaving her favorite dance partner and her swing friends poked through her revelry.

"You wanna do a candle-stick?" Chad whispered in her ear when she came into closed position.

"Sure. One more swing-out and go."

She slid with a whoosh between Chad's legs keeping her body bone stiff. He launched her straight up, flying through the air. Her toes touched the ceiling. She felt her momentum reach its apex when they made a perfectly straight line. He brought her down and safely set her up for the next move.

Friend's faces blurred, one after another jumped in to give June a good-bye whirl. A rookie dancer named Stan hopped in and—for a guy who'd only had three lessons—he was good. She smiled. June hadn't thought so many high school and college kids would be into Jitterbug, but more came every week. A swinging GAP ad even had dancers lindy-hopping in khakis.

Saul cut back in for the last chorus, but whispered something in Janet's ear before he took over. He wrapped up the song with a kick-up dip. June's hair brushed the floor, her legs pointed to the ceiling. Before she could catch her breath, the familiar notes of *Tuxedo Junction* blasted from the speakers. She laughed, remembering when she'd first learned the Shim Sham at the Frankie Workshop. Saul popped her up, and she took her place in one of the parallel lines that had formed for the sequence.

Saul called out the steps. "And you push it and you push it and you cross over, and ya, cross over and ya, Tacky Annie."

Her heart filled with love and sadness in equal parts. Tears threatened to undo her, it'd been a hell of a day.

"Boogie Back and clap," Paul called. "Shortie George, and dance."

June blinked back the tears and found the closest lead.

"And freeze." They froze.

"And dance." She and everyone else changed partners again and finished out the song with frenzied swapping every time Saul called freeze, and dance.

When the Shim Sham was over, June found herself in the center, alone. Her nervousness reappeared, and she blushed crimson. Amy, grinning from ear to ear, advanced with a box in her hands. June slowly opened the box and gasped.

"It's 40s rayon," Amy said.

June wasn't sure what rayon was, but the vintage dress was slinky and pretty. She gave Amy a hug. The tears pressed again behind her eyes.

Next, Janet and Saul gave her a cute pair of lace-up shoes, which Amy assured her were from the early 40s, too. June's heart was ready to burst, her emotions too raw and too close to the surface. Then it was Molly and Jack's turn. They presented her with a white envelope and a smirk.

"I hope it's the right size." Molly winked.

The card pictured an Italian couple swing dancing in the street next to a river. When she opened it, a small plastic card dropped to the floor. June picked it up and recognized Molly's cousin who'd visited the week before. June looked at Molly confused.

"Think it will pass? Julie?" Molly eyed June.

It took a minute, but finally clicked. It was a fake ID, only it wasn't fake. Julie and June were the same height, same eye color, only Julie had red hair.

"Looks like I'm dying my hair." She laughed. "Thank you. Thank you all so much." She could no longer hold it in. Hot tears rolled down her cheeks. She laughed and cried, fanned her face, and gulped the cold water that Amy handed her.

Right after that, Chad suggested they go to 5 and Diner. It seemed fitting to go to their after-class haunt one last time. When they arrived at the retro boxcar restaurant, the long silver bullet glowed in the reflected light. They snagged a table under the white and red umbrellas. Their favorite waitress recognized them and served them first.

June slurped a double-chocolate shake made with real chocolate ice cream and fudge. The jukebox squawked through the outdoor speakers. The newbies jumped up to dance to *Sha Boom, Sha Boom*. The song was so good June couldn't eat her sandwich. She had to dance. But everyone in her group was still eating. She noticed the newbie from her good-bye jam tapping his foot.

"Hey, you. Stan isn't it?" She pointed at him. "Do you wanna dance?"

He almost tripped over the table and was by her side before she had time to take the last slurp of her shake. It was the second time that day she'd felt empowered. *When June beckons, men come running.*

Hopefully, she could hold on to this confidence when she moved to San Diego. And hopefully, she'd find a clue to her biological grandmother. The only lead she had was that her mother and uncle had been adopted when Grampie D was stationed in San Diego after the war. *At least being in San Diego would make it easier to do research and find my biological grandparents.* And she was going. She'd fought and won.

The sweet night air swirled around June's body. The tune sank into her bones, and the joy of dance spread through every fiber of her being from her toes to her fingertips.

Dancing is almost as fun as kissing. In fact, with the right guy leading me around the floor, they're dead even. Please let me find both in my new home.

Violet ~ 1940s
8. I'm Beginning to See the Light
(Harry James)

An hour from dusk, Balboa Park was shadowy, full of sweet earthy smells, and terribly romantic. Charles and Violet walked along the promenade of Spanish style buildings, looking for a place to practice another new aerial Charles had come up with.

"This area was built for the World's Fair. The 1915-16 Panama-California Exposition," Violet explained as they walked.

Scrolling leaves and floral accents loomed skyward on tall columns. Violet had never noticed the sculpted women on the perimeter of the façade before. Their arms rose over their heads, naked breasts hung freely, frozen in plaster. *How many times have I visited the park and never noticed them?* She looked away, embarrassed, not sure why. Charles hadn't been looking up, but watching the people moving in and out of buildings.

"What's the military doing here?" she asked.

"We're taking over some of the park buildings for more hospital space." He pressed his lips into a thin white line.

The war has come to America and touched us all. She wished there was another way to fix the world. A heavy silence lapsed between them.

"Hey." He squeezed her hand. "Don't forget I have a surprise for you. Come on." The smile in his voice was infectious. She pushed her fears to the back of her mind and smiled.

They reached a beautiful, deeply shaded spot where ancient eucalyptus trees dripped long fragrant fingers. The park noises muted behind the thick foliage curtains. Charles directed them to a protruding Magnolia tree root, a gnarly outgrowth reminiscent of *Swiss Family Robinson*, one of her favorite novels. *Had he read it? Was he a reader? There was so much to learn about him. Would there be enough time?*

"Close your eyes," he asked.

The tree root dug into the back of her thighs. Her skin prickled, more sensitive since she'd met him. She adjusted her skirt. He bustled and crunched leaves, arranging the surprise. She wanted to be excited, but remained guarded.

"Hey, no peeking," he said with mock annoyance.

"I'm not."

"Okay, you can open your eyes now."

He stood next to his created tableau of an arranged blanket with a small dainty tablecloth covering the picnic basket, two lit candles, and two plates with what looked like Chop Suey noodles, a bottle of wine, and two glasses. The scene was painfully romantic.

Violet's insides danced a happy jig, her heart started to flutter, and heat rose to her face. She looked at him for what seemed too long a time. Finally, when she spoke, "Wow," was all she could say.

He smiled, then a brief shadow crossed his face, gone as quickly as it'd come. He hopped gracefully over the blanket, coming so close his forehead almost touched hers. His breath was warm on her face. Her heart quickened. He grabbed her hand and guided her toward his surprise dinner.

"Do you like it?" She could see the boy in the man and her heart ached for him. She loved him.

"It's beautiful." *You're beautiful.* She wanted to say.

"I felt like I had to make amends for breaking our date last night. Like I said, my duty watch got switched at the last minute, and I couldn't leave base."

Not trusting words, she nodded.

"You sounded kinda mad at me, and having three sisters, I

have an idea of how you gals think. I thought this would be a nice apology."

"I was just...disappointed. I thought maybe you'd changed your mind about me."

"No, I don't think I will ever change my mind about you. Even if I should."

He looked at her with an intensity that burned and set her heart beating so fast she thought it would lose its rhythm. His face bent to hers, and then he tore away and plopped down on the blanket.

She wanted to cry. *What am I doing wrong?* She collapsed onto the blanket across from him. Her sudden movements flickered the candles.

"Also," he continued not meeting her eyes. "I have a little bit of bad news."

Panic and dread filled her body. Her mind whirled in a thousand directions. *Is he already leaving? Is my time with him at an end when it's barely begun? And what did he mean about "even if he should?" Even if he should what?*

"We're shipping out."

She closed her eyes, squeezing them tight. Her stomach churned and threatened revolt. The big farewell, a romantic dinner in the park, over before it started. She couldn't sit. She couldn't stand. She couldn't breathe. She couldn't move. She opened her eyes. He watched her.

"Hey, hey. It's not that bad. The good news is, it's only for two weeks. I'll be back in time for the finals of the dance contest. Providing we make it that far. Which I think we will. And, I won't be shipping out until after the qualifying rounds."

Did he mistake her panic about losing him with not being able to compete in a local dance contest? She couldn't help being angry. Anger was good. Anger was easy.

"So, this, all this..." She gestured, her hand shaking. "...is to soften the blow?"

His face fell into a perplexed bruise. Her anger slipped away. She couldn't hurt him to protect herself. Her eyes burned as the tears bubbled behind her lids. She didn't want him to see her cry. She couldn't understand why she was so emotional. She hadn't cried in a year. She bit the inside of her cheek, jumped up, and started walking.

The blood rushed in her ears and dulled her hearing, but not her other senses. She felt the warmth of his hand before the touch of his fingers. He gently grabbed the crook of her elbow. She froze, then shook with silent sobs.

He gently caressed her shoulders and ran his hands down the length of her arms. His breath played through her hair. He turned her around and pressed into her shaking frame, holding her tight. His breath whispered in her ear. Her silent sobs subsided. His lips ghosted across her jaw. He wiped her tears with his thumb and rested his cheek on hers.

Wildfire spread through her body. Her heart thundered, shaking her to her core. She was sure he must be able to hear her heart pounding in the quiet of the park. Surely, he felt it on his chest. He tilted her chin. She met his eyes. Pain and compassion looked back at her.

He slid his hands into her hair, his thumbs stroked below her ears. He leaned down, and this time, did not pull away. He pressed his mouth to hers, holding her lips to his. Dizziness washed in waves, breaking across the shore of her soul.

Charles kissed harder, his breath mingled with hers. He exhaled a rough staccato, then slipped to the corner of her mouth, melting across her jaw, tickling her neck. He rested his head on her shoulder.

They stood curled around each other for what seemed an eternity. Violet tried to climb her way back from the depths she'd fallen. Lightness and joy vibrated in their coiled bodies.

He stirred and straightened, pulling back slightly.

"Violet. I was trying so hard for this not to happen."

"Why? What did I do wrong?"

"Violet, Violet, Violet, you gorgeous, sweet, girl. You did nothing wrong. It's me. I'm wrong. This is wrong." He shook his head.

Confusion and hurt played across her face. She wanted to run away and hide, but couldn't tear herself from him. He rubbed his hands up and down her arms, brushing his lips against her shoulder then backed away with resolve, walking back and forth. Violet staggered forward, caught off guard. A gasp escaped her lips. He noticed, looked at her, but kept pacing.

"I don't know what to do. I don't know what to do," he muttered and continued his march. "I should know better." He ran his fingers through his thick black hair. "I have no right, no right."

He grabbed her by the shoulders. "Violet, you deserve better than I can give you."

She paled and rubbed her yearning lips, fighting tears.

"Don't you get it? I'm leaving. Maybe not today, not tomorrow, but as soon as Monday, for two weeks."

"It's only two weeks," she whispered.

"Sure this time it's only two weeks, but it's only a matter of time. I can't promise you a future. I won't be here for you. I knew I shouldn't have started this. I thought I could handle it. I thought we could be friends. I thought...you...I...how can I in good conscious start something I can't finish?" He let go of her arms and ran his hands across his anguished face.

"How can I selfishly set you up for disappointment and hurt? How can I leave you? It's not fair to you. It's not right. I know it's not right."

"I don't care."

"But Violet." He put his hands on her shoulders and looked

her in the eyes. She quivered at his touch. "I don't know when or if I'll be back. I can't ask you to wai..."

She laid a trembling finger on his lips. "I'll wait for you."

June ~ 1990s
9. What's Next?
(Big Bad Voodoo Daddy)

Parking break jammed in. Cars beeped and honked loudly, rushing around her causing her small truck to shudder with every pass. Heavy sobs shook her body. June had stalled her truck on a colossal hill.

I hate San Diego.

The logical part of her brain knew she didn't really hate San Diego. *But no one should have to drive stick shift on these crazy hills.* There were no hills in Phoenix, just nice flat, blocked squares. She rubbed her hands on her face and tried to get a grip, but another round of sobs racked her body.

Living on her own sucked. She missed her mom and dad. She missed her house. She missed her friends. She missed her swing scene. She missed her Julian. She thought the venues in San Diego would be populated with cool, well-dressed lindy-hoppers, like the girls from L.A., but so far the biggest venue, where all the swing dancers went, was no cooler than the Ballroom Academy in Phoenix. The memory of her first night out dancing in San Diego compounded her misery, adding another round of sobs.

She'd donned her 40s rayon dress, fashioned her hair in pigtails and ribbons, and headed out to the Rock-it Swing Spot. It'd sounded promising. After driving around in circles for twenty minutes looking for parking, her mood was severely dampened. She finally found parking a couple blocks away and walked along the busy street until she arrived at the old hall. Swing music and soft yellow light spilled through the antique wooden doors of the

Spanish Mission style building.

Retro couches and chairs occupied the foyer. Old-timey signs hung in front of the bathrooms and two sets of interior double doors opened into a large rectangle room with a stage at the far end. Blocking the entry was an ugly folding table stacked with rows of flyers. Cha Cha Gregorio from the movie *Grease*—not really her, but a woman who looked like her doppelganger—manned the table, another girl at her side.

"Hello. Welcome to Rock-it Swing Spot. Five dollars, please." Cha Cha smiled.

June smiled, dug in her purse, and pulled out a twenty. Cha Cha looked dismayed, then lifted the drawer and threw the twenty on a stack of like bills. June collected her change unsure why Cha Cha would be annoyed at the twenty.

"Thanks." June was about to ask a question, but Cha Cha had already turned to the girl sitting next to her, giving instructions on how to make sure no one snuck in the back.

June maneuvered around the table into the hall. The air was moist and thick from balmy bodies. The dee-jayed music reverberated warmly off the walls and ceiling. Folding chairs lined the length of the left side, water bottles, coats, shoes and towels, cluttered the row. The right side held a line of velvet upholstered chairs.

Most of the patrons were as young as June, which surprised her—and much to her disappointment—very few were lindy-hopping. The usual smattering of older creepy guys and middle-aged women completed the mix.

She laid her purse and sweater on one of the velvety chairs and perched on the edge, trying to look ready to dance. As always, it was the old men who noticed first. A tubby middle-aged guy with a button-down shirt and polyester pants asked her to dance.

After Mr. Tubby, June danced with another man who led

strange jangly moves, not really in sync with the music. It was uncomfortable and did not feel like dancing.

She was on the verge of tears and ready to leave when a cute, young guy asked her to dance. His lead was good, a little groovy and Hip-Hop, but followable. She thrilled to have someone cute to dance with, but he had no zing. The deejay's music choices were flat and too jazzy for her taste. She missed her scene and her Phoenix leads.

She was about to leave when another middle-aged guy came over and asked her to dance. He danced Lindy. After dancing East Coast all night, it was like finding a golden ticket. His lead was solid and easy to follow. He led turns she didn't know, but the tempo was mellow enough that she had plenty of time to figure them out. It was her first fun of the night.

"You must be new. Where are you from?" He began his interview as they danced.

"Phoenix."

"Really? I didn't know they Lindy-hopped there."

"Surprise." She took her time, using the slow beats to style her Swing-out.

"So, are you visiting? Or here to stay?"

"I'm going to school here." He spun her around in a double turn, and she nailed it.

"Nice," he complimented. "Great dress by the way. You should check out Tio Leo's."

"Why?" He pulled her into side-by-side Charleston, which made it easier to talk.

"That's where all the car guys and Rockabilly chicks hang out, some lindy hoppers, too. You'd fit in. You have to be twenty-one though. You are, aren't you?"

"Sometimes."

She wasn't sure what he meant about fitting in, but anything had to be better than the newbie crew at the Rock-it Swing Spot.

He guided her off the dance floor after the song was over and drifted off to find another partner. She couldn't find another hopper, so she gathered her purse and walked back to her car alone, headlights illuminating her tears.

June inhaled deeply and shuddered, finally getting her tears under control. That's really all she hated about San Diego: hills and the swing scene. She took another deep breath and gave herself a pep talk. It really was gorgeous here, and she loved her cute little apartment, old and quaint, within walking distance of cool restaurants and shops. She needed to give it more time. She turned the ignition key, eased off the clutch, and gave it some gas.

June pulled up to the large Mexican restaurant, Tio Leo's, on the outskirts of Old Town. If it weren't for all the vintage cars in the parking lot, she would've sworn she was in the wrong place, but the marquee displayed, *Live Swing: Hot Rod Lincoln.*

Good-looking guys stood under the long red awning, sporting white T-shirts, fat cuffed jeans, slicked back hair, and motorcycle jackets. June drove around the lot and found an open spot in a dark corner. Her vintages shoes clicked on the sidewalk and echoed off the building as she walked around to the front. Her stomach flip-flopped in nervous anticipation.

She glided past the Rockabillies. They watched her while they exhaled cigarette smoke. A little thrill ran through her when she passed. This place was already better than the Rock-it. One fellow, thankfully one without a cigarette, sprinted over and opened the door for her. He was cute with a nice smile. She hoped he danced, and he might find her later.

"Thanks." She grinned.

He looked her up and down. "You're welcome."

Once inside, a tall lanky guy with a band t-shirt and rolled up jeans leaned casually on the doorjamb at the entrance to the bar.

"ID," he said in lieu of a greeting.

"Yeah, sure. Here ya go."

She handed him Julie's ID, trying it with her own hair color. Girls dyed their hair all the time. As he scrutinized the card, she re-thought that plan. She tried to look calm and bored, but worried herself into oblivion. It took three thousand uncomfortable seconds before he spoke.

"Arizona, huh?" He handed her back the ID. "Seven bucks."

Relief flooded her, and she pulled out money and handed it over. She stuffed the ID back in her purse and looked for an empty place at the bar. Men of varying ages took up every seat. She walked up to an empty spot with no stool.

"Excuse me. That's the cocktail stand," a brunette waitress said.

"Oh, sorry, I didn't... should I order a drink from you?" June's blood rushed to her face.

Brunette Ponytail Girl had already turned away and propped her tray on the plastic mat area. She yelled her orders to the bartender. June scooted down to the other end of the bar where a group of older guys sat hunched over Bud Lights. She squeezed in between them and tried to catch the bartender's eye. He didn't even look her direction. A wave of mortification and insecurity swept over her. She straightened up taller and swallowed the lump in her throat.

"You need a drink, honey?" one of the men asked.

She didn't know what that meant. Did he want to buy her a drink—which she certainly did not want him to do—or was he making conversation?

"Uh, thank you. I just need the bartender."

"Joe. Joe," the barfly barked and flagged the bartender.

"You need something, Ray?"

"No, but I think this little lady does." He nodded toward June.

"What can I getcha?" Bartender Joe asked.

June glanced at the line of beer on the shelf and recognized the beer she'd drunk at Amy's.

"Samuel Adams, please." He walked away and returned with a frosty bottle.

"One Sam Adams, that'll be four dollars."

She handed him a five.

"You wanna glass?" he asked, already grabbing for one.

"Yes, please."

He set it in front of her with her dollar change next to it and walked away. Other bills and quarters rested on the edge of the bar. June pushed hers there too and trudged away before the barfly could strike up a conversation. An empty table flanked the dance floor. June darted toward it, baptizing her hand in beer as she plopped down on a stool. Ponytail Waitress sidled by and tossed some napkins on the table, an amused glint in her eyes.

"Let me know if you need anything." The waitress turned and served drinks to the patrons in the corner booth, each person a fashion page from the 1940s.

June wondered if they danced or simply looked good. She'd find out soon enough. The drummer hit his sticks together and beat out the rhythm. The tall bassist pulled the strings so hard she thought they'd snap. They didn't. They thumped and drove the beat into her core. Heads nodded and feet tapped. Girls like June, pulsed, itchy with rhythm. The lead guitarist/singer fingered the melody and crooned into the mic, his voice full and high, edgy and bluesy.

It didn't take long before the floor packed with greaser guys twirling rockabilly girls who tottered on high heels and wore too much make-up. Silver chains that looped from the men's waist to pocket, bounced in rhythm. They danced a style similar to East Coast Swing, but different. *How many versions of swing dancing are there?*

A nice older man asked her to dance. She was desperate enough to say yes and glad she did. He looked her in the eyes and introduced himself as Lucky. She had no idea what he was dancing, but he led nicely, no pulling, no squishing too close. After the dance, they walked back to her seat to find her table over-taken by a couple, drinks already in front of them.

"Were you sitting here? Are these seats taken?" asked the plain, thin girl. Her uniform of black slacks and polo shirt emphasized her shapeless frame. She looked nothing like the vintage set and nothing like the high-heeled Rockabilly girls.

"Um, no. I mean yes." The seats weren't taken, but she'd left her purse to guard her beer, and her sweater draped the stool.

"Good. Do you mind if we sit here?"

Just then the band launched into another song. The man stood and held out his hand to the girl. She shrugged at June as they hit the dance floor. They did Lindy and did it well but looked out of place surrounded by Rockabillies.

At the same time, the vintage group made their way to the floor, and they did Lindy, too. Two of the well-dressed girls headed toward the ladies room, leaving one guy sitting alone. June took this as a sign that she should ask him to dance. She scanned the dance floor for space, working up her nerve. When she turned back to look for him, he was gone.

"Would you like to dance?" He'd snuck up behind her. "You do dance?"

June jumped up quickly and knocked her sweater to the floor. He and she both reached for it at the same time and bonked heads. He picked it up and handed it to her.

"Sorry," they both said and laughed.

"Yeah, I dance." She draped the sweater over her stool and followed him to the dance floor. He started out with East Coast Swing. She smiled, and although he wasn't her type—she liked them tall, dark, and debonair—she was happy to dance with a cute guy her age. His slicked, wavy hair matched her own light brown, though he had ochre eyes, unlike her green. He flashed a perfect smile as they danced. His lead was good and strong, but not too forceful, using his body to guide her.

"Do you Lindy, by chance?" he asked.

"Yes." Her heart soared.

He triple-stepped and sent her out into a swooshing swing-out, one of the best she'd ever felt. She was flying. He anchored his weight, securing her rotation. His style was different and looked more masculine. He had all the cool of the Rockabillies mixed with the skill and dynamics of Lindy Hop.

"Hey, you're okay."

He threw more complicated moves at her—some of which she knew, some she didn't. She fumbled through a few, but nailed enough not to embarrass herself. When the dance was over, she glowed with confidence. He walked her back to her table. She noticed the two vintage girls had returned.

"Ah, what's that you've got over there, James?" asked a dark-haired girl with perfect skin and classic movie star looks.

"Well hey. You gals abandoned me." He turned to June and steered her toward the girls. "I don't know. What's your name, anyway?"

"June."

"Nice to meetcha, June. I'm Clara, and this is Rose. And I guess you've met James. I love your dress, by the way, is it vintage?"

"Yeah, but to be honest, this was a gift. I'm just getting into this style."

The two girls exchanged a knowing look.

"Sit down, June," the one named Clara invited.

Two other couples walked up, and Clara introduced them.

"I hope there's not going to be a quiz," June joked. To her relief, they laughed.

June grabbed her beer, purse, and sweater, and scooted into the booth next to Clara. James and Rose glided onto the dance floor.

"Are you and James related?" June asked Clara.

"No, just friends and sometimes dance partners, although he's pretty wrapped up in Rose. It's hard to get many dances with him. You're lucky. She's pretty sure he's gonna propose any day now." Clara nodded toward the dance floor.

"Wow, they sure dance well together." June felt a pang of envy.

"Yeah." Clara looked away. "They're practicing for The International Jitterbug Championships up in Los Angeles at the end of summer. They're pretty much the best in San Diego. Well, the best at their style."

"I noticed they dance a little different than the stuff I learned in Phoenix and Pasadena."

"Oh, is there swing dancing in Phoenix? Is that where you're from? Or Pasadena?" Clara raised her eyebrows. "Inquiring minds will want to know."

"I'm from Phoenix, but since the dance instruction for Lindy was pretty much limited to one guy, we road-tripped to Pasadena on a regular basis. I even went to a Frankie Manning workshop."

Clara smiled, but her body pulled tight like a snag on a sweater.

"You don't like Frankie?" June drew circles in the condensation on her beer glass.

"No, we love Frankie. We think he's great. We love all his old clips. We study them, but the way Frankie dances now is different than the way Frankie danced in the 1930s and 40s. Don't you think?" Clara asked, as if it was a test.

"Sure. He was really fast in some of those old clips." June hoped that's what she meant.

Clara nodded. "Fast isn't the half of it. Have you ever seen clips of Dean Collins or Lindy from one of the Vitaphones or teen movies?"

June admitted she hadn't and instantly felt inadequate and confused. She thought she knew everything about the history of Lindy Hop.

"This guy Dean Collins—originally from New York—taught a lot of the Los Angeles Jitterbugs to Lindy. He danced in tons of movies and won dozens of contests back in the day. We emulate him and other dancers from the old Hollywood movies." Clara took a sip of her drink.

The other vintage dancers returned. The girls scooted in first, picked up their purses, and checked their lipstick.

Rose turned to James. "Can you get the waitress? I need another drink."

"Sure." He flagged the brunette waitress.

"So, Clara, what have you found out about our new friend? Is she a drinker, into vintage, or a square?" Rose blotted her lips and put her lipstick away.

June was offended by Rose's question. *Why would drinking or wearing vintage make you square or un-square? What a dumb and narrow-minded way to phrase a question.* It felt like another test.

Clara narrowed her eyes and made a face. "Behave, Rose, or we'll cut you off," she joked, but the tension became thick.

"You know what I mean."

Clara sighed and turned to June. "Well, our new friend clearly drinks." She pointed to June's beer. "And she's from Phoenix and is interested in learning about vintage."

"Great." Rose said with no hint of sarcasm. June guessed she'd passed the test, but wasn't sure what that got her, or if she wanted to be where it did.

"And how does everyone know each other?" June asked.

"Rose and James are dating. Larissa and Marty are dating and live together, and everyone else is friends. We hang out, dance together, and spend copious amounts of time watching old videos from the 1940s," Clara answered.

June asked about the couple who'd taken her table. Clearly, they were Lindy Hoppers. Where'd they fit in? Clara explained the subgroups of dancers that populated the San Diego area. June's mind reeled. They didn't have those divisions in Phoenix and everyone got along fine. She liked the look and feel of the Dean Collins style, but wasn't sure about the attitude that went with it.

"So," June asked Clara, after everyone had hit the dance floor, again. "Does that mean you don't dance with the people in other subgroups?"

"Oh, hell no. We dance with everyone. It's really too small a scene to snub anyone. And it's all the same dance, only with different emphasis and body positions."

Clara's answer made sense and June felt better about her new friends. As if on cue, a cute Rockabilly—the one who'd opened the door for her—sauntered over and asked June to dance. Clara smiled approvingly. Obviously, there was no division when it came to cute guys.

They finished the dance, and he asked for another and even though he didn't Lindy, June couldn't help stealing glances of him. His caramel skin, dark hair, and dark eyes made her nervous in all the right ways. They talked as they dance. His name was Vertie, short for Alverto. She'd always been attracted to other ethnicities and wondered if it was her longing for an ethnic identity. Maybe when she found her grandmother, she could claim a cultural history.

When the dance was over, he returned her to her new acquaintances. She made small talk and danced a couple more times before the band played their last song. Clara asked for June's phone number and promised to call—she was dying to take June vintage shopping. June was game, and she needed a friend.

June said her goodnights and went out the way she came in. Cigarette smoke hung heavy in the still night air. The Rockabilly she'd danced with was outside talking to his buddy. She noticed, to her delight, that Vertie wasn't smoking. She did a happy dance in her head and forgave herself for being just a little square. She caught his eye and smiled, but kept walking.

"Hey." He jogged after her. "You want me to walk you to your car?"

She hesitated, trying to make up her mind what a single girl should do. He'd been polite and was so good looking. "Thanks. That'd be cool."

"So, you're one of those Lindy Hoppers, huh?"

"Yeah, I guess." They turned the corner to the dark side of the building. She was glad he'd walked with her.

"You guys sure take up a lot of space on the dance floor," he said with no hint of accusation in his tone. They reached her truck.

"This is me."

"So, I was wondering if you'd like to give me your number?"

She wasn't sure she should, but felt the electricity crackling between them.

"How about you give me your number," she countered.

"Yeah, okay. Gotta pen?"

"Sure do." She dug one out and wrote his number on an old receipt.

He stuffed his hands into his jeans pockets. Silence stretched between them like summer twilight. Neither of them knew what to say next.

"So, yeah, give me a call some time. Maybe we can hang out."

He walked away with a casual saunter, and she re-thought not giving him her number. But it had been a good night, a cute boy and some new Lindy Hopper friends. She was giddy as she buckled her seatbelt and pulled out of the parking lot.

Yeah, I think I'm gonna like it here.

Violet ~ 1940s

10. Milkshake Stand
(The Three Barons)

Violet tried not to think about time hurtling forward, but it was always present, hiding behind every kiss, every embrace. She finished her sewing and pressing for the day and waited for Charles to arrive at the shop.

Since she'd been spending all her free time with Charles, she hadn't seen Jeannie in a week. However, she and Jeannie had talked on the phone. Jeannie twittered about how Paddy had succumbed to her charms and was hopelessly in love with her. Violet had a feeling it might be the other way around. *Would Paddy really would join up after graduation?* The idea sent a sharp pain through her insides, she sighed.

Mrs. Peppy looked up, her eyes filled with concern and compassion.

As much as Violet wanted to take Charles to the malt shop, she was nervous. Most of the kids were polite to her, but none were friendly. She had no idea what to expect from Johnny. If she invited Jeannie and Paddy to sit with them, she'd have to include Johnny, Sue, Ronald, and the new girl.

I don't miss the complicated hierarchy of high school, but I do miss the carefree afternoons spent at the malt shop, finishing up homework, and stuffing nickels into the jukebox. She missed challenging classes and exercising her brain. She even missed lunch in the cafeteria a little. *This is the first time I've admitted it to myself.*

She wanted to pretend she and Charles were high school sweethearts and the world was a perfect easy place, and they had all the time in the world to live and love.

Both Mrs. Peppy and Violet looked up when they heard the bell tinkle. Mrs. Peppy's face lit up almost as much as Violet's. If Violet didn't know any better, she'd have sworn Mrs. Peppy was carrying a torch for Charles, too.

"Good afternoon ladies." He swept into the shop and gave Mrs. Peppy a quick peck on the cheek. "Do my eyes deceive me or do you have a lovely new dress on today, Mrs. Peplinski?"

She blushed and said something in Polish. "Piękny chłopiec." She switched to English. "Beautiful boy, you make this old lady blush."

Charles laughed his throaty laugh, brought out a box from behind his back, and set it on Mrs. Peppy's worktable.

"I don't know that I will pronounce this right, but here are some Chrusiciki which my friend Ski, I mean Marvin, got in the mail today. He was more than happy to share them with us."

He opened the box and the sweet smell of sugar and sharp bite of alcohol filled the small shop. Mrs. Peppy inhaled deeply.

"Thank you, you sweet boy. I have not had this for many years." Her eyes clouded, and she looked away.

Charles tactfully swept over to Violet. "Are you ready my little Jitterbug?"

He swooped down and placed a soft kiss on Violet's earlobe, fire raged through her body, eddying in surprising places. She had to catch her breath.

"I have a little something for you too," Charles said in a fake Polish accent, too low for Mrs. Peppy to hear.

"What would you like to do tonight? There's a new Cary Grant picture, *The Philadelphia Story*, playing at the North Park Theater. Kate Hepburn and Jimmy Stewart, too."

"Well." Violet smiled. "I was thinking we could hang out at the malt shop." *I sound so juvenile.* "It's just that I haven't seen Jeannie since I met you, and we could use a little more practice."

"Sounds great. I'd love to meet your friends."

Violet jumped up, forgetting the book on her lap. It fell to the floor with a thud. He picked it up and examined the cover. She turned red and gritted her teeth. She didn't know what she thought she should be reading, but not that. Maybe *Life Magazine* or a current dime store novel. This book was too literary. She didn't want him thinking she was a dull brainiac.

"Hmmm." He handed it back. She put it face down on her sewing machine. "*The Good Earth*, huh? I really liked that one."

She gawked at him.

"What, squid's don't read?"

She wasn't sure what to say. Most guys who read beyond English class, read Dashiell Hammet or Raymond Chandler novels. A thrill of satisfaction came over her.

"I bet you thought us Navy boys only read comic books and guys like Hammet, didn't ya?"

She laughed and marveled that she'd been caught high-hatting him, at least in her mind. "Yeah, I'm surprised."

"My dad's an English professor at the university and he insists that we all read the classics and Pulitzers." He laughed easily as they walked out the door.

She wanted to hear more about his family and his literary conquests.

"Not that I don't sneak in a little Chandler, when he's not looking," he added with a wink.

"That's swell. The only person who reads in my family is me, not even my mom." The word was out of her mouth before she could stop it. It tasted like sour milk.

"I've never heard you talk about your mom." He paused. "Is she, I mean, has she passed?"

"Are you asking if she's dead? No, she's not dead."

"Would you like to talk about it?"

"Nope." Leaks sprouted in her dam. "No, I want to hear more about your family. Do you have brothers and sisters?"

He stopped walking and looked around. "Sorry to interrupt that train of thought, but do we need to grab the bus to go to this infamous malt shop of yours?"

"No. The Sugar Bowl is a little bit of a hike, but I'd like to walk if you don't mind."

"Oh, I almost forgot." He reached into his pocket and pulled out a crisp white handkerchief with the initials CDM. "Your surprise."

He opened the folded cloth to reveal a dainty nautical anchor hanging from a shiny silver chain. The necklace was beautiful. She gasped. Her heart leapt into her throat.

"Do you like it?"

"Yes, yes, yes."

She threw her arms around his neck and kissed him. Her surprise attack caught him off guard, but he returned her kiss, boiling her blood. She pressed her body into his, wanting more of what she had in the park. He tensed and tried to remove her arms from his neck, difficult with necklace in hand. She opened her eyes to see his embarrassment and caught up quickly. Her face turned a matching red. A matronly lady walked by and gave them an impertinent look. They both laughed.

"Will you help me put it on?" she asked.

"You want to wear it now?"

"Yes, don't you want me to?"

"Yeah, I wasn't sure you'd like it or that you'd think...I dunno." He reached for the necklace. "Here, let me help you."

She turned around to let him fasten the necklace. His hands groped at the tiny clasp. His breath breezed across her neck, prickling her skin. She swept her hair to the side. He secured the clasp, but his fingers lingered, brushing her skin. His breath tickled her ear, sending another round of shivers through her body.

"Is that good?" he whispered.

Oh yes, too good. She wished they were not standing on a street corner. She spun around and continued walking. He held her hand as if it were the most natural occurrence in the world. She couldn't imagine why his handholding was as thrilling as his kisses, but it was.

"So, you were about to tell me more about your family," she said.

"Was I?" He teased. "I've got three older sisters who are married with kids. So I'm Uncle Chassy." He chuckled. "Although since I'll be going on a boat, they've taken to calling me Captain Chas." He winced as he said it.

"Ahhhhh, that's cute," she replied with as much enthusiasm as she could. She'd never even thought about having kids or met anyone she'd want to have kids with. It was something for other girls, girls with normal lives.

"Is it my turn to ask questions, yet?"

"Nope." He rolled his eyes. She continued. "What's your favorite color?"

"Red. Yours?"

"Green. Favorite pie?"

"Apple."

"Favorite book?"

He was quiet for a long time. "Okay, it might be a three way tie between Steinbeck, Fitzgerald, and most recently Buck."

"No joshing. Which books specifically?" She hoped it was books she'd read.

"I like Steinbeck. *Of Mice and Men* was brilliant. Disquieting. And I love the voice of Fitzgerald. He captures beauty and despair in one breath. You know?" He scratched his head, taking Violet's hand with him. "Most folks like *The Great Gatsby*, but I go for, *Tender is the Night*."

She tried to look at him while they walked, but it was difficult. He'd sped up with his animated review. His sincere love of literature completely fascinated her. It thrilled her as much as his touch. Forget the malt shop. She wanted to talk books.

"And then there's the one you're reading, *The Good Earth*. I dig reading about foreign lands and stuff. And I really went for the lead character. It's crazy that a woman wrote it, really getting the man's perspective."

"Wow." Violet matched his stride as his pace continued to increase. "I know what you mean. I couldn't believe it either. The culture was fascinating. So many different customs. I've only read *The Grapes of Wrath*, *The Pearl*, and *Of Mice and Men*, and I have to admit I didn't go bananas over his style. Fitzgerald though, I can really get into. Maybe it's because his characters are so glamorous and flawed. And I'm fascinated with flappers. I could kinda see myself being a one."

"Wee haw. I haven't talked about books since I joined up. Most the fellas don't read much. If they do it's Superman and Dick Tracy comics. It feels good to stretch the old noggin."

He smiled at her, and she realized what was missing in boys like Johnny—a keen intellect. *Intellect is seductive. I'm completely seduced by his mind, not just his good looks and dance moves.*

"So," he continued. "Have you got to the part in the book where he realizes he loves his wife, but doesn't realize that the emotion he feels is love? I think a lot of men are like that." He looked away then rushed on. "And the part where he can't bring himself to slaughter the ox? It says so much about his character. And I found it really neat when they ate the locusts."

She wanted to talk about the love part, baffled when it came to the way men love. She never thought their feelings ran as deep as women's, but seeing her dad's devastation and now Charles bringing up that part in the book, made her think she was missing something.

"Gross." She made a face. "Would you ever eat bugs?"

"Sure, why not. If my life depended on it. Wouldn't you?"

"Oooo, I'd have to be pretty hungry. I think I'd rather have a double chocolate malt." They both laughed.

"I think I can accommodate you there."

The Sugar Bowl Malt Shop stood between Brooks Shoe Shop and a stairwell that lead up to a secretarial school. Violet's and Charles's reflections were distorted in the building's black façade like funhouse mirrors. Long oval windows advertised hamburgers, cold sodas, and milkshakes. The front door, flanked by stacked glass bricks, presented a painted penguin with a scarf.

"So this is your home away from home, huh?" Charles asked.

"I guess so."

He opened the door for her. The smell of sugar and burgers blasted them in the face. A few heads turned their direction. Jeannie jumped up from her booth and moved toward them. Paddy and Johnny looked to see what Jeannie was excited about. When Johnny spotted them, his faced turned dark and pinched. He glared at Charles. Charles grinned in return.

"Vee Vee," Jeannie squealed. "I'm so glad you made it. The joint hasn't been the same without you. We've got a booth. Come sit down."

They followed Jeannie to the tall wooden booth. Spired coat-hooks stood at the end of the tables like fence posts. Opposite the booths, the soda fountain housed the two soda jerks. Wally, Jeannie's older brother, was one of them. Their black and white uniforms matched the penguin on the door. Wally nodded to Violet. He'd asked her out a couple times, but she told him it'd be too awkward if things went sour for them. She couldn't lose Jeannie as a friend. His bitterness about being classified 4-F—for his hearing loss—seemed to rise daily.

The few tables that were usually scattered between the booths and counter were shoved into the front alcove, creating more dance floor for the Jitterbugs.

As Violet and Charles made their way through the rug-cutters, Johnny got up to leave. Paddy grabbed his arm and gave him a look. Violet didn't think Charles noticed. He was busy steering them through the crowd with a protective arm around her.

Violet introduced Charles to Jeannie, Paddy, and Johnny. Charles stuck out his hand. Paddy gave him a friendly handshake, but Johnny waited a little too long before grabbing Charles's hand, giving him the firmest handshake Violet had ever seen. Both boys' knuckles turned white, but Charles kept smiling.

"Nice to meetcha," Johnny mumbled.

"Call me Chas. It's nice to meet you, too. I've heard a lot about you guys."

"Really, that's funny. We haven't heard anything about you Char-les." Johnny drew out his name like a bad word. "So, when are you shipping out?"

Panic built in Violet's chest. She didn't want to think about him leaving. *Is Johnny doing that on purpose?*

"So, what kind of boat are you on, Chas?" Paddy intervened. "You must be out at, uh, Naval Air Station on Coronado, right?"

"Yeah, I'm training on a carrier right now. In fact, we're shipping out for two weeks next Monday for some training maneuvers."

"Wow," Paddy took a sip of his shake. "Have you been on it yet?"

"Only in dock. This will be my first time out on the ocean."

Johnny walked over to the jukebox, digging into his pocket for coins. Charles and Violet sat across from Paddy and Jeannie. The fellas slipped into easy conversation. Jane and Barbara sidled up to the table.

"Hi, Violet, where ya been hiding?" Barbara looked at Charles, the real reason she was making such an effort to say hello. "Or maybe not hiding?" She gave a knowing smile. "Busy?"

Violet wanted to throw up on her. "Yup, I've been busy."

Barbara gave Jane a look and tried again. "So, who's your new friend? Aren't you going to introduce us?"

Paddy and Charles stopped talking, an amused look crossed Charles's face. Violet deliberately ignored Barbara, but Jeannie jumped in before it got awkward.

"Barbara and Jane, this is Violet's new friend, Chas."

"Nice to meet you ladies." He stretched his arm and put it around Violet's shoulder. Her heart flipped and stomach fluttered. She tried not to blush, but the heat rose to her cheeks.

"So, are you as good a dancer as you are a looker?" Barbara asked. She and Jane giggled.

Jeannie's eyes bugged out.

Charles gave them a playful look. "Well, senoritas, you'll have to ask Violet." He looked at Violet with his blue-green eyes and she was lost in his sea. "What do you think Vi? Am I as good a dancer as I am a looker?" His laughter fell like rain.

She ignored Barbara and Jane, looked into his eyes. "Yes."

"Uh, well." Barbara recovered. "You simply must share your jive bomber with us. Would you like to take me for a spin, Chas?" She cooed, and then added, "If you don't mind, Violet. This song's a dilly."

Violet was shocked, too angry to summon a response. Her eyes filled with tears, and she stood to let Charles out of the booth. He hesitated, but Violet didn't want him to see her face. She dropped her purse and bent to pick it up mumbling, "Um, sure."

On his way out, he whispered in her ear, "Sorry, I'll be back."

His breath at her neck sent shivers down her spine. It split her anger, allowing her to regain a little composure. She flopped down onto the bench as Johnny strolled over.

"Scooch over, Vi. Let your old pal Johnny have a seat." She didn't like his tone, but scooted anyway.

"Come on, Jeannie." Paddy tugged Jeannie's hand. "Let's try my new hip dipper slip move, again. This song's knocked out."

Jeannie gave Violet a sympathetic look, but hopped up. Johnny slid over to the other seat, face to face with Violet.

"So, you and that swabbie, huh?"

I don't want to have this conversation. She crossed her arms and leaned against the wall, studying a crack in the paint. Johnny made a couple tries at conversation. Anger, indifference, pride, and confusion played across his face.

She finally answered, "Yeah, I guess so."

He sat quietly for a while. "Ah, Vi, what's he got that I ain't got?"

His humble plea surprised her. She wanted to be angry. Anger was easy, but she could see he was hurt. "I don't know."

"He's not good for you."

"You don't even know him."

"I have eyes, and I can see. He's just using you for a good time."

She balked at the idea, but a buried part of her wakened to that insecurity.

"You're being ridiculous. You've got no say in the matter. And you can be a real creep sometimes. And...and, you don't know what you're talking about." She glared at him.

He scrunched his eyes, the bridge of his nose creasing. "Look, I'm not trying to be a creep. I'm trying to look out for you."

"I can take care of myself."

"I don't think you can. Vi. Don't be like that. You know I'd do anything for you."

"Then leave me alone."

He shook his head and reached for her shoulder, changed his mind, and folded his hands in his lap. "Anything but that."

Panic, fear, and doubt shook her to her core. *Is there some truth to what he said?* Charles was leaving for a long time, who knew how long. She ran her hands along the side of her face clasping them in front of her mouth, blowing air between her sweaty palms. Her mind roiled with Johnny's words. She played with the anchor at her neck, rubbing the cool metal between her fingers.

"Did he give you that? I bet he's got a drawer full of 'em. I bet he gives them to all the girls. What do you think? He'll come back for you? Come on Vi. Tell me you're not that naïve."

"Is there a problem here?" Charles appeared at her side. "Violet, are you all right?"

"She's fine. I can take care of her. Why don't you go back to your boat?" Johnny stood up.

"Apparently she isn't. And you can't."

One minute Violet was standing up to get out of the booth. The next minute Johnny was throwing a punch at Charles. Charles was fast. He dodged and grabbed Johnny's fist, twisting it around Johnny's back, wrenching it toward his head. He slammed Johnny's face into the table. At the same time, Wally leapt over the counter, knocking two malt glasses to the checkered floor. He pulled Charles off Johnny and stood between them.

"Break it up," Wally said.

Everyone in the joint stopped dancing. The only sound was the lilt of Anita O'Day belting out *Stop, the Red Light's On.*

"I'm sorry, but I have to ask both you fellas to leave."

"But Johnny started…" Violet began.

Wally shot her an apologetic look. Johnny gave her the dirtiest, saddest look she'd ever seen. He smoothed down his rumpled shirt, gave a head nod to Paddy and Jeannie, and continued to glower at Violet.

"Don't come running to me, Vi when he leaves you all alone. And believe me, he will." He pushed his way past Wally and Charles and clomped out the door.

The jitterbugs whispered and stared, averting their eyes when caught. Violet didn't need another reason for them to gossip about her. Wally played warden.

"Can we have a minute to catch our breath, and give Johnny a head start? I don't want a repeat outside," Charles asked.

"Sure, take a minute. Vi, can I get you a soda or maybe your favorite double chocolate malt?"

She held herself together by a thread and couldn't answer. If she opened her mouth, she might let out a wail. Jeannie zoomed to her side, but as much as Violet adored Jeannie, she wanted Charles. Jeannie guided Violet, sitting her down in the booth. Violet's emotions were muddled, and she couldn't generate any normal reactions.

"I think you should have a coke, honey. Look."

Wally deposited a soda in front of her. She took a long drink. The cool fizziness calmed her, but she was still shaking inside.

"I'm sorry about that Vi. I didn't want to start anything, but I wasn't going let him slug me."

Violet had no idea why he was apologizing. It was her fault. She never should've brought him there. She'd underestimated Johnny's attachment.

"Excuse me Jeannie, I need to go." An overwhelming feeling of confinement came over her. *I'm trapped. Not by Jeannie. Not in the booth, but by the circumstances of my life.* Jeannie scooted out. Charles took Jeannie's place at Violet's side. He was a balm. She could already imagine the gossip Barb and Jane would spin about the afternoon, but with Charles's arm around her, it was okay.

Charles left a quarter for the nickel soda and turned to Jeannie and Paddy. "Well, nice to meet you."

Violet and Charles walked out of the shop and down the street, Violet was weak and shaky. Charles guided her to a bench.

"Maybe we should take the bus back to the shop? Or maybe you'll let me take you all the way to your house this time?"

"No, I don't want to go home."

She didn't want him to see where she lived, but didn't want to be parted, either. She couldn't suppress the conflicting emotions crashing around her insides. She wanted his arms around her. At the same time, she couldn't stop thinking about what Johnny said. *I've fallen in love with Charles and would wait for him forever. But will he come back to me?* She thought so, but she didn't know.

"Okay." He rubbed his hands together. "What would you like to do? How about the picture show? You know, *The Philadelphia Story?*"

Sitting close to him in the dark sounds appealing. She giggled, the jumble of emotions loosened.

"What's so funny?"

"I was thinking I wish theater seats didn't have arms."

She blushed at her bold admission and looked down. He tucked a curl behind her ear and softly, tenderly kissed below it, running his lips across her cheek. Tiny goose pimples emerged on her skin. He reached for her hand and entwined his fingers in hers. She shivered, closed her eyes, and waited for more. In a flash, he was on his feet. Her eyes popped open, and he ushered her up from the bench.

"Look, we need the bus heading the other direction and here it comes. Let's make a run for it."

He tugged her hand, and they went flying. The wind on her face cooled and cleared her mind. She clung to his buoyancy as they bounded across the street. The brakes of the bus squealed to a stop, and they hopped on, never losing each other's hand.

In the dark of the theater, he leaned over and whispered in her ear, "Are you comfortable? Need anything? Want some candy?"

She was comfortable, yet uncomfortable. An invisible field crackled and sparked around them. *Does he feel it, too?* She was aware of his every movement. She inhaled slowly, trying to calm down before the movie started. The strange yearning desire was almost painful. She needed to touch him, to press her thigh against his, to feel his hand on hers, to feel his lips on hers.

He stretched his arm around the back of her seat, but not around her. She leaned into it. He immediately straightened up and pulled his arm back.

"I'm sorry. Is that uncomfortable for you?" he whispered. His voice was like a lullaby. She leaned closer, trying not to be obvious, but loved the delicious sensation of his breath on her neck.

"No. It's fine." She tried to keep her breath steady and focused as the picture started, but it was impossible to concentrate with him next to her. As handsome as Cary Grant was, he paled in comparison to Charles. She dropped her hand to her side and felt his there. Their fingers accidentally brushed, a powerful spark surged through her body, the yearning pain intensified. He twined his fingers in hers, and it took all her self-control not to throw her arms around him and shower his beautiful face with kisses.

She tried to focus on Kate Hepburn and her pretty dresses and Virginia Weilder's annoying little sister character. Johnny's words came back to her. Insecurity wrestled with hope. *Am I deluding myself after all?*

Charles took her hand up to his mouth and absent-mindedly ran his lips across her index finger, moving his head from side to side. Johnny's echoes dissipated, and she had to hold her breath to suppress a squeak. Shivers so intense her eyes watered, ran through her body. She lost the thread of the movie. She turned to watch Charles as he watched the movie, lips skimming her hand. His eyes were closed. She wanted to be alone with him. A little whimper escaped her lips. He noticed and abruptly put down their hands and straightened up. He looked at her, shook his head, and smiled.

"Sorry about that."

He pressed his lips together, exhaled, and moved their hands to rest on his thigh, staring straight ahead at the screen. She didn't know what to make of it and sat stock still, trying not to move her hand or think about his muscular thigh beneath it. *I can't believe I'm thinking about his thigh.* She watched the movie, trying to clear her thoughts, but the aching persisted.

He turned his head to look at her. She turned to look at him. He focused back at the screen. She longed for him to kiss her, but he didn't. This happened two or three times before, she gave up trying to catch his eye. The picture seemed extraordinarily long — though when the lights came up, and the usher came to show the way out — she couldn't believe it was over.

"That was good. Didn't you think?" he asked, avoiding her eyes.

He let go of her hand and flexed his fingers. He gave her shoulder a little squeeze and guided her up the aisle toward the exit.

"I think we'll have to take a cab. It's a little late for the bus. Should I take you home, or to the shop?"

"The shop please."

She didn't want the night to end, but didn't know what else there was to do. The ferry had stopped running and water taxis were too few. He'd have to take a cab the long way around the Strand to make it on base by midnight.

"Okay, the shop it is." He flagged a taxi.

They climbed into the back of the cab. Electricity sizzled between them, but something was different. He put his arm around her shoulder, more protective than romantic. They rode in silence until the cab pulled up in front of the shop.

The damp night air settled a wet blanket over everything. Condensation dripped from awnings and pooled into small ponds. The low purr of the taxi engine mixed with the crackle of streetlights. He asked the cabbie to wait. Her heart lurched. He was obviously planning a quick goodbye.

They walked to the door, and he leaned in, not pressing his body to hers, only his lips. He turned to go, but she clutched his neck and pressed her body into his, throwing him off balance. He rocked forward, pinning her between him and the door. Her entire body flamed with desire.

He kissed her back, crushing his hard body into hers. His breath quickened. Hers became shallow, her head dizzied. He pulled her tighter. His strong body leaned and flattened her against the damp glass door. The moisture seeped through her sweater cooling her over-heated body. His mouth devoured hers. *This is what I wanted.*

His lips matched her own yearning. He pressed into her, almost smashing his lips into her teeth. Then he pulled back a little, rubbing his lips back and forth on hers like his hand in the theater. Taking a gulp of air, he kissed her again, tugging her lip, parting her mouth, his tongue briefly brushing hers, running across her upper lip. His mouth tripped from hers, kissing into the hollow below her ear, gently, yet firmly sucking on the soft of her neck.

Shudders rushed around her body, resonating in private, newly awakened crevices. She fell somewhere, some place out of time. She knew nothing but his sweet smell, his mouth on her neck, his body trembling against hers. He climbed his way back to her mouth. Her entire being vibrated. His thighs smashed into hers. The curves of her body fit perfectly into his. Her breath came faster and faster, his too, louder and rasping.

"Violet, Violet," he croaked, "I, I, you, you're, driving me crazy, I..." a soft groan escaped his lips as he met hers again.

Honk. Honk. The echo of the horn reverberated off the sleeping buildings.

He drew his head away from hers. She was shocked alert by his sudden stillness. He grabbed her face between his hands, giving her one more, hard, hurried press to the lips. Then he rambled toward the cab, looking like a drunken sailor. She couldn't help giggling, a low rumble stuck in her throat.

"I'll see you tomorrow, same time." His voice was thick. "Same place. Okay?" He brought his hand up to his mouth, rubbing his lips, and looked at her with an indecipherable expression.

The cab disappeared into the mist. Violet caught herself before she crashed to the ground. Her knees wanted to buckle. She grabbed the doorknob, caught her breath, and found her strength. She'd planned on walking home, but decided against it. She let herself into the shop and flopped on the couch in the back room. She doubted Pop would notice her absence, and Mrs. Peppy had said she was always welcome.

She sank into the scratchy mohair couch and replayed the day's events, trying to decipher them. She couldn't quite get her mind to focus on anything except the scene in the doorway. But as she drifted off to sleep Johnny's nagging voice echoed, "Don't come running back to me when..."

June ~ 1990s
11. That's Where My Money Goes
(Indigo Swing)

"So, before we go shopping, there's a few thing you need to know about vintage clothing," Clara said. "One of the most popular fabrics of the war era was gabardine, gab for short. It refers to the diagonal weave and came in cotton, rayon, and wool."

"Rayon. I've heard of that." June nodded her head.

"Yes, now Rayon was created to be a fake silk. Invented in 1898, but didn't gain mainstream popularity until silk was needed for parachutes in WWII."

"That's so cool." June blinked and shook her head. "You know so much about it."

Clara smiled and nodded. "And cotton was different in the 1940s, the fibers were longer. Today's are shorter which is why our clothes wear out faster."

"No way."

"Way. So, that should help while you shop. Let's go."

June wasn't sure how that would help her shop, but found the fashion facts fascinating. Clara dragged her to numerous vintage stores where they drooled over racks of shoes and clothes. June found an affordable pair of cute sandal-like shoes with a wedge heel called wedgies. Clara assured June all the jitterbugs in the 40s wore them with stripy socks. How Clara knew this June wasn't sure, but she didn't doubt her.

As June discovered more about Clara's life, she felt like they'd been friends forever and had a difficult time reconciling the vintage queen working as a receptionist in her dad's veterinary clinic. Clara had gone to college, but hadn't found anything that stuck, though she knew she didn't want to be a vet. Clara's approach to a career mystified June's goal-driven way of thinking.

Clara promised one last shop and then lunch. June was relieved, famished, and running out of money. They walked down dark stairs into a basement shop of their last stop. Ambient house music crushed their eardrums. A tall, thin girl — white hair swirled into an impressively high, cotton-candy beehive — greeted them. Her pale skin, pink eye-shadow, and cat-eye liner gave her the distinct look of a mid-century gothic.

"Welcome to Rags," she yelled above the music. "Looking for anything special?"

"No, just looking. Thanks," Clara yelled back.

June smiled at the sea of chrome rolling racks placed haphazardly in a chaotic maze. They shopped shoes first. Clara spotted 1940s peach pumps and insisted June try them on. They fit perfectly and were surprisingly comfortable and at only twenty bucks, June could afford them. What she really wanted was to spend her money on more 40s rayon dresses. She needed a decent part-time job to give her a little more spending money. They rounded one of the rolling racks and stumbled across James rifling through a rack of men's gab shirts.

"Hey, what are you guys doing here?" He cupped his hand to his mouth to be heard.

"Shopping, of course. I'm showing June the ropes. You remember June, right?"

He looks younger than when we met at the bar. If he wasn't so clean-cut looking, he'd almost pass for Rockabilly. I like his tight fitting ringer-tee and faded jeans. June smiled.

"So, finding anything good?" he asked.

"June's found loads of stuff, thanks to my guidance, of course. I bought some new shoes and an awesome 40s dress for The Big Six Show. How 'bout you?"

"I found this cool gab flap-pocket shirt for fourteen bucks. I think I'm going to get it. What do you think?" He lifted it to his torso.

"That ought to look good on the dance floor. The periwinkle's a good color for you."

"Niiiiice," Clara added.

He tucked it under his arm and continued to rummage through the rack.

"Have you eaten?" Clara asked. "We're gonna grab some grub after this. Wanna come?"

"Sure, let me finish picking through these. I'll meet you guys up front."

The girls continued to comb the racks and found ten different dresses for June to try. Only two fit and were in her price range. June knew it was shallow to get such a thrill out of shopping, but it always perked her up. *Maybe the power to buy had something to do with feeling in control?*

Before they got to the register, Clara ducked into an old bank vault. June followed. Inside, an array of jackets and furs hung on alternated rods. Clara fingered them, studying their price tags.

"Not bad, a little more than eBay, and you can try them on here. No shipping." Clara pulled one out to try on.

"What's eBay?" June yelled.

"Shhh, eBay's a dirty word to these retail shops. I'll tell you about it over lunch. What do you think of this?" Clara held up a plaid jacket. "I think this is perfect. See if there's any you like. These are classic collegiate jitterbug. We call them Pendleton jackets, though they're not all made by Pendleton. It's the style."

June looked closer and found a pretty teal and beige Pendleton with a soft peach accent. She liked it, but it was twenty-five. She put the shoes back. She needed a jacket more.

James poked his head into the vault. "Aren't you gals done yet? I'm starving." He smiled, with bright eyes. June was usually good with first impressions, but couldn't read him.

"Yeah, yeah, we're coming." Clara gathered her merchandise. They paid and marched up the stairs—Clara and James in conversation, June trailing behind.

"So, what's for lunch, ladies?"

"How about Thai?" Clara asked. "There's a great place a couple blocks away."

"I've never had Thai food before," June replied.

"What?" they said in unison.

"You've never had Thai?" Clara asked.

"Um, ya…Phoenix," June said in way of an explanation. "But I'm up for trying anything. Well, almost anything."

"So, where's Rose?" Clara asked James.

"She took off for L.A. to hang with her sister or something."

"Is everything okay with you guys?"

"Sure." He shrugged.

"Cool. Good." Clara nodded. "So, anything going on tonight? Any shows I don't know about?"

"Nope, nothing tonight, kinda dead. Hey, talk to Larissa and Marty. Maybe we could hang at their place and practice. Break down some more steps?"

"Yeah, they've got a good wood floor." Clara smiled. "I like practicing over there. I'll give 'em a call later. I'll let you know if they're into us coming over."

"So what's their story?" June asked.

"Larissa and Marty? True love as far as anyone can tell. They're the perfect couple, no offense James."

"None taken." He shrugged again.

"They live together in a cute old house with killer wood floors and a sweeeet layout. I'm sure they'll end up married."

"Really?" *That's two. I thought Jack and Molly were an anomaly.* "How old are they?"

"Larissa's twenty-four and I think Marty's twenty-six. I don't know. How old is Marty?" Clara asked.

"Yeah, twenty-six or twenty-seven or something. They're good people. Really cool. I don't think Marty's in any hurry to get married, though."

"Really, what makes you say that?" Clara checked her look in one of the old building's big windows.

"Uh, I dunno, they're really happy. Why mess with that? It seems like once people get married they lose something. Don't ya think?"

Clara gave June a sideways look. "Oh yeah, why buy the cow when you can get the milk for free."

James rolled his eyes. "Whatever, Clara. That's not what I meant."

"What did you mean?" Clara raised her eyebrows.

"I don't know. Seems like the trick isn't falling in love. The trick is keeping it going. You hear all those jokes about guys not getting any once they get married. There must be some truth to that. And look at the divorce rate."

"So, we're back to the milk now, are we?" Clara taunted.

"No. Well, maybe, I don't know. There's something about marriage that seems to kill the romance, though. Stereotypes are there for a reason."

"Ah, hell, what do I know? You may be right. I get bored after a couple months myself. What do you think, June?"

June was caught off guard. She hadn't thought much past cute faces, nice mouths, and pretty teeth. She knew she wanted to marry and have kids someday, but that idea was too far away and too abstract.

"I dunno, marriage is..." June switched her bag from one hand to the other. "Tell me about this eBay."

"Ah, one of my favorite subjects. It's this online..."

"Not to interrupt," James interrupted. "But where is this place?"

"Two more blocks." Clara turned back to June. "Now where was I? Oh yes, eBay. It's this online auction that has a whole section for vintage clothing. Sometimes it's cheaper than the shops, but you can get totally screwed on size and condition. Totally cool and worth checking out."

"Do they have men's stuff?"

"Of course."

"What are you doing later? Maybe you and June could come over and show me eBay?"

"Sure, what do you say June? Wanna hang out at James's tonight?"

"Oh, no. I mean yes. Actually, I've got a date." June was looking forward to her date with Vertie, but now she wanted to hang out with Clara and James. "Can I take a rain-check? I'd love to learn about eBay. And James, I'm dying to see those old movie clips you told me about at Tio's."

"Yeah, man, you've gotta check 'em out. There's one called *Groovie Movie* that has tons of cool dance steps. I've done a pretty good job breaking down the footwork. Plus, I hooked up with this guy who's made it his mission to perfect Dean Collins style. I've taken some private lessons with him." James grew more animated as they walked. "You know June, you're a good follow. You could be kick-ass if you learned some of Jewel's styling. She was Dean's partner."

"Thanks." *What did he meant by could be? I thought I was holding my own on the dance floor.*

"Here we are." Clara opened the door. "Royal Thai."

Soft clanging chimes resounded and exotic spices wafted throughout the spacious restaurant. Large ornate tapestries, intricately woven with Thai gods and goddesses, shimmered on the walls. Lavishly adorned ceramic elephants perched on booth dividers. *If the décor and aroma is any indication, I'm going to like Thai food.*

"I love this place," Clara continued. "You know the owner gives cooking classes. Do you like to cook, June?"

"Let's see if I like Thai food first, and then I'll decide if I want to learn how to cook it. I do like to cook though, mostly baking." June smiled.

James's eyes lit up. "Mmm, like cookies and pies?"

June laughed. "Yeah, like cookies and pies." She made a mental note to bake some cookies or banana bread for James. "Doesn't Rose cook for you?"

James and Clara both laughed.

"Rose, no, but I think I'd like to learn to cook. Let me know if you guys do the cooking class. I'd be game."

Clara and James shared their dishes with June. She wasn't crazy about Clara's, but she liked her Hot Thai Basil, spicy hot and full of garlic. James's spring rolls were way better than Chinese egg rolls, too. Overall, June liked Thai and hoped Clara wasn't kidding about the cooking class.

"So tell me more about this date," Clara questioned as they piled their treasures into June's truck. "Who's it with?"

"This cute Rockabilly guy named Vertie."

"That's an odd name. Is he the cute Mexican guy you danced with at Tio's the other night? The one with the gorgeous smile?"

"That's the one."

"He's pretty hot. Too bad we can't get too many of those Rockabilly guys to Lindy."

"There's more to life than dancing."

"Really, like what?" Clara teased. "Shopping?"

"Cute boys?"

"Maybe," Clara conceded, "but boyfriends come and go and dancing is forever. I can go to almost any big city in the world and make new friends by hooking into the dance scene. Don't you think that's incredible? I heard about this dance camp in Herang,

Sweden. Sweden for Godssakes. What are they doing swing dancing there? And Australia and Singapore and France and Germany."

"Wow. Who knew." June navigated the one-way streets to take them out of downtown.

"I know. And I hear Germany and Japan have huge Rockabilly scenes. You know our little group has been talking about forming a club or society to bring instructors over. It's such a pain to go to L.A. and too smoggy. Wouldn't it be cool if we could have teachers from Australia or Germany come to San Diego?"

"Wait a minute. Let's go back. What's up with the Lindy Hoppers and the Rockabillies?"

"They like us all right. We dress nice. Support the bar, but it's not true of most Lindy-Hoppers. If you pay attention, a lot of the hoppers drink free water and don't tip the waitresses. And they wear the worst clothes." Clara rolled her eyes.

"What? That's so shallow."

"What I mean is, some of them wear sweatpants to a bar, a nice bar with a live band. It kinda kills the atmosphere, and I personally think it's disrespectful. I don't expect them to wear vintage, but come on, could the guys put on a button down shirt for chrissakes, and would it kill one of those girls to wear a skirt?"

June had hit a nerve she didn't know was there, and although June would never dream of telling someone what to wear, she could see Clara's point. No one would wear a ratty t-shirt to work or sweatpants to a wedding, but it still smacked of elitism.

"Okay, but what if they don't have money to buy nice clothes," June asked. "It's not like the clubs post dress-codes. Not only that, I think a lot of people get grossed out by wearing something used."

"Look," Clara countered. "There are second-hand stores and discount stores. I'm not saying they have to wear vintage — which by the way, you can find repro and dead stock, so there's no need to wear used—but, you know they don't wear sweats to work. That's why the L.A. dancers look so damn good. Their clubs actually have dress codes. I'm dying to go to The Derby up there."

"Wasn't that one of the places in *Swingers*?"

"That's the one. Maybe we could make a road trip of it? Maybe stay at Rose's parents?"

"But," June argued, not ready to drop the subject. "What if they dress up all day for work and want to relax and not wear fancy clothes in their free time?"

Clara sighed. "Okay, sure. They can wear whatever the hell they want, but it doesn't mean I have to like it, and the rockabillies, well, they hate it. I think respect works both ways. A place like Tio's is a rockabilly joint, kinda like their territory and to show up in sweats is disrespectful. Not only are the fashions and drinking issues, but we hoppers take up more room on the dance floor with our Swing-outs. They get pretty annoyed about it. I can hardly blame them. Some of the hoppers think they're so superior."

"And you don't?" June snuck a look at Clara.

"No, really. In fact, although I love Lindy, I feel more comfortable in Rockabilly joints than dancer venues."

"I don't get it. Why don't the Rockabillies learn Lindy?"

"Now that is the question. I think partly 'cuz no one cool teaches it. I mean, have you been to the classes around town?"

"No, I've only been to the Rock-it and missed the class. And Tio's where I met you guys."

"Good people, good dancers, great instructors, but the Rockabillies are all about the lifestyle, the look, and the cool. There are no *cool* Lindy teachers in this town."

"Yeah, I get that. I think I'm starting to understand, but it's weird."

"And it's a thinking man's dance." She tapped her head,

"There's a reason we have so many engineers, doctors, and professionals in the Lindy scene."

June was uncomfortable with what Clara was implying.

"Hey, I'm not saying I wouldn't date a Rockabilly, or they're thick in the head. If one asked me out, especially one as cute as the one you're going out with, I'd go out with him in a hot second. I'm just trying to explain what's going on here. Let's do an experiment. See if you can talk Vertie into learning to Lindy Hop."

June grumbled.

"Honest, I'm not an elitist. I like everyone. But you'll find it's easier to hang out with people that have the same tastes, likes, and values as you."

"But if you only hang out with people who are similar to you in personality, background, and taste, how can you ever grow as a human being?" June shook her head. "Isn't variety the spice of life?"

"Sure, but do you want a crack ho for your best friend? That would be variety. How much variety do we need? I think, as we get older, we try on different people and different activities until we find where we fit and where we're comfortable and happy. What can I say?" Clara shrugged her shoulders. "I'm comfortable and happy. But hey, that's just me."

Maybe Clara wasn't an elitist, but June knew she had a long way to go before she found her niche. She didn't want to rule out anyone or anything, maybe the crack ho, but maybe there was even something to be gained in a friendship like that.

"I didn't mean to offend you," Clara sputtered. "I think you're really sweet. I'm happy to have met you. I dig hanging out with you."

"You've been nothing but nice to me. I'm glad to have met you, too."

"Good. Now let's go have a fashion dilemma and decide what you're going to wear on your rockabilly date. Where are you going anyway?"

"I don't know. I think dinner and a movie. Got any ideas what I should wear?"

"Let's get to your place and see. You've got to promise to tell me everything. I need to live vicariously. I haven't had a date in ages. If you haven't noticed it's slim pickings for yummy boys in our Lindy scene."

I hadn't noticed.

June's anxiety about not hanging with James and Clara disappeared in anticipation of her date. She and Clara picked out an A-line blue gab skirt and a tight sweater that looked 1950s, cute and subtly sexy.

She wanted to be alluring without being slutty or cheap, but wasn't sure guys consciously noticed the difference. Although she'd heard the stuff they said: *There are girls you bring home to mom and girls you just bring home.* June wanted to be the kind of girl you brought home to mom.

Since she wasn't ready to give Vertie her address, she'd planned to meet at his place. His place turned out to be his mom's place. When his dad died, Vertie was the only one of his four siblings who'd offered to move home. He was obviously not as bad boy as he dressed, but he still had the sexy, unsettling look that curled June's toes.

When June pulled up, she found Vertie waiting outside the Caribbean blue house. June smiled to herself, loving the bright colors in San Diego. She parked and hopped out.

"So, you found it all right?" Vertie walked over and gave her a big warm hug. She nodded. "Nice sweater," he added.

"Thanks." She tugged the edge of her sweater, smoothing it over her skirt. "I had no problem. Great directions."

"You ready then? I thought I'd drive from here."

They walked to his vintage truck. Pale white scrolling designs on the tailgate, wheel-wells, and cab, stood out against the flat black finish. Every corner rounded in a pretty, curvy, sexy kind of way, if a car could be sexy.

"Do you like her? I put her together myself. Just got her pinstriped last week."

He ran his hand along the fine lines of paint like a lover's caress. June had a twinge of jealousy and knew it would be an interesting night. He opened the door, helped her in, and closed it behind her. The inside wasn't nearly as impressive. A clean Mexican blanket hid the wide bench seat. He climbed into the other side.

"So, um, no seatbelts?" June looked around. She'd never *not* worn a seatbelt.

"Nope. Don't need 'em. If they didn't come with her, then you're off the hook, legally."

"Not big on safety in the 50s, huh?"

He flashed his bright smile. His teeth glowed against his coffee-cream skin. Her heart skipped a beat.

"1947 to be exact." He laughed and turned the key. The truck thundered like a small jet engine, no chance for easy conversation. June sat back, feeling wild and out of control not wearing a seatbelt. *Maybe Vertie is one of those guys my mom warned me about, after all.*

After a few noisy miles on the freeway, they exited and made their way through curving hills, pulling down a street lined with cute shops and old cars. People strolled in and out of stores and gathered around the cars. Vertie found a vacant spot between two antique cars: one with no hood, its silver engine exposed like a snail without a shell, back tires bigger than the front, the other turquoise with bright red flames scalloped across the hood and sides. June had never seen cars like this before.

Vertie cut the engine and looked over at her. "I thought we'd hang out, grab some grub, and check out the cars and the shops.

You like to shop don't you?" He flashed a teasing smile. "So, eat first or shop first? Whatever you want."

"How about shop, eat, and then shop some more?"

June started to open the door, but he gave her a look that made her freeze. He bounded around the car and was at her door before she had time to wipe the shock off her face.

"Thank you," she said as he opened the door for her.

Rockabilly guys stood around their cars smoking cigarettes and directed a few "Hey Vertie" greetings his way. He gave them a nod and steered June in the other direction. *Why'd he park here only to snub guys he obviously knew? Is he showing me off? I'm not sure what I think about that.*

"Let's check out this shop. Sometimes they have cool stuff."

"Sure."

To June's dismay the store offered mostly 70s and 80s fashions with a little 50s and 60s mixed in. She plunged through a rack of dresses while Vertie checked the smaller rack of men's shirts and pants. She found a cute—what she called—Doris Day dress, wide flat waist with a shelf bust. She pulled it out and held it up to her body, measuring around her sides.

"That's pretty. Wanna try it on?" He tilted his head toward the dressing room.

"No thanks." It would be strange trying on clothes for him, but she did like the dress. "I'm pretty sure it will fit. It's only $14.99 and the Tiki fabric is too cute to pass up. It'd be perfect to wear to Tio Leo's."

"Cool, got it." He grabbed the dress, walked over to the register, and whipped out his wallet to pay.

"No. You don't need to... I can... NO."

He looked pained and embarrassed in front of the clerk, so June let him finish the transaction. June was unnerved and not sure why. Then it hit her. *I don't want to be bought.*

"Vertie, thank you so much for the dress, but I don't feel

comfortable with people buying me things. I'd love to continue shopping if you promise to let me pay for whatever else I might want."

"Well there's no returns here. I guess you'll have to keep it," he said sheepishly. "So does that mean I can't pay for dinner?"

Another conundrum. How come it's okay for guys to pay for dinner and a movie, but not to buy a dress on a first date?

"What if we go Dutch?"

"Look, you may not be comfortable with me buying you a discounted dress, but I'm not comfortable letting a girl pay for a date, especially dinner."

She could see there was no winning and couldn't think of a good argument.

"And that includes drinks," he added.

"About that..." she started to say. He gave her an exasperated look. "My ID says Julie."

"You're at least eighteen, right? Tell me you're eighteen."

"Oh, yes, quite."

"All right, let's rock."

They strolled in and out of antique stores sometimes pausing for him to admire a slick car and try to explain about the year, model, and rarity. Most of it went over her head, but she liked pretty things, and the cars were quite pretty. Halfway down the street, under a drugstore awning, a deejay played, *Sha Boom, Sha Boom.* June remembered her going away party. An empty place ached inside her.

"I love this song." She stopped and turned to Vertie. "Do you wanna dance?"

"Here, on the street?" He looked around.

"Sure, why not."

"I'm kinda tired and thirsty from walking around." He hedged. "Maybe later?"

She knew he wouldn't dance later, but didn't press him.

"Yeah, that sounds good. I'm hungry, too."

"Great." A look of relief un-pinched his face. "You like Mexican?"

"Is that a trick question?" She smiled. "Of course, I like Mexican."

He grinned and gently guided her into the restaurant. They drank Negra Modelo and talked a lot about cars. He asked if she'd ever been to Viva Las Vegas, the Greasers Ball, or other Rockabilly events she'd never heard of. He enumerated their virtues and piqued June's curiosity, so different, yet similar from her Lindy sub-culture. She talked about her college classes and living on her own for the first time. She mentioned looking for her biological grandmother. He understood how important heritage and family were.

They continued making inroads into each other's worlds, sipping several beers, smudging the nervous edges of their date. By the time Vertie paid the bill, June was ready to head back out into the fresh air. They continued to weave in and out of shops, but June grew tired from her long shopping day with Clara. When he suggested they go, June eagerly agreed.

When they pulled up and parked in front of his mom's house, he cut the motor, but neither made a move to get out of the truck. The faint ping of the engine and distant umpapa of Mexican music kept time with their soft breathing. June knew what was coming next, and her insides curled in anticipation.

"I had a really good time tonight." He looked at her but made no move.

"Yeah, me too. It was a lot more fun than dinner and a movie. Cool cars and cool shops. Clara won't believe she's missed a vintage store. Wait 'till I tell her. What's that area called again?"

"Old Town La Mesa. Mostly rich old geezers with restored cars they don't know how to work on, but it's still cool. Some of the guys from my car club have started hanging out there. I thought you might like it. It's cool you dug it." He grinned and scooted closer.

His smile made June want to kiss him, but she'd wait. "So, what else do you like to do besides mess around with old cars?"

"I've been trying my hand at pin-up photography. I'll show you some time. Maybe I can take some pictures of you?" He waggled his eyebrows.

"Maybe."

"Cool." His knee moved back and forth batting the keys hanging from the ignition. An invisible current buzzed between them. It was hard for June to concentrate on what he was saying. She couldn't stop thinking about his pretty lips and his warm brown eyes.

"So." His lips whispered soft and inviting.

"So."

Silent energy crackled in the cab. He leaned into the space between them. June closed the gap. Their mouths met. His firm lips found hers, soft and sweet. He pulled back, and it took her a second to open her eyes and see him grinning. She grinned back. He leaned in again, this time pressing harder, but keeping his body angled away. His lips parted hers. His tongue brushed the edge of her teeth and lips.

He took his time kissing, slowly tugging her bottom lip with his, dragging his mouth to the corner of hers. She felt warm and fuzzy. She loved kissing, and she loved kissing him. She leaned in closer, and he scooted toward her, wrapping his arm around her waist. She edged even closer and turned her head, letting him kiss her neck. Innumerable shocks leapt through her body.

God he's a good kisser.

He gently pressed her into the back of the seat, angling his body so his chest pressed against hers. She felt his heart beating fast and leaned back as far as she could, their upper bodies intertwined, legs dangling off the seat.

Their bodies hummed and crushed into each other, beginning a soft rhythm. She pressed her toes into the cavity under the dashboard. Her breathing became shorter, matching his. She panicked, shifted and created space. They both came up for air. She looked into his warm brown eyes and smiled. He smiled back. She was glad he did not try to press her for more.

They both sat up. When he opened his door, a whoosh of cool air blasted the cab and sobered her kissing stupor. He quickly jogged around the truck to open her door.

"Don't forget this." He handed her the bag with the Tiki dress and walked her to her car.

"Thanks, again."

"You bet."

When they arrived at her door, he held out his hand for her keys. She handed them over, curious what he wanted them for. He unlocked her door, ducked into the car, and started the ignition for her.

"Thanks," she said as he rose from her car's interior.

"Sure. So, how 'bout I give you a call next time? Maybe we can do this again." A half grin curved toward his eye.

"Yeah, I'd love to." She scribbled her number on a scrap piece of paper.

"Well…" He hesitated and then swooped in for another kiss. He held her lips in his, pulling long enough to quicken her breath, and then released her. She sank into her car, the seat closer and harder than expected. He stood with one hand on the open door, one hand on the roof.

"Later, then."

She wished he would duck in for another kiss, but he didn't. He closed the door and backed a couple feet away. June pulled into the misty cool night, her body vibrating, and her lips tingling.

Violet ~ 1940s
12. That's the Glory of Love
(Benny Goodman)

Violet woke fuzzy and with a terrific headache. Fragments of dreams floated through her wakening mind, dreams of falling and Johnny laughing. The sound of the sewing machine alerted her to the late hour.

She sat up, stretched, and ran her fingers through her hair. She smelled like stale popcorn and dust. Charles's kisses flashed across her memory igniting muted sizzles.

"So, the sleeping beauty is awake?" Mrs. Peplinski smiled at Violet when she came into the front of the shop. "Are you being careful with your sweetheart?" She narrowed her eyes into a knowing look. "Young handsome men can be very hard to say no to."

Violet blushed at the implication. "Um. It isn't like that. We just, he's only...Surely there's no harm in kissing?"

Violet thought about his kisses. *Was he dangerous to my virtue?* Johnny's accusations wormed through the cracks in her wall. She didn't know what to say to Mrs. Peppy. The woman had been like a mother to Violet, but they didn't talk about stuff like that.

I don't need to think about stuff like that. Do I?

"Do you mind if I run home and wash up?"

"Yes, Yes, go home and come back after the noon hour."

Too tired to walk, Violet took the bus and was so lost in thought, she missed her stop and had walk a half mile back to her apartment. When she opened the door, the smell of fresh percolated coffee disturbed her. Her dad never made coffee. She did.

"Pop?" she called.

"Hey honey, is that you?" His voice sounded odd, too loud, and too perky. "I'm in the kitchen. Would you like some coffee?"

He knew she didn't drink coffee. She marched through the living room, down the long hallway, and into the kitchen. She found him at the table in his satin smoking jacket, cup of coffee in one hand, burnt toast in the other.

Then she heard it, water running somewhere in the apartment. Her stomach clenched and palms sweated. *Who was in their apartment? If she was back, then I am leaving. And what is he doing home?*

"Pop, why are you home at this time of day?"

"Well, they had shortages and sent, er, me home until they get more raw materials. This war and the embargos are really doing a number on the factories."

Should she confront him with his obvious lie? It would be the fifth job he'd lost in a year. She was surprised he wasn't in bed smelling like a brewery, which was his usual course of action after losing a job, or maybe that's why he lost them. She decided against confrontation and moved on to question two.

"Who's in our shower, Pop?"

Her dad blushed through the stubble on his face. She was mortified.

"I…I'm sorry, honey. You weren't home last night, and I figured you'd stayed at the shop and my friend… Her name is Helga. I hope to be seeing a lot more of her." He smiled a bashful smile. Violet cringed.

She didn't know why she was so horrified. It was good that he was happy. He hadn't been in a long time, but something didn't seem right about it. She didn't know what to say, or why she felt sick. She'd wanted a shower, but now a strange lady was in her bathroom. Violet had no desire to meet her.

"Okay, Pop."

"Here's money for some food. And treat yourself to a new dress." He handed her a stack of bills. She wadded them up in her fist.

"Pop, where'd you get this money?"

"I had a good night." He smiled.

This was not good. He pitched dice with some of the fellas at the local pool hall. But this was not money he could make pitching dice, at least not with the guys he knew.

"Thanks." She shoved the crumpled bills in her purse.

The phone rang. He made no move to pick it up. After several rings, Violet answered.

"Hello, Yes, Violet speaking." The neighbor picked up the party line, again. "I got it, it's for me." He clicked off.

"There you are." Charles's voice calmed her, but a red flag went up. Her palms sweated and stomach ached. *Why is he calling me when he'll see me in a few hours?* She needed to sit down but didn't want to share her conversation with her father. She slid down the wall and sat on the unpolished wood floor.

"Yup, it's me. What's wrong?" It was an unfriendly greeting, but she couldn't find her manners.

"Nothing's wrong. It's just that I won't be able to pick you right up after work. I got an extra watch when one of the squids cut his hand peeling potatoes, then fainted at the sight of his own blood, fell over, and cracked his head open." He laughed.

Violet found nothing funny about it. She was heartbroken. Surely, things couldn't get any worse.

Then they did. A short, chubby woman with bronze hair, fingers and toes like sausages, exited the bathroom, humming and wearing Violet's mother's old robe. The garment pulled ungracefully across her thick middle. The hem dragged on the floor. Violet tasted bile in her mouth.

"Don't you think that's funny?" Charles asked again. "Vi, are you there?"

"Um, yeah, funny," she replied in a haze. She wanted to look away from the toad lady shambling down the hall, but couldn't.

"I'm sorry. I know we need to practice, but we'll have plenty of time on Saturday. Maybe you can ask Mrs. Peppy for the whole day off?"

"Yeah, sure. I gotta go."

"Okay, I'll ring you tomorrow then?"

"No. I mean, yes, but not here. Call me at Mrs. Peppy's. You have the exchange. Bye." She hung up.

"Oh." The woman giggled. "I hope you don't mind. I found it in the bathroom." She posed and strutted.

"No, I don't mind. It's my mother's."

The woman either saw through Violet's bluff or had already been told the story. The toad lady continued to giggle and make her way to the kitchen. Violet suddenly didn't want to take a shower in her bathroom. She rummaged through her drawer and gathered clothes for a few days. She had no interest in watching her father woo the toad lady. She needed a suitcase, but the idea of going into her dad's bedroom repulsed her. She dashed to the couch, shook the pillow out of its case, and stuffed it with her clothes.

She remembered the money in her purse and thought she might treat herself to some new socks or maybe a new dress, that would make her feel more normal. She wouldn't spend the money. She needed it for bills, but it was fun to think about. Twenty cents an hour wasn't much, even sharing expenses, and she had no idea what would happen next.

Part of her apprenticeship was that she worked Saturdays for free. How would Mrs. Peppy feel about giving her the whole day off? She'd never asked Mrs. Peppy how much rent she'd charge if Violet did want to move in. Her dad and toad lady cooed in the kitchen. She'd ask Mrs. Peppy today.

Violet pressed her palms into her eyes and wished she could

run away with Charles. Run away and live on a private desert island with trees full of bananas and a stream full of fish, animals helping them. Her fantasy had quickly devolved into Snow White. She stopped herself. *Life isn't like a fairy tale.*

Mrs. Peppy looked up in surprise when Violet burst into the shop. The three-mile jog left Violet's hair disheveled and her body sweaty. She could've taken he bus, but she couldn't stand still. She had to keep moving. If she stopped moving, something unpleasant might catch up to her.

"Do you think I could shower here? Ours is…busted." Violet didn't think Mrs. Peppy believed her for a second. Mrs. Peppy eyed the pillowcase and raised her dark eyebrows, but didn't ask any questions.

"Of course, darling, you can stay here any time. Why don't you sleep upstairs tonight in the spare room, instead of that ole sofa. Yes?"

"Thank you. And I can work late tonight, as late as you need." Violet twisted the end of the pillowcase in her hand. "And I was wondering if I could have tomorrow off. It's the…

"Jitterbug Contest," Mrs. Peppy said at the same time as Violet.

They laughed, and a bit of the weight fell off Violet's shoulders. She rushed to Mrs. Peppy and gave her a hug.

"Sorry. I forgot I'm a sweaty mess." They laughed once more.

Violet dashed through the back of the shop and up the stairs into Mrs. Peppy's kitchen, untouched since 1915. An old metal icebox stenciled with flowers perched in the corner. A Magic Chef oven gleamed in black, white, and chrome and glass front cabinets dripped paper lace icing.

Heavy green curtains separated the kitchen from the dining room. Violet walked past the polished mahogany table and matching buffet, continuing into the living room and through to

Mrs. Peppy's bedroom. She found the spare room, tossed her pillowcase on the bed, and headed back to the bathroom, amused by the circular route through the apartment.

The cool water washed away the morning's dirt and stress. She double brushed her teeth making sure not to miss a fuzzy cap. *I could get used to living here, but Pop needs me. Doesn't he? I'll go back sooner or later.* For now, she skipped down the stairs happy about the weekend plan, though disappointed to lose an evening with Charles.

"Is this all there is for today?" Violet surveyed her workload.

"Yes, that is all for today. I think you can go out tonight to the soda fountain or another dance with Charles? And as you can see, I will not need you tomorrow, either. So have fun with your friends and tell me everything about the contest on Sunday."

"I won't be back until late Sunday or early Monday. I promised Jeannie I would sleep over with her after the dance. Don't worry about me."

Mrs. Peppy looked at Violet and raised one eyebrow. "I see."

Yes, I think you do.

Violet watched the clock while trying to stretch the work to fill her day. Time finally inched to 3:45. She didn't know what to do since she couldn't see Charles. She rang Jeannie and was told by Jeannie's mom that she'd gone straight to the malt shop with Paddy and Johnny.

I don't think I could brave the malt shop without Charles.

Then she remembered the extra money in her purse. A little shopping wouldn't be amiss, and she wouldn't spend too much, maybe a gift for Charles. She put up her work and tidied her sewing area, liking the way cleaning used up her energy. She bustled to the closet and whipped out the broom and dustpan singing the Al Dexter tune, *New Broom Boogie* while she swept.

"Well darling, I'm done for the day. Where is Charles? Don't you have a date with him?"

"I did, but then he had to take over a watch. I'm sure I'll see him tomorrow." Violet smiled an unconvincing grin.

What if they pull his leave altogether and he can't make the contest or watch the sunrise? What if I can't see him before he ships out for two weeks? Her stomach hurt. She rushed back to the storage closet and grabbed the vinegar and a couple old rags. She needed to keep moving. She wiped the prints off the door and big picture window, dashing in and out to check for smudges.

Mrs. Peppy watched and shook her head. "Thank you, Violet. Would you like to join me for a cup of tea?"

"Thanks, but I want to get down to McCleary's before they close. Would you like to come shopping with me?"

"Thank you, Violet, you are very sweet, but I am tired. I think I will go drink my tea."

"Okay. See you later."

Violet grabbed her pocket book and scooted out the door. She knew exactly what she wanted at McCleary's and made a beeline to the counter of sparkly hair accessories. She picked up the rhinestone studded hair combs. A buck sixty was a lot to spend on an accessory, but the combs were beautiful and would look lovely in her hair. Then she spied a cute lapel pin that would make a perfect gift for Mrs. Peppy, a yellow fawn with white spots. She put back the hair combs and opted for the pin. If they didn't have anything good to buy for Charles at Beeman's, she'd come back for the combs.

At the counter, a rotund lady jabbered with Mr. McCleary, asking what she should use on her baby's rash. Violet didn't want to be rude, but they could talk all night about which was better, a cream or a powder. She needed to get to Beeman's and back before they closed. She stood on one leg, then the other, fiddling and fidgeting, hoping they'd notice. They were oblivious. Eventually Violet threw her purse on the floor toward the lady.

"Oh, excuse me," Violet said. "I dropped my pocket book. And the pin I wanted to buy. Don't move. You might step on it." She bent down to retrieve her purse, the pin still in her hand.

The lady looked toward the floor, slightly panicked. Mr. McCleary leaned over the counter and scanned the floor.

"Ah ha. Here it is." Violet pretended to pick it up, then showed it to the lady and Mr. McCleary.

"Isn't that precious," the lady said. "Jim, why don't you ring the little dear up?"

"That's so kind of you. Thank you."

Violet pulled a wadded dollar bill from her pocket book and waited for change. Mr. McCleary moved like a sloth in quicksand.

"I don't need a bag, thank you. I'll just slip it in my purse if that's okay?"

"Don't you want a box? I have some small ones here somewhere. Let me look." He ducked down behind the counter. "Ah, here you go young lady." He slipped it into a bag. "Thank you and come again."

The lady and Mr. McCleary restarted their conversation, "This generation's youth is so impatient..."

At Beeman's, new displays of summer dresses and matching short sets in bright Hawaiian fabrics greeted patrons. The store was deserted and near closing time. She hurried to the men's clothing section and considered a sale sweater that would look handsome on Charles, but didn't want to give an off-season gift.

Then it hit her. She knew what to get him, sheet music for his guitar and ukulele. She didn't know how late Lawson's Music Store was open though, and the shop was twelve blocks away. Sheet music would have to wait for another day.

She continued to look around Beeman's, and when she spotted the red, white, and blue stripy socks, she opted for her first idea of buying matching jitterbug socks. Beeman's stocked them in men's and boy's sizes, a pair for him and a pair for her, only a quarter apiece. She grabbed the socks and headed to the counter. No salesgirl. She finally found one in the woman's department.

"Can I pay for these here, please?" Violet tried to suppress her impatience.

"Sure, no problem," the salesgirl said. "Let me go over and see how much they are."

"They're a quarter."

The salesgirl ignored her and toddled toward the display of men's socks. Her high heels clomped on the tile. She wasn't much older than Violet, but had a more mature style. Violet considered her own wardrobe. She dressed like a jitterbug kid. *I ought to try a more collegiate, sophisticated style.* Not tonight though. Tonight she just wanted to make it back to McCleary's.

"Good thing I checked for you. The boys socks are only twenty cents. If I'd listened to you, I would've over-charged you a nickel."

"Yes, thank you for being so observant. I'll make sure to put that nickel to good use." The salesgirl frowned. Violet amended her speech. "Really, thanks. I can get a soda or two songs on the jukebox for a nickel. Every penny counts, especially during war time."

The salesgirl smiled, and Violet handed her a rolled up bill. She rushed out the door and dashed down the block toward McCleary's. The lack of sleep and her disastrous morning caught up with her. Her pace slowed despite herself. Still a block away, McCleary's lights went out. She was too late. She slogged the remainder of the way and rested on a bench to catch her breath.

The saved nickel came in handy. She hopped a bus back to the shop. When she opened the door, a delicious spicy smell made her stomach growl. She moved instinctively toward the scent. To her surprise and delight, Charles stood at the sink, an apron tied around his waist. Red, wet tomatoes glistened like Christmas bulbs in his hands. Violet burst out laughing with joy. Charles and Mrs. Peppy turned and smiled.

"What are you doing here?" Violet asked and rushed over. Unsure how much affection she should show, she gave him a little hip bump. He reached over and gave her an uninhibited peck on the cheek.

"I felt bad about breaking our date, and you sounded out of sorts this morning, so I paid a guy to take my watch. Honestly, Vi, I think you've put a spell on me. I can't stay away from you."

He laughed as he quartered the tomatoes. Guilt squirmed into her gut. She didn't want him spending good money for someone to take his watch. "You didn't have to do that."

"Yup, I did." He deftly sliced the tomatoes and dropped them into a bowl.

"So what are you making here?"

"Fasolka po bretonsku," Mrs. Peppy answered.

Charles leaned over explaining in Violet's ear. "Baked beans in tomato sauce with sausage, I think."

His breath sent a delicious chill down her back and filled her with desire. She wanted to be alone with him, but her stomach growled. She could wait.

"What can I help with?"

"You can pour the beans in the big pot on top of the sausage." An enormous pot simmered with peppery meat. Garlic, oregano, and other spices Violet didn't recognize wafted through the kitchen.

"That is Polish sausage. Much better than Italian kind." Mrs. Peppy laughed. "Now, pour beans over it. Charles, you add tomatoes. Now, we let stew simmer and have a taste of Poland."

"How long have you been here?" Violet asked Charles. They talked in low tones.

"Once I got the watch squared away, I came right over, but you'd just left and Mrs. Peppy wasn't sure which way you'd gone.

The old gal had a twinkle in her eye and sent me off to the market with a list. She thought you might be hungry and forget to eat. And I thought it was a fantastic idea to make dinner for you." His smile lit up the room.

The three of them moved to the living room to wait for the stew to finish simmering. Charles and Violet sat on the couch facing the French doors. Mrs. Peppy excused herself and said she'd be right back. Violet laughed.

"What's so funny?"

She looked down and pointed to the pink bib apron, complete with embroidered flowers, resting sideways around his hips and torso.

"Oh, this? I think this will be all the rage next year. Just you wait. The next Jitterbug contest, everyone'll be wearing them."

They leaned toward each other. The heat from their bodies met before they did. Her skin smoldered with anticipation. She threw her arms around his neck. His hands caressed her back.

"Ahem."

They jumped apart like kids caught stealing. Mrs. Peppy carried a silver tray with an ornate etched decanter. A clear liquid sloshed in its hold. Three matching glasses encased shiny ice-chips. Charles and Violet looked at the contents on the tray and back at each other. Charles gave her a look that she couldn't quite decipher, but thought might be something along the idea of when in Rome, or in this case, Poland.

Classical music drifted from an old Victrola in the corner. Mrs. Peppy set down the tray and poured a little glass for each of them. They followed her lead and took a cup in hand.

"Salutować." She raised her glass to theirs, threw back her head, and drank to the last drop.

"Salutować," they said together and mimicked her actions. Violet tried to throw her head back, but as soon as the liquid hit her throat, it burned like fire. She had to clamp her mouth shut to keep from spraying the contents around the room. Her eyes filled with tears as the fiery liquid cauterized everything in its path.

"Swallow it," Mrs. Peppy said.

"Swallow it," Charles echoed.

She tried again, pushing the liquid—which seemed to have multiplied in her mouth—down her throat. She succeeded and gasped for air, coughing and sputtering.

Charles and Mrs. Peppy found it hysterical and broke out in loud guffaws. After Violet found her breath, she laughed too.

"Care for another?" Mrs. Peppy poured herself another.

"No thanks," Charles and Violet both said at the same time, sending them all into another round of laughter. Mrs. Peppy ignored their refusal and poured more anyway. Violet avoided her drink. They passed the time with small talk while Charles and Mrs. Peppy continued to sample the burning liquid.

"That was fun." Mrs. Peppy patted her thighs. "Thank you for sharing drink with me. Now, I believe it is time to eat. Shall we?"

They stood to walk to the dining room. The blood rushed to Violet's head. Charles caught her as she swooned. She was frustrated and embarrassed that she was the only one affected by the vodka. It wasn't entirely unpleasant, but she'd rather be dizzy from kisses. Besides, she'd seen the ill effects of alcohol and didn't wish to experience them. Mrs. Peppy moved fast and was out of the room clanking in the kitchen before Violet and Charles had time to walk from the couch. Violet's face and body felt flushed, and she sincerely needed to kiss Charles. She reached up and pulled his face down to hers, kissing him aggressively on the mouth. His lips curved into a smile under hers.

"What are you smiling about?" she asked.

"You. You're adorable, and alcohol has a very interesting effect on you. One that I think we're best to avoid. I can barely keep my hands off you, without you being so willing."

He bent down and kissed her with deep kisses that made everything quiver all the way to her toes. She staggered, and they tumbled onto the sofa laughing and falling apart. He stood first offering his hand. "Behave now so we can eat a nice dinner."

They crossed through the curtained doorway. Mrs. Peppy had set a beautiful table, seating Charles at the head, the ladies flanking. Mrs. Peppy served steaming bowls of the Polish stew with big hunks of bread, simple and savory and then led grace in Polish. Charles and Violet mumbled along in English, finishing with a hearty amen.

Their hostess retrieved the tiny glasses and placed them at their settings.

"This is delicious," Violet gushed. "Thank you so much. I'd forgotten to eat, and this is incredible." Violet had never had anything like it, the earthiness of the beans, the sharp acid of the stewed tomatoes, and the spicy exotic taste of the sausage.

"Thank you, darling and you are welcome."

"Wow, Mrs. Pep, you really know the way to a man's heart. If someone else hadn't stolen it, I think I'd give it to you." He winked.

"Thank you, Thank you. I could not have done it without you."

He said someone had stolen his heart. Could it be me? Violet broke off another piece of the hearty bread, the caraway and dill flavor blended perfectly with the stew. She couldn't be any happier, sitting in Mrs. Peppy's dining room, eating good food, next to the person who had stolen her heart.

"So, I don't have to be back on base until Sunday at midnight. What would you lovely ladies like to do?"

Violet wanted to walk around the park all night or stay on the beach, curled in his arms, but it didn't seem right to leave Mrs. Peppy after she'd been so generous.

"We do need to get some practicing in," Violet said. "Where

can we practice? The beach and park are both too dark, now."

"Why don't you roll up rug and practice here? I want to see this dance you do, this Jitterbug."

"Wouldn't we disturb you? We can be awfully loud doing aerials and stuff?" Violet said.

"I would love to watch how you dance. I used to love to dance."

"Only if you promise to dance at least one dance with me, Mrs. Peplinski." Charles winked.

Mrs. Peppy raised her brows. "Yes, but I get to pick the dance." She smiled. "Okay, I clean up the dinner. You ready the room."

Charles and Violet carried their dishes to the kitchen and scurried back to the living room.

"Okay Vi, let's move the couch against the wall. Do you think you can pick up one end?"

"I don't know, but I'll try."

She scooted to one end and tried to lift. It wasn't too heavy, but she wasn't so sure about moving it. Charles lifted his end. Hers got heavier. She squatted to get more leverage, then started laughing.

"What's so funny?"

"I pictured me looking like a sumo wrestler is all."

"You're the cutest sumo wrestler I've ever seen. You have no idea how much self-restraint it's taking for me to stay on my side of the couch." He laughed.

"So what's stopping you?"

He made an exasperated face, tilted his head toward the kitchen, and smiled. "Plus, you do something to my self-control. I gotta watch myself around you. And Mrs. Peppy's Vodka is not helping. You're too irresistible."

"Me?"

"Yes, you, silly." He laughed. "Now lift."

She lifted and had to take baby steps, edging the couch across the room. They struggled, finally moving it to the far wall.

"I've got the chairs." He shoved them all the way to the French doors. They each grabbed one end of the rug and rolled it to the chairs.

"I'll be right back," Charles said. "I've got something downstairs."

He dashed out of the room, and Violet flopped on the couch, tired but excited. The room was big enough to practice in now. What would Mrs. Peppy think about her living room? Violet didn't think she'd mind. Mrs. Peppy was diffcrent than Violet expected—more fun. She'd never thought of old people as fun.

Charles returned with Mrs. Peppy on one arm and a portable radio on the other. He escorted Mrs. Peppy to the chair by the window careful to help her over the rolled rug. He set up the Sonora, tuning to a local big band station. Gene Krupa's, *Let me Off Uptown*, kicked out of the little speaker. He extended his hand to Violet.

For her, their connection was like walking on water— miraculous. When his hand joined hers, she became an extension of him. They whirled around the living room, hitting every beat, playing off the flute, emphasizing the drum, flitting their feet, improvising steps to the boogie piano. Her muscles responded to his calls as he led her around the floor. She piked at the waist and leaned into the swing, feeling her thighs flex, twisting her torso. The center of the universe was the two of them spinning on a top.

They grinned and knew something extraordinary was happening between them as their bodies moved as one. Their connection went beyond a basic physical attraction. Their movement wasn't just dancing anymore. It was something else, something grand, beyond them and part of them.

He wound her up for a dip, not letting her go, keeping her close with a little lean. His eyes sparkled, her skin glowed, their hearts beat fast. He kissed her with so much passion and fierce emotion her eyes filled with tears.

The sound of clapping broke the spell.

They'd both forgotten Mrs. Peppy was there. Charles released Violet from his hold, grinning from ear to ear, not the least embarrassed. Violet was as red as the tomatoes in the stew.

"Bravo," shouted Mrs. Peppy. "You will win the contest unless the judges are blind. I did not think I would like this Jitterbug, but you make it look beautiful as the waltz. Poetry in wild motion. Yes, Yes. I wish I was young enough to dance this dance. Bravo."

Charles's eyes twinkled as he walked over to Mrs. Peppy. "I believe it's your turn. And by the way, I do know how to waltz. May I have this dance, Mrs. Peplinski?"

Mrs. Peppy giggled and took Charles's waiting hand. Violet turned the Victrola's crank handle and placed the needle on the record. It surged to life emitting a sweet, soft Waltz. Mrs. Peppy straightened up to her full, tiny height and held her carriage like a duchess. Her right hand dropped to pick up her long black skirt. Charles wrapped his hand delicately around her waist and expertly glided her around the floor. She looked younger and he older.

With every turn, his eyes found Violet's. They smoldered with an underlying gleam. She shuddered at his look, a tiny bit of fear gripped her. She realized she was afraid of her passion for him. And what frightened her more, she didn't care.

They continued to swirl until the Victrola slowed, stretching the notes into long funny noises. Completely mesmerized, Violet had forgotten to wind the crank. Mrs. Peppy looked grateful and red-faced when Charles deposited her on her chair.

Violet trotted to the kitchen to get Mrs. Peppy a glass of water. As she was chipping ice off the block, Charles stole up behind her. His hands snaked around her sides, crossed her stomach, and pulled her to him. He nuzzled his face into the back of her neck and ran his hands up and down her sides, stopping at the place where her hips began to curve. He pressed down. Then finding the slope of her neck, he nibbled and sent shivers to dark places.

She was helpless, filled with desire, and a sharp pulsing ache she didn't know what to do with. She felt safe, yet not safe. Her breath became shallow. She surrendered to his kisses. His hands continued to press into her hips, the weight of them carving prints into the gabardine of her skirt. He turned her round, her back to the cool of the icebox. His hands ran up her sides and grazed the edges of her breasts, igniting a wave of shudders.

He pushed her arms above her head, pressing elbows. His fingers tangled in hers. His body crushed into her as he kissed her. Kisses on her eyelids, her cheeks, her lips, her chin, her neck, the edge of her blouse. His breath was hot and ragged on her neck, his lips cool and moist. One hand released hers, but the other held her fast and hard. His free arm clutched around her waist jamming her harder against his taut body. His teeth tugged at her bottom lip, and he ran his tongue across her teeth. She opened her mouth and received his kisses.

A slight groan escaped her lips or his. He let go and backed away for a moment.

"Whoa." He tried to breathe. She tried to breathe. "My gosh, Violet, I, I'm sorry, I..." He gulped for air. "Got carried away. Please forgive me?" He ran his fingers through his hair.

The world started to blur, and she began to crumble to the floor. He caught her. "Are you okay?"

"Um, water for Mrs. Peppy."

"Are you sure you're okay?"

"Yes."

"Yes?" he questioned.

"I'm fine," she squeaked.

"Wait here. I'll take this to Mrs. Peppy." He looked as dazed as she felt.

She blinked at the kitchen, the stove, and sink, all too bright and mean without him standing in the midst of it. She didn't know what to think about what happened except that it kind of scared her and yet...

Charles returned and fetched two more glasses. The sharp sound of chipping ice jarred her senses and sobered her. She felt like she did when she'd drunk the vodka, but much, much more intense.

He squinted, eyebrows hooding his eyes. His lips pressed together in a hard line. "So, um Mrs. Peppy offered to let me sleep on the couch, but I think perhaps I should sleep on the sofa in the shop. That would be more proper. Don't you think? Or really I should go back to base and give us some space."

"Did I do something wrong?"

"No Violet. I did. I meant only to kiss you and then...I, I got carried away. Like last night. I promised myself I wouldn't lose control with you." He looked like he was in pain. "Can you forgive me?" He walked over and took her hands in his.

"Of course I forgive you. There's nothing to forgive. It's not like I wasn't kissing you back?" She smiled, but he still looked pained. *What is he was thinking?*

"We need to slow down. Agreed?"

"If that's what you want." She paused. "Wait, does that mean the beach sunrise plan is off?"

"What do you think?"

"Loads of kids hang out at the beach all night. They have bonfires until the sun comes up. I say yes. After all, you're going away for two weeks." *I need to store you up.*

"All right." He ran his hand through his hair. "I guess it's good I'm going away for two weeks. We need a little break."

"It is not good. It's horrible, awful, and not fair. I want to go with you. Can't you stow me away?"

He flashed his dazzling smile, a hint of concern lurking at the edge. "What am I going to do with you?" He ruffled her hair.

When they returned to the living room, they found Mrs. Peppy asleep on the chair, her head lolled to one side. Her glass precariously balanced in the crook of her arm. She looked like an old Victorian doll, well loved by its owner. Violet gently nudged her awake and suggested she go to her room.

Charles and Violet worked at putting the living room back together. *Why was he so upset? Our kitchen kiss was no different from our kissing last night.*

After they set back the furniture, Charles suggested they sit and read a little. That sounded like a silly idea to Violet. She read when she was alone or bored, and she wasn't alone or bored, but this idea seemed to make him happy. He'd stay overnight, but down in the shop on the mohair sofa, a good compromise. She'd get to see him for breakfast.

Charles sat at one end of the sofa with book in hand while Violet leaned against the arm of the sofa, bare feet curled under her. They both read *The Good Earth*. He'd brought his copy from the barracks. He wasn't kidding when he said the novel was a new favorite, and he'd read it again so they could have an in-depth discussion about it.

She couldn't get comfortable or focus on her book, not with him sitting at the end of the couch. The familiar electricity buzzed between them. If she didn't know it was the streetlights crackling through the open doors, she'd swear she could hear it too. She put her feet down and tried to sit up and read. She tried fluffing the pillows. She tried bringing her knees up to her chest with the book resting between them. She flopped around and put her back to the arm of the couch. Stretching her legs, she accidentally nudged Charles with her toes. He looked at her and smiled, picked up her feet, and laid them across his lap.

He seemed perfectly content. She was overwhelmingly frustrated.

"So, do you think we're ready for tomorrow?" she asked.

"Yeah, we've got a lot of tricks worked out and fast footwork, too. And you can follow anything I throw at you. We're so connected."

"It's kinda crazy how connected we are. It's like I can read your mind."

"It's almost creepy."

She made an alarmed face.

"Nah, just kidding. I like it. I've never met anyone like you."

Johnny's comments coiled in her head.

"So, is that a good thing or a bad thing?"

"Good, I think. Yeah, good."

"You think?"

He opened his mouth to say something then hesitated. "Ah, never mind." He picked up his book.

"What?"

"Okay, look. I know you don't want to talk about it, but I am leaving Sunday for two weeks. And I will be leaving sooner than later for a long unknown amount of time. I just...I want you to know where this is going. I don't want to hurt you."

He put down his book and methodically rubbed her legs, as he talked. She doubted he had any idea what kind of tremors shot through her body at his touch.

"No. I don't want to talk about it." What was she supposed to say? "Anyway, I'm a tough cookie."

"Tough are you?"

He grabbed her foot and tickled it. She kicked and twisted trying to get away. In moments like this, her world felt normal. But there was an underlying current that ran below all their interactions. Lately she felt like she was on a ledge of a tall building.

She sat up and scooted closer. He gazed at her and tucked a piece of hair behind her ear. She grabbed his hand and kissed his palm. He cupped her face in his hand, looking at her with his sea-green eyes. He was gorgeous.

Why does he have to be in the Navy? Why couldn't I have fallen for a guy like Wally or Johnny? Although there was no guarantee they wouldn't enlist or be drafted either.

She scooted closer, trying not to scare him. She wanted to kiss him, but it occurred to her there were so many things she didn't know about this handsome man.

"Charles, I never asked you how old you are."

"What if I said I was twenty-six?" He ran his hand through his thick black hair.

She heard Johnny's words in her head. Then he burst into a laugh. She looked at him confused.

"Nah, I'm joshing, I'm eighteen. Would it be so odd if I were twenty-six?"

"Hmm." She contemplated, not sure why, but she thought it would. There was a big difference in life experience between eighteen and twenty-six. She closed her eyes for a minute, maybe more than a minute. When she opened them again, he was staring at her, looking bemused. She wanted to ask more questions, but her brain was thick and fuzzy.

"Hey, sleepyhead, let's get you into bed."

"Okay," she mumbled.

He picked her up from the couch in one swift motion. If she were more awake, she would've demanded kisses, but instead, she smiled and let herself float away. He carried her to her room and set her down gently on the bed. She barely registered she was no longer in his arms as he tucked a blanket around her. She felt safe. He brushed her cheek with his lips, a soft sizzle resonated across her body.

"Good night, Violet." Then he whispered something she

couldn't hear, something that sounded like, I love you, but she must have been dreaming.

June ~1990s
13. Smack Dab in the Middle
(Steve Lucky & the Rhumba Bums)

"I thought I'd pick you up early so I could hear all about your date with Bernie before we get to Marty and Larissa's," Clara said when June got into her car.

"His name is not Bernie. It's Vertie."

"Whatever. So…."

"He's a very good kisser."

Clara squeaked.

"He bought me a dress. Don't you think it's inappropriate?"

"It's a little odd, but who cares. What kind of dress? Was it cute?"

"But don't you think it's like being bought. Like he thinks I owe him something?"

"Hell, no. You don't owe a man anything. I don't care if he buys you the Taj Majal." Clara banged on the steering wheel.

"But what if he buys you an engagement ring?"

"That's different, but what you owe him is honesty and fidelity."

"Right."

"So, what kind of dress?"

"Super cute. 50s style, totally Tiki fabric. I can't wait to show you. And I found some new shops for us. Have you been to downtown La Mesa?"

"Downtown La Mesa? No. Who knew anything was there? Let's go tomorrow. What else?"

"We walked around and looked at cool cars. He explained a bunch of crap about the cars. Went in one ear and out the other."

They laughed. "Then we had some Mexican food and beers and talked. And he had an idea about where to look for my grandmother. He suggested checking churches, especially Catholic ones for adoption stuff."

"That's a good idea."

"Oh, and you know what else? He's a photographer. He does pin-up stuff."

"Rockabilly pin-up or vintage pin-up?"

"I don't know. Who cares? Do you think I should do it?"

"Do what?" Clara winked.

June blushed at Clara's implication. "Not that, I mean the photography."

"Seems like one could lead to the other."

"No. He was quite the gentleman. He got the door and dinner. Did I tell you about him starting my car for me?"

"That's sweet, but he doesn't sound too perfect a gentleman if you were sucking face on the first date."

"Come on. There's no harm in that."

"I'm just jealous." Clara looked at June sideways. "Okay, to be on the safe side, we should schedule a photo shoot together. That way he can't seduce you."

June rolled her eyes. "Yeah, I'll talk to him."

"Great, we'll have to get to planning. I know Marty has at least one Elvgren and one Varga pin-up book. We'll check them out when we're there tonight. Then, we'll need to do some costume planning and scout locations. I certainly don't want any cheesy pictures on cars or motorcycles. We want sexy without slutty. Don't you think?"

"But . . ." June tried to interject.

Clara continued. "I say no to nudity. But yes to swim suits, vintage lingerie, and stockings with garters. There's always the sexy secretary, and the patriotic red, white, and blue babe, and the cute homemaker in the kitchen with her skirt getting caught on a drawer exposing her gartered thigh."

Clara sounded like she knew what she was talking about. June was convinced.

"And you know what else would be cool? If he took the pictures in black and white and then hand colored them. I wonder how you do that. I might have to do some research. Maybe there's a class I could take? Let's pick an era. I vote for 40s. What do you think?" Clara asked, finally including June.

"Honestly, I think whatever you think. I really don't have your experience or expertise in vintage style."

"Goody. So, you won't mind me taking over? I'm sorry. Please let me know if I step on your toes. I can follow direction, but it's hard if there's not a strong lead." Clara looked over at June and laughed. "That's probably why my following isn't as good as it could be. I'm always hi-jacking the lead and doing my own thing. It drives most guys crazy. James is about the only one that can handle it. And that guy that teaches class on Sunday at the hotel."

Did Clara have too much coffee? She is totally spun, but very entertaining.

Clara found close parking, and they quickly walked up the wide stairs of the 1920s craftsman house. A Squirrel Nut Zipper's song blasted through Larissa and Marty's front door. Clara knocked and walked, not waiting to be let in. They manueverd through the dancing couples, the furniture pushed back against the walls. Rose was back in town and dancing with James. Larissa and Marty were busy practicing Charleston variations. Samantha spun with Kris, while Dave sat in the corner perusing a book.

Nobody stopped dancing, but all said hi or gave a nod in acknowledgement of June and Clara's arrival. When the song ended, they gave hugs and cheek kisses all around. June felt like she was back in Phoenix. It felt like home.

"Oh good, you guys made it. I've been waiting to start the

video until you got here." James pushed play. "Okay, now check this out."

A dancer who looked like the tattooed guy June had seen in Pasadena—sans the tats—moved in an old time Lindy style, refined and elegant. His partner triple-stepped with long spider legs in a blur of amazing swivels. The dancer girl sat back leaning into the swivels, accentuating the beat. It was a gorgeous, feminine style. It also looked harder than the Swivels June had been doing. *I have to learn those Swivels.*

"See this guy?" James pointed to the screen. "This is Dean. He's a badass. And that chick, that's Jewel. Best partner he ever had. Check out how they counter balance and how dynamic it makes their Swing-out. Now, if you compare that to Frankie in *Hellzapoppin'* they look really similar on the three and four. The big difference is on the seven and eight. Frankie does a lay-out with his body, where Dean does a pike, but it's got the same power and same rubber-band effect."

June had no idea what James was talking about, and it showed on her face.

"C'mere Rose." Rose went to James and took his hand. "Okay, check it out." He did a swing-out that looked like Dean's. "See how you have to bend and create tension here on the three and four?" He stopped Rose midway through the dance.

Once frozen in position, June could see it. Their backs were straight, giving the illusion of standing upright, but their knees were slightly bent, feet closer to each other creating a V-shape.

"Can I try?" June blurted, too excited to edit herself.

Everyone laughed. "Another convert," Kris said.

"Sure. Do you mind Rose?" James asked politely. Rose shook her head and sat down.

"Okay," James instructed. "I want you to go to the three and four, walk, walk, triple-step and stop. Don't swivel and don't continue. Freeze."

June did exactly what he said. When she got to the count where they were facing each other, she froze as instructed. He put his hand on her chest above her breasts and pushed. It felt weird with his hand on her chest. She rounded her shoulders.

"No, don't collapse. Keep your back straight. Now bend your knees and almost fall back into my hand. You've got to trust me."

Trust is a funny thing in partner dancing. It's hard, like Clara said, to give up control and with this style you have to trust the lead even more.

"Now, listen. You can't do this with all dancers. Only if you feel it. You've got to have the counter balance and then you can give it back. Okay, now try the rest of the swing-out."

James sent June through the remaining four counts. She felt the power and whoosh of the swing-out, but wobbled off balance.

"Not bad for a first try." James nodded.

She tried again, and again, and again, slowly walking through the steps, adjusting her body and trying to feel the counter balance. She could tell her movement wasn't quite right, but didn't know how to fix it.

"Kris, come take over with June. I wanna find another clip." James handed June off to Kris while the others lounged and sipped cocktails.

"Hey, do you know switches?" Kris asked.

"I don't think so. What are those?"

"Clara c'mere. Can you show June switches?" Kris dropped June's hand and took Clara's.

June watched as Clara orbited around Kris, keeping her back straight, sitting into twists, bringing her feet together after every step. She maintained a lady-like stance that looked almost exactly like the girl in the video.

"Do you get it?" Clara asked.

"I think so." Clara handed Kris back to June, and June tried again.

"No. Sit back more," Clara instructed.

"Pike. Do you know what I mean by that?" Kris asked. "Bring your feet closer to mine but lean your butt away, keeping your back straight."

Was that even possible? Larissa and Marty were on their feet as well as Clara and Dave, all doing switches. June was overwhelmed and discouraged. It was too much criticism.

"Maybe she needs to have more visual." James pointed at the TV. "Check it out. I want you to compare Dean to Frankie and then watch this other clip with some dancers who are similar to Dean. Man, don't you think Dean is like the Fred Astaire of Lindy?"

June prickled. She knew they were trying to help, but it wasn't helping. She didn't want to stop dancing and watch an old video. She wanted to keep practicing until she got it, but everyone sat back down and watched the video.

Larissa leaned over and whispered, "You want a drink? I made Lemon Drops."

"Sure, thanks," June replied.

Larissa bustled into the kitchen and came back with a martini glass full of shadowy liquid. A lemon rind curled in the center, salt crystals rimmed the glass edge.

June gingerly licked the salt, surprised to find it sweet. She sipped through the sugar rim, lemon and a clean bright alcohol taste easily slipped down her throat. *I like it.*

She wanted to ask Larissa about it, but James pointed at the screen, demanding her attention, vigorously enumerating the finer points of vintage swing dancing. June listened, but knew she was more of a kinesthetic learner. Finally, James was on his feet, and Marty took over the DVD player.

"Okay, let's give this another whirl." James took June's hand. "Do you know send-outs?"

She was at a loss and shook her head no, swallowing a hard

lump in her throat. *After all my dance classes and workshops how are there so many steps I don't know?*

"Right. Well, why don't you try to follow? It's a basic six-count pattern. Check it out."

James led it, and June followed, not perfectly, but she didn't lose the rhythm. She smiled and felt better, less self-conscious. He smiled too, led a Send-out, and then pulled her in for the new and improved Swing-out.

Whoosh. June was amazed. Her heart and soul soared. It was the best swing-out she'd ever felt, and she trusted him. She matched his counter balance. They finished the dance, and he thanked her, a contemplative look on his face. He moved on to Rose and danced with her the rest of the night.

June took a break and sipped another Lemon Drop, plopping down on the couch next to Clara. Clara leafed through one of the Pin-up books. Kris and Dave gave, not so subtle, hints they wanted the girls to dance.

Samantha flopped on the couch next to June. "I need a break. One of you will have to take over."

June eagerly hopped up and took turns dancing with Kris and Dave. They taught her more new moves. She danced and laughed, clinked her martini glass, and basked in the glow of new friends. *Maybe Clara's right. Friendship isn't about being elitist, but finding company you enjoy.*

Everyone finally settled in to watch the complete hour and a half of James's dance clips, but attention was not fully on the television, conversations wandered. James suggested June apply at Macy's for an opening in the shoe department where he worked. Marty let Clara borrow his Elvgren pin-up book, and she'd already marked eight pages with yellow post-it flags for the future photo-shoot with Vertie. *Vertie. How would he fit in?* June hadn't proposed the idea of him learning Lindy, but something told her it would be a hard sell.

June folded her laundry while she waited for Clara to arrive. Her thoughts turned to their earlier conversation and her nerves bubbled below the surface.

I miss Gramma Gigi. I miss Julian. Why won't these feelings go away? Why do I feel so isolated and disconnected? I can't stop thinking about my biological grandmother. Would finding her give my life more weight?

She replayed her last conversation with Clara.

"Having a baby out of wedlock was not as acceptable then as it is today. Not that it's ideal now, but back then it was scandalous. What would you do if you were pregnant?" Clara had asked.

June hadn't known how to answer. She couldn't even think about it, which was one reason she was still a virgin. All choices sucked. She didn't think she could go through with an abortion, but the choice should be there if she needed it. Adoption seemed best.

"I don't know, Clara. That's beside the point. We need to focus on clues that will help us find her."

"You're right. When was your mom born?"

"1942."

Clara scribbled in her notebook. "So, your mom had you when she was thirty-eight?"

"Yeah, my mom's older than most of my friends' moms." The creepy feeling rushed through June's veins again. *I won't think about my mom dying. I won't.*

"If your mom's mom was young—and I bet she was—she could still be alive today. She could be in her late seventies or early eighties. I think there's hope." Clara scrunched up her face. "Maybe the father was a soldier who never came home."

"Maybe. Grampie D said they adopted my mom and uncle when he was stationed in San Diego. It's a long shot, but I have to keep trying."

"I know. I'm here to help. We can find her." Clara winked.

Even with Clara's help, they'd exhausted all of their leads and found nothing. The only new suggestion was Vertie's. June's mystery grandmother could've had her baby at one of the Catholic orphanages that straddled the US and Mexico border in the 40s. Vertie's great grandfather had come to America in the 1920s and it wasn't until the 1950s that the border was made less permeable.

The click of Clara's heels preceded her and snapped June out of her ruminations. Clara swept into the room with an exuberance that brightened June's studio apartment. June put aside her laundry and got out her notes for their upcoming adventure.

"Hello Darling," Clara said in a Betty Davis way.

"Hello, Sweets." They'd watched *Some Like it Hot*—filmed on location at Hotel Del—and June had picked up Tony Curtis calling Marilyn Monroe *Sweets*.

Clara, as usual, had been a woman obsessed, insisting they watch old movies and take notes on everything the women wore. Clara'd filled an entire notebook full of pictures dedicated to their photo shoot.

"Clara, have you ever thought about writing a book about living a vintage lifestyle?"

"I have been toying with the idea of creating a magazine. Look out, I may be recruiting soon."

"I have come far under your expert tutelage." June gestured to her latest vintage ensemble. "I totally get the vintage thing. It really does accentuate the look of the dance. And it suits me to a tee. Thank you, Clara."

"Any time, Doll. Now look what I've got for us." Clara displayed an Asian tapestry depicting a Chinese village. "We can use this to sit on, as a backdrop, or draping. I got it at a thrift store this morning. Isn't it perfect?" She didn't give June time to answer. "And look at these." She pulled out two antique Chinese parasols with wooden handles.

"They're so pretty."

"And check this out. I don't think it works, but it'll make a good prop."

June had to look twice before she figured out the little black box was an old-time camera with a double lens in the front. "Cool."

"We can pretend to take pictures of each other while Vertie is taking pictures of us."

"You're brilliant." June played with the camera looking through the lens.

"I know." Clara fluffed her hair. "I've also copied some classic pin-up poses from an old *Screen Star* magazine. Oooo, that reminds me. I found this totally awesome store that sells nothing but old ephemera."

"Sorry to seem dense, but what's ephemera?" June hoped it wasn't something every dancer knew.

"Ephemera refers to paper nostalgia, old photos, menus, magazines, dance cards, and greeting cards. Any collectibles made out of paper or items people would usually throw away," Clara explained without a hint of condescension.

That's one of the things June loved about Clara. She had her definite opinions, but she didn't fault people for not agreeing or not knowing.

"Okay. I get it. You'll have to take me to the ephemera shop some time."

"Of course, Darling. So, should we make up a story about why we're at the beach taking pictures in front of the Del? Are we two dolls on vacation? And who's taking our picture? A hot sailor we met on the beach? Or maybe some other locals? Don't you think we need to have a scene?"

"I guess so." June thought for a minute. "Why do we have the

Chinese stuff? How do our Asian accessories fit in?"

"Good point." Clara stopped leafing through her idea book and looked toward the ceiling. She pursed her lips and then curved them into a smile. "I've got it. Our sailor boyfriends sent them to us from China—since they were our ally in WWII—and we've planned a beach outing with a cousin who's visiting. We decided to bring our exotic goodies along and take pictures of ourselves to send to our overseas beaus."

They both started laughing and knew it was going to be a fun day no matter what.

June and Clara lounged on the circular tree benches in front of the Hotel Del, looking like young Hollywood starlets. June in borrowed—from Clara—1940s sunglasses and a vintage one-piece swimsuit, sarong slung around her waist and Clara in a three-piece matching skirt ensemble. The girls stretched their pale legs and awaited their photographer. A group of Japanese tourists asked if they could take their picture, and the girls eagerly complied.

June liked the formality and manners of the Japanese culture. America had become so informal. Maybe that's what drew her to the 1940s.

"Hey, Clara, if you could be magically transported to the 40s, but you had to stay and live out the rest of your life in that time, would you?"

"Do I go with the knowledge I have now? Or do I only know what was known then?"

"Good question. Give me an answer for both scenarios."

"Okay. Maybe if I had no knowledge of what I know now. But I think that's a big maybe. And a big fat hell no, if I know what I know now and was stuck there. I think the misogyny would drive me insane. I might have to kill someone." Clara laughed.

"Yeah, I agree. I was thinking in today's world, I can take all the good parts, the manners, the fashion, the values, the overall style and use it with all the choices I have today. I mean, most likely if I was eighteen years old in 1940, I'd probably be getting married. Or going to college to look for a guy to get married to, and then using my degree to make better cocktails for the hubby's boss. That's not appealing in the least."

"Yup, even though I love this vintage lifestyle, I'm happy and grateful for the choices I have," Clara agreed. "Let's say a silent thanks for all the women who fought to give us the opportunities we have today."

"Amen, sister." June clinked an imaginary glass. "Can you picture being married right now? Pushing out babies and changing cloth diapers? Gack. I shiver just thinking about it."

Clara took off her glasses and looked at June. "I don't think it would be so bad. I think I'd make a really good mother and wife."

"Okay." June didn't see Clara as the in-a-rush-to-get-married-have-babies type. She knew Clara was a couple years older, but barely twenty-two.

"Do you really think being married would be so bad?" Clara asked.

"I don't know. I honestly don't think about stuff like that."

"Don't you want to be in love?"

June had Clara pegged for a cynic and was surprised by this side of her. "Sure, but to be honest, I'm kinda afraid of everything that goes with it."

"Like what?"

"I don't know, stuff, just stuff." June didn't know if she should tell Clara she was a virgin and that she was abnormally fearful of getting pregnant. She certainly wasn't ready to share about her brother's accident or her panicky episodes. "Love is complicated isn't it? Have you ever been in love?"

"Sort of. I don't know. I think there are all kinds of love and that love grows as you grow. I remember in fifth grade there was this cute boy I really, really liked, puppy love, you know. Well, I remember going to the movies with him. When we held hands I felt so filled up. I was sure I was in love and I would marry him some day. Then three weeks later, he's holding hands with Jenny Gray. I was devastated and swore I'd never love again. But I did, and each time the feelings grew bigger. I think it's worth taking the risk of being hurt. Don't you?"

June laughed uncomfortably. She'd never really let her guard down like that. Her feelings of love were complicated and filled with loss.

"Come on now, how about that guy? He'd make pretty babies don't you think?" Clara pointed to Vertie who strode toward them, a camera slung around his neck, a tri-pod in one hand and white satiny discs in the other.

June jumped up and gave him a hug and a swift kiss on the cheek. Clara swooped in and gave him a friendly hug as well.

"Can I help you with anything?" June asked.

"No thanks. You guys looked great where you were sitting. Let's get some pictures here and see where it goes. I'm not sure how well it will work in the deep shade, but let's try."

He set up his camera and took a few shots of June, then Clara, then both of them. Clara worked the angles of her body and posed like the pictures she'd collected. When they'd finished with the bench shots, they walked around the Del trying to be inconspicuous, but failed miserably. They lingered too long by the gazebo in the courtyard, and a crusty old security guard asked them to stop monopolizing the grounds. They scurried down to the beach where Clara pulled out her last surprise: a vintage travel bar complete with stainless steel shaker, four drinking cups, a measurer, pourer, and curly wire strainer, all in a small rectangular suitcase.

"Vertie, would you be a dear and run back to the hotel and

get us a few mixers. I was flustered by the guard and plum forgot," Clara said in photo character.

"Sure." He tipped his head. "Anything you prefer ladies?"

"Lemonade would be divine, but whatever you like, darling."

For a second, June could see Clara ensconced in cocktail parties for the boss, two little ones sleeping through the adult glamour, while their parents entertained. Did people still do that? If they didn't, June had no doubt that when Clara found her true love, she'd bring it back in style.

Vertie tromped back with a brown box filled with three lemonades, crackers, cheese, and fruit.

"I found a deli in the basement. You guys have to check it out. It used to be a grotto where they kept wine. It looks like a cave."

"Sounds divine." Clara poured one of the lemonades into the silver shaker, took out her bottle of Vodka, and measured a shot. She closed the top and shook it like a character in an old movie. Vertie was as amused as June. He opened the cheese and crackers. Clara wielded the wire strainer and poured into one of stainless serving cup.

She handed the first one to Vertie. He sipped and smiled. "Not bad."

He took another slug and downed the entire contents. She refilled him and moved on to the other containers of lemonade, doling out a drink to each of them. June began to feel a little warmer and a lot more relaxed.

They spent the afternoon posing for pictures, using the props, and having a wonderful, silly time. At one point when Vertie was photographing Clara solo, he beckoned June over.

"June, come here. Take a look."

June shuffled through the sand to the tripod and tried to focus through the tiny hole. Clara was in miniature sitting on the sand, umbrella in hand, the Chinese blanket spread beneath her. She looked amazing. Vertie moved behind June. His breath was hot on her neck. He whispered in her ear while clicking the camera. He moved closer and pressed his body against her back and bare legs, nibbling her neck. She was afraid she'd fall forward and knock the camera over, but he snaked his hand around her stomach and pulled her to him. She wasn't entirely comfortable with his attention, but not uncomfortable either.

Clara did her best poses while trying to ignore Vertie's groping of June, but gave up and began to pack up. Vertie was too busy kissing June's neck to notice. June was worried about Clara and mad at herself for responding to Vertie. She forced herself to wiggle away. Vertie looked annoyed. *Should I help Clara or placate Vertie?*

"So, I guess we're done with the photo shoot?" June asked.

She didn't want anyone to be angry, and although Clara didn't look mad, she didn't look happy, either. Vertie looked positively frustrated, but June was used to frustrating boys. She supposed she'd need to give him *the talk*. Boys usually took it as a challenge, but when they realized she wasn't putting out, the lack of phone calls and dates turned into lame excuses.

Vertie grumbled. "Yeah, I guess we're done. Hey June, why don't you let me drive you home? I'm sure Clara can take care of herself."

June didn't want to abandon her friend and wasn't sure she wanted to go with Vertie. Her body wanted to go, her nibbled neck and yearning lips said yes, but her brain said no. She didn't want to piss him off. But not pissing someone off was not the right reason to go with them. *Why were relationships so confusing?*

"Oh, shoot Vertie, I made plans with Rose and James and some of the other hoppers. Would you like to come? We're going to work on some dance stuff." June glanced at Clara and saw her trying to conceal a smirk.

"Thanks, but I've got to meet up with some of the guys and pull a carburetor. I thought I could give you a lift home. No big."

Once he'd slung his camera over his neck, June trotted back to him, thinking the camera would be a safe buffer between their bodies. He anticipated her approach and shifted the camera to his back. He squeezed her in a close embrace and kissed her long and hard. It made her toes curl, but scared her too.

"Ahem. Ahem."

Vertie waved Clara off and brought his hands to the back of June's head. He was a good kisser. Her knees started to wobble, and she pulled tighter around his neck. He smiled under the kiss and pulled away. She had to catch her breath. Clara gave her an exasperated look and ambled over to offer Vertie a good-bye hug. He gave Clara a huge bear-hug and planted an unexpected peck on her lips. She startled for a second and then recovered.

"Oh you naughty boy, you." Clara patted his shoulder. "Thanks for a swell day, Cookie. We'll be seeing ya."

The girls walked to their car, arm in arm and happily shot.

Violet ~ 1940s

14. Beat Me Daddy, Eight to the Bar (Will Bradley)

"What do you think, Jeannie?" Violet twirled the shop phone cord around her finger. Her thoughts turned to Charles and Mrs. Peppy upstairs, cleaning up breakfast.

"That sounds like a great idea. Of course I have to check with Paddy, but he got on really well with Charles at the malt shop before Johnny and Charles had their scuffle."

Violet winced, but at least now she didn't feel guilty doing the contest with Charles.

"So, what should we eat? Chinese? Italian? Mexican?" Violet asked.

"I'm thinking. I'm thinking. What are you wearing?"

"I don't know yet. I think something red and white or blue to match Charles. Why?"

"We should skip Italian then. It's never smart to wear white to an Italian restaurant."

"Oh. I hadn't thought of that. Well, we could do Charles's favorite Chop Suey place?"

"That sounds good to me. I think Paddy likes Chinese, although he's mostly a meat and potatoes guy. Did I tell you he's been over three times this week for dinner? My mom just loves him, and I think my dad does too. I caught my dad staring at him intensely. It's a good thing I learned to cook from my mom. He really loves her cooking. Wouldn't it be swell if I married Paddy and you married Charles?"

"Don't you think we're kinda young to be thinking about marriage? I always pictured myself getting married after college."

"We are not too young," Jeannie said. "Loads of kids get married right after high school, and with the war on, you gotta grab your man. My mom got married right out of high school. Didn't yours? Uh, I mean, it's normal for girls if you find the right fella. Well, if Paddy asks me, I know what I'm gonna say."

"Do you think Paddy is your one true love?"

"Oh, I don't know. He's awful cute isn't he, and nice and polite and..." Jeannie giggled. "Did I tell you what a swell kisser he is?"

"No, you didn't." Violet smiled. "Oh Jean, I'm so happy for you." Violet knew Jeannie wanted her to give details about Charles, but the connection she and Charles had seemed too special to compare with Jeannie and Paddy. "Would you say you're in love with Paddy?"

"Of course, silly. What kind of question is that?"

"Let's say he joins the army and he doesn't come back for a couple a years. Would you wait for him? How long?"

"Oh, I don't know. You think too much. That's just beside the point."

"You're right. I do think too much."

"Now, what time should we go to dinner? What time do you have to be there to sign up for the contest?"

"The doors open at 8 o'clock."

"So, we should go for dinner around six? Or maybe even five? Yes, let's make it five. It'll give us plenty of time to eat, rest, and catch a taxi to the dance hall. Should we meet there? You know Paddy doesn't have a car. We always ride with Johnny. Oh, speaking of Johnny, did I tell you he switched dance partners? Looks like Ronald's leg wasn't all that bad, so he's doing the contest with Sue and Johnny's going steady with the new girl, Millie. Too bad she wasn't there at the malt shop that day, huh?"

"Yes, too bad." What an understatement. "Five sounds great. See you there. Hey, are you gonna do the contest with Paddy?"

"He keeps pestering me, but let's be honest, I haven't got a chance. My money's on you sweetie. See you at Chop Suey."

"See ya later, alligator."

Violet hung up the shop phone and dashed up the stairs to Mrs. Peppy's spare room. She laid out her gifts for Charles and Mrs. Peppy then carried them out. Charles and Mrs. Peppy stood when Violet entered the room.

"Would you like to sit here?" He gestured beside him.

"Thank you." She smiled. "But first, I have something for you both. The other night I went to buy rhinestone hair combs for myself and saw this and thought you'd like it. I wanted to thank you for all your kindness." Violet presented the little box to Mrs. Peppy.

Mrs. Peppy tugged at the ribbon and opened the box.

"This is lovely. Thank you so much, darling. I love it." Her eyes glistened, and she pinned the miniature deer to her lapel.

"And now, for you." She turned to Charles. "Not nearly so spectacular, but what I wanted to get you wasn't available at the time." She handed over his gift.

He methodically opened the package, taking the utmost care in preserving the ribbon and the paper. He smiled ear to ear at the simple socks.

"This is great. Thank you, Vi." He hesitated and then kissed her on the cheek. *Yup, the tingle is still there.*

"You know what would be really swell?" he asked. "If you had matching ones. We could wear 'em in the contest."

Violet ran back to the room, grabbed hers, and came out flapping one in each hand. He burst out laughing. Mrs. Peppy and Violet joined in.

"There is something extraordinary between you two. It is uncanny how like-minded you are. Yes, that is why you dance to well together. I know. I knew that kind of connection." Mrs. Peppy closed her eyes and lost herself in an old memory, her face a twist of happiness and melancholy.

"So, what's the plan, Ms. Woe?" Charles asked.

"We're meeting Paddy and Jeannie for dinner and then going to the dance hall."

"Sounds swell. When and where?"

"You mean you can't read my mind."

"Almost, but not entirely. You are a very intriguing specimen." He waggled his eyebrows. "All right then. It doesn't make sense to have a big lunch, perhaps a little snack at the coffee shop around the corner? Mrs. Peppy would you care to join us?"

"Thank you, but no, I think I will like to listen to some of my old songs."

The neon Chop Suey sign glowed reddish orange in the dusk, casting a gaudy light on the entrance. Charles pulled the wrought iron handle of the yellow and red door, allowing Violet to walk in first. Paddy and Jeannie were already waiting in the foyer. An attractive hostess loomed behind Violet's friends. The hostess smiled and nodded as Violet gave Jeannie and Paddy hugs.

"Hiya, Gate. You look adorable. I love your dress. Are those umbrellas on the fabric?" Violet asked.

"It's my new rayon. I picked it out special for tonight. See the little parasols, perfect for this restaurant."

"Turquoise and pink are marvey on you."

"And look at you," Jeannie replied. "You look like the quintessential jitterbug. Navy gab skirt, red and white striped jersey shirt, and saddles. And are those new stripy socks?"

Charles overheard and lifted up his pant leg to reveal his matching socks. His dark blue pants and white button down shirt with red sweater vest matched perfectly. They certainly looked a team.

"Ah, you table is ready." Violet loved the hostess's thick accent. "Please come this way." The hostess ushered them past the bar. Black lanterns cast dim light on shelves filled with exotic ceramic glassware. They continued to their red-clothed table, yellow chairs matched the lattice of the doors.

Charles pulled out Violet's chair, and Paddy did the same for Jeannie. The girls made sure to sit together so they could chat and let the boys get to know each other better.

"Hello, my name is Hou-Chin." His accent exotically Chinese, too, but more refined than the hostess's. "Can I bring you drink? Mai Tai? Scorpion? Maybe Navy Grog?"

They looked at each other questioningly. Charles spoke with command and a surety. "Yes, thank you. I think we'd all like to split a Volcano. Four straws, please."

"Ahhh, very good, sir. I be right back with your drink."

"So Charles, what'd you order there?" Paddy looked game for anything.

"It's an icy concoction of rum and fruit juices my buddy tried a while back when we first found this joint. It's not too strong, and well, it's festive. I feel festive. Don't you?" He smiled his glorious smile, his dimples dipped into his handsome face.

"I hope it tastes better than Polish vodka," Violet said and Charles burst into laughter. Paddy and Jeannie exchanged a look of shock.

Jeannie leaned over and whispered. "Vee Vee, I don't want to be a square, but I don't drink alcohol, and I know my mother and father wouldn't approve."

"It's okay," Violet whispered back. "I think it's mostly fruit juice, and if we don't like it, we'll make the fellas finish it up. Okay?"

"Okay-dokey." Jeannie crinkled her eyes.

The waiter returned with a giant ceramic vessel filled with a flaming liquid island, encircled by a pink slushy moat. Jeannie's eyes were as big as baseballs. Paddy eyed the drink gleefully while the waiter handed out straws to everyone. No one wanted to be the first one to try The Volcano.

"Ready to order?" Hou-Chin looked to Charles.

"Thank you. Not yet. Can you please give us another minute to look at the menu?"

"Very well. I be back in a minute."

"I would say bottoms up, but since we can't lift the bowl, how about, straws ready. One, two, three, sip."

They followed Charles's command. Their four faces moved closer to the glass bowl, then they dipped their oversized straws into the icy moat and sucked. Chilly, pure cold, then juicy pineapple with cherry filled their mouths. Underneath it all, Violet recognized the caustic bite of vodka. She looked over at Charles who grinned while still sipping. She gave him an accusatory squint. That did it. He released his lips from the straw and threw his head back in laughter.

Paddy and Jeannie put down their straws and looked from Violet to Charles.

"Okay what's the gag?" Jeannie asked.

"I swear," Charles said through his mirth. "I had no idea there was vodka in this drink. I thought it was rum." He erupted in another round of laughter. "Okay, Okay." Charles got his laughter under control. "When we were having dinner with Mrs. Peppy, she poured us this very strong Polish vodka."

Jeannie shot Violet a shocked and accusatory look.

"Vi, graciously drank it, but almost ceased breathing. It's too hilarious that there's vodka in this drink since she disliked it so much."

"Oh." Jeannie rolled her eyes. "I have to admit, I didn't taste anything offensive in this drink at all. I think I'll have another sip." At that, they all reached for their straws and followed Jeannie's lead.

By the time Hou-Chin brought the check, they were well sated and a little light-headed. Their faces glowed in the dim restaurant light. Charles and Paddy became newfound pals. They both blew out the center flame and bravely drank the liquid within and appeared no worse for the wear, albeit a little louder and sillier.

Hou-Chin brought them each a special dessert of fried bananas. No one had had them before except Charles. The sweet smell of syrupy caramel made Violet's mouth water though she was full. Jeannie rolled hers around on her plate, nibbling only little bits.

"Well, ladies. Shall we?" Paddy put down his money for his and Jeannie's half of the check.

Charles snatched the check. "Nothing doing. It was my idea, and Uncle Sam's paying me well enough. I'm treating."

Paddy tried to protest, but gave up. He reached for Jeannie and rubbed her back. Both fellas rose and scooted out the chairs for the girls.

"Thank you," Jeannie and Violet said at the same time and giggled.

"Should we head to the dance hall? Or do we have time for a walk?" Paddy asked.

"We've got about forty-five minutes to knock around. I don't know too much around here, but we could take a cab to the hall and walk around there. Whatever you girls want," Charles said.

Violet looked at Jeannie. She shrugged in response.

"I think it's livelier around Pacific Square," Violet said. "Let's head that direction. Plus, I get anxious about being late for anything." Her nerves were waking the butterflies in her stomach. She wasn't only nervous about the contest, there was the Johnny factor.

Charles hailed a taxicab and asked the driver to drop them seaside. The dance hall was close, and it would be a nice walk. Violet was grateful. The evening air was cool and dry, exactly what she needed to clear her fuzzy head. They arrived at the hall with plenty of time to sign up for the contest.

Violet knew if she and Charles didn't make the cut tonight, there would be no second chance. He'd be on a boat off the coast for the next two go-rounds. Tonight they'd be going up against thirty couples in a tap-out bout. Three couples from each night would go on to the finals. Violet noticed a lot of familiar names as she scanned the list: Barbara and Frank, Dick and Jane, Sue and Ronald, Johnny with…Mildred? Violet's stomach hurt.

She signed her name and Charles's names then turned to Jeannie. "So, are you gonna do it with Paddy?"

Jeannie surprised everyone by grabbing the pen and signing them up. "Oh sure, why not? After all, Paddy does have his new slipper dip kick or dip slip drop, or whatever it is, move." They all laughed and Violet forgot about the pit in her stomach.

"Ha ha. Looks like we'll see you on the dance floor." Charles clapped Paddy on the back.

"Don't be so sure we can't take ya," Paddy teased.

"Let's try to get a table." They walked toward their usual perch.

Violet spotted Johnny, heading up the gang from the malt shop. Violet froze. Jeannie looked to see what was wrong and spotted them.

"I have a feeling it'll be all right. Let's give it a try." Charles squeezed her hand.

Violet took a deep breath and ordered her feet to move. As they approached, Johnny's body tensed. He looked from Violet to Charles, to Paddy to Jeannie with a hard look, fists clenched at his sides. He took a deep breath, relaxed his hands and responded to someone talking to him from behind. He then pointedly moved to sit by her. It wasn't a girl Violet recognized. As angry as she was with Johnny, she suddenly felt very protective and hoped this girl was good enough for him. Even though Johnny was not right for Violet and he'd been a creep to Charles, he was like a brother.

"What's the rumpus?" Ronnie asked when they reached the group.

The air hung heavy, enemy territory during a cease-fire. Charles and Violet, and now Paddy and Jeannie, by association, were the enemy. Violet was so tired of being the odd man out.

Charles, gregarious as ever, thrust out his hand. "Howdy, I'm Chas. I don't believe we've met yet."

Charles's friendly manner caught Ronald off-guard, and he quickly grasped Charles's hand in a polite shake. "Right. My name's Ronald and this here's Sue."

"Mighty nice to meet another one of Vi's pretty jitterbug friends. Vi tells me you and Ronald cut a mean rug." Charles winked and Violet thought Sue would swoon. Ronald accepted the compliment, and some of the tension dissipated.

"Hello. If it isn't the ducky jive bomber." Barbara squirmed in between Ron and Charles. "You must save me a dance. I'm sure Vi plans to share. Don't you Vi?"

"Actually I don't. Sorry Barb, I have to save him for the contest. I have to save him for me."

Violet smiled, and her self-esteem rose a notch. *I'm not going to let the mean girls walk all over me anymore.*

Charles looked over at Violet, amused, and winked. He laughed boisterously. Everyone else laughed, too, except Johnny. From then on it was easier. Dick came over and introduced himself while Jane explained that she'd already met Charles at the malt shop.

Finally, Johnny saw no other way. He was forced to acknowledge their presence. Still seated, he looked over and nodded his head to Paddy and Jeannie, then looked at Violet and Charles. He gave Violet a look of pity. The magnanimous feelings she had for him disappeared.

"Hey there, Johnny. Good to meetcha, again." Charles offered his hand.

"Yeah, same here," Johnny said and glared at Violet.

"Hi, I'm Millie." A tiny redhead bopped up next to Johnny.

He realized his rudeness and jumped up. "Sorry, er, Millie, this is, Paddy, Jeannie, Charles and..." He paused at Violet's name for a second too long. "Violet."

"It's great to meet you all. Wow, the rumors don't lie. You do look like a starlet." Millie pumped Violet's hand. Johnny glowered.

Violet's ego rose for the second time, that night.

"Why don't you come over and see me some time, and I'll teach you my beauty secrets," Jeannie said in an awful Mae West impression.

Violet couldn't love Jeannie any more. Everyone laughed so hard they all had tears in their eyes. Violet, Charles, Paddy and Jeannie were invited to pull up chairs. The fellas went for cold drinks. And even though everyone was being nicey-nicey, Johnny sat as far away from Violet as he could, which suited her fine.

Millie bounced over to chat with Violet and Jeannie. A junior and a recent transplant from Pennsylvania, she was open and frank, and there was nothing not to like about her. Johnny appeared annoyed at her rapt interest in Violet and Jeannie and promptly asked her to dance. Jeannie and Violet watched at how easily Johnny tossed Millie around. Her tiny lithe frame minimized his awkwardness on the floor as she flitted around. Jeannie and Violet looked at each other shocked.

"Jean." Violet leaned over. "Is it my imagination or are Johnny and Millie total murder on the dance floor?"

"Honey, I think you've got your work cut out for you. There's your competition right there." Jeannie twisted her mouth and lifted her brows. "Don't worry, kid, they're taking three tonight. The rest of 'em, including me and Paddy, are off the cob compared to you guys. Get out there and knock 'em dead. You know you'll catch the judge's eye. You both look like movie stars."

"Jeannie, you're so good to me. What would I do without you?"

"I don't know. Go off and leave me for a sailor?" Jeannie joked, but Violet caught the bit of truth in her jest.

The Andrew Sisters, *Bounce me Brother with a Solid Four*, beat out a solid melody that made fun rhythms for their feet to play with. Violet's nerves were getting the best of her until Charles wrapped his arms around her and looked intently into her eyes. She relaxed into the music. Her heart knew his beat.

The room was a blur with Charles her only anchor. Every time she came around from a spin his eyes would find hers. Their souls synchronized to the hot rhythm. Violet flew away for a Swing-out, his tension changed, and she knew what he wanted. She gave an extra push and glided around his back to land by his side. He dropped to one knee, and she sat on it. They pecked like chickens, scratching out the rhythm. She grinned, filled with candid joy. Then they jumped up and crossed to eight-count patterns. Her feet sprang against the wood floor with each push.

The way they moved was magic, not one ounce of hesitation, flowing like liquid gold. As the song ended, Charles maneuvered her into splits. She hit the slide as the last note reverberated off the ceiling. She buzzed with happiness. The crowd went wild. She glanced around and saw ten couples left on the floor. She and Charles were still in. The judges would increase the tempo for the next round. She looked up at Charles. He beamed his glorious smile like heaven shining down on her.

"Good job, Gorgeous. Ready for more?" He winked and gave her hand a squeeze. The music started before she had time to reply. They'd saved some of their best moves for this. She scarcely recognized the tune. *Solid Potato Salad* was outrageously fast, and she loved it.

Bam. Charles tossed her out. She ducked. He swung his leg

over her, pulling her through, for not one, but two Slide-throughs. She rocketed across the floor. The slick surface zoomed below her bottom. It felt good and looked good, too. On the second slide, he lifted her up, resuming their fancy footwork.

The musicians sped up the song in a wild frenzy, but Charles and Violet were solid on the beam. They both knew it was time to bust out the six-count Collegiate Shag. They kept it tight but fun. Heads and torsos level, feet flying in kick-ups and stomps. He led a Send-out, keeping the crazy six-count footwork. They returned to closed position. He leaned back and slid his foot, his thigh under hers, forming a diagonal. The familiar crash of desire rushed through her body as they touched. She reveled in the sensation while still maintaining her rhythm. She was of two minds, one aware of his beautiful body pressing against hers, the other aware of the tension, footwork, music, and position she needed to be in.

Charles skillfully turned her around so they were back to back, both of them leaning into each other. His back muscles twitched and stretched as he slipped beneath hers to supports her back. He lifted her from the floor, tumbling her over his head until she was standing in front of him, hitting the crazy Shag beat. The crowd roared and the judge nodded approvingly. The song sped toward its finish.

Charles threw fast pitch Swing-outs into a perfect Rhythm-circle, spinning like a top. He stepped out and went into a triple Free-spin. Violet improvised tap steps to the beat. She caught his lead hand as he came out of the Free-spin and into one last Swing-out. His arm windmilled across her body leading a Quick-stop drop, the Jitterbug curtsy. She held her position. Thunderous applause washed over them. They were one of three couples left on the dance floor. The judge walked over and Charles twirled her out of her pose to stand beside him.

"One of your three champions for the night and a crowd

favorite." He asked their names in a low voice. "Charles Mangino and Violet Woe, Congratulations. We'll see you jits here three weeks from tonight to battle it out for Pacific Square's First Annual Spring Fling Swing Contest."

The judge proceeded to the other couple announcing them with as much flourish as he did Charles and Violet. He arrived at the last couple, an adorable little redhead and a lanky, cute guy who glared at them with an unreadable look.

"May I present your last and third winners of the night, Johnny O' Shea and Mildred Elliot. Congratulations to all our jittering jitterbugs."

Jeannie, Paddy and other kids from the malt shop tackled them with accolades, pats on the back, hugs, and handshakes.

"To the beach for a bonfire," Charles called.

"Killer diller. Yes. You said it, brother," resounded.

Violet didn't want to share Charles, but before she could voice a protest, they'd divided into two cars. Against Violet's hopes, Johnny and Millie were going, too. They were part of the evening's victory, but tainted her joy.

Their group stopped by the Mrs. Peppy's shop on the way and picked up the blankets and snacks Charles had fortuitously stowed inside. The beach would be fun, but Violet longed to be alone with Charles for their last night together for two weeks. *Two weeks. Only two weeks. For now.*

Violet woke to discover Charles curved the entire length of her body. His head nestled in her neck. His chest pressed against her back, thighs glued tightly to hers, even his feet twined around hers. A thrill electrified her body, igniting every place he touched, but none more so than her thigh, left exposed from her tangled skirt. Orange coals glowed faintly while gray smoke rose against the blush of morning. The sun inched its pale fingers to the plaid blanket where they lay. She tried to see if there were any other sleeping couples, but couldn't see anyone without disturbing Charles. His body felt delicious. She tried to breathe slow breaths, but her exhale trembled.

Long shadows stretched toward the water's edge. His breathing changed. His hand unconsciously rubbed up and down her bare thigh in a long oval pattern. Goose-pimples dotted her entire body. She dizzied and found it necessary to breathe through an open mouth. His legs twitched, his hand pulled her closer. He pressed harder into her body. His breath hot at her neck. His body moved slightly against her, a low gasp escaped his lips.

He tensed and froze finally awake. His hand groped for the edge of her skirt, found it, and smoothed it back into place. He took a gulp of air and exhaled slowly.

"Whew, there now. That's better, isn't it?" His voice was thick and deep.

"Is it?"

He kissed her softly on the back of her neck. "Good morning, Gorgeous," he cooed in her ear.

"Good morning."

She rotated to her back so she could look at his handsome face. He propped his head on his elbow, his other arm chastely draped across her lower abdomen. He beamed at her, and she forgot to breathe for a second.

"Gum?" He rolled back and dug in his pocket, not waiting for a response. He popped a stick quickly into his mouth and unwrapped one for her.

"Open up."

She obeyed. He delicately placed the chewing gum on her tongue, his thumb lingering, scraping across her teeth, pulling at her bottom lip. She closed her mouth and kissed his thumb as he slowly dragged it back and forth across her lips. He ran his hand from her forehead to neck, following the edge of her hairline. She sizzled through every pore in her body. He shifted his weight almost on top of her, but slightly askew. They both hurriedly tossed their gum into the coals. His mouth was on hers, devouring. His lips pressed into hers. She tried to breathe, but it was shallow and ragged. The familiar falling sensation rippled through to her toes and fingertips. She was electrified. She kissed him back strongly and arched her body toward his.

"Violet, Violet," he whispered her name like a song. "I...you have to tell me when to stop. Is this okay?"

She tried to find her voice. It clung somewhere deep inside. "Yes, yes, I want this," she replied in his ear, tugging and kissing, sliding her mouth into his sweet smelling neck.

He ran his hand up and down her body over her clothes, grazing the edge of her breast. New sensations flared everywhere. His mouth smashed into hers. His hand pushed on her hipbone. His body wriggled beside hers. She pressed into him. He squeezed their bodies together tighter, slightly rocking. Her hand caressed the back of his neck, her other stroked his firm strong bicep. She marveled at the complex movement of muscles in his back. Her breath respired unevenly mixing with his staccato exhale.

His tongue darted into her mouth, cool with a hint of mint, curling and probing. He rolled her onto her back. His full weight pressed her into the sand. She felt miniaturized, crushed beneath his hard body. She pulsed against him, her body undulating under his. His kisses came harder and quicker. Her body quivered and found his rhythm. Their rasping exhales competed with crashing waves.

"Am...I...crushing...you?" he asked between delicious kisses.

She shook her head no. His breath moved to her neck, lips brushing into the hollow, tiny nibbles became gulping bites. Her body trembled beneath his. He leaned his torso slightly away running his hand over her breasts, tugging at her shirt, but keeping his hand atop the jersey fabric. She arched toward his groping hand.

She struggled for breath. His eager mouth climbed from her neck to pull at her lips. His hand glided over her chest, clutching and gripping. She'd never let anyone touch her like that before. Her whole body trembled. Her hips rhythmically smashed against his hardness, and she could no longer think. Her breath became a short pant joined with his. Their movements began to escalate.

Then from far, far away she felt a twinge of panic. Even though she wanted this, even though he felt so incredible...But his kisses...clouded her brain and his body felt so good, so warm, she was thinking something...ah, his hands...something she should be thinking...something important...

As she tried to form a coherent thought, he pulled back before she could articulate her fear. They let the space between their bodies cool their breathing. The air rushed too quickly in and out of her mouth. She tried to take long, slow breaths finally comprehending the warning her brain tried to send.

Charles found his voice before Violet did. He wrapped himself snugly, but chastely around her.

"Violet, I, I, don't know what..." he sighed. "I don't know what you do to me. I've honestly never felt this way before. I feel like a crazed maniac when I'm with you, and yet I can't stop wanting you. I can't stop wanting to touch every part of you. I can't get enough of you." He looked into her eyes.

What's behind his stormy gaze?

"You don't set any boundaries for me, and I'm finding myself increasingly unable to set them for myself."

"Oh."

"Don't I scare you? Or have you done this before?"

She finally caught on to meaning. *I should have told him to stop or slow down, but I was about to, wasn't I?*

"No. I certainly have kissed boys before." She prickled at the accusation. "But no, never like this." His face relaxed into a contented smile. "Never so intensely. Never so willingly. Am I doing it wrong?"

Charles chuckled softly, "No. You're doing it too right. Are you sure you're only seventeen?"

"Yes. I'll be eighteen next month. You're the experienced one. Don't you sailors have a gal in every port?"

"What funny ideas you have. No, Violet. I do not have a gal in every port. I've had girlfriends, dates, even a steady for a while, but I keep trying to tell you Vi, I've never felt this way. I never wanted to be so close to anyone before. I keep embarrassing myself and putting you in a compromising position, pushing you further than I should." His brows knit together.

She wanted to believe him, but she was confused. She knew she loved him and felt safe with him, but Johnny's words ate away at her trust. Surely, this gorgeous, intelligent man couldn't have been saving himself for her. *Maybe he is using her for a good time before he goes away. But, if that's it, why did he stop?*

"Please say something, Vi. What are you thinking?"

I love you. You're amazing. I don't want my life to go on without you. Don't go. A small boat in a large sea, enemy planes attacking. Blood, death, and war. Don't die. Please come back. I want to believe every word you say. But fairy tales are not real and you are so very fairy tale.

How could she explain?

"Vi, I'll understand if you don't want to see me again. It really might be better to be friends before . . . ."

"Are you crazy? Don't you know? I...I love you. I'm hopelessly in love with you." She said it. She shouldn't have said it. She shouldn't have thought it. She shouldn't have felt it. An awkward silence followed. Her walls started to crumble. A fear rose inside her, but she did mean it. She loved him even if he didn't love her back.

"No," he replied dashing her last hope. "No, Violet. I'm in love with you, recklessly, insanely in love with you. I love you. Violet Woe. What are we going to do? I can't undo being in the Navy, but right now I would give up my country for you. I can't leave you now that I've found you. We could run away to Mexico." He hugged her close almost crushing her.

"As much as I want that, you're too honorable and you know it."

"It sounded brilliant for a second didn't it?"

He looked into her eyes, not closing his and kissed her tenderly and with so much emotion, her eyes blurred with tears. One fell. He gently brushed it off her cheek. She tucked her head in his chest and let the rest of her tears fall.

June ~ 1990s
15. Work Baby Work
(Royal Crown Review)

"So James, what's your swing story? How did you get sucked into swing dancing?" June organized a rack of sale shoes at Macy's.

"Am I sucked in? I guess I am." He tossed her a shoe from under a chair. She caught it and arranged it on a Lucite stand.

"I was working with this chick a couple years ago. She was going to some swing dance lessons, and what did I think of that. Would I be interested? And truthfully, I was not interested in swing dancing, but I was interested in her. And I'd always loved old gangster movies. Like the ones with James Cagney and Edward G. Robinson, and I dug the music. I don't know. Big Band music's always knocked me out. It seems full. Know what I mean, Kid?"

"Yeah." He'd taken to calling her *Kid,* and although it was endearing, it was also patronizing.

"This chick was real cute. We guys'll do some crazy shit if we think it'll get us laid."

June scrunched up her face and threw a shoe at him. He caught the shoe and smirked.

"What? I'm a guy. You know it's true. I can't help it if I like hot babes. I didn't make me this way."

"Is that all guys ever think about?"

He picked up an empty box. "I can't speak for all guys. But yeah, I'd say young guys without much else going on pretty much think about getting laid most of the time."

"Really?"

"Okay, not all the time, but come on. If a chick is even remotely hot, it crosses our minds."

"So, do you think men and women can never be friends 'cuz the guy is always thinking about sleeping with the girl?"

"Maybe." He hesitated. "I don't know about all dudes, but I can turn it off. Like, I really try not to think about anyone in a sexual way besides Rose, but sometimes it pops in my head. I can usually dismiss it or redirect it."

Does he think about me that way? She wasn't sure what she wanted the answer to be. She liked James as a friend and wouldn't want to screw up any of her new friendships. From the little things he said, she didn't think he thought about her that way, anyhow.

"How?" She scooted a chair back into place.

"How what?"

"How do you dismiss it?"

"Oh. I usually think about a new dance step I'm trying to work out, or a paper for school, or a recent boxing match I watched," he explained. "What about you?"

"Me? What do you mean, what about me?"

"Don't you ever think about it? How much do chicks think about sex?"

"I don't know." She turned as red as the patent leather pump in her hand. "I think we, or I think more romantically. I think about kissing a lot, but I don't know about thinking specifically about it." She did think about it though, about how to avoid it, but she didn't want to tell him that. "What does Rose say?"

"Rose? I dunno, I've never really talked with a chick like this before. You're different, kinda like talking to a dude."

"Is that a good thing or a bad thing?"

"I dunno, it's cool. It's nice to get a chick's perspective."

"So, back to how you became a swinger?" She punched the word swinger. Swing dancers hated to be called swingers.

"Right. So anyway, this cute chick, what was her name, Tanya, yeaaaah Tanya." He smiled.

"So, I go to this dance class with Tanya and I find that I kinda dig it. And I'm pretty good at swing dancing. We date for a while." Another smile. "And then she moved, but I kept dancing and I met Clara, Rose, and the others. Eventually hooked up with Rose. Been with her for over a year now." He tilted his head as if surprised by that revelation.

"So, Rose. Is she the one?

"I dunno. She's a real pretty girl and a hell of a dancer when she puts her mind to it." He shrugged.

June nodded.

"Hey, well, you better go close out your register." He playfully swatted her butt with his moneybag.

"Hey."

"Uh, well. It's almost time to go and I wanna get outta here. I can't wait to hook up with everyone at the Cat Box. Should be a rad show. How were your sales by the way? You've caught on real quick for only being here a couple weeks." He looked at the receipt. "Good sales. Wow, you're just behind me and I've worked here for three years."

"Thanks." He'd given her an actual compliment. She shouldn't be such a praise junkie, but she couldn't help it. And James never said anything complimentary about her.

She started closing out, excited about going to the notorious Casbah—affectionately called the Cat Box. The Big Six band, from England, was playing and she couldn't wait to see them live. She'd blown off a date with Vertie. He was going to Tio's to see the Lucky Stars. She'd seen a lot of him and really liked him, but was dying to Lindy. No luck getting him interested in learning Lindy. She hated to admit Clara might be right.

She lost her count and tried to focus on the money, not the bands and dancing. James crept over and jingled his moneybag, obviously impatient. She counted in her head, eight, nine, ten....

"Eleven...eight...fourteen." James messed with her.

"Shut up." She lost her count again and re-tallied, putting the one-dollar bills in stacks of twenty. James continued to harass her with random numbers.

"James, what the heck. I thought you wanted to get out here?"

He laughed. "Sorry Kid, you're just so fun to tease. And I love your reactions."

She glared at him with as beady eyes as she could muster, but of course, her face betrayed her, the corners of her mouth turned up to a smile. "Oh, save it for Rose."

"Eh, Rose is so stoic. I can never get a good reaction out of her. Here look out." He nudged her over and took control. He whipped through the count. His fingers flew across the ten-key pad as he input the checks and cash. June barely had everything in the zippered bag before he was done. They raced up the escalator and waited in the money line. Luckily, there was only one cosmetic girl and the guy from men's suits in front of them.

They punched their timecards and headed to the bar.

James quizzed June on her biology terms for her test on Monday as she drove. When they made it to the bar, they had to circle the block three times for parking, finally finding a spot four blocks away. The steady rush of cars on the elevated freeway mimicked the ocean. The bar crouched under the overpass in a small squatty building much grungier than she'd imagined.

A heavily tattooed guy sat outside on a stool with a SOLD OUT sign hung on the door behind him. "Are you on the list?"

"Yeah, June Andersen and James Clark." Their names were out of his mouth before she had time to remind him that her ID said Julie Wright. June looked at James in a panic. It only took him a minute.

"Hey, and uh, June couldn't make it. So Julie here is using her ticket. Is that cool?"

What if he doesn't let me in? Panic peeked through her excitement.

Tattoo man checked their IDs and waved them into the outer courtyard. June shook her head at her needless worry. James winked.

Guys and girls chatted, chain-smoked, and strutted around the courtyard, performing a timeless courting dance. Ratty, but arty concert posters plastered the tall cement wall. The smell of musty concrete mixed with nicotine and hung in the air like fetid ghosts. Energetic swing music blasted from the first of three doors. Packed bodies jammed the threshold of the first two. The far door outlined figures moving deftly around green felt tables.

"That's the back bar," James shouted. "Let's grab a drink in there since it's so packed up front."

Next to the pool table, the cramped space held a curved bar with old school video games against the opposite wall.

"No one's at the Pac Man table. Go, go, go," James commanded. June darted over and took an empty seat at the console.

He made for the bar and yelled, "Whaddaya drinking?" The low hanging, 1960s bulbous light brushed the top of his head.

"Beer." The place didn't look like they'd make a good Lemon Drop.

"What kind?"

"Whatever." She shrugged her shoulders. James came over and dropped two quarters into the machine before she could decide whether she wanted to play. The beer tasted as skunky as it smelled.

"Just a quick game. It's really crowded on the dance floor when it's a sellout." James pressed the play button.

He went first. He was good and fast, like the ten key at work, but too greedy. He tried to go for too many dots. On June's turn, she got within a hundred of his score. He gave her a funny look, took a slug of his beer, and launched into his attack. They played countless games with June digging in her purse for quarters and James running to the bar for change, insisting on another rematch.

With their eyes on the game, they didn't notice Rose and Clara come in. James lifted his head as the ghost caught his guy. The machine made its classic falling bomb sound with bloops and bleeps. He jumped up when Rose reached the table. She looked from June to James to the four empty beer bottles. James looked sheepish, but quickly wrangled Rose around the neck, pulling her close for a kiss.

"I hope you don't expect a kiss from me," June said to Clara, trying to break the tension. Clara and June laughed. Rose did not.

"How long have you guys been here?" Rose glared at June.

"Ha. Long enough for me to kick June's ass at Pac Man." He laughed, oblivious to the trouble he was in with Rose and the fact that they'd tied.

Rose rolled her eyes and looked perturbed. At least it looked a bit like anger. James was right, Rose never showed much emotion, but now anger radiated from her body directed at June.

"Let's go dance." Rose dragged him off.

"Is Rose mad at me?" June asked Clara.

"No, she's mad at James, but it's easier to take it out on you. Give her some space and stick to dancing with Kris, Matt, and Dave tonight." Clara tilted her head. "Plus, there's ample hoppers you can sink your teeth into. We have plenty of foot fodder for the night."

"How's the band?"

"Hot," Clara replied. June looked confused.

"Both." Clara read June's mind. "It's a sweat box in there, but the band's on fire. Wait till you hear them."

"What do you mean, wait? Aren't they still playing?"

"No, dummy. You missed the first set playing moronic video games. Come on. Let's get you a real drink and some air. It's stuffy in here." Clara returned from the bar with two pale maroon colored drinks in short glasses.

"What's this?"

"Does it matter?"

June sighed. "No, I guess not."

They grabbed their drinks and walked into the courtyard. Clara bumped into a short dark guy in a plaid suit. Half her drink splashed onto the sticky, cement floor.

"Surry sweets," he said with a lovely English accent. "Didn't mean to do that. Let me get you another, luv. This here's, Al." He nudged a tall, thin guy toward them. "Al, entertain the ladies while I get them new drinks, won't you?"

"Hullo," Al said in an equally cute English accent and plaid suit that matched his friend. It took June a minute to put it together. These guys were with the band. June pulled at her skirt. Another band mate joined his friends, this one even cuter than the other two.

"Hey brother, aren't you going to introduce me to your lovely friends, then?" he asked.

June could listen to them talk all night. They were older than she expected, late twenties, early thirties. She laughed to herself, her palms sweated, and stomach fluttered. They were celebrities.

"So which one of you fellas dance?" Clara raised an eyebrow.

They smiled, jockeyed for position, and said simultaneously, "I do."

Everyone burst out laughing. The drink spiller returned and was introduced as Pat. That made three guys and only two girls, good for Clara and June, bad for the guys.

"Who wants to dance first?" Clara asked.

"Can you ladies Jive?" the cute one with the dark hair and light eyes asked. June looked at Clara for help.

"Everything in triple steps, right?" Clara replied.

"Sure, close enough. Let's go, luv."

The tall one grabbed Clara's hand and dragged her through the crowd. The cute one, eyed June and although she felt bad leaving the short one holding the drinks, the cute English boy was already maneuvering her through the crowd. As they passed, people patted him on the back, showering him with accolades. They squeezed into the center of the mismatched tiled floor. She spied her other friends at a cocktail table near the tiny dance floor. The cute English boy's name was James too. It sounded different in his accent, more like Jams.

Butterflies prickled her stomach as she tried to follow a dance she'd never done and not think about the fact that he was famous. His lead was firm, easy to follow, and he smiled encouragingly. She relaxed into the dance. *Clara wasn't kidding when she said it was all triple steps, constant push turns, bouncy and peppy.*

June tried to make her triple steps smooth like American James had taught her, but with the English guys the jive was all about the bop. She gave up and surrendered to the vertical rhythm. He guided her into repetitive side by sides and Sweethearts-turns, looked her in the eyes, and smiled. Every time English James brought her close to his side, she felt a little zing. *What is my relationship with Vertie? I guess I need to find out.*

The room was hot. Sweat dripped down her neck and back. Rivers of water coursed down the back of her thighs, tickling behind her knees, and pooling into her shoes. She sloshed happily around the dance floor with the cute musician from England.

It took her most of the dance, but she finally nailed the Jive rhythm and bounce. She couldn't wait to call Amy and tell her about dancing with the guys from The Big Six.

I wonder if these vintage bands also have vintage ideals and morals. Was it different for girls in the 40s? Was my grandmother a jitterbug?

She danced with the plaid trio several times, before their

band-mates gathered, and tapped invisible watches. It was time for The Big Six to hit the stage.

English James gave her an unexpected kiss on her cheek, blood rushed to her face. She was supposed to like Vertie. And she did. But she liked English James, too. Clara got a kiss on each cheek from Pat and Al. June didn't know how Clara felt, but June felt like the belle of the ball.

"Well now, this is some unexpected fun, don't you think?" Clara asked.

"I'm having the best time ever." June gave Clara a big hug, and she squeezed back. "Of all the chicks in the bar they could have danced with, they danced with us."

"Yeah, and they want us to hang around after the show. What do you think?"

"What do you think?" June asked.

"I think we should dance some more." Clara moved toward their friends' table.

The band lit up the stage and the dancers claimed their space on the crowded floor, pushing the standees to the outer edges. June danced with her regular leads and a guy she'd met at the Rock-it. She made sure to steer clear of James and Rose and received no more dirty looks from her.

When she came out of the bathroom, she ran into James. "Hey, wanna rematch?"

"Are you crazy? Don't you want to watch the band?"

"Sure, sure, it's so crowded it makes me a little crabby, and Rose is in a weird mood."

"I don't want to add to that. Besides, I love dancing to this band. I gotta get back out there." June started to go.

"Hey, I haven't danced with you tonight." He smiled big and easy. "Wanna dance?"

"Thanks, but I already promised this song to George."

It was stretching the truth a little, but she really didn't want to get between him and Rose. He was oblivious to the fact that their Pac Man game had pissed off Rose.

"Who the hell is George?"

He was clearly not used to getting turned down for a dance, guys rarely did.

"Look, I don't know Rose well, but I think she's a bit bummed out 'cuz you spent a lot of time playing Pac Man with me and didn't come and look for her first."

"Oh, you think so?"

"Yeah, I do." June ran off to find a dance partner.

James had said dancing in a crowd is like bowling for drunks and boy was he right, and I'm the ball.

June swirled and bumped, knocked and rocked around the floor, but still managed to dance and do Swing-outs. The music was good and the energy high. Even though she dripped with sweat, she felt connected to the music and all her leads.

She kept one eye on her cute English dance partner as he banged away on the keyboard. The band kicked the vibe into overdrive, and when she thought it couldn't get any better, the bass player picked up his stand-up bass and stepped off the stage. The dancers made room, creating a semi-circle around him. He slapped and thumped, and although June still had the urge to dance, the deference was unanimous. Everyone quit dancing and watched the man work.

Then the sax player hopped off the stage and zigzagged around the room. He leaned up against a pretty girl in a short black skirt. She wiggled and gyrated against his sprinkling rhythm. He arched his back and fingered the brass buttons on his sax. The instrument's wail filled the room with the sweet sound. He strolled over to his bandmate, then the beater man came out from behind his drum kit and started drumming on the edge of the stage, keeping a perfect beat.

The other musicians brought the sound down low and soft so

everyone could hear the acoustic drumming. While they played softly, he rhythmically hit his sticks on the edge of the bass, they clicked metrically, wood on wood. June ached to dance, but couldn't take her eyes off the guys and wouldn't dare disrespect their spotlight. He drummed the sax, tapping the bigger bend of the golden instrument, the sound soft and tinny, then continued to the table where James had joined Rose, both looking blissfully happy. The drummer beat the edge of the Formica table, tinkling the half-empty glasses like high hat and cymbal. Everyone held a collective breath listening to every beat he created on the variety of surfaces. Rose's eyes glowed with the attention in her corner of the room.

The drummer transitioned from the table to tap up the side column at the stage corner. He made his return, drumming everything in his path. The rest of the boys continued to play softly. The audience leaned in, bending toward the plaid clad stage, caught on the end of an invisible fishhook. The Big Six reeled them all in.

The beater man returned to his drum kit. With the first stroke of his wooden sticks the band exploded in full force, full volume, full energy, and June was convinced they were going to blow the roof off the joint. George sent her out into the tiny open space. She butt-bumped into Clara, colliding on beat like it was choreographed. The English lads noticed and smiled at Clara and June, the girls smiled back before their vision was obscured by flying elbows and whipping hair.

Clara, Samantha, and June sat in the booth at Denny's all night coffee shop. Pat and English James invited the girls up to the Derby in L.A. They'd be happy to put the girls on the guest list, and if the girls were so inclined, join them for supper.

We were inclined.

Clara kept her glee contained, but vibrated with excitement at the offer. She accepted for all of them, although Samantha declined since she had to work. If June was on the schedule for Sunday, she'd get James to cover for her.

Clara and the English boys talked of the Derby's swanky interior and its rise in popularity since the *Swingers* movie. The Los Angeles landmark was originally a chicken shack when Cecil B. DeMille bought it and turned it into the fourth Brown Derby. Unfortunately, the Brown Derby the boys were playing was not in the shape of a Derby hat, like the original one had been, but it was the only one left of that era.

The boys insisted June and Clara must have dinner with them at Louise's Trattoria—the restaurant that shared space with the Derby—and try the Cobb Salad since it was created by the original owner of the first Derby restaurant, Bob Cobb.

June and Clara arranged to meet them at the restaurant at 5:30. June entrusted Clara to retain the details, since everything had begun to blur and run together for her. The boys kissed the girls' cheeks, and they said their good-byes until the Derby.

"Do you mind crashing at my place? I'm too tired to drive you home?" June yawned.

"Of course not," Clara replied.

June's head barely hit the pillow before she drifted off, wondering if English boys kissed the same as American boys. She woke shaking. Sharp visions of the accident flashed in her mind. Her brother's cry as he went over the edge. Her mother's wail resounding off the tall mountain. June's heart hammered, and her head ached. Her body was cold and hot at the same time.

Am I having a heart attack? Am I dying? Am I going crazy?

She needed to clean something. She needed the lights on. She needed to organize her room, but she didn't want to wake Clara. And she didn't want Clara thinking she was a freak. She stumbled in the dim window light and grabbed a basket of laundry, dragging it into the bathroom. She began folding. Waves of chills undulated through her body. *You're not dying. You're fine. This will pass. It was only a dream.* It seemed like hours before the chills and her beating heart settled down. When they finally did, she climbed back into bed and slept soundly until morning, grateful that Clara didn't wake.

Clara scurried out as soon as she woke, babbling about planning for tomorrow. *It must exhausting to be Clara sometimes.* June would've rather gone back bed, but she was still a little jittery from her panic episode. Instead, she jumped in the shower and let the hot water rinse her salty, sweaty body. The shower only helped a little. She still felt icky.

She could cancel her date with Vertie and go back to sleep, but she bucked-up and took two aspirin.

What was I thinking when I agreed to the afternoon date. I have to to work the closing shift. I can do it. I can work, go to school and have a social life. Can't I?

She wiggled into her dress. The high waist of the Tiki dress accentuated her flat stomach and flattered her figure. Gold, brown, and black fabric fell in layered tiers with yellow piping accenting each section. The dress reminded her of the skirt Nancy had worn so long ago. Her life had changed a lot since the night she'd thought of Nancy as the girl in the Jitterbug dress. Maybe one day she would feel like the girl in the Jitterbug dress and hopefully there'd be dancing at the BBQ-Car Show. And maybe Vertie would dance with her, even if it was only East Coast Swing.

The doorbell rang before she had time to blot her lipstick. Vertie greeted her with an awkward hug and a swift hard kiss. She didn't tingle.

"You look ready. Let's get a move on. We're going to meet up with some friends I ran into last night, okay?"

"Vertie, what's our deal?" She ran her hand across her midriff and gritted her teeth. "Are we free to see other people or are we exclusive?" She should've wait until later to ask, but couldn't hold it in. English James floated in her mind.

"I don't know. What do you want?"

That was the crux of it. What did she want? What she really wanted was to be able to see other people and for him to not to, but that wasn't fair.

"To date?"

"Cool. Sounds like what we're doing."

"We're dating. But we could, if we wanted to, date someone else, I guess. Right?"

"Sure, whatever." He pulled his comb from his pocket and slicked back his already perfect hair.

"So, are you dating other people?" She grabbed her purse and dropped her lipstick inside.

"Not right now. You?"

"Not right now." Which was technically true. She'd leave it at that. He didn't seem interested in pursuing more of a relationship and since she was clueless as to what she wanted, it was probably a good thing. Still, it bruised her ego a little.

Violet ~ 1940s
16. Heebie Jeebies
(The Boswell Sisters)

The apartment shook, shapes blurred. Her stomach curled with fear, and started to drop. Violet stood, ready to run outside, but when she did, the couch stopped shaking and the room settled. It took her a second to realize she was shaking. Her body was quaking, not an earthquake. Tears streamed down her face pooling at her collarbone, soaking into her shirt. She couldn't stop. She fell back down onto the couch, sinking into the worn cushions. She had no control.

She shouldn't be so sad or dramatic, but the ache in her chest felt like someone was sitting on it. No, someone was tearing it open and clawing it to bits. She didn't understand why she hurt so deeply. His deployment was only two weeks.

She took a deep breath, hoping it would help, but it only fueled her torrent. She felt heavy, but at the same time, light, so light and insignificant that she could float away, every molecule of her being drifting off like dandelion seeds on a breeze.

What she hadn't wanted to admit to herself was that this was only a prelude. He would soon be leaving for a long, long time. She'd cocooned herself in a fantasy world and without his presence to bolster her, she sank into self-pity and despair.

Tears continued to stream down her face. She needed him. She needed to be in the park where he first kissed her, to sit on the cold tree and pretend he was whispering in her ear. She needed to be laughing in Mrs. Peppy's kitchen. She needed to see him walking into the shop. She needed to sit in the dark theater and pretend he was sitting next to her. She needed to feel his arms around her, smell his pine fresh scent.

She felt sick. She was going to be sick. Her stomach clenched. She wove her way down the narrow hallway, pressing her hands against the walls to keep steady. She sank beside the toilet and lifted the lid. The smell of stale water and faint bleach steadied her. The tile was cold against her calves and feet. *How can it be this hard to love someone?*

She needed to be numb, needed to remember how to be numb. She gripped the porcelain edge of the tank and heaved. Maybe she didn't have the strength. Maybe she didn't deserve him. *Was love supposed to be so painful? How did the other navy girlfriends and wives do it?* Why couldn't she pack her feelings away like she did with her mother?

He'd opened her heart and now she couldn't stop feeling, crying, and yearning for him with every fiber of her being. She couldn't turn off the movie in her head of the attack on Pearl Harbor. It could happen to him in the Pacific Ocean. The ocean was big. The world was big. Death lurked around every corner.

She could drink, like her Pop. Mrs. Peppy too, the way she sipped her Vodka. Charles deserved better. If she could hold on to hope. Will him to come back to her whole and strong. If she clung to that thought, mind, body and soul, it would give her strength. *Could love and hope be enough?*

She woke in darkness, her cheek pressed against hard tile, legs cramped and cold. Her stomach muscles hurt and she was drained, but oddly calm, resolved, like she'd settled an onerous debt. She felt woozy when she stood and had to catch herself on the toilet tank, gripping the edges with both hands. She shook her head to clear it, but that only made it worse.

Charles was gone from the city, her life, her existence, gone for two weeks with no possibility of phone calls or letters. She took a deep breath, bracing for more tears, but found herself emptied. She groped her way to the icebox in the kitchen. She found cheese and a stick of salami, bit off a hunk of each and chewed methodically. She felt a little more in control.

A moonbeam streamed through the tiny window, enough to find a candle and match. She couldn't suffer the glare of electric lights. She cut slice after slice of cheese and salami. Memories of the candlelit park dinner, the first time Charles kissed her, stabbed across her heart. She remembered the warmth and joy of his kiss, a prickle of desire flickered. She leaned back, grinned at the memory, and poured herself a glass of milk. The cool creamy liquid slid down her hot throat. It felt good. She felt better. She was a woman in love and there was no time for tears. She needed a plan.

The San Diego early morning yawned. The paper boy shouted headlines and scandals like an alarm clock. Her local bus rattled down the street and milk bottles clanked on doorsteps. Foghorns blasted in the distance. It all sounded hopeful.

"JUNIper 302," Violet said to the telephone operator. She waited while the operated repeated and rang Jeannie's phone.

"Hello, Jackson residence," Wally answered. Embarrassment pinched Violet, and for a second, she wished she could have fallen in love with Wally. *It would be so much easier if you could choose who you fell in love with.*

"Hi, uh, Wally, is Jeannie home?"

"Yeah. Who's calling?"

"Wally, it's me, Violet."

"Sorry Vi, I didn't recognize your voice. Are you okay? Are you sick or something? You sound funny."

"A little spring cold I guess." Usually good at small talk, she couldn't think of anything. "So, is Jeannie around?"

"Yeah. JEEAANNIEEEEE," he yelled.

Jeannie clomped down the stairs. The sound echoed over the phone as did her mother's scolding at her for stomping and Wally yelling. Violet's heart yearned for a mother like Jeannie's.

"Hiya, Jeannie here." Her voice was cheerful.

"Hi, Jeannie." As soon as Violet said Jeannie's name, tears dripped down her cheeks. She bit her lip and inhaled deeply.

"Hey, Jeannie." Violet's voice cracked. All the love she had for Jeannie flooded her senses. Violet closed her eyes and thanked God for the many kinds of love in her life. "I was hoping..." She took another quick breath. "That we could get together after school? I thought maybe we could do some shopping. I have an idea and would love your input."

"Sure, honey, you know you can count on me. You wanna meet me at the malt shop? Everyone's buzzing about you making the contest finals."

"Maybe you could meet me at Peppy's? I'm not sure I'm ready to face the crowd right yet."

"Of course. I'm sorry. Really, Vee Vee, I'm so sorry for you."

That did it. More tears trickled down Violet's cheeks, but she kept her composure and noted it was almost the same words Jeannie'd said about her mom. "Thanks. I better get going. See you later, gator."

"Should be a cinch. See ya after school." They hung up at the same time.

If Violet thought the day was long waiting for Charles to get off work, it was excruciating waiting for him to come back from the boat debt. She tried to find new ways to fill her time at Peppy's. By two o'clock, she'd completed the workload, cleaned the windows, and swept the entire shop. Her mind drifted and ruminated about things she didn't want to think about.

"You are trying to put Charles out of your head? How long will he be gone?" Mrs. Peppy pursed her lips and fixed her knowing eyes on Violet.

"Two weeks," Violet answered. "I think I'll dust out the old couch and the dressing room curtains."

Mrs. Peppy nodded and continued to pull the needle through the dark fabric.

Violet sprinted into the back room, grabbed a step stool, pulled the curtains from the rod, and took them to the back alley for a good beating. It felt good. After the dust was out, she rehung them and wrestled with the old mohair couch, dragging and pushing, only to find it didn't fit out the door.

A poof of dust swirled around her when she plopped down on the sofa. The memory of sleeping on the couch after kissing Charles came back to her. He'd slept on the couch, too, the night he made dinner. She lay down and closed her eyes, trying to picture his face, his body, his smell, and touch.

"Hey, lazy bones. I thought we had a date?"

The voice disturbed her dream. Why did Charles sound like a girl? Violet eased out of her slumber. A shadow of frizzy hair blocked what little light there was. Violet quickly sat up. Her head swam, but at least she wasn't crying.

"Gosh, what time is it Jean?"

"It's only four-thirty, but I knew it'd be a cinch to spring you early. And here I find you sawing logs on the clock. Let's get you up."

Jeannie pulled Violet's arms. Violet lurched forward and gave her best friend a big hug.

"Thanks." Violet had to bite her cheek to hold back the tears, but she was getting better. Violet had been down this quiet road with Jeannie before.

"So, what's the grand plan for the day?" Jeannie sat on the arm of the sofa.

"You know we've got the big semi-finals, and hopefully finals of the dance contest coming up." Violet didn't want to say, *when he gets back.* "And I thought I'd make a special new dress for it. I need your help picking out a pattern, fabric, and accessories."

"Oooooo goody."

Violet stretched, yawned, and asked Jeannie to help move the couch back into place. Even though Violet worked in a tailor shop, Mrs. Peppy didn't have a large selection of new patterns and women's fabrics. She worked from her experience and mostly tailored men's suits.

They said good-bye to Mrs. Peppy and walked toward the bus stop.

"Walker's has the best selection of McCall patterns in stock and great new rayons and jerseys." Violet said as they walked. "What do you think, should I go with a rayon, cotton, jersey or gab?"

"I don't know. We'll have to see the fabrics. I don't know as much as you, but I do know what I like when I feel it." Jeannie giggled. "I've had some heavy dates with Paddy. I don't want to kiss and tell, but I will. We've kissed quite a bit."

"You've been holding out on me, huh?"

"You know I can't keep anything from you. His kisses are murder and he's such a sweet lamb. He takes my breath away and curls my toes. If you know what I mean."

She did know what Jeannie meant, but couldn't think about him right now.

"Oh honey, I'm sorry," Jeannie said. "I shouldn't have mentioned it. I didn't mean to bring up a sore subject."

"I won't go into a decline. I'm happy for you and Paddy. When did you finally clobber him?"

"Saturday, after the contest at the bonfire. Gee, that was a swell time. I'm glad you're okay to talk about it."

Violet smiled and tried to hold on to the happy memory. "Barb was even tolerable that night."

"I know, and can you believe Johnny and Millie? What a surprise that was. They cooked with helium on the floor. Not as dance hall as you and Chas, but they really suit each other. Don't you think?"

"I guess I should worry about them as competition, huh?"

"I don't think so. You and Chas really swing. Although Johnny and Millie were cooking, they swing like a rusty gate compared to you and Chas."

"Do you really think so, Jeannie?"

"Christopher Columbus, yes. Now, tell me more about this jitterbug dress you're planning."

"The only thing I know for certain is that I want to do something nautical, sailor-ish, or at least red, white, and blue." *Yes, this is a good distraction.* "I've got an idea in my head, but I don't know if a pattern exists for it. I want it to be modern and classic at the same time. Does that make sense?"

"Not really, but you can show me." Jeannie smiled, hooked her arm in Violet's, and they boarded the bus.

They arrived at Walker's in fifteen minutes flat and wove their way through chattering housewives to the rayons. Violet ran her hand across the beautiful fabrics, imagining all the lovely dresses and blouses she could make if she had the time and money. They focused on anything with anchors, wheels, or ships. Jeannie spotted one first.

"Vee Vee, over here," Jeannie called. "What do you think of this one?"

"Neato, but not sophisticated enough."

"Oh, you didn't tell me sophistication was on the list, too."

"Isn't it always for me?"

They gave up looking at fabrics and headed to the catalog table. The long angled counters held thick book in place by a wooden ledge. They pulled up stools and flipped through the McCall pages of *Spring and Summer Fashions: Chic for the High School Miss, Glamour Frocks for the Prom*, and *For Boyfriend Exclamations*, but saw nothing similar to what Violet had in mind.

"Look at these hemlines. Getting shorter. The boys'll like

that." Jeannie flipped another page.

"Even the fashion designers are frugal in wartime." Violet closed the McCall's and moved on to Butterick. Jeannie found a nautical pant pattern with a jumper sailor shirt, but Violet was looking for a dress.

"Ooo, wouldn't this be dreamy for Prom?" Jeannie pointed to a sleeveless gown with an elegant silhouette in the Hollywood Patterns catalogue. "You know you could come to Prom if you wanted. We could double."

"I don't know. Wouldn't it be weird since I don't go there anymore?" *I would love to go to Prom with Charles. He'd probably think it was juvenile.*

"We could get you tickets. Remember how much fun the four of us had at dinner? Promise me you'll think about it. And promise me you'll think about making me a dress?" Jeannie added, half joking.

"If you bought the fabric and notions, why not." Violet was excited to have another project to keep her busy. "But first I've got to get my contest dress made."

"Look at this one." Jeannie showed her a Hollywood Pattern of Anne Rutherford.

"It's perfect. Cute long full sleeves. Fitted at the wrist with rows of piping. A tailored bodice flaring out to an A-line skirt. Doesn't show piping at the hemline, but I think it'd be nice to add. Maybe a big anchor appliqué." Violet began to feel normal. Hopeful.

"Whatever you say," Jeannie replied.

"I'll have to tack down the collar flap so it doesn't flop when I happen to be upside down." Violet smiled at the memory of Charles flipping her around.

She brought the pattern number to the gal behind the counter and crossed her fingers they weren't sold out of her size. Jeannie settled on a beautiful gown pattern from McCall with thin straps and matching bolero. Violet still needed fabric. They found a simple white rayon gabardine that she'd trim in red or blue cording.

"I could go for some goo and moo. Wanna find a diner around here?" Jeannie asked.

"Pancakes for dinner sound swell. If we can find a joint that serves breakfast all day."

"You want Topsy's." The housewife in front of them balanced a baby on one hip, thread and trim on the other. "It's two blocks west of here."

"Thanks." Violet and Jeannie helped the woman carry her sewing notions to the checkout.

Violet was afraid to go to bed and afraid not to, but mostly afraid to stop moving. She swept, dusted, and scrubbed every surface until finally exhausting herself, though still too early for sleep.

She couldn't concentrate on much, but could picture him reading *The Good Earth* in his bunk on the boat, maybe reading the same book at the same time she was. The familiar hurt crept back. She grabbed her pattern and read the entire package, pulling out the inner instruction sheet. *I can make the dress in time for the dance contest.*

She fell asleep thinking about anchors, cording, and snowy white fabric. She dreamed of bright, red blood staining her pristine white dress. She didn't know where all the blood had come from, her or him? A series of clicks, gunfire, cannons or bombs, echoed in the background. She was confused and panicked. The edges of reality creeped into her dream, pulling her awake. Pop stumbled through the door. He wasn't close, but she could smell the booze on him. She didn't want him to know she was awake and kept quiet until he stumbled down the hall to his room.

Her dream faded, but she was left hollowed and panicked, her heart still racing. She sat up and shook her hands, trying to get the icky feeling away. She opened the French doors and let the cool breeze calm her until she was numb enough to go back to bed. This time she let herself think about Charles and wrapped clear memories of his dimpled smile and his sweet lips on hers. She could almost hear his voice saying, *I love you, Violet, I love you.*

June ~ 1990s
17. Jump Jive and Wail
(Brian Setzer)

"Hey James, did you clock me in?" June rushed into the shoe department looking around for the manager.

"Of course. I got your back, kid. Plus it's not like we get paid hourly. We're straight commission. Mike doesn't need to know you were a little late, does he?" James winked and smiled.

She smiled back and wanted to give him a hug, but didn't.

"How was your date with Veggie?"

"Ha, ha, very funny." *How did he know I had a date?* "It's Vertie and it was...okay."

"Just okay, huh?"

"I'm not sure where it's going. And I'm not sure where I want it to go."

"Man, that's all your chicks' problems. You always have to define things. What's up with that, anyway?"

She crunched up her face and narrowed her eyes. "I don't know. Why are you so cranky? Wait. Let me guess, Rose?"

"Yeah, she's all about what are we doing. Where are we going, blah, blah, blah."

"You've been going out a while and honestly, James, if you don't know how you feel now, do you think more time will change that?"

He took a deep breath and exhaled in a rush. "Damn it, I think you're right. I just don't want to admit it. I mean. I like Rose, I really do, and maybe I could love her. I don't know. She's so pushy sometimes."

"But if you don't love her by now, I don't get what time's

going to change?"

"Well, maturity. Right? You know, we dudes keep our emotions on the down low and take a while to catch up to you chicks." He carried a box back to the stockroom. June followed, grabbing a shoe for her customer.

"Sounds like you're making excuses to me."

"Does it?" He ran his fingers through his hair. "So what's with you and Veggie?"

"Vertie."

"Whatever. I think he's playing you."

"Me? I don't think so. I don't put out."

"You don't? Why not, are you Uber-Christian or something?"

"No," she blustered and blushed. "Hey, is the schedule up? Am I working tomorrow?"

"Yes, and yes. And you're not changing the subject. This is too juicy. Here's something I didn't know about our little Junebug."

She ignored him and went to check the schedule. The strong smell of leather permeated the office area. June found it intoxicating, like Arizona earth after a good rain. San Diego usually smelled like ocean and refried beans.

He followed her to the desk. "Come on, you can tell your good buddy James."

She continued to ignore him and ran her finger down the schedule, looking for her name.

"Frigid?"

She rolled her eyes and flipped to the second page.

"Some odd intellectual cult?" He waggled his eyebrows.

June tried to keep a straight face, but it was hard. He was funny. She found her name and saw she was working 8:00 to 4:00. That wouldn't do for her Derby adventure. Now she'd have to talk to James.

"Had a bad accident like Frida Kahlo? And it would be too

painful?" He hovered around the desk.

She was surprised he liked Frida Kahlo and knew a bit about her history.

"Hey, can you come in early for me tomorrow? Clara and I are going to go see The Big Six in L.A. and we need to leave by 3:30 at the latest."

He smiled big. "On one condition, you tell me what your hang up with sex is."

"Hellllloooooo. Anyone working here?"

They rushed back onto the floor, a stylish lady held a black pump, dangling it from her index finger. James helped the woman. It was his turn. Another woman came over and asked directions to the ladies room, but overall it was a slow night. James finished with his customer and sauntered over smugly.

"Ah, where were we?" He smirked.

"We weren't anywhere."

James shrugged and started to walk away. "Whatever you say. Should I get Clara on the phone and tell her you won't be able to make it tomorrow night?" He smirked again.

"Okay, it's not really that big a deal. I've got nothing against sex. It's just I have kinda an old fashioned way of thinking and am waiting until I'm married." She couldn't tell him about her panic episodes or her brother or her parents pretending it never happened. "I'm not judgmental about others." She turned away from him, her face on fire. "I know what's right for me, and for now, it seems right."

"That's cool. I can dig it."

"Oh, I'm so glad you approve. So, I guess you'd be a male slut in comparison?"

He squinted his eyes and shook his head. "Why do we guys have to be one or the other, a player or a religious zealot? Let's say I'm not a slut, but I've had…a couple steady girlfriends."

That surprised her. He was good looking, witty, fun, talented, intelligent, interesting, nice, and a tiny bit mysterious. How could he not be player?

The quiet between them was deafening.

"Hey wasn't that a great show last night?" James finally broke the silence.

"Absolutely."

"Did you see that guy drumming on our table? Rose talked about it all night. I think she's a little jealous that you and Clara got invited up to L.A. and put on the guest list." He talked like he really cared about Rose. June didn't know what his problem was, but hoped he'd work it out.

"It's so dead in here let's practice. I want to teach you Collegiate Shag."

June scowled. "Where's Mike? Isn't he lurking around?"

"No worries. He's the manager on duty and there was some crazy guy in woman's lingerie running through intimate apparel screaming, *You can't make me pregnant, you can't make me pregnant.*"

They laughed.

"Man, we get all the nutters at night. Mike's up in the security office dealing with the guy. Let's not make this night a total waste. C'mere and let me teach you to Shag."

"All right, lay it on me, but if we get in trouble you're taking the blame."

"Yeah, yeah, yeah, you worry too much. You know what'd be cool? If I had a video of Collegiate Shag to show you."

June rolled her eyes.

"Okay, check it out. It's the same rhythm as East Coast, slow, slow, quick, quick, but instead of rocking side to side, back step, you tap step behind and replace then hop, hop."

"What?" *Why is it every time he explains something, I don't get it? Men make things harder than they need to be.* "Just show me."

He did, and she got it right away.

"Nice job. Okay, now let me explain the break, same rhythm,

but we hold instead, and your leg goes back as mine goes forward, then we switch. Get it?"

"Just do it."

He grinned and led the break. It was easy. He used his body to push hers down. Any follow would be able to get that break. She loved the dance. Collegiate Shag was rhythmic, fun, and Jitterbug.

"Here, let me...." He put his hand on her hips but immediately took them off as if she were a hot stove.

She felt a little spark and wondered if he felt it, too. He placed his hands back on her hips weighting her stance and spoke quickly.

"Uh, sink your weight into your hips and use them as shock absorbers. You want to keep a straight upper body, but let your lower legs go."

She cleared her head of random thoughts and sank into her hips. She wished they had music and couldn't wait to try it on the dance floor. Hopefully, people at the Derby would know how to Shag.

A customer strolled into the department. The pair separated awkwardly and stopped dancing. After the customer left, June begged James to show her more. He ran down the list of all the Shag moves he'd learned from workshops and gleaned from old videos. June started to get ideas of steps that could work in the confines of the Shag rhythm, but didn't feel confident enough to suggest them. She was still in awe of James's knowledge and talent. *He's a good looking guy, but on the dance floor, he's...hot. I never realized that before.*

As promised, James arranged with Mike to come in early, which allowed June to go to the Derby. She'd worn a vintage dress to work—no time to change before she and Clara headed out—and was surprised at the compliments she received throughout the day.

Shoppers packed the store and before she knew it, James glided through the department ready to take over her shift. She gave him a Clara-style Katherine Hepburn salute and raced to her car.

June drove to Clara's, but Clara drove to L.A. The drive was a blur of June rubbing her tired feet and Clara multitasking while driving. They made good time — arriving ten minutes early — but Clara refused to appear too eager and insisted they sit in the car for fifteen minutes.

June spied the guys making their way into the club. The band's matching bright red suits made them look like off-season Christmas elves, but very handsome. Clara insisted they wait another ten minutes until June thought she might explode with anticipation. Clara finally shut off the radio, checked her lipstick for the third time, and climbed out of the car. The smoggy air stuck to June's lungs and skin. She made a face.

"I know. The smog is horrible isn't it? Makes you appreciate San Diego. It's the very worst this time of day, too. Great for pretty sunsets, but hell for breathing." She laughed. "Are you ready?"

The Derby didn't disappoint. The club was the epitome of old Hollywood with dark wood, deep reds, velvet, and brass. Before the hostess could even get a word out of her mouth Pat and English James spotted the girls and rushed over.

"These lovely creatures are with us." Pat smiled at the hostess. "And we'd like to take our dinner in the bar." The boys kissed each of the girls on the cheeks.

"Don't you two look dressed to kill?" English James said.

"Thank you." Clara and June suppressed the titters that bubbled below the surface. Clara always played the sophisticate. And tonight June did too, feeling older than her eighteen years.

The guys led them down a row of velvet curtained booths

opposite the enormous bar. June had never seen a bar so big—not that she'd seen a lot of bars—but this one seemed extraordinarily long and wide. They arrived at a large booth. White linen napkins fanned across the plates. Wine glasses glinted like rubies in the low light with red velvet curtains framing the black and gold marbled table. Clara and June scooted in next to the other two band members. Pat and James flanked them like sentinels, English James next to June.

"What are the curtains for?" June asked.

"For Privacy." Pat stood and pulled the curtains across the table arc. "Private enough to do just about anything." He winked.

Pat re-opened the curtains presenting a view of the ornate columns that encircled the bar. Crisscrossing diamond beams rounded toward the high ceiling, completing the opulence. The dance floor and stage anchored the other end of the room. The dance area was smaller than it appeared in the movie *Swingers*.

I'll have to remember to tell Amy.

When the waitress came to take their drink order, June followed Clara's lead and ordered a Lemon Drop. The guys ordered drinks she'd never heard of, a Sidecar, something on the rocks, and a Manhattan. It all sounded swanky and glamorous, and June felt like a movie star.

The description of the dishes had her drooling, and she was thrilled to find the restaurant had their own southwestern version of the famous Cobb Salad with fresh avocado, scallions, and white corn.

June glanced over the top of her menu at Clara. *Was it un-classy to split something?*

"So, what looks good to the ingénue?" Clara asked.

"Honestly, everything." Everyone laughed at June's enthusiasm and agreed.

"You ladies order anything you want. It's on us." Pat grinned.

"Thank you." Clara raised her glass in a classic movie star

toast. She took an elegant sip. *I hope I can learn to be as classy as Clara.*

It turned out, it was not uncouth to share. Clara and June decided to split the pan-seared crab cakes with mango aioli and the angel hair pomodoro. The guys ordered so much food, June couldn't keep track. She barely noticed when a full drink replaced her empty one. Even though she didn't believe there was any way she could fit dessert into her stuffed belly, they ordered five different delectables.

June stole tiny bites of each and was pleasantly surprised at how much she liked the hummingbird cake. The flavors complimented her tasty Lemon Drop, which she was fairly certain they'd ceased putting alcohol in.

The other Big Six musicians rousted Pat and English James for an equipment and sound check. The girls thanked the guys for the wonderful meal and said they'd see them on the dance floor. June scooted all the way round the booth to sit next to Clara.

"June, look sweetie, I don't want to be a nag, but you need to slow down on the Lemon Drops. We've got a long way to go tonight. Why don't you drink water for a little while?"

"I'm sure I'll dance it off." The ingénue comment had come back to bite her. "I don't see you drinking water?"

"Well darling, I've had two and you've had three or four. Honestly, I'm not sure. I want you to have a good time and not end up puking in the powder room."

June wanted to protest, but Clara was right. She never wanted to be one of those girls. She grabbed a water glass and took a big drink.

June and American James shagged across the floor.

Clara almost spit her drink when Rose and James walked into the Derby during the first set. June had wanted to run up and give James a big hug, but kept herself in check. She followed Clara's lead and let them come their way, while continuing to elegantly sip their Lemon Drops. Rose and James stopped and said hello, then immediately hit the dance floor. Rose had yelled to Clara, "get me one of those," as James whisked her away. June and Clara had barely seen them all night. Though June was repeatedly asked to dance by a variety of leads, it felt like she'd waited all night to dance with James. Luckily, Rose was dancing with someone else.

James raised June's right arm above her head, her torso toward him with enough room for their feet. The movement started at her hips, thighs working, feet flying fast, keeping the rhythm. He led a front break. She felt the heat of his body under hers and tried not to think about it. She repeatedly fell in love with him on the dance floor for the three-minute song. She thought ideas she didn't want to think about James. She caught English James's eye. *I'm just transferring my affection for English James to American James. Okay. It's just dancing, nothing more.*

All eyes were on June and James, the only Shaggers on the floor, the song murderously fast. He gave her hand a little tug and led a Shag Swing-out. The air swished by her, momentarily cooling her dewy skin. She concentrated on keeping the rhythm while traveling around the floor, taking bigger steps, using her thighs to pull her knees up, but always keeping her upper body still. She felt silly and playful.

He brought her into a closed position raising her right arm again, pulling her against his body. He felt good, really good. James had a nice body. She hadn't noticed before, but decided not to think about that now. She thought about his hand dropping behind her back, turning her body open, and bringing her to his side.

They twisted their hands, curling them around without letting go, their feet kicked out the crazy beat. The heat of the dance filled her head making her dizzy. When she looked for a spot to focus on, she couldn't quite get the faces to stop swaying.

James's body dipped down. She followed. His arm clutched tightly around her middle and his other braced under her knees. Whoosh. The world flipped upside down. Her stomach jumped into her mouth. She swallowed hard and closed her eyes. James landed her solidly, but when she opened her eyes the room was spinning. Black spots danced before her eyes. They looked like beautiful little fairies. *Had the band brought them from England?* And that's all she remembered before she blacked out.

Violet ~ 1940s
18. Topsy
(Count Basie)

The days crawled by, and Violet made slow progress on her dress. She managed to keep her self-pitying to a minimum. Pop had been around the apartment more, too, no German lady. Violet didn't think she could've handled that particular diversion.

The nights were the hardest. *To have felt the warmth of waking in your love's arms, to find yourself waking alone. You could never sleep properly again. Every bed was too big, every couch too wide, every space too open, every blanket too cold.* It was much harder to contain her thoughts and fears in the quiet of night. She had horrible nightmares about drowning, dreams of bloodshed, bombs, sinking ships, and falling. She couldn't focus on the dress.

She lay quietly on the couch and stared at the dark ceiling. Finally rousing herself with a pep talk. *I will work hard and fast for Mrs. Peppy. Today I will start sewing on my dress.* Jeannie'd badgered her to go to the malt shop, but she didn't think she could get her legs to move to the music. And there was no one there she wanted to dance with.

The door rattled. Pop was home, later than usual. Before she could flop back down and feign sleep, he greeted her.

"Hey pumpkin," he slurred. "Sorry, did I wake you?"

"No Pop, I'm awake." She studied the shell of a man he'd become and felt a pang of love and sympathy. For the first time, she began to understand his pain, though she couldn't understand how he could give up so easily. His apathy angered her. She ached and feared for Charles's, but refused to give up living.

"Pop, you've got to get yourself together. It's been almost two years. She's not coming back. She's never coming back." *If I were never to see Charles again, would I become my father?*

"Come on Pop." She tried to get him off the couch and into his bed. "You need to sleep it off. Go lay down. You'll feel better when you wake up."

He wiped his soggy nose and eyes on his sleeve, not looking at her and stumbled down the hall. She swallowed any remaining emotion and launched herself into her morning routine.

Violet pricked her finger and immediately dropped her pattern pieces, bringing her finger to her mouth. She didn't want to stain the white fabric. Her tongue licked the tiny poke of blood. She closed her eyes and imagined Charles's mouth around her finger. Her pulse started to rise. She quickly opened her eyes before she fell further into her fantasy.

"Are you all right?" Mrs. Peppy asked.

"I poked myself with a pin is all."

"So, that is dress for big contest?" Mrs. Peppy checked Violet's handiwork.

"What do you think? Should I do two color trim or one?"

"You want classy or theatrical?"

"Classy, but I also want to stand out on a crowded dance floor."

"Darling, you will always stand out on dance floor." Mrs. Peppy shook her head and went back to work.

"Thank you." Violet filled the two words with all the love and respect she had for Mrs. Peppy.

Violet continued working on the sleeve. She'd never been good at joining the sleeve seams and side seams like many pattern instructed. She preferred to join the sleeve after all the side seams were sewn.

Violet loved the three dimensional puzzle of sewing and finding the best order of operations. She couldn't attach the collar without adding the trim first. And she needed to decide on the trim.

The bell jingled and announced the mailman, Ernie.

"Good morning ladies. I've got a package here for a Miss Violet Woe."

Violet looked up, shocked to hear her name, and almost sewed over her finger. *Why would I get a package and at work of all places?* She gathered the dress pieces off her lap and piled them onto the sewing table behind her machine. Ernie waited patiently at the counter.

Mrs. Peppy feigned indifference, but her dark eyes peeked from beneath her forehead.

Ernie dug into his bag and pulled out a small package wrapped in plain brown paper. Violet's mind jumped to the idea that something horrible had happened to Charles, but then she wouldn't receive anything, his mother would.

Still, she was afraid to open the package. She knew it had something to do with Charles, maybe a good-bye letter, good-bye gift, or both. Her stomach churned. Ernie fumbled in his mailbag, adjusting various letters and packages. Mrs. Peppy stopped sewing. Violet looked up, realizing they were waiting for her to open her package. *What if it's something bad?*

Ernie clicked his tongue. "Are you going to open it or not? I haven't got all day now," he teased with a sweet chuckle.

Mrs. Peppy's eyebrows raised in anticipation. Violet glanced at Ernie and back at the package. The strong taped-up packaging gave no corner for Violet's to easily peel. Mrs. Peppy handed her the seam ripper she was using on Mr. Cole's pants. Violet gently drew it from the wrinkled hand and carefully jabbed the long point into the edge of the package, ripping it open like a seam. An envelope and small white box tumbled out onto the counter. Violet didn't want to read her note in front of them, but their curiosity needed to be sated. She lifted the lid of the box. Nestled in soft white cotton were the rhinestone hair combs she didn't purchase at McCleary's.

"Ain't those purdy." Ernie let out a long whistle. "Looks like you've got yerself an admirer."

"Ahh, she does at that." Mrs. Peppy nodded to Ernie.

Ernie and Mrs. Peppy waited expectantly for her to open her note. In the silence that followed, they exchanged a look.

"Have a nice day ladies. See you tomorrow." Ernie exited the shop.

How did he know? When? How? The mail. He's on a boat. Her mind filled with a million questions, her heart swelled five times its size. She removed the combs from the box admiring their simple elegance, silver teeth with a clustered row of small and medium rhinestones. They looked exactly like hair combs Jean Harlow wore in the movie *Grand Hotel*.

Corny as it seemed, the fact that he recently touched them made her want them on her body, like his hands touching her. She pushed them into her hair, swirling her dark curls around the teeth so the combs bit in, securing makeshift rolls.

She dashed through the cutting room to the tiny bathroom at the back of the shop. The mirror reflected her glowing face, smiling for the first time in a week. She turned her head from side to side, wavy hair brushing her shoulders. The rhinestones sparkled in the dim light. She closed the toilet seat lid and sat down, opening the envelope.

My Dear Little Violet Flower,

If I have timed everything correctly, you should have received this package halfway through my deployment and although we do not have mail delivery on the ship for such a short jaunt, I wanted you to know that I think of you every moment I'm away.

I know you, and I know you will not hear my words until you have discovered the mystery of how and why. That's one of the many things I love about you, your inquisitive, brilliant, insatiable mind.

You may not recall, but when you gave Mrs. P and me our gifts you mentioned hair combs you didn't purchase for yourself. I asked Mrs. P which shop you'd purchased her deer pin from. Do you remember that night I cooked you dinner at her house?

How could she forget? She remembered every moment, every single moment she'd spent with him. She continued reading.

Well, the store had several different rhinestone combs. So, I don't know for sure if these are the exact ones you liked, but I thought they looked the most like you. I hope you like them. After that it was easy to package them up and convince a bunkmate who was not going on ship to mail them at the appropriate date and Viola, there you go, your surprise.

Please keep your chin up and for gosh sakes keep your dancing up. I will be home soon and cannot wait to hold you in my arms and shower you with kisses and turn you round the dance floor.

All my love,

Chas

Tears dripped on the paper smearing the ink of his attractive handwriting. She pressed a tissue into the droplets, hoping not to mar the ink. She intended to read it again and again. She wrapped her arms around herself and hugged tightly, pretending it was Charles. She smiled through happy tears. He held her in his heart. He was thinking of her as much as she was thinking of him.

She didn't know how long she sat in the bathroom, but she reread the letter many times, practically memorizing his words.

Footsteps echoed outside the door, followed by a familiar voice.

"Vee Veeeeeeeee." Jeannie knocked impatiently on the bathroom door. "Vee Vee, are you in there?"

"Yeah, just a second, Jean." Violet hopped up from the seat and splashed cold water on her face, rubbing the back of her neck with a cool washcloth. She took two deep breaths and assessed her face in the mirror. Her eyes were a tiny bit red, but presentable.

"There you are. I thought you were going to move in there." Jeannie grabbed Violet's arm, hooking her elbow, and pulled her out of the small room. "Look, you're coming with me to the malt shop and I ain't whistling Dixie."

"But, uh."

"Look at you. You need a milkshake. And how."

"But Jean, I really have to finish my dress I was…"

"Nothin' doing. You're coming with me." Jeannie dragged Violet through the shop. "I'm kidnapping her for the rest of the day. I hope you don't mind," Jeannie said as they passed Mrs. Peppy.

Mrs. Peppy waved her on, smiling her mischievous, conspiratorial grin. Sometimes Violet thought the whole world was in on a secret she wasn't privy to, but today it was okay. Everything was going to be okay. She let Jeannie lead out of the shop and down the street to the bus stop.

"So, are we hoofin' or ridin'?" Jeannie asked, not letting go of Violet's arm, perhaps afraid she'd turn tail.

"You know what?" Violet looked up at the sky. "It's such a gorgeous day, let's walk." It was like coming out of a cave. The sun was glorious on her shoulders, a fresh spring breeze on the air.

"What's with the sparkle in your hair? Are those new? Did you go shopping without me?"

"You can't believe it. Charles sent them from the boat."

Jeannie gave her an uncomprehending look. "Well, not from the boat, but he arranged it all before he left so they'd get mailed out from the base, and I'd get them half-way through his deployment. Isn't that amazing?" It sounded even more amazing out loud.

"Oh honey, you've got him hook, line, and sinker."

They put their heads together, laughing and skipping all the way to the Sugar Bowl.

Icy thick double-chocolate malt slid down Violet's throat and cooled her over-heated body. She'd danced non-stop since walking in the joint. The scene was much better than she'd imagined. Everyone greeted her warmly and congratulated her on her and Charles's win. She barely prickled at the mention of his name.

Wally even came out from behind the counter and turned her around the floor a few times. She'd forgotten what a good dancer he was. The jukebox blared the Andrew Sisters, *Sing, Sing, Sing.* Wally twirled and whirled. Her atrophied leg muscles caught up quickly. It was good advice to keep dancing. She'd always found joy on the dance floor. *How could I have forgotten?* Wally sent her spinning in a shoulder-twist, the three-sixty fast rotation and quick catch always made her feel miraculous. Wally's was great, but Charles was better.

She smiled big at Wally though, gleaming at his earnest face, letting him know he was doing fine. Some of the other jits stopped dancing and let Wally have the floor. He so rarely danced anymore. The jam circle was a nice show of respect for Wally. And Violet was having so much fun, she didn't mind being the center of attention. She loved a good swing-out, waiting for the tug, meeting in the middle, building the centrifugal force until being flung out again. There was no other dance like the Lindy.

Wally spun her back into the crowd, bowed, and hopped back behind the soda fountain. To Violet's astonishment, Johnny and Millie jumped into the spotlight. Johnny eye-balled Violet as he spun Millie in rapid turns. Violet was amazed that he could dance so well with his eyes fixed on her. She couldn't read his face, but his expression sucked some of the joy out of the room. She switched her focus to Millie and watched as she twirled around him in multiple ballerina spins. Violet envied her trained form, but missed the raw edge and wild excitement that made Jitterbug so racy. Still, Millie was delightful to watch.

Jeannie scooted up beside Violet.

"So, how ya doing, Kid?"

"Great. What's the rumpus?"

"Johnny said anything to ya, yet?"

"Nah, and that's fine by me. I don't need anyone laying an egg on my day."

"You said it, sister. So, Paddy and I, and some of the other kids are gonna go catch a picture show. Ya wanna come along? We've got Ron's jalopy, and there's plenty of room for you."

"Is it all couples?"

"I dunno. Wally might come along, but he doesn't count. He's only my brother."

"But I wouldn't want him getting his hopes up again. You know how he is with me."

"Sure, sure, but that was in the past. Come on. Come out with us."

They squished into Ron's jalopy. The fellas rode on top of the seat backs, their legs dangling. The girls squeezed between them.

"So where's Millie?" Violet whispered.

"She had to go home and have dinner with her family. A Great Aunt is visiting from back East, and we couldn't un-invite Johnny. Although, I'm surprised he came," Jeannie whispered.

"This oughtta be swell," Violet muttered. Between keeping Wally's hopes at bay and avoiding Johnny's dagger eyes, the evening certainly had enough to keep her thoughts off Charles.

They tumbled out of the jalopy and dashed for the box office, a little late. Ron had been forced to take side streets to avoid any coppers who might've had a problem with three fellas not actually sitting inside the car.

Violet dashed for the powder room as soon as they hit the joint, the milkshake sloshing in her gut. She checked her hair in the mirror and smiled at the combs. The warmth of Charles's thoughtfulness glowed in her skin.

As she left the powder room, a gal bumped into her knocking one of the combs to the floor. Before she could scoop it up, a dark blue tennis shoe caught the corner of it.

"Oh, it's you." Johnny picked up the comb. "Here." He shoved the bent comb into her hand and quickly walked off.

Violet suddenly felt fragile and bent like the comb. She fixed it back in her hair and went into the theater. Jeannie waved at Violet. The sight of her was like a rock and helped calm her.

She sidled down the row to take a seat next to Wally. Johnny came in and eyed the set up. She tried not to look at him, but it was ridiculous to ignore him. She glanced his way and gave a wry smile. He gazed past her, looking for another seat, any seat, anywhere, but there were none. He scooted in beside her, slamming into his seat, shaking the entire row.

"Whoa. Easy there, Tex," Wally said.

Johnny rolled his eyes and scowled at Wally. Wally ignored him and turned to Violet. "How ya doing Vi? Can I get you anything?"

"No thanks. I'm not hungry."

She'd eaten more at the malt shop than she had all week. The greasy burger turned in her stomach queasy. Or maybe it was being trapped between Johnny and Wally.

Wally leaned over, too close for comfort. "Why the devil did he bother to come if he was gonna be such a drip?"

"I don't know."

The curtains parted and the houselights went down. They showed a newsreel about an aircraft carrier, touting how it was one of the most dangerous places to work. "Our boys are specially trained and aim for zero error. Rarely does a sailor get blown off the flight deck," the narrator announced.

Watching the planes catapult off the edge of the ship and knowing that Charles was on deck, made her stomach churn. Fresh fears found purchase in her imagination. Her stomach rolled again, and a fine sheen of sweat broke across her back. She didn't want to see her deepest fears illuminated across a movie screen.

Johnny leaned over to Violet. "So, I see you're alone."

"I see you are, too."

"For now."

"Same here."

"Yeah, and then what?"

He hit his mark. She swallowed hard. Her eyes burned, the familiar ache of tears welled behind them. She didn't want to give him the satisfaction.

"Popcorn?" Johnny held the bag under her nose with feigned friendliness.

She grabbed his soda pop instead and sipped hard, letting it overfill her mouth, burning her throat, trickling into her lungs. She coughed and sputtered. The cola tickled the back of her nose and stopped short of blasting out her nostrils, the perfect cover for her watering eyes. Wally took notice and whacked her on the back. She leaned over and let a few tears spill. Wally handed her his hanky. She dried her eyes, composed herself, and thanked him.

And then what...and then what, echoed in her mind. She shut it away and watched the actors prance around in their perfect black and white world.

After breakfast, Jeannie and Paddy walked Violet to work, but not without a promise to meet at the malt shop tomorrow after school.

Work was busier than Violet would've liked. She daydreamed about meeting Charles's boat when it came into port. Her mind drifted away from her work, and she messed up her stitches on a cuff twice. He'd put her on the list to get on base, and she planned to wear the dress. If she could finish it.

With the day's work finally done, she took out her dress and worked the topstitched darts in the skirt. Then she attached the skirt to the bodice and created the zipper placket, the slide fastener sewn into that. The Jitterbug dress was almost a reality. The last big step was to attach the sailor collar and sew the clothing label inside.

She laid the blue then the red trim across the fabric, still undecided. The embroidery appliqué that came with the fabric didn't fit her vision, either. She took off her necklace and studied the silver anchor, remembering the day Charles gave it to her—his hands on the back of her neck, his warm breath at her ear. She shook her arms and fingers trying to calm the passion in her body.

The light cast a stylized shadow of the anchor. She sketched it out, drawing several sizes before picking one that would work on the edge of the skirt. Then using the same navy fabric as the neckerchief, she cut out the applique.

But before she could sew the anchor on, she had to finish the trim. With blue tailor's chalk, she drew two perfect lines for trim on the collar, sleeve cuffs, and skirt hem. The chalk line was an efficient trick she'd learned from Mrs. Peppy to sew trim without having to pin and unpin. Violet carefully followed her marks, feeding the red trim under the needle. Mrs. Peppy walked by and nodded approvingly. With that done, she could attach the collar. She added an embroidered star in each corner of the back flap, another hint of blue.

"Do you think it's too much?"

"No, darling, it's perfect. I can't wait to see it on you."

Finally, it was time to sew the anchor. First, Violet zigzag stitched the edges so they wouldn't fray. Then she ironed and was ready to hand-stitch the applique onto the skirt.

"It's time to go home, darling. You finish on Monday."

Violet looked up and blinked. The evening shadows reached into the shop and even with electric lights, the space was too dark to sew. She put her dress away and crossed her fingers that there would be enough time to finish the Jitterbug dress.

June ~ 1990s
19. What's the Matter with You
(Lavay Smith)

A soft blue light pulsed against June's eyelids. She was cold. Her throat burned. Her eyes fluttered open with fuzzy consciousness. Pale green walls reflected dull fluorescent light in what her mind told her was a hospital room. Thin blankets lay across her aching body, a hard mattress beneath her.

Fragmented memories flickered across her mind: hand trailing flocked wallpaper, upside down faces, hair tucked into her dress, a low swirling toilet. Someone's arms carrying her to a car and pushing the seat prone, the taste of bile. Her stomach convulsed involuntarily at the memory. The rest of her body awoke, feeling like someone had scooped out her insides and scraped her throat with a blunt instrument from tongue to stomach.

Too many pieces of her memory were missing. *Had I made an ass of myself in front of the Brits? Had I broken anything? Hit my head? Where was Clara? Did James drop me?* June stretched her brain to put together a sequence of events, but it was a blur. *I'm an idiot.*

She wiggled her toes, lifting each leg and rotated each ankle, then knees, and hips. Each limb and joint were fine with the exception of her burning throat and hollow insides. A pitcher of water and empty cup sat next to the bed on a stand, no cards or flowers. That seemed like a good sign.

"Knock, knock."

She whipped her head too quickly toward the sound of the voice. It hurt. She was surprised and happy to see James poking his head around the corner.

"Come in," she rasped then winced, her voice scratchy and deep.

"Hey, Kid."

He walked in and dragged a chair to the bedside. *Wait. What do I look like? What do I smell like?*

"You sound like hell. Here, drink this." He handed her the cup but then snatched it back. "Eh, I wonder how old this is. Let me check if you can drink anything, yet."

An attractive Asian lady wearing tropical print scrubs and a nice smile entered the room, moving with efficiency and grace.

"I see our sleeping beauty is awake." The nurse looked at her chart. "How are you feeling? Throat a little raw?"

June nodded her head, afraid to talk, but dying to. Thankfully, James asked one of the questions she was thinking.

"Is it cool for her to drink water?"

"I'd start with little sips, but she should be okay. I'm Nurse Pham, but you can call me Janell. Food Service will be in to take your order soon, and I expect you'll be released later today. Let me know if you need anything."

Two questions answered.

"I'm going to refill this for her. Is that okay?"

Nurse Pham raised one eyebrow. "I guess you know where everything is by now."

He jogged out the door while Nurse Pham checked June's IV, took her temperature, and wrote notes on the chart.

"Do you need anything, Miss Andersen?"

Sure, she needed to know what day it was. Where her time went. Why she was here. Why James was here and where Clara and Rose were, but she didn't ask. She was afraid of her raw throat, but more afraid of the answers. She wanted to cry, but stopped herself and closed her eyes.

"Not asleep again, are you?"

She opened her eyes to find James hovering bedside with a

lopsided grin. She hadn't heard him come in. He grabbed the bed controls—which she didn't know existed—and maneuvered her into a sitting position. That was better, less helpless. The pitcher dripped condensation from its plastic exterior. She gave him a weak smile. He gave her a cup.

She sipped micro amounts as instructed. The water was nice and cool, but her stomach clenched as it hit. She held her breath, closed her eyes, and counted. The moment passed.

"So," she whispered. "What am I in for, Chief?"

"I'm not surprised you don't remember. You were wasted."

She groaned. He laughed. She wanted to throw something at him, but it did lessen her embarrassment.

"Hey, it's a rite of passage. Everyone has to have one whopper of a drinking story, and you don't do anything half-assed. You go for gold."

"What am I doing..." She looked around. "...in here?"

"Oh, that. I guess you don't remember much?"

"Are ya gonna fill me in or keep smirking?"

"Maybe just a little more smirking. Where to start."

"How about start when we finished our dance."

"So, you remember that." He nodded his head and pursed his lips. "That was a hell of a dance by the way. You really pick stuff up fast. So anyway, we kicked ass on the dance floor. I threw you into a back flip and landed you perfect at the end of the song. The crowd went wild. People clapping and then I heard Rose yelp. Her voice cut through the applause. I followed the sound. She was on the other side of the dance floor in a heap. Some dude leaned over her, another girl at her shoulder. You'd gone off mumbling about the bathroom. I ran to Rose. Tears streamed down her face. And that's when I knew something was really wrong. She never cries, I mean never. The girl's the definition of stoic."

June nodded her head, remembering he'd said that before.

"Rose's face was twisted in a contortion of pain, both her

hands around her foot. I shoved the guy away—almost provoking a fight—and scooped her up. By now, Clara was there with a bar towel full of ice. Rose's ankle didn't look good. The top of her foot was already swelling. She was physically shaking, not making a peep, tears rolling down her face."

This was not the story June was expecting. Where did she come in? She didn't interrupt, but nodded her head and took another micro sip of water.

"So, it's clear to me there's something seriously wrong with her foot. I got bits of story from the girl who hovered at her shoulder. Rose was dancing with someone she knew from L.A. At the end of the song, this girl next to them did a Judo-flip aerial with her dance partner. He came down and landed square on Rose's foot, full force, his whole body weight."

James shook his head. A host of emotions played across his face. He continued the story.

"So, I turned to Clara and told her I was gonna take Rose to the hospital. She's from L.A. I'll go wherever she usually goes. I assumed Clara would want to come, but damned if she doesn't give me one of those disgusted looks and rolled her eyes. Just thinking about it pisses me off again. But she pulled it together and told me she was going to find you and let the guys know what's going on. Trying to give me a guilt trip about how disappointed they'll be. Like I gave a shit what some skanky British musicians were gonna think."

At the mention of the Brits, June couldn't help interrupt, "Uh…"

He chuckled. "So, you wanna know where you come into the story. Keep your pants on. So, Clara came back and told me you were passed out in the bathroom. Women." He rolled his eyes. "So, I carried Rose to my car and had Clara sit with her. Then—to the shock of many primping babes—I marched into the girl's bathroom, found the stall you were in, scooped you up, and carried you to Clara's car."

June recalled a dim memory, but hadn't remembered it was James.

"So yeah, they admitted you for alcohol poisoning. They even pumped your stomach. How cool is that?" He grinned.

Now that she knew the details, she was even more mortified. "Do you think that was necessary?"

"I don't know. You could've probably slept it off, but who knows. You were really out of it, and no one knew how much you had to drink. We thought it best to err on the side of caution. Some kids might still be alive if their friends had erred on the side of caution and brought them to a hospital. So, there you have it."

She couldn't argue with that even if it was embarrassing.

"How is Rose? Where is she? Where's Clara?" June grimaced at the pain in her throat but more at her own stupidity.

"Are you okay?"

"Yeah." She took another sip of water.

"I gotta go check in on Rose. The nurse said they'd probably release you later today. I'll drive you back. Rose's folks aren't too happy with me right now, and Rose is gonna be up here in L.A. for a while. I've been ducking in to see her as much as I can while staying out of her father's way."

The thought made June strangely happy. Not that Rose's folks were mad at James, but that James would drive her home.

"Wait, what about my parents? Did anyone call them? What about Clara?"

He looked at the floor. "Clara had to…go. And neither she nor I called your folks. The student insurance covered you and you were going to be fine. So what was the point of worrying them?"

Relief that her mom wasn't worried mixed with the pain of being abandoned by Clara flooded her senses. She closed her eyes to block the tears.

"Hey Kid, don't worry about it." James patted her shoulder. "It'll all work out."

June gazed out the window replaying the last twenty-four hours as James drove.

A random event changed my life again. And again dance.

James asked her to be his dance partner and start practicing with him for the International Jitterbug Contest. Rose wouldn't be recovered in time and might not even finish out the semester at UCSD.

Rose's father was specifically angry with James. "James should've taken better care of his daughter. He shouldn't have been dancing with another woman. What was the big idea taking a girl dancing and not dancing with her?"

Rose acted annoyed at her dad for yelling at James, but she hadn't defended him. James admitted feeling guilty about Rose's injury, but felt worse that Rose didn't stick up for him. Rose's father forbid Rose to see James or hang out with any more derelict swing dancers.

It was Rose's idea for June to take her place. June was surprised and honored that Rose had picked her over Clara. *Could I do it? It was a lot to learn in a short amount of time.*

"So, do you wanna go?" He turned down the music and tapped her shoulder.

"Go where?"

"To Amvets," he repeated. "I need to do a little thrifting. You got any cash? You know they don't take credit. I swear I always find something cool, and I don't have enough cash. So I have to stash my item, run to the bank, and hope no one finds it before I get back." He exited the freeway.

"Yeah, I've got some cash." She made a face.

"What?"

"I never come here. Parking sucks, and I hate parking by the

Nude-y place. It creeps me out."

"The Nude-y place? Is that even a word? What? Are you afraid they'll see you walking by, run out, nab you, and force you to dance topless for drooling middle-aged men? You big prude." He joked, but it wasn't too far from her fear.

"You know I'm a prude. So, you seem pretty familiar with the place. Go there often?"

"Sure, all the time."

June was shocked and more than a little disappointed, but he couldn't keep a straight face and busted up laughing.

"Haaaa, you should see the look on your face. No, I don't go to titty bars. The concept's pretty lame, really. Why do I wanna see half naked girls I can't touch? Seems kinda desperate to me. Now, with that said, I'm not against the occasional bachelor party or boys night out."

"Humph." She crossed her arms. "But don't you think by supporting those places, even for a boy's night, you're saying it's okay. These aren't real women, not real people prancing around. Or yeah, it'd be cool if my mom or my sister or even my daughter was a stripper?"

He was quiet for a minute.

"No, it would not be cool for my sis, or if I ever had kids one day…but maybe…maybe that's our societal bias?"

June frowned. "Then it seems like a good societal bias. It objectifies women, demeans them, and devalues the importance of a healthy sexual relationship based on respect and mutual admiration. Don't you think?"

"You sound like a women's lib ad. And, I think you put too much importance on sex, but you may have a point."

"What makes a woman decide that selling her body is a good choice or her only choice? It'd make sense to legalize it, regulate it, and tax it. Seems like it might be cleaner and safer, but I've heard the debate on NPR that it only helps the Johns and the Pimps, the women are still oppressed. But, should sex be for sale? I don't think so, but I don't know why."

"Whoa, down girl. I'm too tired to argue. And look, I found a nice parking space right in front, nowhere near the sinister nude-y place."

"How do we get into these kind of discussions, anyway?"

"I don't know Kid, you tell me."

Holy shit. Holy shit. Holy shit. This is so cool. June pulled a cute 1940s sailor dress from the rack, almost too short, though. Too many vintage dresses she'd found had been hacked off and turned into mini-dresses. She blamed the 70s and prayed this one had been hemmed and not cut. She flipped the skirt up and found four inches of hem. *Yes! I can't wait to show James.*

She was so excited she wanted to stuff it under her shirt and run out, not to steal it, but to make sure someone didn't take it from her. She had this weird daydream where she found something cool at the thrift store and someone would come along and say, "Sorry that's not for sale," or a greedy collector would try to snatch it out of her hands. She knew it wouldn't really happen, but her mind jumped into paranoia mode.

She was so excited about the dress she was tingly. The sailor scarfy thingy was intact with adorable piping on the sleeves, albeit a bit dingy. She hoped Clara's Biz Bleach cure-all could fix that.

"Boo."

June jumped five miles high. "Dang it James." She punched him playfully in the arm. "You scared the hell out of me."

"Hey, whatcha got there? That looks cool."

"Check it out." She held up the dress, slinging the hanger over her head, stretching the sides around her curves. James eyed her from head to toe. She started to blush and turned away in a spin.

"That is sweeeeet. Could be exactly what you need for the

competition. Yeah, we could do a whole sailor theme thing. I can check out the Army/Navy surplus next week. See if I can find any old uniforms. Whaddaya think me hearty? Wanna get naughty-cal with me?"

She rolled her eyes and groaned. "It's a great idea. I'll need to do a little work on the dress, but it'll be perfect. I love the nautical theme."

She pictured herself gliding around the floor, the white skirt whipping around her legs. It was the perfect Jitterbug dress. Everyone's eyes would be watching and cheering them on. She was getting too far ahead of herself. She'd never done anything like it before.

What if I can't pull it off? What if James and Rose can't get me ready in time? What if I cave under pressure? What if I have a panicky attack in the middle of the competition? What if I'm not good enough?

Violet ~ 1940s
20. And her Tears Flowed like Wine
(Anita O'Day)

The change of season played tug-a-war with the sun. Sky and sea whispered a promise of warmer days as Violet skipped down the street. She had to stop. She looked ridiculous. *Two more days, two more day, two more days.* She wanted to sing at the top of her lungs. *Two more days and he'll be home.* She couldn't wait for him to see her in the Jitterbug dress. Would he recognize her when he got off the boat? Would she recognize him in a sea of white uniforms? Would he scoop her up and kiss her in front of a crowd of people? She hoped he would.

She was too jittery. Funny that the word Jitterbug came from jittery. It was a widely held belief that when the dance was invented someone thought it looked like jittering bugs and the name stuck. Now she was the girl in the Jitterbug dress and boy did she need to burn off some of that jittery energy. Maybe Jeannie could meet her at the malt shop. After all, she had to keep up her dancing for Charles.

She looked up, amazed to find herself home, already. The ole joint didn't look so bad today. She took the stairs three at a time stretching her legs, playing a game with herself. Her legs quivered, but she pushed all her muscles forward, reaching for the rail. She was a mountain climber climbing Mount Everest. A couple more pulls and she was the first American Jitterbug to reach the peak.

Oh my gosh. Oh my...Pops.

She abandoned her childish game and raced to his side. He lay passed out on the ground in front of the door. The neighbor's cat lapped at the dark red ooze from a wound at his temple. Violet stood up. She sat down. She shooed away the befouling cat.

She didn't know what to do. She ran downstairs and looked up street—for what, she didn't know. She ran back upstairs and tried to push her father in a sitting position. *How long has he been here? How could anyone not notice? Where's the neighbor? Where's her house key?*

I need to get to a phone. Yes. I need to phone a doctor. Do I have the strength to drag him inside? I can't leave him in a pathetic heap on our stoop.

Hot tears dripped down her face. She wiped them away. She had no time for tears and clamped her jaw, drawing a deep breath. She let the air rush out, taking all her uncertainty away. First, she would try to rouse him.

"Dad, Dad, Daddy, Pops." She tapped his blood-encrusted cheek. Nothing, not a sound. She felt his warm breath and knew he was alive and breathing. She heard footsteps click on the stone steps and turned expecting to find her neighbor, or Jeannie, or even Johnny.

"Violet, Violet."

He rushed up to her. Everything moved in slow motion. She wanted to scream. *NOOOOOO. Go away, go away, go away.* But her mouth couldn't open fast enough. Her brain short-circuited and found no words. She was torn in ten directions.

She knew how she must look in his eyes, a solitary girl with a tear-streaked face leaning over a disheveled, putrid smelling, roughly shaven old man, tattered cats licking bits of blood. Charles hurdled the space between them. In his hand was a bouquet of purple violets mixed with tiny white flowers. Their sweet scent mixed with the decaying odors of the landing. She froze.

His beautiful face looked down at her with alarm, concern, and disgust? Yes, she was sure she saw disgust in his eyes. His idea of her must be shattered. A million questions ran through her head, but foremost was what would happen now and how this would change them.

Ossified between a kneel and a crouch, she teetered. She half rose to meet him and her leg muscles buckled. In painfully slow motion, the flowers dropped and bounced on the dusty cat-hair floor. Her father listed sideways and slid, leaving a bloody smear on the door. She tumbled pathetically, pitifully into Charles's hands. Then everything sped up, like the first time they met, but instead of being her best day ever, it was her worst.

"Violet? Violet?" His face was so close she could smell his clean scent above everything else. The heat rose to her face, and she looked away.

"Violet, what's wrong? Are you hurt?"

"No," she whispered. "I…I need to help my father."

"This is your father?"

She couldn't answer, only nodded.

"Right," he said not letting go of her.

She twisted out of his arms, wanting to run away and hide, but more wanting to climb inside his skin and lose herself.

"Can you help me get him inside?" She jiggled the doorknob.

"Where's the key?"

"The key. Yeah, the key." She walked in circles looking for her pocketbook then forgot what she was looking for.

"Come here." Charles tried to embrace her, but she ducked and scrambled for her purse, a thin layer of cat hair already coated it. She pinched it open and forgot why she opened it. She sensed Charles behind her and felt the heat of him. Every tiny hair and molecule on her body strained toward him, filling the empty space with energy. It was ruined. She'd ruined it. Her Pop'd ruined it. Her mom, her damn mother had ruined it.

He touched her shoulders, his breath tickled the back of her neck. She couldn't fight what her body wanted and what her mind knew wasn't hers anymore. He turned her around into a pressing embrace. She crumpled into his very being. He kissed the top of her head. His hands moved from her shoulders to the nape of her neck. Fingertips cupped the edge of her face, tilting it to his. His eyes searched hers with a pleading look and then his mouth came down on hers. His lips were cool water. His mouth the darkest, sweetest chocolate, but she knew things would never be the same.

"I'm sorry," he said. "I'm sorry. I know it was selfish, but I...I missed you so much. We ported a day early." He straightened and ran his fingers through his hair. "Okay, let's fix this."

Before she had the key in the lock, he slung Pop over his shoulder. She couldn't help register how manly, how much like a hero Charles looked in his starched white uniform. Pop looked like a sack of dirty laundry. Charles bounded through the door and looked left and right.

"This way." She guided him down the long narrow hallway to the bedroom.

There was no time to tidy her father's room. Although she cleaned regularly, the room had a dingy appearance and smelled of fermented alcohol. Charles, gently set Pop down on the bed. The springs squeaked and bounced like a box car at the end of the line. Charles bent over him to examine the wound. It continued to weep gooey, thick blood.

"How about a warm wet washcloth," he asked calmly.

"Be right back."

She rushed from the room like an actor in a horrible melodrama, only this was real life, her life. She returned with a couple of warm washcloths, some gauze, antiseptic, and dry towels.

"Perfect." Charles grabbed them all, and held her hand in his. His eyes searched hers again. She pulled away, letting her hand slip against the cool smooth of his skin.

"I'm going to go phone for a doctor." She backed out of the room.

When she got to the hall, she questioned if she should call a doctor, if she had enough money. She didn't want Charles to offer his help, she knew he would. How much was a house call? She held the phone in bewilderment and didn't call.

She crept back to Charles. He bent over her pop like an angel in white. He turned to look at her even though she'd made no noise.

"What'd the Doc say?"

"Um."

She didn't want to lie, and she didn't want to embroil him in any more nonsense that was her life. He was an imaginary part of her life, a dream part. Her Pop in bed, gash on forehead, was her real life. *Why did my real life have to intrude on my imaginary one?* Charles waited for an answer.

"I didn't call."

"I've done all I can do. Honestly, I don't know what else a Doc could do except tell you to take him to a hospital. It's hard to tell how much blood he's lost and what kind of wound it is. I'd say if it doesn't stop bleeding soon, you ought to consider a hospital."

He sat on the edge of the bed. His eyes bored into her. She wanted to hide.

"I'm sorry," they said at the same time.

"You're beautiful."

"What?"

"I said. You're beautiful." He crossed the floor to where she stood, reached for her then paused, and leaned against the door jam. She stared at the floor. She couldn't look at him. She didn't want to see the pity in his eyes.

"I'm sorry," they said again. His eyes looked as confused as she felt. *What is he sorry for? I'm the one who's sorry, sorry that I dragged him into this.*

"Please…let me…just…I'm sorry for intruding. I'm sorry to have charmed your address out of Mrs. Peppy. And I'm sorry you feel you have anything to apologize for."

She crinkled her face and started to open her mouth. He beat her to it.

"Violet, I don't know what you think. Or what you think I think."

She took a breath readying herself to speak. He put up his hand.

"But," he continued. "You are not your circumstances. I'm not crazy about you because of what you do, where you live, who your parents are or even who your friends are. I'm crazy about you because…you're amazing. You make me feel alive, like I'm bigger than myself, like there's a real tangible reason to go to war. You fill me up in places I didn't know were empty."

She looked at the ground not knowing what to say. *He's being chivalrous. No one could want this.*

"Violet, look at me."

The room was still. She knew what she had to do.

"Violet, I love you. Shouldn't that be enough?"

Silence stretched into the truth, but she couldn't speak it.

"Let me give you some space. I know I've been pushing too hard. With my deployment coming up, I just…I've been pushing. I know. I'm sorry. What if I promise to be your friend. Be your really good friend and your…dance partner. How 'bout that, Beautiful? Don't shut me out."

She was numb and confused, but relieved that he'd found a way out. She could be chivalrous, too.

"Yeah, that would be best."

"Well then, Miss Woe, I'll…be, uh… seeing ya." He began to lean in for a kiss, but circled back on himself and stood tall.

What have I done? What should I do? "Huh?" She shook her

head.

He started to walk away. Something inside her began to tear.

"I'll, uh, let myself out...unless there's something else I can help you with?" He hovered.

"What?" She looked up.

Part of her didn't want to let him walk out that door. Not part of her. All of her ached to draw him back, to feel his arms around her, to bury her head in his chest. *Don't go. I love you. But he must go. It would be best for him.* She wouldn't be selfish.

"Nothing," he mumbled.

He walked away. She was stunned that she didn't dissolve. *This is how it's supposed to be. They never could've happened. How much harder it would've been months from now. This is better.*

"You are awfully quiet today?" Mrs. Peppy worked a buttonhole on a jacket.

Violet bent over a bit of hand sewing on a cuff. "I'm sorry, did you ask me something?"

"I'm sorry darling, was it wrong to give him address? You seem not yourself. Is everything good with Charles?"

"Yeah." Violet paused. "It's Pop. My dad's ill. I'm worried about him. He's in the hospital."

"Oh darling, I am so sorry. You know you can stay here if you don't want to be alone."

"Thanks Mrs. Peppy. I'm sure he won't be in the hospital long, and I'd like to clean the place. Have it nice for his return. I'll be okay."

Violet liked the idea of living alone, totally alone. She'd need to get used to it.

"You know I worry for you. Well, it's nice that Charles is back? Will we see him today? Maybe lunch? Supper?"

"No, they have some drills or something, I think."

"I saw the flowers he brought. Weren't they lovely? When I

saw him with flowers, and look on his face when he'd missed you at the shop. I give him address. I had feeling he was going to sweep you of your feet. No? Did he not?"

"We talked about when we could get together to practice for the contest is all. We're really just good friends you know. Dance partners."

"If you say so."

"I'm done with this coat. I'm going to go clean up the back room. I think it needs it. Will you please send Jeannie back when she comes in? Thanks." Violet walked away not waiting for a response.

Mrs. Peppy's questions were too probing and uncomfortable. Violet couldn't bear the scrutiny of her dark knowing eyes.

She phoned Jeannie and made sure they were meeting at the shop. She didn't say a thing about Charles. Why should she? They were just friends and she could love her friends. She loved Jeannie, so she could love Charles the same way. She hoped they could at least be dance partners. His Swing-out, Sugar-pushes, and air-steps flashed in her mind—the way she felt on the dance floor in his arms.

Will I get to feel it again? Will it feel the same?

June ~ 1990s
21. Feelin Kinda Lucky
(Big Sandy)

Five, six, seven, eight. June finished the Lindy Swing-out. One, two, her hands hit the floor. Her biceps twitched as she kicked her feet over her head widening her legs into a V, trying not to kick James's face. She did.

"Ow," he yelped.

She flipped back down, her momentum halted. "I'm sorry. I thought I had it that time." She wheezed, her face pink.

"June, you're killing me. I don't know what else to do to get you to do this move right. I'm afraid you're going to take out an eye. Maybe we should cut it?" He rubbed his brow, a bruise already coloring his skin.

Her limbs felt like bricks. Her stomach clenched. She didn't want to fail in front of her friends. Tears welled behind her eyes.

"Excuse me." She ran to the bathroom and sat on the toilet.

What was I thinking? I've been dancing less than a year. I'll be competing against people who've been dancing for years. From all over the world. No. I'll tell James I can't do it. Maybe if I had a year, but not months. The tears came hard and fast.

"June," Larissa knocked on the door. "You okay. Take a break. Come have a drink."

"Just a sec. I'll be right out." She hitched her breath, wiped the tears from her eyes, and ran cold water over her fingers, pressing them under her eyes.

"Larissa, do you have any powder or make up?" June cracked the door.

"Oh sweetie. I know James can be an ass. But you can do it.

Here, have a sip of this." She handed June a Lemon Drop. "Scoot over. Let me fix your face."

Larissa fixed June up, and they rejoined everyone in the living room.

"Give me a minute to hook up the inputs and we can watch your rehearsal." Kris pulled wires and moved toward the screen.

"Do we have to?" June was nervous enough to see what she looked like on video, and in front of all those critical eyes, she wasn't sure she could take it.

"Don't worry doll, we all know the camera adds five pounds," Clara quipped from her perch.

"The truth is I'm afraid of how I look dancing."

"You mean you've never seen yourself dance?" Larissa refilled Clara's Lemon Drop from a glass pitcher.

"Little glimpses in mirrors, but that's it."

"Honey, if any of us looked as good as you, James would've asked any one of us to step in for Rose. Wouldn't you have James?" Clara gave him a sideways glance. "Don't sweat it. Wait and see. You'll be surprised at how good you look. You've almost got it."

"Well, the Kid's got talent. What can I say? Can I pick 'em or can I pick 'em?" James said in a Groucho Marx imitation.

James and Clara's exchange bothered June. Maybe it was being talked about in the third person. Or maybe it was that James hadn't really given her his critique, not that she wanted it. She knew she was disappointing him.

"All right, lights, camera, action." Kris pushed play and everyone watched James and June dance on screen.

They should've videoed when she and James first started practicing, not at the end. They'd been at it for hours. Her legs and brain were tired, and she knew she looked terrible. She watched as she and James danced the Collegiate Shag. She hadn't been dancing Shag long enough for it to become second nature, and she could see the difference in James's relaxed hop and her stiffer bounce.

James walked backwards until they hit the seven-count, and he popped her up with a jump, her knees level with his head. She landed solid, but took an extra count, muddling her Swing-out. Everyone could see it.

Her face fell. She'd been trying to hit that move all afternoon, and had failed that, too. They continued watching. June knew what came next. The kick in the face. They all winced and laughed as June's foot connected with James's brow.

She was a mess, and they all saw it. She needed to tighten up everything and smooth out her hoppiness. Her Swing-outs needed more styling. The timing on the jump needed fixing. The only thing that looked good was the Jitterbug dress.

"Overall, good job kid." Clara's Lemon Drop sloshed in her hand. "Except for those delays and, of course, the handstand. I'm sure you'll get there."

Compliments came from the rest of them, but they were being kind. *What does James think?*

"Yeah, we've got some stuff to work on." James ran his hand through his hair, a half-hearted smile on his face.

Not what she needed to hear. Why couldn't he find something good to say? Exhaustion filled her with lead.

"I'm tired." June forced a yawn, slowly breathing in and out to cover the threatening tears.

"Okay, everybody. Let's call it a night." Larissa began picking up glasses and herded everyone toward the door. She stopped June and gave her a sweet hug then turned her around. "Oh look you've split your seam."

"Damn. I knew I should've reinforced the seams, but I wanted to see how the sailor dress would look." *It looked better than I did, like it was made for dancing.* "Thanks for pointing it out."

"You're welcome." June, James, and Clara lingered on the

porch while everyone else left. Larissa closed the door behind them.

"So, I'll see you gals tomorrow, right?" James looked at Clara.

"Yeah." June gritted her teeth. *I'll talk to Clara about her taking my place. I can't do it. Maybe James will have time to get Clara ready instead?*

"Whatever you say boss." Clara gave her two-finger, Katherine Hepburn salute.

June shuffled down the stairs. Clara and James remained on the porch. Clara grabbed his arm and talked in a low voice. Was Clara going to tell him he'd made a mistake choosing June?

"If I didn't know any better," June overheard Clara say. "I'd think you were a little afraid to be alone with the kid."

It bothered June that Clara had picked up James's kid diminutive.

He rolled his eyes. "Don't be ridiculous. I'm all in with Rose. You, better than anyone should know that. Besides, Rose chose her."

"Okay, okay. Whatever you say. You know what you're doing." Clara walked down the stairs to June. "Let's roll, kid"

"Oh great. Now you've got Clara calling me kid, too."

James laughed and walked to his car. June wanted to say something else. Tell him she'd work harder, but he'd already climbed into his car.

The two girls walked to June's little truck. June slid behind the steering wheel—driving again—something she'd been doing more often. Clara banged the door shut.

"Did I do something? You think it should be you instead of me? Is there something I should know about you and James? Am I interrupting something? I'm terrible aren't I?"

Clara sighed. "Look, the truth is. I'm jealous."

"But, I'm not…"

"Wait. Let me explain. No. Let me back up. Yes, there's a

thing, but it's not what you think. When we all first met I had a boyfriend, but James and I had something, a killer dance connection for one. We danced great together, but I'm not the kinda person to play a guy, and I wasn't ready to give up on the guy I was dating. Well, by the time I was, James was already involved with Rose. The best thing to do was to leave it in the past. So, although I don't have the hots for James anymore, I always thought we'd end up dancing together again, being competitive dance partners. Rose picked you for her replacement, not me. I guess that hurts a little, too."

"Oh, no. You must hate me? And I'm not good enough. I know I'm not. I'm so sorry."

"No, that's just it. I adore you. I think you're awesome. And what really sucks, is you are a better dancer than me. Or you will be when James and I get through with you."

June grimaced. Part of her rejoiced that Clara thought she could be better than her, but part of her wanted her to say she was already better. She pulled onto the freeway.

"Okay. So that's it. Sorry if I've been such a bitch lately. It's only my bruised ego."

"I thought you were still mad at me about the Derby thing."

"Oh well, there is a little of that, but really I was more pissed at the time. I'm over it now."

"Really?"

"Yeah, really. Hey, not to change the subject, but have you made any headway on the whole finding your biological grandmother? I haven't heard you mention it in a while. Not since we called the birthing centers and hospitals."

"There's been so much going on, and I had this horrible Doc/Arg essay due yesterday. Though, I did find out some interesting facts. Like for one. Did you know that adoptees have two birth certificates? One that they make up and give the parents who adopt them with their names. The other, with the real birth mother's name, gets locked up somewhere in non-public secret files. I think I've hit a dead end. Not only do I have no clue where my mother could've been born, even if I did get the right place, I'd never get a look at the secret files."

"If I were more sober, I might have an idea. Wait, wait, inspiration darling…I've got it. Hire a PI."

"What? Like a detective? How 1940s film noir." June smiled and turned off on Clara's exit. "You would think of that. I could never afford one, though. Any idea how much they are?"

"No, but I like it. Maybe we could do a short film about it. You know totally *Big Sleep* it out. Follow around our Private Dic with a video camera."

"What's *Big Sleep*?"

"*The Big Sleep*? You're kidding? It's only the best Humphrey Bogart movie ever. Well, it might be a tie with *To Have and Have Not*. Maybe I'll bring it over and we can watch it after practice."

"Cool. I've only seen *The Maltese Falcon*. My dad loved that one and insisted on watching it whenever it was on. I thought it was a little boring."

"Me too. And the chicks in that one are not near cute enough. No good dresses to get excited about. Yes, I think that tips the scales for *The Big Sleep* vs. *To Have and Have Not*. But the dialogue and the chemistry between Bogie and Bacall in *To Have and Have Not* is so good. Maybe we'll have to watch both."

"Really? Can you really bring them? It'd be cool to do something besides dance."

"We've been a little hard on you haven't we?"

"A little. I don't think I can do it."

"Of course you can. We all believe in you June."

"You do? I planned on telling James to train you, instead of me." June had to blink to keep the tears from her eyes. "And I don't mean to sound corny, but thanks for being my friend. You inspire me, Clara."

"Glad I could be of help. And you are NOT quitting." Clara tipped her head. "Now get my drunk ass home before I change my mind about you."

They laughed, and June felt better, though not totally convinced. Clara insisted June take the dress to a good tailor she knew. June wished she'd learned to sew, neither her mom nor Gramma Gigi did. *I wonder if my biological grandmother sewed. Maybe Clara would take sewing classes with me.*

June dropped off Clara and watched her complicated friend saunter to her door. Clara let herself in and waved good night, her imitation Kate Hepburn two-finger salute, vintage perfection. *Maybe I won't feel so pathetic in the morning.*

June shook the steaming pot, holding the dish towel around the top—no pot holders at James's bachelor pad. The oil sizzled and splattered keeping time with the explosive kernels. She thought of Amy and how she'd persuaded June to give up microwave popcorn in favor of old-fashioned stove popped. She missed Amy.

James's and Clara's voices rose in heated debate from the living room, though June couldn't make out their words above the pinging popcorn.

June was glad to be done dancing for the night. Clara persuaded her to not quit. She wasn't convinced she could do it, but agreed. For now. The sessions were exhausting and hard on her ego with James nit picking and Clara backing him up. June knew they were only trying to help, but there was only so much criticism she could take in one sitting.

She'd volunteered to make popcorn while James cued the movie. If none of them fell asleep watching *The Big Sleep*, they'd move on to *To Have and Have Not*. When she walked into the living room, she found Clara at the door.

"Are you leaving?"

"Yes, Duckie. My dad needs me early tomorrow at the office and I've got to get my beauty sleep. Besides, I've already seen these movies half a dozen times." She walked out the door before James or June could protest.

"I guess it's just you and me, Kid. Still up for that movie?"

"Yup. You sure it's cool?"

"Of course." He shrugged. "Why wouldn't it be?"

Why wouldn't it be? Right? Why'd I say that? It was not like she and James hadn't spent copious amounts of time alone at work, but being in a guy's apartment by herself always sent up a warning flag.

"Here's the popcorn. See if this isn't better than microwave."

She plopped down on the couch, setting the bowl on the low coffee table. James hopped over the couch, bouncing her a good foot off the frame. They reached for the popcorn at the same time, their hands touched, and they jerked away.

"Sorry," they both mumbled.

"Uh, do you mind if I kill the lights?" He jumped back over the couch already moving toward the switch. He flopped back down, making sure to keep a distance between them. It was funny that they could be so close dancing, but sitting next to each other in the dark was awkward.

He stuffed another handful of popcorn into his mouth and pulled the bowl to his lap.

"Wow, this is really freaking good. Hands down this beats microwave popcorn. That reminds me, when are you gonna bake me some cookies? If I recall you promised me some home-made cookies?"

June laughed, having forgot. She had said something about baking cookies a while ago. James's earnest look gave him a boyish charm, and she got an idea.

"How 'bout this. Next time we practice, I'll bring all the ingredients and teach you how to make 'em. Plus, there's nothing like having them right out of the oven." It would be a nice feeling to do something better than James.

"Sounds great." He stuffed more popcorn into his mouth. "I'm interested in learning to cook. Hey, next time you talk to Clara, ask her about that Thai cooking class. It sounded cool."

"I'd like to check that out, too. Maybe between the two of us we can remember to ask her." June laughed and elbowed him in the ribs.

They sat side by side and watched the black and white images flicker across his television. June sipped beer and munched popcorn. He hoarded the bowl. It was better, less weird, but she still didn't feel completely at ease with him. The 1940s world of stunning costumes and snappy dialogue sucked June in—she even developed a little crush on Bogart.

James replenished their beers and set them on the table. They both lunged for them and knocked heads. June slipped off the couch trying to catch her bottle before it went off the table. She saved it just in time. James grappled and rescued his, plopping back down on the couch. He immediately reached for June, rubbing the bonked spot.

"Sorry, Kid, you okay?" They laughed, giddy and tired.

"Yeah, my head doesn't hurt nearly as much as my back and my feet."

"I'm sorry. Am I pushing you too hard? You've got to speak up. I want to improve your dancing, but I don't want to kill you. It won't do any good to have over-worked muscles, anyway. Let me see if I can work out some knots."

Before she could answer, he slipped behind her and began rubbing her shoulders. She felt strange again, but as he massaged, she melted into a stupor. She leaned forward letting him work his fingers up and down her back. She couldn't concentrate on the movie plot at all, but the people sure looked pretty. When she leaned back, he switched his hands to her shoulders and arms, massaging the full length all the way to her fingertips returning to her neck. His firm fingers worked into her hair and behind her ears. He leaned in to say something, his hot breath on her neck, an involuntary chill ran down her spine.

"Uh." He paused and launched himself backwards, jumping over the couch. "I forgot what I was gonna say. You seem pretty tired and I'm beat, too. Let's call it a night and…finish this, I mean finish, watching…this another night. I'm too tired to concentrate on the movie, anyhow."

Before June could maneuver herself back to a sitting position, James was across the room turning on the light. The bright glare stabbed her eyes, stark and fuzzy at the same time.

"Can I help you clean up? Let me wash the popcorn pan."

"Nah, that's okay. It's the least I can do for sharing your culinary expertise." He chuckled. "Okay, I'll see you tomorrow at work, and if it's slow we can work on some other Shag moves. Or, we can wait to meet the gang at the Hep Spot to… practice. I think I'll see if Rose is well enough to come down. Maybe she can sneak away from her family. I'd love for her to see what we're doing. What we're, what I'm, what new…dance…stuff…you've picked up."

He reached over the couch and gave her a sterile pat-on-the-back.

"Are you okay James?"

"Yeah, why wouldn't I be? I'm frigging tired and hit a wall. I just remembered I have to get up early and finish some edits for a paper."

"Okay Chief, whatever you say. See you tomorrow."

She let herself out while James stayed glued behind the couch.

For the past couple of weeks, no matter where June and James practiced, as soon as they were done he'd scoot out the door. June lay in bed trying to sleep, but thoughts of his weird behavior kept her awake. She couldn't figure out what she'd done wrong. *He probably regrets his decision to dance with me and just doesn't know how to tell me.*

She replayed the night at the Hep Spot. Everyone was dancing—not critiquing, for a change—and James wanted to run through more contest moves. June suggested they just dance, pointing out they hadn't just danced in ages. She felt like she was too much in her head, disconnected from her body. Technically, she was a better dancer, but she'd lost her joy and still didn't feel good enough. She tried explaining this to James and didn't know if he understood, but he'd sighed and said okay. Sighed, like it was a chore to social dance with her.

Count Basie's, *Shout and Feel It* blared out of the sound system. The first strums of the guitar went straight to her center, and when the orchestra kicked in, she felt it in her bones.

James started out leading their choreographed combinations. June wouldn't have it. She stole the lead and hung onto the Swing-out for twelve counts doing a side-to-side tap step. For a second she thought he was going to be pissed, but then he watched her feet and mirrored them. From then on, it was heaven. He danced unrestrained, and they both let their guard down.

June missed the grab on a Shoulder-twist but didn't flinch. They both clapped, hit the beat, and boogie-backed with Kick-ball-changes. They reenacted a 40s Vitaphone—*Groovie Movie*—in synch and of one mind. He brought her into a Rhythm Circle and the room blurred around them. They grinned at each other and she felt the joy. He came out of the Rhythm Circle with a Free Spin. She waited to catch his hand, stomping to the beat, finally finding something to do for those counts. Her skirt swished around her legs. Her shoulders bounced in rhythm. She caught his hand and with the momentum, he pulled her in hard for Balboa—another swing dance she'd recently learned.

He led a Throw-out and collected her, spinning her into a Waltz-y turn he'd never do in a contest. She pressed flush against his body, her leg between his, switching her weight as they went round and round. His taut muscles trembled under his vintage gab pants, twitching and pulsing as he used his legs to rotate. Her chest smashed into his warm torso and of course she fell in love for the three minute song. The dance made a sap out of her every time. Her Lindy crush an illusion, but she gave into every bit of feeling and nuance. Her heart spun with her body.

James played along and gazed romantically into her eyes. The song wound toward the end. He dipped low. Her hair brushed the floor. James's lips were close to her throat. His breath tickled the tiny hairs on her neck. Their legs and hips pressed into each other's, a momentary wave of desire swelled so strong in June, she dizzied. She closed her eyes half expecting a kiss. James popped her back up and scuttled two feet away, looking up at the big institutional clock.

"I have to go finish a paper." He ran out of the hall.

His erratic behavior was making her more insecure. She sensed his growing disappointment in her dancing. Her dreams and panic episodes were increasing. And if disappointing James wasn't enough, the detectives she'd contacted were too expensive. She'd never find her grandmother. And finals were around the corner.

The stress was too much. She could put her grandmother quest on the back burner, but school, James, and her anxiety needed to be dealt with. She knew her panicky episodes were tied to Julian, but didn't know how to deal with the pain and fear. She needed someone she could trust. She didn't have anyone.

For school, she could join a study group and buckle down. For James, she'd have to suck it up and confront him. But first, butter him up with baking. Homemade chocolate chip cookies would help any problem.

Violet ~ 1940s
22. In the Mood
(Andrew Sisters)

Day two and still no Charles. Violet hoped they could be friends. She would've written him when he went overseas and who knew what could've happened when he came back. They could've started over.

"Hey, hellllooooo. Anyone in there? Vee Vee, Wally asked if you wanted your usual double chocolate." Jeannie waved her hand in front of Violet.

"Um, yes please, that'd be swell."

She wasn't sure if anything she ate would stay down. Her burger and double chocolate stayed down yesterday, but yesterday she was more hopeful. She hadn't said anything to Jeannie. Jeannie would probably think her glumness had to do with Pop being in the hospital.

The doctors and nurses said even though people were unconscious they recognized voices. She visited him daily and read bits of the newspaper to him. The doctors didn't say much else, but she overheard one of the nurses gossiping. The head wound was from a bullet. A bullet? What had her father gotten himself into?

"Vee Vee, Vi, Vi, Violet."

"Uh, Yeah?"

"Where is your head today? Is it your Pop? Poor kid. The bobby-sox brigade is going to the beach for some flames and games. You wanna swing over there? We can get our shakes to go?" Jeannie looked toward the soda fountain. "Hey Wally, make those double moos with wheels, we gotta scram."

"Yeah, yeah, two double moos with wheels." Wally poured the shakes into large paper cups, topping them off with whip cream. The red cherries smeared pink in the fluffy topping. It looked good. It looked happy. Violet tried to look happy and dug in her purse for some coin.

"Quit the floy floy Vi. I don't want any of your clams. Just save me a dance next time around."

Wally hasn't entirely given up on me. Maybe he could be a pinch hitter for Charles in the contest? Why hasn't Charles come round to practice?

The ride to the beach was unremarkable. Violet was out of the jalopy—shoes off, toes in the sand—before everyone unpacked. The sand felt good beneath her feet with the ocean air shaving a bit of melancholy from her. Jeannie wasn't letting Violet out of her sight, though.

"I thought you might wanna take a powder and talk. What's the haps?" Jeannie asked as they walked away from the gang.

"Nothing." Part of Violet ached to tell someone, anyone, what a mess she'd made, but thought it unfair to heave her problems on someone else. Better to grin and bear it on her own.

"I know there's something cookin' besides your Pop being laid up. Just 'cause I'm Genial Jeannie and don't have your grades doesn't mean I don't see the goings on underneath. Is it Charles?"

"Christopher Columbus." Violet took take a breath. "Am I that transparent? Have I done something to make you feel like a dope?"

"No sweetie, and don't try to change the subject. This isn't about me. You know you can tell me anything."

Jeannie was true blue and never judged her or gossiped about her. "Oh Jeannie, I've lost him." Violet wrung her hands. "I've made a complete mess of things."

"Come on, it can't be all that bad, tell me about it."

"I sent him away. It was awful. I came home and found Pop passed out on our landing. The neighbor's stinky cats mewing all around him. Then Charles surprised me with flowers. And he was in his dress whites. And I couldn't find my key. And the flowers fell to the dirty floor. And Pop smelled like alcohol, and his rumpled clothes, and the blood and Charles looking so perfect, and Pop and I looking so...and Charles carried him in and cleaned him up. And my ugly apartment and...and...and...." Violet took a breath. "And I didn't want him to be any part of it. Any part of my sad ugly life so I...I sent him away." She stopped talking. They walked in silence.

"Well, you'll just have to get him back."

"No. That's just it. I let him off the hook. It's the kindest thing I could've done. It's for the best."

Jeannie stopped walking and grabbed Violet's arm.

"Who says it's for the best? You? Why don't you let the fella make his own decisions? Vee Vee, I'm sorry, but what makes you think you have the right to choose for him?"

"I uh...I...But I thought I was...being...noble?" *Now that I say it aloud, it sounds silly and childish and...pompous. Is that my pride? My own fear?*

"Seems like the noble thing to do is let people make their own choices. I mean, isn't that what this war is all about? Hitler and his buddies want to take away our choices, take away the world's choices?"

"I never thought of it that way." The idea knocked Violet off her feet. She plopped down in the sand. "Jeannie, how'd you get to be so smart?"

Jeannie plunked down beside her. "I dunno. Maybe 'cause I always think I could be wrong, so it opens me up to listening to all sorts of ideas. There's all different kinds of smart. Isn't there?" She wrapped her arm around Violet's shoulder and gave her a squeeze. "So, the question is, how do we get that anchor clanker back to you?"

The thought of having him back gave Violet hope, but she was afraid to give into it.

"I don't know." She picked up handfuls of sand and let it slip through her fingers. "I don't even know how to reach him on base. He's always come to me."

"We can work on it. Come on. Let's get back to the gang."

"You know, Jean, I think I'll sit here a minute longer and see if I can think of something."

"Are you sure? No moping? No throwing yourself into the ocean?" She laughed trying to lighten the mood. Violet laughed too.

"Nope, not throwing myself in the ocean. I just want to sit and watch the waves. Okay?"

Jeannie hesitated then stood. "Alright, but come over before it's dark." She skipped back toward the others.

Jeannie sounded just like her mom. Violet was envious. She wished she had a mother in her life. She resolved to tell Charles the whole story, if she got him back.

She watched the waves and dug her feet into the sand, scooping handfuls of grains, patting wet clumps around her ankles. A driftwood stick became a pencil. She wrote Violet Mangino in the sand. Erased it and wrote again, Violet May Mangino.

An unidentifiable figure walked toward her. For an instant, she imagined it was Charles, but the shape and stride were wrong. He cast a shadow on her bare shins.

"Hey."

"Hey, Johnny."

"So um, I heard about your Pop and all. He's a pretty swell guy. I, uh, just wanted to say I was sorry to hear it, is all."

"Thanks."

"You don't have to be sarcastic." He started to walk away.

"Oh, I'm…no, I wasn't being sarcastic, really, thank you."

He made a sharp U-turn but kept his distance. "I guess you probably don't need anything from me, since you've got your swabbie and all, but…uh, Violet, if you do ever need anything. All you gotta do is ask."

Before she could edit herself, she hopped up, closed the distance between them, and threw her arms around him. At first, he didn't hug back, but then he gave her a long slow embrace. She stepped away before it became something else.

"What was that?" Johnny sputtered. "Don't think your swabbie would like that too much, would he?"

"Thank you."

She wanted to tell him how darn lonely she was, but she couldn't lay that on him. She'd already been down that road and it led to no end she was interested in. Was that the same as making a decision for him? No, she knew what she wanted, and it wasn't Johnny.

"Uh, and I was kinda sent to fetch you and bring you back."

"Jeannie," they both said at the same time and laughed.

"I love that girl. She's too good for me."

"Don't say that," he said with such dejected sweetness that it almost broke her heart. "There isn't anyone that's too good for you."

They walked toward the crackling fire and sparkling jitterbugs. Ron tuned his guitar, Paddy sharpened sticks for marshmallows, and Jeannie, with the help of Sue, arranged blankets on abandoned stumps. Violet marked the contrast between herself and her friends. She sat down next to Jeannie and pasted on happy. Even though Jeannie thought Violet could get him back, Violet wasn't so sure, but she was determined to make happy as best she could.

When the bonfire broke up, Johnny offered to drive Violet

home. He didn't talk much or try to pull any of his old moves. Violet had to admit, he wasn't as one-dimensional as she'd thought.

Violet wasn't up for going to her empty apartment. So, she had Johnny drop her at the shop. She slept again on the old mohair couch instead of in the guest room — transient. Her head hit the sofa, and she fell hard asleep.

Even though nothing had changed, she felt lighter when she woke. Maybe it was having someone like Jeannie to talk to, Johnny too, or maybe it was because she had hope. The city shimmered in soft hues as she strolled back to her apartment. Eucalyptus trees dripped long fingers toward the earth, hazy in the morning mist. Frying potatoes greeted her nose, and the sweet smell of flowers cut through everything with a pungent ripeness. She didn't remember there being so many flowers in her neighborhood before. The sweetness filled her up.

She hopped up the steps and found herself surrounded by violets and gardenias, a river of purple and white. They flowed across the floor, tumbled off the top step, and rippled down the neighbor's landing. Every windowsill and ledge dripped with fragrant flowers. And there in the corner, on the rusted metal chair, Charles lounged, fast asleep.

Violet's senses, overwhelmed by the heady scent, couldn't process what her heart felt. Her chest tightened, her eyes filled, emotions toppled expectations. *Is he really here?* Her entire being filled with light. The sun inside her burned its way out, erupting from every pore, sure she would disintegrate. Tears of joy rolled down her hot cheeks.

He was here. He was here and he loved her. She was loved by the man she loved. His eyes flickered open, drooping heavily back to sleep, but in a swift, frantic movement, he was up on his feet crushing her in a solid embrace. Their bodies collided and crashed, falling into each other and out of time. The searing heat of his radiance melted them into one. He didn't try to kiss her nor her him.

Unknown seconds, minutes, or hours passed. Their fires slowly balanced. Her limbs and senses returned. She found the edges of where his body began and hers ended. His hands stole up her back, finding the nape of her neck. He tilted her head, angling her face toward his. She waited for his kiss — her perception of time skewed — it took an eternity for his lips to reach hers.

His breath caught in his lungs. His body pressed into hers. The dizzying scent of the gardenias enveloped them. Every hair on her body prickled. He bent slightly. She felt the heat of his mouth before his lips touched hers. Then it was fire, warm, radiating heat. His lips were life, water she needed to survive. She drank deeply. Their mouths parted, swirling and probing, responding to unasked questions.

Her heart pounded fiercely, and her breath quickened. His mouth tumbled down her jaw to her neck, down her chest. He knelt, his head at her stomach. She hugged him to her like a child and lifted his face, stroking his hairline and cheek. He reached into his pocket with one hand and held her hand with the other.

"Violet. I love you. Will you marry me?"

He flipped open the tiny box, a ring flashed a brilliant wink. He smiled and looked hopeful. She sunk to her knees, level with him, and gazed into his beautiful face. Brimming with emotion, she laughed and cried. All fear, worry, longing, dreaming, loving, crashed into her at once. Her body shook. She found his hands and kissed them, bowing her head to rest her lips on their joined hands. He let go of one hand and tucked a dark curl that had stuck to her wet cheek.

He searched her face with beseeching eyes. She hadn't answered. She laughed as more tears rolled down her face, screwing up her mouth, trying to get the words out.

"Yes, yes, a thousand times yes."

His brows relaxed, and his free hand stroked her shoulder.

"Do you like it? Do you like the ring? It was my grandmother's. I was two days to Tucson getting it for you," he said exposing the boy in the man. He slipped the ring on her finger.

"It's beautiful." She wiggled her fingers. The simple round-cut diamond set in silvery filigree, sparkled in the light.

She shifted from side to side, not wanting to break the spell, but her knees hurt. He sensed her discomfort and helped her to her feet.

"I'm sorry for not getting back sooner. And, I wanted to ask your father's permission, but..." he trailed off. "How is he?"

Reality cleaved the moment. Her life outside Charles seemed so far away, but there was no escaping the convergence. Everything would be okay. Even though her life was a mess, Charles still wanted her and everything that came with her.

"Pop's not well. He's in the hospital. After..." She didn't want to relive the ugly scene, but it was time to stop sweeping things under the carpet. "After you left..."

He gave her a hurt look.

"I mean, after I sent you away." He nodded and tucked another hair behind her ear. "I phoned the doc and he insisted on the hospital. Pop's been there ever since and hasn't awakened."

"I'm so sorry." He squeezed her tight.

She hugged him back, and then looked around. "It's so pretty out here. I don't want to leave the flower glade. My own secret garden. But would you like to come in?"

"So you like it?" He flashed his boyish grin. "I wasn't sure what to do. It didn't seem right to ask you at the shop and I didn't know how to get you away for a surprise. I wanted to inspire you. Violet, you must know I love you. I can't imagine life without you. Nothing in your life will come between us. You are not your circumstances, whatever they may be."

She unlocked the door and looked back at the flowers. "Let's grab some of these beauties and bring them in. I don't want the neighbor's cats ruining them." She ran her hand across the silky petals.

Suddenly everything was easy. She grabbed two. Charles grabbed two. They rushed into the living room and set them down. At first, they merely walked swiftly, then somehow it turned into a race. He eyed her and took longer strides, reaching over her to grab more. They repeatedly rushed in and out of the apartment scrabbling to grab the most. He was faster, but she was wily. Ducking under his full arms, she miscalculated and tumbled Charles and herself onto the sofa, laughing with hands full of flowers. The petals knocked against them and fell like rain, releasing their heady scent as Violet and Charles crashed onto the sofa cushions.

Charles liberated his hands and embraced her, showering her with sweet soft kisses. She released her grip on the flowers and wrapped her arms around his neck, pulling him further on top of her. His body pressed the length of her. His foot reached back toward the door and slammed it shut. Their thighs pressed, her hips swiveled and found the spot where their bodies fit.

It felt like home, but no home she'd ever felt before. She was aware of her rising desire, his warm body pinning her to the couch, but there was something deeper and richer in her emotions. Her love for him mingled with her desire. She pulled him closer and savagely kissed his face, tugging his mouth to her. He brushed her teary cheeks and pulled away with a questioning look. She grinned and laughed. He laughed with her.

She plucked at his shirt, wanting to feel his skin touch hers, needing to get as close to him as she could. Her body smoldered, and heart and mind rejoiced. He grinned and helped her tug his jumper over his head. It caught on his ears and they both laughed.

She gingerly kissed his chafed lobes. He scooted back, sat up, and brought her with him, his legs straddled hers keeping her close. He pulled her sweater over her head. Their eyes met. He whispered soft kisses on her lips and cheeks. His hands fumbled at the back clasp of her brassiere. She raised her arms above her head, freeing her torso of clothing. His eyes traveled down her chest. She simmered and felt safe, utterly safe that he would not judge her, hurt her, or embarrass her. He looked in her eyes for approval and found it.

His hands skimmed over her shoulders slowly, fingertips softly brushing her skin. He skimmed her breasts with shy hands. Chills tiptoed down her spine. Her nipples tightened and ached. He continued down her body exploring every curve, resting for a second at her hips, and then rising again scooping, grabbing, and kneading. His mouth was on hers, their shaking bodies wriggled against each other, trying to hold back the crashing desire.

He pulled back again, looking into her eyes, asking permission. She gave it. She gave him everything he wanted, everything she wanted. He worshipped her from head to toe, kisses and nips and caresses, the smoothness of skin on skin. The incredible warmth and dichotomous cool sheen of their skin. She explored his body, delighting in how each area reacted to her touch.

She tried to memorize each and every freckle, mole, and hair on his body and wondered how he got the crescent shaped scar on his knee, and would ask if she could find her breath. Instead, she found the spots that made him breathe harder and quiver. He held himself back. His shaking hands took their turn sliding over every curve, pressing into her hips and slipping between her legs. He explored and teased until both their bodies begged for release. They committed everything to each other.

After the shudders and spasms subsided, they collapsed into a tangled heap. His face matched hers with a few joyous tears. He rubbed hers away with his thumb, oblivious to his own. She wanted to talk, but there was nothing to say. He held her tight, absent-mindedly rubbing her thigh as it lay across him. Their smells mingled with the cloying flowers. She wanted this for the rest of her life, forever. She wanted every part of him, mind, body, and soul, and in return she would give him all of it back, freely.

They rested in sweet silence. "I want you to know you can tell me anything." He kissed her temple.

"Do you want to hear about my mother?"

"Only if you talk about it?" He shifted and opened his eyes. "Nothing you say will change my opinion of you."

"Okay." She took a breath. "When she first left, Pop would ask me what he did wrong. He would come home late in an alcohol haze and cry silently. I hated her. I hated her so much I didn't want to let myself feel anything but hate. Hate was clear. And easy."

She paused. He waited.

"Pop was a mess of self-doubt. He'd ask, *Wasn't I a good husband? Didn't I love her enough? Didn't I give her enough?* At first, I didn't know what to say, but eventually I found the words that he could hear. I told him that she didn't love us back. It wasn't me or Pop. It was her. She was selfish. I repeated it, trying to convince myself, hoping it was true. Some nights I would lay awake for hours wondering if there was any way to change the past. I'd wrack my brain looking for a key to restore our former life, but mostly to restore Pop."

Charles rubbed her arm and looked at her without pity or judgment.

"She wasn't always bad," Violet continued. "When I was little she taught me to sew and would sit at my tea parties and drink tea with me and my dollies. I can still feel the softness of her slender hands as she held mine when we would walk home from church."

He pulled her closer.

"She always smelled like violets. She said it was her favorite flower, and she'd named me after them. I learned later that a violet's scent comes and goes. It contains a compound that inhibits human smell for moments in time. The smell disappears, like she did. Every once in a while—when I smell violet perfume—her beautiful face smiles down at me, and I'm a five year old girl, again. Only I'm not."

He smudged a tear off her cheek.

"Do you want to know why she left? I mean besides the fact that she didn't love us enough. It would be better if it was dramatic or beautiful or even tragic, but no, it was low. She was low. She was having an affair. I know that doesn't sound so awful. I'm sure many people have affairs—they always do in movies and society gossip columns—but not real people, not people you know, not MY mother. Not to MY father. And the worst of it was, she got caught. At school. In his office. My principal. They were caught in his office, on his desk. She made a mockery of love, a mockery out of trust and love. The trust Pop had in her—I had in her."

Violet balled her hands into fists.

"And found by a student. A student. There was no denying it. She and my father fought, and when the screaming was over, he was broken, and I was tainted. Hardly anyone would talk to me at school. If they did, it was awful boys, saying awful, vile suggestive things. I was my mother's daughter and the apple doesn't fall far from the tree. I wasn't her daughter. I was my father's. I had to quit school to work and take care of Pop. I couldn't stand to be in that school with all those girls whispering about me and...and...."

She took a gasping breath.

"...I miss her. How could my mother who sang me to sleep, who brushed hair off my forehead to kiss me goodnight, who'd sit by the fire and read me Elizabeth Barrett Browning poems of undying love, be this woman?" Violet sobbed.

"I miss her. I miss the her she was. How could she do that to us?"

The old memories, her fears about Charles, and her worry about her father shook her body with jumbled emotions. Charles wrapped his love around her distress and rocked her like a child until the last bits of hate drained away. She shuddered and took a cleansing breath.

"Thank you. I've never let myself feel the loss of her. I'd only let myself feel the anger and hate. Thank you."

He brushed new tears off her face, softly kissing her cheeks and each wet eye. She was reborn, perfect, and whole. They found themselves in their passion and made love again.

June ~ 1990s
23. Back in Your Own Backyard
(Dean Mora)

June had butter, flour, sugar, brown sugar, chocolate chips, baking soda, salt, eggs and of course walnuts. After she buttered him up with homemade cookies, James wouldn't be able to resist her questioning. She intended to get to the bottom of his odd behavior whether she lost a dance partner or not, but not until after work.

The sale day at Macy's had her running her ass off for pennies. There was nothing worse than a snob, except a cheap snob. When she passed James in the stock room and told him her cookie plan, she didn't give him a chance to say no.

Since she was off work before him, she had time to stop at the Salvation Army by his apartment. On her way to the thrift store, she spotted an old-timey tailor shop and a little voice in her head told her to circle the block and park. She still had the torn dress in her car—not having had a chance to try the tailor Clara recommended.

When she walked through the door, the shop bell jingled above her head and the smell of scorched fabric tickled her nose. With the long counter—which spanned three quarters of the shop—to the antique cash register and wooden folding chairs, June felt like she'd stepped back in time. Two sewing machines rested on ancient tables, one occupied by a petite, attractive older lady, the other vacant.

"Hello, what can I help you with today?" the woman asked, not rising from behind her machine.

"Well, I have this dress. It's um, a…an old dress."

June was suddenly embarrassed to have brought an old ripped dress to be fixed. She'd never been to a tailor before, but was fairly sure they didn't see too much vintage clothing. A feeling of timidity and another emotion she'd not felt before almost made her turn around. *Will she think I'm impoverished?*

"Uh, I think it's from the 30s or 40s. I got it at a...." She paused. "At an antique store. I really love it and want to wear it in a dance contest...a swing dance." June couldn't shake her embarrassment. Or was it pride?

The woman stopped sewing and walked to the counter, an inquisitive peak in her eyebrow. Up close, she appeared to be in her seventies, but still nice-looking with crow's feet and smile lines.

"You're a dancer, are you?"

"Well sort of. Not a ballroom dancer or anything fancy. I do a little Jitterbug...uh, Lindy Hop." June mumbled Lindy Hop. Most people who didn't swing dance didn't know what Lindy was, even old timers.

"Did you say Lindy?" Her eyes focused and gleamed. "Now, you wouldn't know to look at me, but I was once a Jitterbug. Only then we didn't call it the Lindy Hop. We just called it The Lindy." She smiled, and her eyes glassed over. "Do you know why they called it The Lindy?"

"Wasn't it named after Charles Lindbergh?" June clutched the bag refolding the top, not sure if she should take the dress out.

"Humph. When I was a girl, we all knew it had nothing to do with Lindbergh. The writer reporting on a dance contest thought it would sell more stories if he connected the new dance craze to Charles Lindbergh."

She winked.

"It's really all about this fella George Snowdown. It's too bad it's not called the Snowdown. That would have been a fine name for it. Well anyway, Snowdown was the first to let go of his partner in The Charleston and sort of fling her out. When the reporter asked what he was doing, Snowdown said The Lindy." She leaned in conspiratorially. "Which was a vernacular term for a girl, or woman."

June shook her head, not understanding.

The woman waved her hand dismissively. "Sorry, I'm rambling on a bit. It was a long time ago. Oh, I used to love to dance. Show me what you've got there. I'm sure I can fix you up." She reached for the bag.

June let go of her grip, though the ignominy crept back. The lady might be an old Jitterbug, but she had to think it was bizarre to wear someone's old, used clothes. June slipped the dress out of the bag.

"I pulled the side seam here and here. I took out the shortened hem, but the original hemline needs help. Actually, I'd like to reinforce all the seams."

The woman picked up the dress and wore the strangest expression on her face—a cross between someone seeing a ghost and receiving birthday present. She turned it over, flipping the garment inside out. June waited. The heat rose to June's cheeks and an uncomfortable feeling and fear that the woman might be a little crazy.

"Ahhhhh," the lady sputtered. "It's here. It's mine. It is mine." Her eyes filled with tears, and she clutched the dress.

June wasn't sure what she should say, or do. The woman was clearly crazy. June looked around for help. Her stomach tumbled. Was the woman having a stroke? Would she have to call 911?

"Are you okay?" June squeaked.

The woman laughed through her tears. June's hands began to shake, and a wave of chills washed over her. She didn't know what to do.

"Yes, yes. See this tag? See this? This is me." The tailor pointed to an old frayed tag at the neckline. "Oh dear, I'm sorry,

I'm not making any sense am I? You don't look so good." The woman came around the counter and stood next to June. "Don't be alarmed, honey. I'm not crazy...yet." She winked. "Can I get you a glass of water? Why don't you have a seat?"

June didn't know what the woman was talking about. She spoke in gibberish as tears streamed down her aged cheeks. She guided June to a row of chairs. June sat. She offered June a cup of water from an old ornate water cooler. The cooler looked as old as the shop, but the water came out clean and clear. June took a long sip.

"Are you okay, Ma'am?" June asked.

The woman smiled kindly, her eyes twinkled. "Strange and unbelievable as this seems, this dress, this dress right here. I made it. A long, long time ago. For a dance. For a sailor beau." She stood quietly, holding the dress, a curious expression on her face.

June took a gulp of water, draining the cup.

"Look here. See? That's my label: Violet Woe Designs for Peppy's Tailoring." She showed June an old hand-stitched label. "Old Mrs. Peplinski gave me a pack of those labels when I made this dress. I only ever used three of them. I'd forgotten all about those. This shop used to be hers." The woman looked around. "Funny to think it's mine, now. I'm Violet. What's your name?"

"June." A thousand questions ran through June's mind, but she had no idea what was proper to ask.

"Oh, I loved this dress. I realize it's hard to believe looking at me, but I made this for a big Jitterbug contest." Violet quieted again. Emotions played across her open face.

June was discomfited and didn't know what to say.

"You have no idea how many memories this dress brings back."

Violet hugged the dress to her chest and closed her eyes. June thought it one hell of a coincidence that the dress she'd found in a thrift shop once belonged to the woman in front of her. But if the dress was from San Diego and the woman was from San Diego, maybe not.

"You don't look old enough to have been a Jitterbug in the 40s," June blurted.

Violet smiled an impish smile. "Thanks, sweetie, but trust me, I am."

"Can you tell me about it?" June jumped up. "I mean, what it was like to be a Jitterbug the first time around. What it was like to hear all that great big band music when it was new?"

"Unbelievable." Violet sighed. "But, I've rambled on enough. You don't want to hear about my old Jitterbug days."

"Yes, yes I do. Please."

"Well now, if you're sure." They sat down. "How much time do you have, honey?"

Oh crap, oh crap, oh crap. I was supposed to meet James two hours ago.

She should've called him, but she'd gotten carried away talking to Violet. He wouldn't believe the story about the dress. She barely believed it. Maybe they could call Clara. *What on earth is taking James so long to answer the door?*

"Uh, helloooo…" He cracked the door, the chained pulled tight across the small gap. June smashed her face in the open space. He stepped back and grabbed the towel around his waist. June would've been embarrassed if she wasn't so excited to tell him about Ms. Woe.

"What the…Oh, it's you. Damn June. After waiting for two hours, I figured you weren't coming. I jumped in the shower. Just a…come on in." He undid the chain.

"Thanks. Wait 'till I tell you about my…"

"Give me a sec to get some clothes on?"

James veered toward his bedroom, still hugging the towel around his waist. It took her a moment to realize he was naked under there. She giggled, and then noticed what a nice back he had. She'd never seen him with his shirt off. *Not bad.*

His shoulder blades tightened as he gripped the towel, his shiny, clean skin glistened. No man pelt either. She didn't go for hairy men.

What was she thinking? She didn't go for James. He was her good friend...who kept avoiding her, which was why she was here with cookie ingredients. She trotted off to his kitchen.

"Watcha doing under there?" James asked, returning in a ringer-tee and cuffed jeans.

"Ouch." She bonked her head coming out from under the cupboard.

"Seriously, what are you doing?"

"I'm looking for a cookie sheet."

"You mean for...cooking...cookies? I don't have one of those. What would I use one of those for?"

"I don't know. Pizza?"

"Ever hear of delivery? Single guy here."

"I guess I didn't think of everything. Well, you got anything flat that could go in the oven?"

"I can't think of anything. Oh no. Does that mean no cookies?"

June kept looking. The broiler pan, not quite flat, but it might work. "How about tin foil? Do you have any of that?"

"Now that I do have."

James retrieved the foil from an upper shelf where June would never think to look. With his classic smirk, he handed it to her. His hair was wet, messy, and boyish. His shit-eating grin had returned, and he seemed his old self.

"So woman, are you gonna make me some cookies or what?" He rubbed his hands together.

"Uh, no. First of all, I'm NOT your woman, and second of all I'm not going to make cookies for you. I'm going to teach you how to make cookies for yourself."

"Okay Julia. Let me have it."

"Julia? Hello. June."

He rolled his eyes. "Duh, Julia Child, cooking chef extraordinaire?"

June grinned. She and her mom watched Julia Child on PBS when she was a kid, little wine for the sauce, a little wine for Julia. James was definitely back to his old self.

"Okay, we need a big bowl for mixing. Some people like to use two bowls, but that's another to wash. If you mix your wet ingredients first, then add your dry, you save washing." June tried her best Julia impersonation, which came out sounding slightly Italian.

"Bowl." He handed her a bowl. "And that was a horrible impression."

"I know." She shrugged. "Mixing spoon?"

He rummaged around in a drawer and pulled out a mangled metal spoon. It would do. "Spoon." He handed it over.

"Okay. First we cream the sugars with the butter and shortening."

He gave her a sideways look with a mischievous smile as if she'd said something naughty. She rolled her eyes and hit him with the spoon.

"Ow."

"Are you going to take this serious or not? Baking is a serious science."

"Yes, doctor."

"Anyway," she continued, "you MIX the shortening, butter, and sugars. I use half butter and half shortening. It's a little trick my Grammy taught me. They're less greasy and keep longer."

"You're the boss."

"Then you add eggs and vanilla." They both took a whiff of the sugary vanilla concoction. She handed him the spoon and bowl. "Here, you stir."

His stirring was awkward at first, but he quickly found a rhythm. His forearm flexed around the bowl. Cooking looked good on him.

"Oh and you don't want to use an electric mixer," she added. He gave her a look. "You don't even have an electric mixer do you?"

He smiled and touched his finger to his nose, using the spoon to gesture, splattering June with batter. He laughed and reached for her cheek to wipe it off. She caught her breath and turned toward the counter, dipping in the makeshift measurer — a coffee cup — into the flour. With the next dip, she got the brilliant idea to payback his accidental splattering. She pinched back a bit of flour and launched. The powder hit him square on the side of the face, barely missing his eye and sticking to his damp skin. June fell back laughing.

He abandoned the bowl, lurched for the bag, grabbed a fist full, and pelted white rain at her head. The powder dusted her in a white cloud, and she tried not to breathe, but it was too funny. She dragged her sleeve across her mouth, gulped air through the fabric, stole the bag of flour, and ran. He gave chase. She foolishly backed herself into a corner of the kitchen. He lunged at her, trying to retrieve the bag, but she ducked under his arm and ran the length of the kitchen and into the living room, dripping a trail of white snow.

He was fast and on her tail before she could make an escape plan. She tried to put the couch between them feigning left and right, but he was on her like a shadow. She flung flour at him across the couch. He expertly dodged and attacked at the same time. In one bound and a hop, he flew over the couch, tackling her to the floor. She tried to army crawl, but he clung to her legs, pulled her back and gained her waist, reaching the crumpled bag of flour. They were laughing so hard she was almost crying. She raised the bag above her head, but he lunged the rest of the distance and retrieved the weapon.

His body smashed her to the floor, his face inches from hers. They stopped laughing and looked into each other's white dusted faces. He wiped a hunk of flour from her cheek. Desire and electricity sparked between them. He leaned in. She knew he was going to kiss her and didn't know what to do. She closed her eyes.

Suddenly James sprung upright. Her eyes flew open.

"Truce?" He grinned down at her with his hand extended.

"Um, yeah," she replied confused, relieved, and a tiny bit disappointed. "Truce."

"Wow. This place is a disaster, but damn that was fun. You're a real crack up, Kid. Hey, we can still finish the cookies, can't we? I'm starving for 'em." He grinned and rubbed his stomach.

"Yeah, sure." She decided right then and there, it was her over-active imagination and Violet's talk about her Jitterbug sailor. Of course, James wouldn't try to kiss her. They were just friends. "Let's put in the first pan, and we can clean between batches."

"No problem. Nothing a shop-vac can't handle." He jogged to the closet and pulled out a red and black monster of a vacuum. "This baby can handle anything. I'll get this bit around the couch if you wouldn't mind getting the kitchen." He handed her back the torn flour bag.

"Oh sure, give me the messiest bit."

"Who started it?"

"What do you mean *who started it*? You started it by flinging creamed sugar at me."

"What? That was an accident. You're the instigator." He laughed.

She rolled her eyes. "Cookies first. Follow me." He did. They added the chips, and she showed him how to measure out even portions. "Hey, James, can I ask you something?"

"Sure, shoot." He spooned the dough onto the makeshift sheet and plunged it in the oven.

"The last couple of weeks you've been acting really strange. You didn't seem like you wanted to hang out with anyone, especially me." She turned her back and continued wiping up the spilt flour.

"Sorry. I've been totally preoccupied." They finished cleaning the kitchen, and she followed him to the living room. "Can I tell you a secret?"

"Of course you can. If it doesn't sound too corny, I've come to think of you as one of my best friends." *Maybe James is the one I could tell about my panic and my brother.*

"Me too, Junebug." He turned on the vacuum, did a quick sweep, then turned to June. "You can't tell any of the others. I haven't told anyone I was even thinking about this. And I haven't got it all worked out. And I don't want Rose to get wind of it, until I do, but...." He paused. "I'm going to ask Rose to marry me," he whispered as if someone were listening.

"WHAT!" June yelled. "I mean, Wow. I thought you weren't sure...that you...that she was the one. Aren't you the kinda guy that doesn't buy the cow? Didn't you say something about marriage ruining relationships?"

"Did I say that? I don't know. I just figured, I don't want to lose her, and I feel like I'm losing her. I haven't seen her since the accident, and she's barely called. It seems like the right thing to do. You know, Rose is a really good girl."

"Are you trying to convince me, or yourself?"

"I don't need to convince anyone of anything."

"Okay, great. I'm happy for you." She gave him a quick hug. *Why do I feel like crying? He's not the one to share my secrets with.*

"Thanks. I knew you'd get it."

"Should we stop practicing for the contest?" Her voice cracked. She pictured her dress at Ms. Woe's shop. What was the point of working out a trade with Ms. Woe for a dress she wouldn't be wearing in the contest?

"What are you talking about? First of all, I haven't worked it out yet. It's the deciding that's made me feel…secure about…things. It's been weird not having Rose around. I'm all tense and thinking, weird stuff. Sorry if I've taken it out on you and the gang. It's all going to be good. I think she'll say yes, but there's her father to get by—he doesn't really like me right now. You do think she'll say yes, don't you?"

"She'd be crazy not to."

The sweet smell of baking filled the small apartment.

"Cookies." They said at the same time. The awkward edge fell away as they retrieved the first batch and put in another.

Relaxing with cold beer and warm cookies, June told James about the dress and the woman who made it. The gap between them closed, and they settled back into their comfortable friendship. June retold Violet Woe's story: the Jitterbug sailor, the rivals for her affection, the malt shop, the dance halls, and what life was like for a young woman in the 40s.

James jumped in, sharing his knowledge of fads, slang, and other bits he knew about the war era. They both admitted envy at not having juke joints or malt shops. June told how Violet had to quit school to take care of her dad and how June couldn't imagine that happening today. James chastised her, pointing out how sheltered she'd been. Those situations did happen today, only not as much at their socio-economic level.

James couldn't wait to meet Violet Woe. They both wanted to hear more about Violet's Jitterbug contest and James—like June— hoped Violet might be interested in watching them dance. He suggested inviting Clara, which June agreed to, but reluctantly. June wanted to keep Violet for herself and James for a little while longer. The dress, the contest, and meeting the old Jitterbug seemed like something special.

Violet ~ 1940s & 1990s

24. Sentimental Journey
(Dinah Shore)

"Jeannie, you can't believe who I met. I know I've got to stop talking to myself but I know you're up there listening. Well, I want to believe you're listening, and I'm not going batty. The darnedest thing, this young girl comes in, cute as a button. She reminded me of us when we were young. She comes in here and guess what she brings? My old Jitterbug dress. You remember the one I made for the contest.

"I went and told her all about our jitterbugging days. I don't know why—the dress, her shining eyes. I've got myself all stirred up. It was so long ago, but I'm swimming in memories. I can't stop thinking about him. I know we made a pact a long time ago never to bring him up, but this dress. Why now?"

Emotions strained Violet's quiet morning. She embraced the dress, blubbering like an old fool. Memories came crisp and clear. She was eighteen again.

Cold shower tiles on her back, warm water drizzled over her head. Water splattered, hit the floor, and their skin. His skin was like silk. Although they'd made love several times before, this was new.

He glimmered. Water rolled over his cheeks, dribbling across his goofy grin, silly and sexy at the same time. She marveled at his easy countenance. He grabbed the shampoo, squeezed its contents into his big hands, and deposited the mixture on her head. Slowly rubbing the crown of her head, his thumbs massaged her temples. His hands kneaded her hair and scalp like dough. She understood cats a little better.

His hands slid over her body, sensually, but not sexually. She shuddered. She tilted her head readying for a kiss that didn't come. Instead, he worked the lather down her arms to her fingertips, gently pulling each one. She admired his strong thigh muscles taut against his skin.

He continued soaping, running his hands down her back to her hips. Deliberately, and with the lightest touch, he brushed between her legs, barely grazing her most sensitive spot. She closed her eyes and swayed as the hot water ran out. She ached for more.

Charles popped up and smiled.

"Let's get you rinsed off before you freeze." He turned her around and stepped to the side letting the cold water splash her buzzing body. She sobered, stomped, and did a little dance while he turned off the water. He tied a towel around his waist and beckoned her into a dry one. She stepped into it and leaned against his bare chest, basking in his clean, fresh scent.

"Ready for tonight?"

"Ready as I'll ever be."

The memory slipped away as Violet waited for the kids to arrive. She knew those kids were adults, but they looked so young. She couldn't help calling them kids.

Did Jeannie and I ever look so young? Maybe it's all the sunscreen they wear? Maybe it's my old age? Time has a devious way of playing tricks on your perception.

June and her friends wanted to hear all about the big Jitterbug contest. Violet dug out the trophy to show them—her name on it. She hadn't looked at it in years. She'd forgotten the engravers had etched Violet Mangino instead of Violet Woe. Charles and Violet Mangino. *Would it have made a difference?* An old ache rippled across her heart.

After all these years, she couldn't believe she was asking herself these same questions. She wept softly, hugging the cold trophy to her chest. So much loss and so many secrets. *I've opened a door I can't close and part of me doesn't want to keep it closed, anymore.*

The bell jingled, and the chatter of young voices followed. She wiped the tears off her face and waded out of her past to greet her new, young friends.

"Hi, Ms. Woe," June chirped.

"Now June, how many times have I told you not to call me that? It makes me feel old." She laughed at her own joke. She was old. "I insist you call me Vi."

"All right, Vi. You got it."

"And who is this charming young lady?"

"Vi, this is Clara, Clara this is Vi."

"It's nice to meet you, dear. Aren't you adorable in your outfit? So much like me and my friends fifty years ago."

"And this is James."

"Nice to meet you James. And don't you look like a young jitterbug." James beamed.

Follow me upstairs to my apartment. I've dug out a few old pictures and my Jitterbug trophy, here."

Violet tucked the trophy under her arm and led the kids up the back stairs, through the kitchen, and into the spacious living room. "Make yourselves comfortable."

"Wow, this place is awesome. It looks like it hasn't been touched since World War II. Look at this couch and this fabric." Clara ran her hand down the arm of the sofa.

"Let's see now." Violet smiled. "After Pop passed away I moved in with Mrs. Peppy and convinced her we needed to update the place. We went to work using the new tropical touches that were all the rage during the war. I convinced her to update the kitchen and the bathrooms as well. We had a grand time redecorating. The redo gave the furniture and her a new life and was a great distraction for me."

"A distraction from the war, I guess?" June asked.

"Yes, something like that." She wasn't willing to share that part of her life. This younger generation might find it impossible to understand the limited choices available to her as a young woman in the early 1940s.

"You'll have to excuse me, the apartment and the shop haven't changed much since Mrs. Peppy left them to me in her will. I rented the shop, but left the apartment vacant and untouched while I gallivanted between Vegas, L.A. and across the sea. Eventually making it back here."

"Lucky for us." James rubbed his hands together.

Violet nodded. "When my boyfriend, Wally, died..." She never could bring herself to marry him, and he graciously never pushed it. Bitter at being excluded from his great war and resentful about his divorce, Wally was always kind to her, but then he'd loved her for a long time.

June and Clara looked at each other in the heavy silence.

A deep pain pierced Violet's heart. I should have come back to San Diego sooner. Just two years after Wally died, Jeannie had a heart attack, sudden and unexpected. There were secrets, important truths Violet had wanted to tell Jeannie. Maybe Jeannie knew, but if she did, she never said anything. Only once did she ever ask if Violet had any regrets about not being a mother.

Violet bit back the tears and memories and continued her story.

"I got all this old furniture out of storage and moved back in here. The place could use some work though. A new coat of paint and I'm thinking about reupholstering the furniture with something more neutral."

"No!" exclaimed Clara. "I mean, it's in such good shape, and it's gorgeous and totally period. This is my ideal. Sure, I can see how a fresh coat of paint and maybe a refinish to the hardwood floors would be good. Please excuse me for being so bold. It's lovely the way it is." Clara finished nearly out of breath and panic-stricken.

Violet laughed heartily. "Well, if you feel that way about it, I guess I better leave it."

Everyone laughed and sunk into her perfectly preserved furniture. She couldn't help being amused.

"So, you want to hear about my famous Jitterbug contest, huh? It's not really that exciting. I can't imagine why you kids would want to know, but if you've really got nothing better to do than listen to an old lady, I'll tell you." The dread of Charles's departure stole upon Violet, anew. Her stomach clenched and a deep sorrow spread into her veins. The memories burned hard and fast as she began her story.

"It was 1942 and we gathered at the malt shop the night of the Jitterbug finals. The joint was packed with everyone from our grade as well a few of last year's grads. Two local couples had made the finals: Charles and me, and Johnny and Millie. Millie was ready and looked like a quintessential bobby-soxer. She'd braided her hair in two long plaits, bright pink ribbons on the ends. Her pink flowered rayon dress alternated with black insets, shiny black buttons dotted the bodice and puffy sleeves finished off her ensemble. Oh dear, I'm sorry I get carried away with details, too many years of working with fabric and clothing. I'm sure you don't want to hear about that."

"Yes we do. I can picture it now. Do you think you could reproduce her dress?" Clara was almost drooling.

"I don't know. Maybe, but it would take quite a while. The hardest part would be finding the fabric. I don't know why it's so hard to find nice rayon these days. Everything went the way of polyester you know. Worst invention, if you ask me. I'd rather be wrinkled in linen and silk than pressed in polyester."

"Me, too." Clara and June replied.

"Now where was I? Fashion, yes, so that's what Millie wore, and honestly, I cannot remember a thing Johnny wore. He was always a snappy dresser, but no image of him comes to mind. I, as you know, was wearing the Jitterbug dress. The dress I cannot believe you found and brought to me. June dear, did I tell you the skirt used to have an anchor appliqué toward the bottom?"

"Really? Do you think...could we..."

"Reproduce it?" Violet finished. "Yes, I think we'll have to. So, what else? I wore the most darling red suede wedgies that wrapped around my ankle. Not too different from the ones you're wearing, Clara."

Clara beamed at her. Violet looked down at her aged ankles. *Who put those old lady feet at the end of my legs. Aging isn't fair. Well, at least the legs still look good.*

"I keep getting off topic. I'm sorry, dears. Charles, my dance partner, wore his dress whites—that's the uniform sailors wear in spring and summer—and of course his non-regulation Jitterbug socks."

"Stripy," June, James, and Clara said at once.

Caught off guard, Violet looked at them questioningly.

"Old clips from the 40s and 50s." James jumped up. "We noticed all the kids wore stripy socks, and most the old-school Jitterbugs have taken it up. Especially us who try to stay true to the WWII style of Lindy."

Violet was delighted. *They may know more about jitterbugging than I do.* "Tell me about these old clips. What do you mean?"

"Do you have a VCR? I have a ton on tape, and I could show them to you some time," James replied.

"I do. Let's plan that. Maybe make a night of it?" She immediately felt foolish. These young kids didn't want to hang out with an old lady like her.

"That would be so great," June said. "Maybe...maybe James

and I could show you some of the footwork we've figured out?"

"I'd love to see you dance." Violet smiled and patted June's knee. "All right, back to my story. I'll try not to digress or we'll be here all night."

She told the story as if she were reliving it....

"Ah come on Vi, you can't lay an egg on going in the old jalopy with us," Jeannie whined.

The jukebox blared through the packed malt shop. Violet leaned over and talked low in Jeannie's ear.

"I know Johnny's not being a crumb, but things aren't exactly copasetic either. Ronald and Sue's buggy is full, and I don't want to push my luck. And honestly, I just want more time with Charles." *Alone.* Violet finished in her head. She needed him, physically, emotionally, achingly. She wished she could share everything with Jeannie, but was afraid she wouldn't understand.

Jeannie looked at Violet and the ring on her finger. "I know he's your chief charm. Don't worry about me. I won't go into a decline over it. We'll see you over there then."

"Thanks Jean." Violet gave her a quick hug, grabbed her sweater, and went to find Charles. Barbara trapped him beside the jukebox. The girl needed to take a powder, but even Barbara couldn't clobber her mood.

Violet caught Charles's eye and realized with certainty that he'd kept his eye on her every second they were apart. An invisible thread connected them. When he spied Violet, he gave Barbara the brush off. Violet smiled as he made his way toward her. His progress across the floor was so similar to the first time he walked across the crowded floor at the dance hall—dress whites, olive skin, sea-green eyes, uniform taut across his chest and shoulders. She took a deep breath, trying to contain her longing. Desire rushed unheeded, electrifying every nerve. Charles leaned down and talked deliciously into her ear.

"What's the rumpus?" He lingered at her ear sending shivers down her spine. It took a moment for her to reply.

"I talked to Jeannie, and we're all clear. The gang is making a break for the hall. We'll meet them there."

"Hmmm, is that so? Well Miss Woe, soon to be Mrs. Mangino, how much time do we have?"

She got his meaning and blushed, admitting to herself, she longed for a little more time, too.

"Not enough," she replied with a smirk.

"Okay, Gorgeous. You wanna grab the trolley or a cab? Ordinarily I'd fancy a walk with you, but I don't want those gorgeous gams of yours tired out?"

"What, these old things?" She picked up the edge of her skirt, pointed her toe, and turned her leg to the side.

He looked her over from top to bottom and back again, drew a breath, and shook his head. "Now look here Gorgeous, you'd better tuck that leg back in if you want to make it to the Jitterbug contest. There's only so much a red-blooded American can take." He laughed good-naturedly and hailed a cab.

Twenty minutes later Violet and Charles exited the cab and approached the hall. The line was out the door. Violet grimaced and rethought not going with the gang. Charles sensed her anxiety, grabbed her hand, and politely ducked through the throng until he came to the door. He maneuvered them to a pretty girl sitting behind a table.

"Excuse me Ma'am, but we're in the finals of this here Jitterbug Contest, and we're wondering where we check in."

"Oh, you're late. Hold on a minute." The gal jumped up and motioned toward someone they couldn't see. A young kid came running over.

"What do you need, Judy?"

"Can you run over to Gil and ask him for the roster sheet for the contest." She looked them up and down. "No never mind, take these two with you and make sure Gil's got 'em on the list. If not..." Judy made eyes at Charles. "Chuck 'em out the door on their jitterbugging keisters." She laughed.

The kid looked taken off guard and none too sure of Violet and Charles, but he followed directions as Judy turned around to the grumbling kids in line. Charles moved lithely through the packed dance floor, swerving around a couple before a girl was flung into their path. Charles's reflexes were quick.

The trio made their way toward the stage where the band had already begun. Judy's assistant ushered them through a battered door, directing them down a short hall into a room where young couples pinned numbers onto their shirts, skirts, and pants.

Violet and Charles smiled and followed him through the room of competitors. Other couples sized them up, whispering to each other, smiles faltered. The whole room buzzed with determined energy. In the corner, another guy with a clipboard chatted with an older, dapper gentleman. He started to speak as they reached him.

"Ah ha, you must be Violet Woe and Charles Mangino. You're late. We're about to start. Please put these on and no grumbling about the numbers. They were picked randomly."

The man handed them their numbers plus a handful of safety pins. Violet sighed. She was not superstitious, but a chill ran down her spine.

"Lucky thirteen, killer diller," Charles said with his happy lilt.

"I love you," she whispered in his ear.

He smiled and hugged her, then grabbed the guy with the clipboard.

"Hey, uh, could you change that name from Violet Woe to Violet Mangino?" He winked at the guy. "You know so they get our name right on the trophy."

Violet raised her hand toward his face allowing the diamond ring to sparkle in the stark light. Clipboard guy rolled his eyes and made a notation.

"So it's official then?" Violet didn't see Johnny slink up behind her.

"It's none of your business," she blurted before she could stop herself. Was that like admitting it wasn't true? Not that it mattered what Johnny thought. As far as she was concerned, her heart, mind, and soul were married to Charles even if the state of California didn't have it on record, yet.

"Good for you, Vi. Good for you." Johnny gave her a hard look, then turned and stuck out his hand to Charles. "Congratulations she's...she's...that's a good girl you got there."

"Thanks. I know."

Johnny and Charles shook hands and stared each other down. Johnny dropped his hand and looked away first.

"Oh, hi Vi. Looks like you just made it." Millie scooted up beside Johnny. "We were a little worried about you. Jeannie's about to go into a decline. Too bad there's no time to let her know you made it, but she'll see you soon enough. We're about to be on."

The orchestra beat out a version of Benny Goodman's, *Sugar Foot Stomp*, good and fast. The intro started out big, not as solid as Violet liked, but good horns. Charles made it work with tight easy swing-outs, and she sailed across the floor. The clarinet took an early solo and played it sweet and hot. Violet and Charles grinned at each other and dug the jive.

His eyes twinkled, and she fell into his sea. She felt strong and whole. He swung her out into a quick-stop drop then led her into switches, riding the clarinet. The trumpet kicked in and bam. Charles pulled her up to his right shoulder, her head dangled over his back toward the floor. She laughed with pure joy. He tossed her back into Facing Charleston. The trombone slid and so did she, right into a Boogie-Drop split, slipping between his legs. Usually he would pull her back up, but in a flash, he leapt forward and crouched at the floor. Even though they'd never done this move, she got it, and knew what he wanted. She did a forward roll across his back, relishing the feel of his strong back below hers. Both of them straightened up and hit the Charleston.

The crowd roared, energy surging, but she only had eyes for Charles. The square-back collar on the Jitterbug dress flapped like small wings, matching the flight of his jumper. They soared across the floor—her feet barely touching the polished wood. The song ended without a real wind-up, and to Violet's surprise, she was scarcely out of breath. She could dance all night in this perfect time and place, in synch with the crowd, the band, and Charles. Life was magic.

The judges tapped out over half the finalist, leaving ten couples on the floor. She looked around but didn't see Johnny and Millie. She was sad and surprised by her genuine regard for Johnny and Millie. Before she had time for contemplation, the bandleader tapped his rostrum.

"You know we've got this right, Gorgeous?"

She squeezed his hand in return.

The first notes Count Basie's, *Shout and Feel It* echoed across the silent hall, four eight-counts of a sumptuous, simple guitar solo. Charles pulled her into the Balboa step and she almost swooned as she pressed against his warm body. His leg pushed hers. Her left side brushed his. The orchestra came on strong, and Charles led a Throw-out, immediately followed by a Swing-out Toss. She launched upward and tucked her legs. The whoosh of air cooled her heated body. She soared, feet level with his head, landing opposite him. She hit the floor solid with no slide or extra bounce. They did Swing-out after Swing-out, Charleston, spins, slides, mirroring footwork and a crazy assortment of acrobatic flips that all flew perfect.

She wished she could tell Charles how she felt, but thought he knew. She connected not only to Charles and the music, but also to everyone and everything, melting into the air around them. Everything was one, she was all, and being all, she was love. It was the only way to describe it. She was there, and not there. She was everywhere. Inside and outside of him.

Her feet pressed into the floor. Her muscles tightened, loosened, lengthened, and tightened again for the next step. Her thoughts were not dual or separate from her dancing. They were one. The memory of laying with Charles, making love with him, the glow when they both reached their peak mingled with the dance, with her life, with the moment.

Violet didn't divulge all those details to the kids, but related most of the story much like she remembered it. The timeworn ache echoed across her mind and body.

"So you guys totally beat everyone? It's too bad they didn't have video then. I would love to see some of those moves you described," James said.

Violet laughed and dabbed a loose tear from her eye.

"We sure clobbered them that night. It's was so long ago, but I can remember it as clear as you kids sitting here."

"So, what happened to him, to your partner?" Clara asked.

"Well…" Violet stuttered. *I should have seen it coming.*

"But…" Clara started again.

Violet caught June narrowing her eyes at Clara. *Sweet June.*

"So, what was it like to hear Big Band music the first time around?" June asked.

"The music was new and exciting and full of life. We'd been brought up listening to classical music and a little Dixieland. Then, out of nowhere it seemed the classical musicians—long hairs, we used to call 'em—started working with the Jazz musicians. I don't really know the history, or when the music changed. I just know that when I heard the sound coming out of the radio, I wanted to jump around and tap my feet. It was wild and..." She paused.

"And what?" They leaned in.

"Let's just say the music felt connected to those things forbidden. Those things not talked about in my generation."

"Oh, you mean sex?" Clara said.

Despite her age, Violet blushed, surprised that an old lady like her was still capable of blushing. She'd forgotten how bold this generation was. Not that it was a bad thing, either.

"Yes and no. Maybe in a sense, but it's almost like the music woke something primitive in us. I think much like Frank Sinatra and Elvis did for the generation after mine, and perhaps what each new music type does for that coming-of-age generation. Although hearing all the different types of music throughout my life, I can't help believe there was—and still is—something very special about big band swing. Of course, I'm biased by my experiences."

"No, I don't think you are. I know what you mean." James jumped up. "Sure there are some rock songs that have a similar affect, but overall there's something...."

"Full," June finished.

"Yeah. Full." James looked at June in astonishment.

"If you say so," Violet agreed. "Like I said, I'm biased and could listen to swing music all day."

"So, when are you going to come out dancing with us, Miss, uh, Violet?" Clara asked.

"Oh, well, I hadn't thought of it. I haven't danced in years," she replied. *Who'd would want to dance with an old lady like me?* "Maybe I'll just watch you kids some time."

"You're on," they said.

What have I gotten myself into? She smiled and couldn't wait.

June ~1990s
25. Wednesday Night Hop
(George Gee)

June pulled into the alley behind the shop where Ms. Woe told her to park, reminding herself to call Ms. Woe, Violet. June let herself in the back door as instructed.

"Helllloooo. Violet, it's me, June," she yelled as she climbed the creaky stairs. Familiar big band music greeted her ears. She made her way through the kitchen and dining room toward the sound, recognizing the familiar swing of horns and reeds, but couldn't place the voice.

Violet strolled out of the bedroom in a light blue A-line skirt that swished when she walked, topped with a matching striped shirt. She looked half her age, and June had to blink to put into perspective what she was seeing. Still trim and curvy, Violet Woe was a tiny wisp of a woman. Her waist looked unrealistically small and her feet, in white Keds, looked like children's. Her chin-length, silver gray hair was perfectly coiffed into soft barrel curls framing her petite face.

"Wow Miss, um, Violet, you look like a jitterbug."

"Do I? Thank you. Not bad for an old broad, eh?"

The music started to slow and drag, the trumpets stretched into elephant calls. Violet scurried to the old record player and lifted the heavy needle.

"Ah, listen to this old thing. I kept so much of Mrs. Peppy's antiques. They were old when I inherited them, and now they're ancient, a bit like me." She chuckled to herself. "Such a nice soft sound, pretty Victrola, isn't it?"

"Yes, it's gorgeous." June kept it to herself that she preferred the sound from her CD player.

Violet sighed and ran her finger across the edge of the old Victrola. "I know I will have to invest in one of those disc players, but this brings back so many memories."

June didn't know what to say. She never knew what to say or how to act when people became emotional.

"Now, we can't live in the past can we? So, where are you taking me this fine evening, June?"

"There's a concert in Balboa Park to top off the Cultural Event Weekend. They don't usually do them until the summer, but tonight is a big band dance under the stars at the organ pavilion. Only, now that I think of it, it might be too cold for you."

"Let me grab a sweater and put on some stockings. We'll bring a blanket and see how it goes. Shall we?" She patted June's hand. "Don't worry dear. If I get too cold, I'll grab a taxi home."

June looked alarmed.

"Now, don't give me that look. In my day we always took taxicabs. I'm not going unless you promise me I can take one if I get too tired or too cold."

June tried to object, but Violet raised her hands in protest. June promised, but with fingers crossed behind her back. They made their way to June's truck.

"By the way, who was that playing on your Victrola? I recognized the voice, but can't place it. Was it Ella Mae Morse?"

"No, but you do know your 40s songbirds, don't you? No, that was Anita 'O Day. I loved her with Gene Krupa. That man could play the drums. Oh, you should have heard him live. They were my favorite. When I sang, I tried to sing like her. You know she wrote a book about her life. *High Times, Hard Times.* You might enjoy it."

"You sang, too?" June turned off the freeway.

"A little. Seems like I've lived many different lives in my time. Now tell me more about yourself, June. I know you're quite the brainiac. Tell me about your friends, about Clara and James. Is he your boyfriend?"

"No, no." June blushed. "James and I are just dance partners."

"Really?"

"He's like my best friend. We work together, dance together, hang out, and sure he's sweet and funny and kind and cute, but, no. There's nothing between us. He's actually in love with this girl Rose. The one who broke her foot."

Violet gave her a skeptical look.

"Anyway, he's going to ask her to marry him." She'd said it. "But you can't say anything to the others. I'm the only one who knows."

"Don't worry, dear. I can keep a secret."

The parking lots closest to the Organ Pavilion were full, but June found a spot by the museums.

"It's not too far to walk is it?" June asked Violet when they got out of the car, amazed at how spry Violet was.

"No, this is fine." Violet slipped her sweater over her slender shoulders. "Oh my goodness, I haven't been in this park for a long time. Did you know that during the war they used these building as overflow for the hospital?" Violet pointed at the ornate buildings as they walked past.

"No I didn't. I'm still getting to know San Diego."

"And how do you find it?"

"So far I like everything except the parking and the canyons. I can't tell you how many times I got lost when I first moved here. And with my truck being a stick shift, I still have a heck of a time on these hills."

"Yes, this city didn't use to have so many people. And it sure didn't have so many cars, although it's always had the hills." She chuckled. "In my day, everyone rode the trolleys and took taxicabs. In some ways, there was more community with communal transportation. Anyway, you're a fine driver, June.

Thank you for picking me up. It's not that I don't drive, but I prefer not to if I don't have to."

They walked down the Prado and admired the gorgeous buildings, passing the lily pond, continuing toward the smaller fountain in the middle of the roundabout.

"So, tell me more about this Jitterbug contest you and James are practicing for."

"I'm really nervous about it. Rose and James were supposed to be competing and like I said, she got her foot smashed. I'm not as good as Rose."

"Ah, that was the accident. You didn't say how it happened."

"It's kinda my fault, but kinda not. I don't know. I think if he hadn't been dancing with me, he would've been dancing with her, and her foot wouldn't have been broken."

"He, you mean James?"

"Yeah. We were at this club in Los Angeles, a kind of famous place. Maybe you've heard of it, the Derby?"

"No, sorry. I don't know it."

"Anyway, I was dancing Shag. Hey, do you know the Collegiate Shag?"

"Why yes, it had a good run of popularity for a while. We used to mix it in with our Lindy. Some jits would simply Shag, never bothering to learn the Lindy. Seems like they called it Flea Hop or Single Balboa, but I might not be remembering right."

"Cool. I'll have to ask James about those other dances. He's our local dance historian." June could listen to Violet's stories all night. "What were we talking about before I got side-tracked?"

"The contest and Rose's unfortunate—or perhaps fortunate— accident." Violet had a gleam in her eye and smiled conspiratorially.

"I hadn't really looked at it that way. Do you believe in fate?" June switched the blanket to her other arm.

"I don't know, maybe. I think we make our own fate, but I

have to say, you bringing me that dress after all these years is certainly serendipitous. After losing Wally and Jeannie, you're exactly what I needed. I sure wouldn't be in Balboa Park, going to a concert, meeting young people, and considering taking up dancing again."

Maybe Violet's right. Maybe I'm what Violet needs, and Violet's what I need. June liked the idea that they were what each other needed. "Did I hear you right? You said you are going to dance?"

"I may swing a wing or two." Violet smiled her impish grin.

The music rumbled its way between buildings and through trees, long before they reached the Organ Pavilion. If it wasn't June's imagination, Violet picked up the pace as they made their way closer.

They met the low stone wall that opened onto a concrete floor where hundreds of metal chairs were bolted to the ground. The seats were nearly full. A portable dance floor lay between the raised stage and the first row of chairs, already populated with local swing dancers and other free-style dancers.

The 1914 ornate arch dwarfed the large band. Rows of white lights followed the concrete arc and flanking promenades. To June's surprise, Clara whirled on the dance floor with James. How he beat her to the park she didn't know. As they did a swing-out, Clara caught June's eye and tilted her head, nodding to the right. June looked to where Clara's eyes led and spied a cluster of familiar faces. In the middle, like a queen bee, perched Rose. A vintage wool blanket covered her lap.

June and Violet zigzagged down the aisle to where her friends gathered. June made introductions. Rose offered Violet a drink from Clara's mini-bar, but Violet declined. Rose frowned and continued to mix cocktails, handing one to June.

The sweet minty liquid tickled her taste buds. June thanked Rose and gave her a warm hug. Rose looked as fabulous as ever in black gab slacks, pullover sweater, and plaid Pendleton jacket.

"Mmmm, Rose, this is yummy. What is it?"

"It's the latest and greatest, although not a traditional vintage cocktail. It's my new fave. My mother's been making these at her last few parties. The originals are rum, lime juice, mint, and simple syrup, but Clara and I came up with a mango/blueberry. And think of the health benefits. Cheers." Rose clinked June's glass. "Doesn't Gramma Jitterbug drink?"

"I don't know. I don't know her that well, yet. But she's a really sweet lady, and you should hear the stories she tells. She knows all the dances we do. She was there when they were new."

"Violet," June yelled over the music. "This is Rose. Rose this is Violet."

"Thank you, dear. Rose was sweet enough to introduce herself and offer me a drink."

The band wrapped up the song and Clara and James sauntered over. James gave Violet a hearty handshake and Clara gave Violet a light hug. He leaned in and kissed Rose, lightly brushing her perfect matte, red lips. June had never seen James so attentive. Maybe she was wrong, James and Rose were right for each other.

"Glad to see you made it, Vi. Am I going to get a dance with you?" He flirted.

"Maybe if you're lucky." She winked.

"Hey Rose, you wanna try this slow one?"

He helped her stand, conveying her across the aisle to the dance floor. For a brief moment, June had a pang of jealousy, but James looked happier than he had in weeks. They swayed to Harry James's *It's Been a Long, Long Time*.

"So that's Rose?" Violet asked.

"Yup, that's Rose. Isn't she beautiful?"

"She reminds me of a girl I once knew in school. Her name was Barbara. But what is beauty if it's not tempered with kindness?"

June didn't know what to say to that and took another sip of her drink. She was itching to dance, but she didn't want to leave Violet sitting alone. "So, how's my dress coming along?"

"You mean my dress?"

June laughed. "Okay. Split the difference. How's our dress coming along?"

"It's almost done. I just want to replace the missing anchor appliqué."

"I forgot about that. Do you have any pictures of you in that dress?"

"I had one, but sent it with my dance partner when he shipped out. I'd hoped to have another copy made, but never got the chance."

"That's too bad. It would've been fun to see you in it. Heck, I think it'd still fit you."

"Aren't you sweet? Your mother did a very nice job in bringing you up. I doubt you'd even recognize me, anyway. I used to have the nicest brunette hair." She touched her hands to her silver locks.

"You could always color it again. I thought about coloring my hair red."

"I did color my hair for many years, but when you get this old and this gray, you end up having a skunk stripe within a few weeks. It's too much. I haven't thought of doing anything with this gray in years."

"I'll say it again. You look really great for someone who was a jitterbug in World War II."

"And I will thank you again." Violet patted June's knee.

The song ended and James scooped up Rose and carried her back to her seat. June jumped up to give Rose back her seat. James set Rose on her perch, and she offered him a drink.

"Thanks, I'll have one in a minute, babe." He again, uncharacteristically pecked Rose on the cheek. "I've got to grab this pretty lady for a dance. Would you do me the honors?" He extended his hand to Violet.

She stood. Even though the song was a nice medium tempo, June was nervous for her. What if she fell and broke something. Weren't old people always breaking their hips? But if Violet was going to dance with anyone, she trusted James the most.

He started out slow, not even doing swing-outs, but stayed with easy six-counts. She smiled a devilish grin, and he led a Dean Collin's send-out. She nailed it, and again June couldn't believe Violet's age. She looked like the girls they'd watched on the old videos. He led sugar-pushes, turns, and swing-outs. She followed everything.

June was mesmerized and so was everyone else on the floor. Most of the dancers on the floor had formed a circle around the dancing pair. June wanted to rush over and join the circled audience, but felt badly about deserting Rose. She turned to ask if Rose needed help or wanted to hobble over.

"Go." Rose waved her off. "I'll stay here snug under my blanket. Besides, it's not like I haven't seen James dance a million times."

June started to point out that he was dancing with Violet, a 1940s jitterbug, but gave up. June squirmed her way into the front lines, planting herself next to Clara.

"Would you look at her go? I want to be her when I grow up," Clara said.

"Yeah, me too."

The bandleader spotted the spontaneous swing jam and cued his clarinetist, who stepped forward and took a solo. James and Violet picked up on the riff, and he led her into mirrored facing Charleston, transitioning into shadow. The drummer noticed the jam and gave them extra rhythm. James and Violet matched him beat for beat. The crowd went wild. Most of them were on their feet, many standing on chairs to get a better look. James and

Violet busted out switches, and she shimmied her hips through the rotation. June thought she was better than Clara, Rose, and herself combined.

James led a lindy-circle, and as soon as he had her in a closed position, he did a quarter turn and led her into Collegiate Shag. James did a bit of a scoop step whereas Violet did a replacement step. James caught her style and mimicked her replacement step. June filled with joy, her eyes brimming with tears. Clara had the same delight and sparkle in her eyes.

When James brought Violet into the Shag break, she whispered something to him. He leaned back, she forward, giving the illusion that he was kicking her legs out from under her. Then, instead of straightening up, he continued to walk backwards with a slight drag, melting into the cheering crowd.

Local instructors took over the jam spotlight. Their style was different but fluid and jungle-like, bouncier than James and Violet, but still enchanting. Then Lucky, an older gentleman—and regular at Tio Leo's—grabbed Clara and took her to the center, spinning her eight turns in a row. Clara twirled easily, but June saw her eyes glaze and her body wobble when she came out of the spins.

June suddenly felt someone push her into the circle, balked, but quickly realized it was James. When they hit dead center, his strong hands tightened around her waist, pushing down on her hipbones. She bent her knees, feeling the energy build, then pushed off the parquet floor. He lifted her over his head, her legs flared out, landing effortlessly. She smiled and felt like she was home. He pulled her backwards into a boogie-drop, popping up into the shag break. The night air, the big band music coursing through her veins, and meeting Violet, combined into an ideal mix.

The band began winding up for a big finish. James sent June out, followed by three rapid swing-outs. She flew. On the fourth swing-out, she gripped his shoulder, pushed off the floor, and whoosh. She propelled around his back in a Helicopter, landing by his side. They both extended one leg forward, one back, in a lunge and pecked liked chickens to the last quivering note. In that moment, June wanted to kiss James. She glanced at him and saw him starring at her, his grin as wide as hers.

Happy, shiny faces glowed, and people clapped and stomped. James stood and helped June up, breaking whatever spell she was under. They turned toward the band and directed the clapping to them. The bandleader tipped his hand in thanks. James returned the gesture. With his hand still around June's waist, he led her back to where Rose and the gang rallied. He quickly dropped his arm on approach. June felt sheepish, though she'd done nothing wrong. Rose had a smile on her lips, but fire in her eyes. June mumbled a quick thanks to James and scooted away.

"That's the best I've seen you and James dance," Clara gushed. "Too bad it was so short, but you did get the big wind up at that end of the song."

"Me? What about Violet? Did you see them?" June turned to Violet. "Are you sure you're not a ringer?"

"It's been a while, but it's surprising how the dance steps come back. And James. Why he's quite the lead. You'd be hard-pressed to miss anything that boy led. Strong, but gentle." She smiled with a faraway look.

"You and Lucky were great, too." June nodded to Clara.

"Thanks. Good old Lucky." Clara got a gleam in her eye. "Violet, have you met Lucky?"

"How you doing Violet? Are you cold or tired?" June trampled Clara's question. "Would you like me to take you home?"

"Now what did we agree on, June? I may be old, but I'm not an invalid."

"Obviously." Clara and June said. "After watching you dance, the furthest thing from it," Clara added. "So, will you train my friends here?"

"Train them? My heavens, what could I possible teach them? They looked perfect."

June's face fell.

"Well, if it's that important to you, dear." Violet patted June on the back. "Honestly, I don't know what I could possibly add, but if you want me, you've got me. What else do I have to do?"

June perked up and both Clara and she clapped their hands like kids. June recognized the scheming look in Clara's eyes. What could she be planning next?

Violet ~ 1990s & 1940s
26. The Devil and the Deep Blue Sea
(Eddy Duchin)

The halcyon dawn roused Violet from sleep. Sea mist covered the city in a blanket, streets faded into fuzzy gray walls, spider webs shimmered, and eaves dripped like leaky faucets. Violet's consciousness coalesced and she was amused to find herself thinking poetically, finding it hard to believe she was still a romantic after all these years.

The open air from the French doors refreshed her tired old body. Her hips and ankles ached from the evening's dancing, but she felt alive for the first time in years. Old memories, old faces, and old hurts eddied in her mind. She sipped her tea while the emotions swirled. Her youthful passions burned sharp in her heart, but her old body reeled in confusion.

"Jeannie, are you up there? Are you listening? I went dancing last night. You should have seen me swing a wing. Remember that old saying? And would you believe all our old dance steps came right back to me. Of course, I can't move as fast as I did in our day, but I was moving."

She rubbed her feet and twirled her ankles.

"This young handsome fella led all our old moves. What are these young kids thinking, wanting an old broad like me around? They wanted to hear all about the big bands and our malt shop. Did I mention they wear our old clothes too, they call it vintage. In our day, we would've given the stuff to the Rag Man. Now, they collect it. I guess that would make me vintage. Perhaps they're collecting me. I wish you were here so we could be vintage together."

She yawned and stretched.

"June's sleeping in the bed I used to sleep in when I lived with Mrs. Peppy. Funny how history repeats itself. Now I'm the old seamstress from a bygone era."

The floorboards creaked. "Good morning, sleepyhead. You're up early," Violet said as June emerged from the bedroom. "I pegged you for a late sleeper. Can I offer you some tea? I'm sorry, I don't drink coffee."

"I am a morning person, usually." June yawned. "I don't know why I'm so tired. I may look awake, but I don't feel awake. Thanks, I'll try some tea. You look wide awake."

"One of the few perks of old age. You don't need as much sleep during the night, but then you nap in the middle of the day. Maybe it's a wash. My teapot's full. Let me get you a cup. Is it too cold for you with the doors open?"

"No. Actually, it feels really good. What a cool view of downtown."

June yawned again and curled up on the couch like a cat, tucking her legs beneath her. Violet didn't know why, but so many things about June reminded her of herself. Violet shuffled into the dining room and retrieved a teacup.

"Here you go, sweetheart." Violet handed June a cup. "Do you think you're up for some sewing today? Or do you need to have caffeine to make your brain work?" She wanted June to sew the appliqué on her—their dress.

"No, I don't usually need caffeine." June held the cup to Violet and Violet poured the steaming liquid into it. "But I gotta warn ya, I'm no good at sewing. My Grammy tried to show me how to embroider, and I was hopeless."

"No one is hopeless, and sewing isn't rocket science. It's knowing how, and practicing that knowledge and skill. In fact, it's a lot like dancing. You learn the muscle memory of using a needle, and your brain becomes accustom to how things go together. Just like people learn to hear the beats in music."

"I never thought of it that way. I figured you have the skill or you don't."

"You either have talent or you don't. But skill can be learned. And in something like sewing or dancing, there's a lot of skill involved. In fact, I would hazard that sewing takes less talent, more skill. So, you're in luck." Violet smiled at her young apprentice.

"Cool. I'll give it a whirl." June took a sip of her tea. "Mmmmm, this tea is good, what is it?"

"It's Earl Grey with lavender, one of my favorites. It's the oil of Bergamot which gives it its distinct flavor and the lavender mellows the tang."

"Well it's yum."

"I've got some work to catch up on. When you're awake and ready, come down to the shop, and I'll get you started. Feel free to take a shower. There's towels in the closet."

"Thanks. I was only going to brush my teeth, but a shower sounds fab. Thanks for the loan of the nightgown, by the way."

"Do you always travel with a spare set of clothes and a toothbrush?" Was this younger generation so cavalier about their values? Perhaps every generation thought that about the next one. It was possible Mrs. Peppy thought that about her. She'd given her reason.

"That's Clara's doing. She suggested I always have an extra set of clothes, clean underwear, and a toothbrush at all times. At first, I thought she was crazy or easy. Um, she's not, easy."

"In my day we called them able-grables."

"Cool slang. Well, Clara isn't that either. But, you never know where the day will take you. I'm personally NOT in the habit of crashing at people's houses. And I'm certainly not a...that is... Anyhow, the extra clothes and toothbrush came in handy last night and this morning. Not a bad policy. I think I'll go brush my teeth now."

Violet chuckled and shook her head. June scurried back to the bedroom. When Violet thought about it, sleeping over or crashing at someone's wasn't that different than her generation spending the night at the beach with a bonfire. *Though in many ways, my generation was more innocent.*

"So, the first thing I do is outline the appliqué with tailor's chalk. There's always some give to the fabric." Violet began her instruction.

"Give?"

"Yes dear, that means stretch."

"Oh, okay. Let me try the first part first, and then we can move on? I'll start with the outline. And maybe you could check it when I'm done?"

"Of course. Now here you go. You're all set up. Give me a holler when you're ready." Violet went to her machine and finished sewing a hem. She could do it with her eyes closed, but pretended to be engrossed in her efforts. She didn't want to make June feel any more self-conscious than she obviously did.

"Um excuse me, but is there a trick to getting the chalk to move smoothly across the fabric?" Frustration and determination etched June's face. "Mine looks like a road divider."

June was doing fine, but she needed to get over the idea that she couldn't do it. "Let's see, don't press too hard with the chalk and keep the fabric taut. That ought to do it."

"Thanks." She let June struggle a minute more, and June figured it out. "Hey, would it be okay if I put in a couple pins while I outline. I don't want my outline moving either."

"Why yes, of course. I guess I skipped that part didn't I? That's exactly what you're supposed to do. See, you're more of a natural than you think. And really, sewing is a lot of common sense. And you obviously have that."

June beamed and returned to her work, bowing her head over the jitterbug dress. Violet watched June concentrate. June's lower jaw jutted out slightly. She was adorable. Violet's heart swelled.

After fifteen minutes, June looked up. "Okay, I'm pretty sure I got it. I'm going to go ahead and pin it up. Will you show me how you want me to stitch it now?"

"Absolutely." Violet set down the suit jacket and inspected June's work. She'd done a nice job with the outline and pinning. "Can you thread a needle?"

"I'm not as inept as all that." June laughed. "Of course I can."

"Okay. Well, here you go. Nowadays I have to use a needle-threader."

"Is that one of those triangle wire thingies? I think Gram used them, too."

"That's them. They work great, but I feel I'm cheating. I can't get my eyes to focus that close no matter what glasses I put on. Well now, I see you've done it. Good. So, what you want to do is take the needle through the back and poke right in about a quarter inch from the edge." June tried but pushed the wrong way. "Do you mind if I show you?"

"Please do. I'm especially visual. James always tries to explain a dance move, and I don't get it. But when he shows me or leads me, I get it no problem."

"He's a good looking boy, isn't he? Nice and polite, too."

"Yeah. Not really my type. Like I said, we're just friends."

"Oh that's right, you told me that, didn't you? Well, anyway, watch as I poke the needle through the back but keep it under the appliqué. You want to feel around until the needle hits the fold. Then push the needle horizontally through the fold and again next to the edge. Do you see?"

"I do." June settled into her work.

"It's such a pretty dress isn't it?" Violet ran her hand over the edge of the dress.

"I love it, but…"

"But what, dear?"

"Never mind." June shook her head. "It's dumb."

"I'm sure it isn't."

"I have this weird idea about clothing. How they become part of you. Or part of your personal mythology. And this dress is part of your history, your mythology. How can it become part of mine? That sounds silly doesn't it?" June set her needle down.

"No, I understand. Sometimes the way you dress becomes your signature and a way to express yourself. It's an art form. Dance is an art form. You're an artist, June."

"Me? An artist? I don't know about that. I just know I want to be the girl in the Jitterbug dress."

"You will. The dress only exists for me in the past. And we don't live in the past. We live in the now. Just like all the other vintage clothing you've acquired. This dress is no different."

"Yeah, I guess you're right." June picked back up her work.

"That said. I wish you could've seen me in that contest. I told you all about the contest, didn't I?"

"Yes, but I'd like to hear more. Like what happened after. What'd you do? Where'd you go? Who'd you celebrate with?"

"You really want to know all that? To be honest it was very bittersweet. You see…"

At that moment, the doorbell jingled and Clara rushed in.

"Violet. Violet." Clara stopped to catch her breath. "Is June…oh, there you are. I didn't see you sitting back there."

Violet was alarmed and didn't know if this was normal behavior for Clara. Judging by June's reaction, it was not.

"For goodness sakes, Clara dear, what's the matter?"

That seemed to do it. Clara regained her usual nonchalant composure. Although, as she sauntered to the water cooler for a drink, Violet saw Clara was taut as a tight rope.

"Okay ladies, are you ready for this?"

Violet liked how Clara included her.

"James…after you left last night…James…." Clara took a swig of water. "James, did it. He did it. He asked Rose to marry him. She said it was only a matter of time, but I didn't think James would really do it."

Violet looked at June's face and noticed a shift, resignation maybe, but then June's pert smile was back. Clara was oblivious.

"June, come on, you don't look that surprised. I just dropped a bomb. This is James, our James I'm talking about."

June's mouth curved into a smile that didn't quite reach her eyes. "I have to admit I knew. He said he was going to ask her. He swore me to secrecy. I didn't think it would be this soon, though."

"What? He didn't? And you kept it from me? Well how do you like that? I don't know whether to be mad at you or not. I would've told you." Clara scrunched up her face. "It is what it is. And it is exciting."

"And she said, yes?" June asked.

"Of course she said yes. But here's the kicker, and I only know this because I talked to Rose alone. She's not going to tell her father. She wants it to be their secret for a while."

"And what does James think of that?" Violet asked.

"I don't know. They left after that. I'm sure she told him in the car on the way home or something. I haven't talked to either of them today. I felt like, you know, it would be a bit too intrusive. Besides, Rose has to get back up to L.A. today, anyway. We can grill him tonight."

"But I thought you and Rose were close?" June asked.

Clara shrugged. "Sure, close for Rose, but, not the same kind of close I am with you and James."

They lost me. Either someone was your friend or they weren't. Violet didn't remember friendships being that complicated.

"Anyway, do you want to hear the whole story or not?" Clara looked like she might boil over if she didn't get to tell her story.

Violet and June nodded their heads.

"All righty then. It was before the last set, and I guess James had spoken with Bill, the bandleader, and told him it was Rose's birthday."

"It was?" June interjected. "I didn't know. I feel awful. I didn't wish her a happy birthday."

"No. It wasn't her birthday. Just listen. So anyway, Bill does the whole announcing, *We've got a special birthday in the house and would she come up to the stage.* Rose looks around, like she's embarrassed to be the center of attention, but we know she loves it. She gives James a questioning look. He shrugs his shoulders and tells her to go with it. That's one of the great things about Rose. She's always up for a bit of adventure. So, James scoops her up, carrying her like, well, like a bride, and sits her down on a chair on stage. Bill puts a tiara on her head, but we're all still thinking birthday or maybe half birthday? I'm trying to figure out what James is playing at, but never guessed this. We all sing a pretty swinging version of *Happy Birthday* and then, and THEN, well you can guess what happened next." Clara paused for a breath.

Violet and June were on the edge of their seats.

"And then what?" June squeaked.

"Then James gets down on one knee, and oh my God, you should have heard the gasp from the crowd. Everyone thought it was a birthday thing. It gets real quiet, so quiet you can hear the buzz of the amplifier. He reaches into his pocket and pulls out a box with a pretty little ring. Who would have thought James had it in him?"

"And she said yes right away?" June asked.

"Well, she batted her eyes. Acted all surprised, then threw her arms around his neck. And then said yes. And guess what she said to me after he brought her back down off the stage while he was talking with Marty and Kris?"

"What?"

"She said, *See I told you it wouldn't be long, but I'll have to do something about this ring.* I think she's still sore at the fact that James had a thing for me before they met. Don't you think?"

"Did you and James date?" Violet asked.

"Not really, we were kind of like Rick and Ilsa in *Casablanca*. But I always thought there was something lingering, you know. Which, no offense to June, is why I think Rose picked June to be his partner, instead of me."

June winced at the remark.

"So you don't think it had to do with June's superior talent?" Violet asked.

"Oh, gosh, yes. June's an incredible dancer. She is now, anyway. She was all raw talent when we met her. I don't mean for a second to demean June at all. Sorry, did it come out that way? June, you know I adore you. And Violet, June knows I'm a wee bit envious. We've already talked about that. So, that's that. What do we think about James and Rose?"

Violet was exhausted just listening to Clara and also disappointed for June. Being the old romantic, Violet saw June and James together. *Maybe I saw what I wanted to see. What I wanted to be, the happy ending I never had.*

"Do we still have a contest to win? This doesn't change the fact that this girl Rose can't dance any time soon does it?" Violet asked.

"I already asked James about it." June piped up. "We're still on."

"Glad to hear it, kid." Clara nodded.

"Speaking of dance contests, before you busted in, Violet was about to tell me more about her great contest."

"Oooo, yes please. Do you mind if I stay and listen?"

"Okay girls, but you have to promise to listen AND work. Clara, you don't know how to rip seams do you?"

"As a matter of fact, I do. Hand me a seam ripper and point me in the right direction. I'm your gal Friday."

Violet walked to a pile of pants and handed the stack to Clara along with a seam ripper. "Ah that was a lovely picture, *His Girl Friday*. It astounds me you know so much about my era. Wasn't it with Cary Grant, and who was the woman? She was a brunette, thin, funny. In *The Women* with Norma Shearer?"

"Rosalind Russell," Clara replied.

"Yes, Rosalind Russell. You clever girl. I think the only other woman who could keep up with Cary Grant was Kate Hepburn. June, have you seen that picture?"

"What picture?" June asked, not following the conversation.

"*His Girl Friday*," Clara and Violet replied.

"No, I haven't. Do you have it on video, Clara? We're due for another movie night."

"I don't have that one, but we can rent it at Ken Video."

"Do you really like old movies?" Violet shook her head.

"Absolutely. I love the clothes, the hair, the sets, the writing, the dialogue. I mean nobody talks like that in real life, but you wish they did." Clara grinned with delight.

"My story isn't nearly as exciting as a Cary Grant picture, but I'll have a go at it. Where did I leave off? Oh yes, after the contest." Violet sank into her memories….

"We've been on stand-by for weeks, when do you think we'll ship out, Cheese?" Marvin asked.

Violet hadn't been listening to their conversation, but now her ears perked up. She didn't know if it was the firelight or the uniforms, but suddenly Charles and his Navy pals looked older, years older than her malt shop friends. Their faces reflected the joy and camaraderie, still buzzing from the jitterbug contest. Charles's and his buddies' faces looked pained in comparison. *Had Marvin just said they're on stand-by? Did Charles tell me they'd*

been on stand-by? He'd said something about their unit's deployment,
but I assumed it would be weeks or months. Violet thought back to the
time they talked about it, it was a good memory…

"What's for dinner, dear?" They'd settled into a routine of
playing house. That night he strolled around the corner, fresh
from a shower, a bath towel around his waist, his hair damp and
messy. Her heart flipped and body warmed as his thigh flashed
from under the towel. She tried not to look, turning her attention
to the gurgling pot of spaghetti sauce, and stirred. The smells of
tomato, garlic, and oregano filled the small apartment.

He snuck up behind her, put his arms around her, and
nuzzled the crook of her neck. She closed her eyes and inhaled his
clean damp scent. It mingled with the tartness of the sauce. He
pressed his body down the length of her, hugging around her
middle. She stopped stirring and leaned into him. His damp chest
cooled her back.

"Mmmm, that smells good." He nibbled her ear. "Can I
help?"

His hands shadowed hers on the wooden spoon and pot
handle. She scooped a spoonful of sauce and raised it to his
beautiful mouth. He blew gently on the spoon, not taking his eyes
off her. She loved him so much it hurt. She swallowed down the
welling tears. He tested the red liquid then turned the spoon to
her, their heads touched and lips shared the spoon.

Violet turned off the stovetop burner. He plopped the spoon
back in the pot. Their hands groped for each other, smashing their
mouths together. He hiked her leg up, holding it against his upper
thigh. She staggered forward and leaned him into the icebox on
the opposite wall. The narrow kitchen saved her from pushing
him to the floor. She felt wild.

Charles felt it too and tore at her blouse, unbuttoning and
kissing down her neck. Her hands snaked around his head, neck,

and back. They kissed voraciously, writhing half-naked, in the kitchen. The city sounds drifted through the window echoing their passion. The trolley bell clanged as her skirt dropped to the floor. His hands glided under her loose tap-pants, massaging her bare skin. He twirled her to the rumbling trucks and forced her against the cupboards. The counter top was cool and hard beneath her bottom as he lifted her and set her down. A horn honked in the distance. He parted her legs kissing from her knee, working his way slowly up her leg, tickling and tasting every bit of skin beneath his lips.

She shuddered and wanted more, lifting his head and tugging his hair. Her waiting mouth attacked his lips, neck, cheeks, forehead, and eyes. His fire burned through her. He dropped the towel. She scooted to the edge of the counter. His hands shifted the loose fabric of her underwear. Arms wrapped around her thighs drew her to him. She clung to his neck, using his shoulders for balance. He sliced her in two, again, and again, and again. She bore down on him. She couldn't stop. He couldn't stop. They couldn't stop. Aching, pulling, filling, sliding, rubbing, they raced to the same destination, reaching their peak at the same time. A ship's horn cried loudly in the harbor. They gasped and collapsed into each other's shaking bodies. He carried her crackling body to the sofa.

"Are you okay?" he asked. "That was, I didn't..."

His look of concern made her smile. She put her finger to his lips. "I did."

"Sometimes...sometimes I feel so desperate." He stroked her cheek. "Like we're living on borrowed time and I...want to give you so much more. You deserve more. I knew the moment I saw you I would be helpless not to fall in love with you, but still, I...well, you know."

She did know, and she didn't want to talk about it. Yet couldn't help ask. "So, any new news on when you're shipping out?"

"No, we're on stand-by now. We did have a leave date for two months from now, but they've got us on the ready. It could be weeks or months who knows...."

No wonder she'd forgotten he'd told her about his deployment. She'd tucked that bit of information away and now here it was in front of her.

"What do you think?" Marvin asked again, a little more emphatically.

"Hard to tell, but they've had us pack our sea-bags. So it's probably sooner than later." Charles replied.

"This waiting gives me the heebie jeebies. I just wanna get on with it, you know? Put my training into action. Do something real." Marvin threw a twig in the fire. "I feel like I'm holding my breath. Know what I mean?"

Charles nodded and rubbed Violet's arm. She scooted closer. A couple of the other fellas leaned in and listened to the conversation.

"Vee Vee, did you hear me?" Jeannie asked. "Do you want a marshmallow?"

"Sorry, Jean, I wasn't paying attention. A marshmallow? No thanks. I'm not feeling so swell all of a sudden."

Whenever she thought about him leaving, she pushed it away and told herself, he may be leaving but not today. She tried to tell herself that now, but she was too tired and jangly to believe it. She needed to move, shake out her limbs, make the bad feeling go away.

"Do you think you'll see any combat?" Ronald asked.

"I sure hope so." Marvin poked at the fire.

"Probably not," Charles said. "Working on a carrier is one of the safest places you can be in the Navy. Unless you're stateside in an office."

Why do they have to talk about this? Violet's eyes and face burned. She was thankful for the cover of darkness. She tucked her head into Charles's arm.

"That didn't save any of the guys in Pearl Harbor," Ronald replied. He popped a burnt marshmallow into his mouth.

"I guess not," Charles answered.

"Besides, we saw a Vitaphone Short about working on an aircraft carrier deck, and it's one of the most dangerous places in the world to work. Isn't it?" Ronald continued.

"Yes and no. It can be dangerous if a plane misses the wire, but that rarely happens. We're all trained extremely well. You know we just spent a couple weeks off the coast doing practice maneuvers, and our pilots are the best," Charles replied, proudly.

Violet watched Charles's handsome face and wondered if he was trying to convince himself, too. She was not convinced, and her heart ached. Marvin poked the fire, Lee snuggled up with Jane, and Clyde danced with Barbara. Would all these young men come home? Despite the patriotism and brave talk, this was no training drill. Soon enough, the war would be real for them. They would be forced to kill or be killed.

How could a man live with himself when he killed another? How would my caring, loving man be changed by war? A cold shiver ran down her spine. Her mother used to say it meant a goose was walking over your grave.

"So, we celebrated with a bonfire and party at the beach." Violet concluded her story not relating the intimate details of her memory.

"What happened after that? How soon did Charles ship out?" Clara asked, not stopping to wonder if she should. June shot her a look. "It's terribly romantic isn't it?" Clara mused.

"It might seem so, from this distance, but at the time it was...."

"Not that I'm for war or anything, but it seems like the reason your generation, or that period in history, is referred to as the greatest generation, is because of the war and the changes that came with it." Clara rushed on. "Look at the patriotism, the fashion created by the rationing, the music, and everything."

"Oh, girls, Clara, you're romanticizing. Those years were hard and often grim. History has a way of making nostalgic gobblygook. The war wasn't all waving flags and kissing sailors." Violet rubbed her forehead.

"But look at all the progress made by women. The shortage of men forced women into the workplace, which opened up more opportunities for them. Isn't that amazing?" Clara continued. "Now women aren't expected to stay home and be housewives. Now we have a choice, thanks to women like you."

"Yes, I suppose you're right in some ways, but still, the war and the destruction was an awfully big price to pay. And are we women any happier?" Violet asked.

"I think most woman are. At least our choices aren't as limited. Freedom is always worth the price."

"That's easy for you to say, now isn't it?" Violet retorted.

"Anyway," June cut in, "why don't you tell us about when they did ship out? Did everyone come and see the boat off like they said they would? Did you have a swing jam on the dock? Was there a band? Is this something you'd even like to talk about?"

Sweet, polite June. I really like her.

"Well girls, it wasn't like in the movies. In fact, most things aren't. We thought we'd have a couple more weeks and I was certain we'd be married by the time Charles shipped out."

"And you weren't?" June asked.

"No." Violet sighed and shared another memory…

The clock hands crawled around the dial. Violet had never

been so aware of time in her life. She was so distracted, she had to re-sew Mrs. Darling's skirt hem three times. Charles would get his blood results back, and they'd go to city hall and be married. Jeannie would meet her at the shop after school, and Jeannie and Marvin would witness their nuptials. If the clock would only cooperate.

When the phone rang, Violet almost sewed over her finger. She jumped up and dropped a tin of pins. She left them and sprinted to the phone.

"Yes, hello. I mean, Peppy's Tailoring, how may I help you?"

"Hey, Gorgeous, it's me. How are you?"

His voice sounded pinched and thin. She could picture his jaw set tight, brows furrowed. She didn't like it.

"What's wrong?"

Mrs. Peppy stopped sewing. The shop became so quiet Violet could hear her heart thumping. Charles was silent for three long beats, though she heard rumbling and murmuring in the background.

"Nothing's wrong." He paused. "We've...I've been given orders. We're shipping out in thirty-six."

Time stopped. She froze. Mrs. Peppy froze. Violet took a breath. Time rushed forward, too quickly. *Make it stop.* Violet had expected to be a blubbering mess, but something inside her clamped down and steeled her nerves. "So, do you have any leave time? Or are they keeping you on base until you deploy?"

"Yeah, just a minute. I heard you," Charles said, his voice slightly muffled, the sound of scuffling behind him. "Look Gorgeous, I need to tell you something else. They can't find my blood test results. I'll have to do another, and there's a long line at Medical. I've got Ski standing in line for me, but half the Navy is trying to get hitched before we ship out. They put me on the priority list, but it doesn't look good for getting to the courthouse today."

She breathed in slowly, closed her eyes, and found strength. She refused to add to the pain he was trying to hide.

"Tomorrow it is. I'll tell Jeannie. We'll have to ring the bells tomorrow."

"You're amazing, Gorgeous. What a trooper. Don't worry. We'll make it happen. I won't leave without you being my wife. They've got extra corpsmen coming in tomorrow morning to help process everyone. My liberty expires at twenty-two hundred tomorrow. I'll come over there..."

"Then go already." A voice crackled in the background with more grumbling. "Stop hogging the ameche."

"Can it, if you don't want a knuckle sandwich," Charles said in a scary voice she'd never heard before. His tone betrayed his anger and disappointment. One part of her wanted to laugh, the other wanted to cry.

"Sorry about that Vi. There's a line of fellas waiting to get on the ameche. I'll go see how far along Ski is in line and come right to you. Wait for me, doll. We'll have a good time tonight, anyway."

He hung up. She stood there with the phone to her ear, her insides roiling. Mrs. Peppy's machine whirred into action as the shop's door jingled.

"Good afternoon, Mrs. Peppy," Jeannie said. "Where's...."

Jeannie abruptly stopped talking. Violet hung the earpiece on the hook and numbly walked to her machine. Jeannie came toward her ready with a hug, but Violet knew if she let Jeannie hug her, she'd break and crumble. Jeannie reached for her and Violet pushed her sewing between them, snipping a loose thread.

"So um..." Jeannie looked from Mrs. Peppy to Violet.

"Charles has been given his orders. He ships out tomorrow night. He has to be on board no later than ten p.m. tomorrow."

Jeannie gasped. Mrs. Peppy sighed.

"But, we're still going to the courthouse today, aren't we?"

"Nope. Navy laid an egg on that plan. They've lost Charles's blood test results, so he's standing in line to do another."

"Oh." Jeannie's mouth made odd shapes. "What about...."

Violet had thought through all the possibilities already. There was no solution. She couldn't take Charles to her doctor. Doctor Hardy's results took three days. But then another thought struck her. If they'd lost Charles's blood test, had they lost hers, too? She'd had to turn it in when Charles applied for his test.

"Jeannie, I've got to get another copy of my results to turn in with his new test, so they can compare them. Who do we know with a car?"

Jeannie frowned. Mrs. Peppy stopped sewing, reached into her top, and pulled out a five-dollar bill.

"Take this. Call cab, and go."

Mrs. Peppy almost broke Violet with her kindness, but her mind was already three paces ahead. Violet gratefully grabbed the dough and phoned for a taxi.

As soon as the cab arrived, Jeannie and Violet jumped in and rushed over to Doc Hardy's office. Young men and women filled the lobby. Some sat patiently holding hands while others paced and smoked cigarettes.

Gertie, the receptionist, recognized Violet and smiled, then looked alarmed. "What is it, Violet," she asked with concern. "Is it your father?"

"No Gertie. It's Charles."

"Was there an accident? Is he hurt?"

"No, it's just that he's shipping out early and they've lost his blood test and I...do you have a copy of mine?"

"I'm sure we have a copy on file. Yes, this sudden deployment announcement has made quite a mess for us. They..." Gertie swept her arm indicating the full office. "All want blood tests. Doc Hardy's had me call the lab to see if we can get a rush, but the best they can do is a twenty four hour turn-around and I don't know that it will be enough time to get all these kids hitched."

"Oh." Violet realized her case was not unique or special. The thought filled her with hope and determination. If these couples could do it, so could she.

"Gertie, I'm in a bit of a hurry. Can you find my test results?"

"Sure thing, sweetie, let me…"

Doc Hardy walked out from the door behind Gertie.

"I'm ready for the next one, Gertrude." He looked up. "Oh, hello Violet, what are you doing here? Everything okay with your father?"

"Yes, no change."

Guilt jabbed her conscious. She'd barely thought of Pop, nor had she spent much time at his bedside. Since there was no change, she'd selfishly spent time with Charles. Was she being punished for that?

Gertie pulled the carbon copy out of her typewriter and handed it to Violet. Jeannie was already on the sidewalk hailing a cab.

"Vee Vee, you know I'm pulling for you, but what's the plan? How are we going to get on base and get this to Charles?"

"I don't know. I'm making this up as I go along. I thought we'd get a cab over to the base, and then wait at the gate, and see if we recognize anyone. Maybe Lee or Clyde or Ski, or even Charles will make their way out."

"Just making sure you had a plan, sweetie."

"Did you make it in time?" Clara asked.

Violet was so lost in the past she forgot the girls were there.

"Shhhhh Clara, let her finish the story."

"We did make it to the base, and we did see Ski and Charles walking through the entrance to hail a cab. I explained to Charles that he may need another copy of my test. He hugged me and called me brilliant. He and Ski took off at a run, trying to get to Medical before they closed. Jeannie and I breathed a sigh of relief. And even though the fellas could've signed us in, we decided to wait at the gate since we'd only have slowed them down."

"I'm confused," Clara said. "Did you get the blood tests by morning?"

"Yes, we did, but the next day didn't quite turn out like we hoped."

"Oh Clara, please let her finish."

Violet laughed, surprised that her story should be so enthralling. She wished Jeannie was there to help tell it. Violet remembered more than she told the girls...

Violet woke to the rise and fall of his lovely smooth chest. She wanted to stay there forever, but she also wanted to get married. The earlier they hit the courthouse, the better. She gave herself a couple more minutes of staring at her man. He looked so boyish when he slept, all signs of worry and age erased. She snuggled into the crook of his shoulder, her body too aware of his. Her passion stirred sleepily, but steadily, curling and tingling in her center. A morning breeze drifted through the open window, cleansing the musky scent of last night's love. She ran her hand up and down his torso, down around his stomach, and followed a downy trail to his manhood. He stirred. She continued to run the tips of her fingers up, down, and around. His breathing changed, and he grabbed her hips and shifted her on top of him. He feigned sleep as she nipped his neck and lips.

She liked being on top and in control. Small groans escaped his mouth as he awakened. She rubbed her body in slow, tight circles, guiding his to where she needed it.

His hands tried to quicken the rhythm, but she was in command and continued her slow teasing rotations. She leaned forward and arched her back, pressing her lower abdomen against his. The breeze chilled her damp skin and tiny goose-bumps broke across her body. She pulled the covers over their lower bodies and met him on their climb.

Her mind cleared to one single purpose, one single thought, one single timeless moment when a million stars exploded. She was pulled through a black hole and shot out the other side. She collapsed and let the rush of feelings and emotions course through every fiber of her being. Her body shook with spasms. Tears flooded her eyes before she could stop them, his too. They lay clinging to each other, his arms nearly squeezing the breath out of her.

When would we be able to hold each other again?

They laid in silence, weeping their joy and fear. The day turned bright, taking the morning mist with it. They tumbled onto the floor, laughing, tangled in the sheets.

He brushed aside a dark lock of hair as he'd done so many times before. She tried to memorize the gesture and lock it away. They gazed into each other's eyes. The sea in his stormy eyes looked like eternity, though time marched on. She loathed the day's end.

They donned their championship jitterbug clothes. After all, they'd met on the dance floor. She didn't think Jeannie would do it, but she actually skipped school—truant officer be damned. Charles and Violet, Marvin, Jeannie and Paddy met at Topsy's Diner. Paddy insisted on ditching with Jeannie.

They shoveled the goo and moo. Violet thought she'd be too nervous to eat, but finished her plate and half of Jeannie's. Jeannie, on the other hand, was nervous enough for both of them. She continually fiddled with Violet's hair and dress and kept hugging her.

"Isn't it swell?" Jeannie said for the billionth time that morning.

Marvin rolled his eyes and gave Charles a comical look.

Paddy patted Jeannie's hand and tried to grab the tab, but Charles beat him to it.

"Nothing doing. This is the wedding brunch after all, and it's my treat." He gave Violet a wink and a hug.

Violet didn't know how he did it, but Paddy got Johnny's car for the day. They piled into Johnny's ole jalopy and headed for the courthouse. The old building perched majestically on an island of manicured grass, the ocean a backdrop. The good thing about its odd location was you could always find parking. But as they drove down Grape and turned onto Harbor Drive, they were blocked.

A blue clad officer in white gloves directed traffic. He waved a few cars through but turned most around. Paddy pulled up alongside the officer.

"Ahhh Patrick McGuire, and what might ya be doing out here on the road, behind a wheel of a car I know tisn't yers. Shouldn't you be in school where ya belong?" His tone was part threatening, part teasing.

"Good Afternoon Officer O'Donnell." Paddy knew most of the cops in San Diego. He was related to half of them. "What's the rumpus?"

"Eh, don't give none of yer slang. Yer gonna hafta turn this jalopy around. Tare's a big back up at the courthouse due to the fleet moving out. Everybody's got the bright idea that they oughta get hitched before they go off to save the world."

"You don't say." Paddy smiled and gestured to Violet and Charles.

Officer O'Donnell looked them over. Jeannie and Paddy in front, Violet between two sailors in their dress whites, all of them grinning like a bunch of idiots. The fficer smacked his hand on his head.

"So waddaya say Danny, can you let us through?"

"That's Officer O'Donnell to you." Violet couldn't tell if the officer was ribbing Paddy or if he planned to get the truant officer on the radio. "Yer lucky I'm feeling magnanimous today. Now listen, I don't tink yer find any parking by the courthouse proper, but thare's an empty warehouse off a Harbor Drive and Hawthorne. Might be a little bit of a hike, but yer young, ya can do it. Now get outta here before I change me mind." He took off his hat and swatted the side of the car as Paddy inched forward.

Violet exhaled and took a big gulp of air. She squeezed Charles's arm.

Since Officer O'Donnell turned most the cars around the traffic eased, but as they got closer to the courthouse, the road became thick again with cars double and triple parked. They came to a standstill, hemmed in by oncoming traffic. Still a couple blocks away. Paddy laid on the horn to no avail. From where they sat, they could see a line snaking out of the courthouse, down the lawn, and all the way to the first boat dock.

The familiar bite of panic tugged at Violet's stomach, the double goo and moo gurgled unhappily. The smothering traffic fumes didn't help, either.

Jeannie read Violet's fear, reflected her panic, then took command. "Okay, this is what we're gonna do. Charles, you take Vee Vee and get in line. Marvin, you walk to the front and look for someone official, and see if there's some paperwork they can start filling out." She reached to the floor and brought up a pen and pencil. "Take these."

Violet gave her an incredulous look.

"What? They were with my schoolbooks. Paddy and I will go find the warehouse, park, and meet you back in line."

Charles and Marvin jumped to action. Both of them hopped out of the back. Charles held his hand out for Violet. She stood and let Charles scoop her up over the side of the car. He gently set her down on the pavement. She gave Jeannie a hug and Violet, Charles, and Ski moved toward the throng.

"I know you told me there are around five thousand people on your carrier, but this is strictly from Dixie? What gives?" Her nerves prickled, but she tried to stay up-beat.

"Well, Gorgeous, it's not only our ship, it's the battle group. You got your carriers, destroyers, frigates, cruisers. That's a lot of men leaving for...."He stopped and looked at her, putting his arms around her shoulders. He gave her another squeeze. "Ahhh Violet, I...."

"I think I'll run up ahead and see about the paperwork stuff." Marvin dashed up the line.

"Violet, why'd you have to go and make me fall in love with you?" He grinned from ear to ear.

"You? What about me? Why'd you have to be such a killer diller jitterbug and a sailor 'ta boot?" She gave him a quick kiss, and they continued to the end of the line.

Marvin came back and reported that they'd run out of forms but had sent a runner to the printers for more. He assured them it'd be okay by the time they got close, the forms would be back. Already, five couples had lined up behind them, their faces as hopeful as everyone's.

A fella up the line had a portable radio tuned to the local station loud enough to hear Harry James blowing his horn.

"Are you thinking what I'm thinking?" Charles pressed his forehead to Violet's. She tilted forward letting him take her waist and gave him her right hand. They leaned slightly and triple-stepped, swinging-out across the lawn. Another couple did the same. Like dominos, it went up the line until the music faded too soft for a jitterbug to hear the beat.

Paddy and Jeannie found Violet and Charles in mid dance. They joined in and Marvin clapped out a solid rhythm. *This life, this moment, feels good. Dancing in the clean, California air. A perfect day to get married.* The hushed ocean splashed on one side, the city purred on the other. Violet's shoes collected grass stains as she glided, turned, and swirled around the lawn. She and Charles couldn't help pulling bits of competition moves. She tumbled gracefully over his back, upside down, and around. She worried about staining his dress whites, but he chose his tricks wisely, aware of his body and uniform.

They danced their way up the line, taking breaks, changing partners, and making new friends with the other hopefuls. Finally, the sun dropped into the sea and they were told to go home. Time had run out. Jeannie chattered incessantly as they walked to the car, maybe afraid to stop talking, afraid of what the silence would bring.

Although disappointed, Violet was secure in the love she and Charles had for each other. She felt married in her heart and that belief would have to be enough for now. They piled back into Johnny's jalopy and drove toward base. Paddy pulled over a couple blocks from the gate to say their good-byes.

Violet gave Marvin a hug and a peck on the cheek. Jeannie hugged both fellas and wept dramatically. Charles and Violet started toward the gate, Jeannie began to follow, but Paddy held her hand and said they'd wait in the car. Marvin told Charles he'd see him pier-side and jogged ahead.

Charles and Violet walked slowly, his arm around her shoulder, hers around his waist. They pretended to be an old married couple out for an evening stroll.

"This is it, Gorgeous." They turned and faced each other. The breeze blew a curl across Violet's cheek. He tried to tuck it behind her ear, but the wind teased it out again. His finger caressed her cheek. She grabbed his hand and kissed softly. It would be a long time before he could tuck her hair again.

"You know I'll come back for you. And we'll write. And I'll send you surprises and…."

Violet stood on her toes and kissed his open mouth. All her love flowed into the kiss. Time had run out with nothing more any of them could do. He kissed her tenderly. She felt the whole of the world press into her lips. She hadn't wanted to cry, but silent tears slipped down her cheeks. He wiped them away for the last time. She watched him walk through the gate and disappear into a sea of white. Just when she thought she'd lost him, he turned around and waved. His face glowed like the sun. She let it fill her up, and then he was gone.

"And that's the last time I saw him."

June ~1990s
27. No More Nothin
(The Lucky Stars)

"That went well, don't you think?" Clara poured herself an ice-water after everyone had left June's apartment.

"I know you'd been thinking about starting a vintage magazine for a while. I'm glad to be part of it. Writing for you might be tricky around finals, but I'm honored to be the vintage society's secretary and do interviews and stories, too. School's going to take priority, though."

"Of course. We're all doing double duty. James will be music editor and layout. Larissa will work on ads. I'll do classic movie reviews, fashion, gossip, and will act as President of the the Lindy Society." Clara plopped down on June's rattan couch. "Do you think that's the right name? It might sound like we're an aviation group, especially with Lindberg Field being our airport."

"Not sure." June tapped her pencil against her teeth. "But the timing for a preservationist dance society and a swing dance magazine is perfect. Squirrel Nut Zippers, Big Bad Voodoo Daddy, and Royal Crown Revue are being played on alternative rock stations everywhere."

"How about V-Fads?"

"I don't get it?"

"Vintage Fashion and Dance Society? It has a nice vintage ring to it like V-day."

"I'm still not clear who our readers are." June cleaned up the extra glasses and dumped them in her sink. It'd been a little strange having everyone in her studio apartment, but they all fit and loved her burgeoning tropical décor. She sat back down across from Clara.

"People who like vintage fashion, but don't dance. Rockabillies who like the music, fashion, and history, but aren't big dancers. And the lindy hop community whose main focus is dance. We've got our work cut out for us. And I think you should interview Violet and get her jitterbug story."

"She's told us her story. I think I could write it from memory."

"She hasn't told us the whole story. Aren't you dying to know what happened to her sailor? I mean, they were supposed to get married. It's so mysterious."

"I think it's too personal. If she wanted to tell us, she would've." June pulled a loose thread on a throw pillow.

"Come on, June. You want to know as much as I do."

"You're right, but what if it's bad. What if he died?"

"I don't think he did. Wouldn't you have some kind of shrine or memorial or something? Pictures of him in uniform. No, I'm convinced something else happened."

"Why don't you do it? I'm no good at figuring out mysteries. Hell, I can't even find my biological grandmother."

"Still no leads? I think you need to break down and ask your granddad what agency they adopted your mom from. Tell him you're doing a project for school. Your mom doesn't even have to know. Besides," Clara added, "Violet adores you. She's practically adopted you."

"You think so? I actually like hanging out with her. And by the time she's done with me, I just might be able to sew us cute dresses." June pushed aside thoughts of her mom and Grampa. She couldn't explain to Clara about the accident and how fragile her mom was.

"Ooooo, that would make a good article too: Sewing Vintage. I like it. Good angle."

"Clara, you've got a one-tracked mind."

"What? I've got are several tracks: writing, editing, organizing, dancing, bossing." They laughed.

That was one of the things June admired about Clara. She knew her faults, embraced them, and poked fun at herself.

"And did you notice Kris?"

"Notice what?"

"He was totally making googly eyes at you through the entire meeting. Haven't you noticed him asking you to dance whenever you and James aren't working on contest stuff?"

"Not me. Nobody likes me. You all treat me like your kid sister."

"Oh no, do we? Well, maybe a little, but trust me. No one really thinks of you as a kid. June, you're a hottie."

"Me?" June blushed.

"You have blossomed under my tutelage." Clara teased. "No seriously, June, you better start living up to your potential. You've got the goods to break a lot of hearts."

"I don't know about that, but thanks. I've been spending so much time with work, school, dancing, and now sewing, I haven't had much time for boys."

"You and me both, sister." Clara put down her pen and looked thoughtful. "Maybe we need a girl's night out. Something other than swing dancing. Somewhere where a lot of boys will flirt with us. Maybe an 80s night downtown in the Gaslamp?"

"What would I wear? I've got nothing but vintage anymore. I think I've forgotten how to be normal. I wear vintage to school, to work, or new stuff that looks vintage. What the heck would I wear to meet normal boys?"

"We can still do our vintage. We just need to tone it down. Most guys don't notice. I mean they'll notice we don't look like all the other cookie-cutter girls, but that's to our advantage. Besides, men notice pretty, and we're pretty." She laughed.

"You're so conceited."

"No, I'm self-possessed and confident. There's a difference."

"I'm sure there is, but I'm not sure I know what that is. I could stand a little bit more confidence these days. Especially after Vertie lost interest. Too bad, he was such a cutie."

Clara shrugged. "Yeah, but, what do you think of Kris? You didn't say anything about it. Will you go out with him if he asks?"

"I don't know. He's all right, but I don't get any twinkles in my toes, you know?"

"Yeah, me either." Clara leaned back and tapped her pen against her cheek.

"Wait, did he already ask you out?"

"Sure, but it was a while ago. After my boyfriend and I broke up."

"You never talk much about it. Can I ask what happened?"

"Oh you can ask." June face scrunched up with hurt. "Just teasing, June. You don't have to take everything so seriously. I thought he was the one, except he didn't dance and really had no interest in learning. It eventually broke us." Clara took a long sip of water and looked away.

"You couldn't see yourself married to a man that didn't dance?"

Clara looked back and made a face. "No, I was perfectly happy dancing with my friends. I realized a long time ago that you can't get everything you need from one person, but he couldn't hang. I guess it drove him nuts, watching me dance with other guys. He was convinced they all wanted to take me home and were making love to me on the dance floor. We had too many stupid fights about it. Honestly, I couldn't give up dancing. I tried, I really did, but was miserable. In the end, I chose dancing over him. So I guess he wasn't the one after all."

"I'm sorry."

"Yeah, well, it sucks 'cuz it's slim pickings in our dance scene. All the cute ones are already coupled up. And the one's that aren't, are players. It's ridiculous." Clara stuffed her notes into her folder. "I did get asked out by one of my dad's clients. Well, he gave me his card and said he'd like to take me to dinner."

"Are you gonna go?"

"I don't know. He seems like a real grown-up. Let me help you wash up the dishes. It was my meeting, anyway."

"Sure, thanks." They walked the four steps to the sink. Clara filled the sink with water and soap. June took out a clean dishtowel. "What do you mean real grown-up?"

"Most of the time it's like our little subculture is suspended in time. Real grown-ups don't spend the amount of hours we do dressing up, dancing, watching old movies, and hanging out. Sometimes it feels artificial." She sighed and handed June a plate.

"Lots of people have lifestyle hobbies. Like surfing. When I first moved here, I couldn't believe people would go surfing before work, after work, and on the weekends. It seemed so teenager-ish to me, but people surf their entire lives, and they're real grown-ups with grown-up jobs."

"I know you're right. I'm just feeling off." Clara sighed, rewashing the same fork three times. "You know, I think I've been down since the whole James and Rose thing. I have to admit, I'm jealous."

"Do you still have feelings for James?"

"No, it's not like that. I'm jealous that I don't have "a" James, not that I don't have James. Does that make sense?"

June nodded and kept drying.

"I have a hard time when I don't have any admirers."

"But you've got me?" June smiled.

"I know, but that's not the same as male attention. I want the story book ending."

"Do you really think it exists?"

"Honestly, I'm banking on it."

June and James were three songs into their practice at his apartment when June wondered where Rose and Clara were. James had said Rose was coming down for the weekend. She pictured Rose sitting around James's apartment eating bon-bons and laughed to herself.

"What are you grinning about?" James sent her into a swing-out.

"Oh nothing, a funny image that popped into my head."

"Share."

She shook her head *no* as she spun in and readied for the next move—fireman's carry and toss. She bent and launched herself upward. He pulled and steadied her on his shoulder, but didn't toss her out. Instead, he twirled her in a circle like a professional wrestler.

"Ha, ha. Now you hafta tell me." James held her legs and let her head dangled toward the floor.

"Not fair." She dizzied, blood rushing to her face. "Put me down."

"Nope. Not 'til you tell me what's so funny."

"You're such a baby." June was determined not to give in. *If I hang upside down long enough will I pass out?*

"Oh, I'm the baby? I'm the baby? Well, if I'm the baby, you're the kid."

"I'm only a kid to you. I'll have you know, many guys find me attractive." June tried to wiggle herself into a position that wouldn't end up with her head crashing to the floor, but she couldn't find any leverage.

"Yeah. I bet they do." He set her down on the couch, a funny look crossed his face. She tried to stand but fuzzy snow floated in front of her eyes. She swayed.

"Whoa there, Kiddo." He caught her and held her steady.

"And stop calling me Kid." She gave him a playful punch.

"Okay, sor-ry. Are you okay to stand on your own?"

"Yeah. I was just dizzy there for a sec."

"Sit down for a minute." He guided her to the couch and sat her down, sitting down beside her, a respectable distance. "It's cool if you don't want to tell me what you were thinking. I know it's been different hanging out since Rose is around. I mean, it's great having her here. You and I don't talk like we used to. She's a good coach, though. Don't you think?"

"Sure." *He's acting weird again.* She couldn't keep up with his mood swings.

"So where is she, anyway? And where's Clara? I thought they were meeting us here tonight. Clara wanted me to find out more about Violet's mysterious past. I may have some information for her."

"Oh crap. I forgot to tell you." James smacked his forehead. "Clara called and said she decided to go out with a guy from the office. Said you'd know who she's talking about."

"Oh yeah, I do. Interesting."

"Why is that interesting?"

"No reason."

He rolled his eyes. "You're full of mysteries tonight aren't you? Clara's teaching you well. Did I ever tell you I like-liked Clara for about five minutes?"

"No, but she did."

"Really? She told you? What'd she say?"

"She said by the time she broke up with her boyfriend you were already in love with Rose and that was that."

"Hmmm."

"Hmmm, what? What's up with you tonight? Do you have feelings for Clara?" She sat up straight. She didn't want to admit it, but she didn't think Rose was right for him.

"Clara, no. We're good as friends, but...." he hesitated. "But can I tell you something and you won't tell anyone else?"

"Of course. You told me you were gonna ask Rose to marry

you and I didn't tell anyone, not even Clara."

"Yeah. She was kinda pissed about that. But come on, I couldn't tell Clara. She wouldn't have been able to keep herself from telling Rose. And I wanted the surprise element."

"So what's the big secret now?" June turned toward James, pulling one knee up, resting her chin on it.

"It's no secret. It's just that Rose hasn't told her family. That I asked her to marry me. That she said yes. That we're engaged." He looked down at his hand, pulling at a hangnail. "It's really bugging me."

"Why don't you tell her it's bugging you?"

"I can't talk to Rose that way. That's not how we work. But I can talk to you about anything." He looked up. "I've missed talking to you."

"Thanks. Soooo, what are you gonna do about it?"

"Nothing comes to mind."

"Did you just quote *Princess Bride*?"

"Yeah, do you know that movie?"

"Are you kidding. It's one of my faves?"

"Mine too. Rose thinks it's—what did she say—insipid."

"No way, she's crazy."

"I know." He smiled and hopped up. "Do you mind if we skip practice tonight? I'm not feeling it."

"No problem. I'll go work on my Violet story."

He gave her a hand up. "Did you discover something?"

"Maybe. When I was helping Violet clean the shop, we found a box of old airmail letters. She told me to throw them out, but I put them in my car. I haven't read them yet, but I'm dying to."

"Whoa, seriously? She told you to chuck the whole box? Seems like if there was any kind of story, she wouldn't tell you to chuck it?"

"Yeah, I don't know. Maybe the opposite is true. At any rate, Clara told me I have to be a detective."

"No offense, but you're not the detective type. You still haven't gotten any closer to finding your grandmother right?"

June squinted her eyes at James and grabbed her purse. They walked to the door. June wanted to take offense, but he was right. She was a thinker, an analyzer, but not much of a spy.

"You think if I pretend it's a box of old letters we found at a yard sale, it won't be like I'm invading Violet's privacy?"

"I don't know. Like I said, they can't be all that important if she's chucking them. Go for it."

"I was hoping Clara would help me read through them, though. There's about twenty of 'em."

"Bring them up. I'll order pizza and help you read them." He opened the door, leaning on it with his arm extended.

June ducked under his arm, then turned. "Wait, what about Rose? I thought she was coming over?"

"Yeah, I thought so, too." He ran his hand through his hair. "She and her sister were going to a Spa, and she was gonna sneak away and hang out with me. She must of gotten tied up with her sis."

"I'm sure that's it. Nothing to worry about."

"I'm not worried. Who said I was worried?" He shrugged. "Go get your crusty letter box and let's see what we can find."

June ran down and quickly retrieved the box. She set the letters on the coffee table, picking one at random. The delicate letter was lined with dark creases like spilled coffee, the paper a pale yellow onion skin. June was afraid the letter would crumble in her hands, but it was stronger than it looked. A lot like Violet. She read aloud.

My Dearest Violet,

I can hardly believe we've only been at sea XXX week. I think about you every moment I'm awake and see you in my dreams. I've tried to write everyday and started several letters, but have had trouble completing one. We work twelve hours on, twelve hours off and between sleeping and eating there's very little personal time. As I adjust to this routine I will write more, or at least write more coherently.

We've pulled in for a brief stay although I cannot tell you where. This has allowed me a day to rest and write. I'm surrounded by **XXXX** and when you get this letter and gift, it will give you an idea where I've been. I cannot even tell you the kind of weather we enjoy. I can say I've seen first-hand the devastation our enemies have inflicted on us and even though I wish I were with you, I know this is the right and necessary path.

I've placed the picture from the contest above my bunk and look at you every night before I sleep. I miss you as I've never missed anyone in my life. I miss your smile, your laugh, your touch, your smell. I miss your funny little apartment and I miss seeing your eyes light up when I'd walk into Mrs. Peppy's shop. I miss dancing with you. But mostly I miss holding you, feeling your skin against mine and waking with you in my arms. I close my eyes and imagine I'm lying next to you.

I've not received any letters from you, but they seem to come in batches and out of order. I think it's the same for outgoing. So please do not worry if some time goes by without getting a letter. Know that you are in my mind and heart and my words will find you when they can.

Love,

Charles

June gently rested the letter in her lap and looked at James. He looked as thoughtful as she felt. "So, what do you think of that one and what with all the XXXs?"

"The Navy censoring parts that might give away location? And, I think we, modern people, are losing our romance."

"In what way?" He surprised her again. June set the letter on the coffee table and turned toward him. He turned toward her.

"It seems like people, men, expressed themselves more eloquently than we do today, than I do. Even in old movies they're more lovey-dovey. It doesn't sound corny. Its sounds natural. If I talked to Rose that way, she'd roll her eyes and ask me what I'd been smoking."

"You think so? Have you tried? I wouldn't roll my eyes. I might if I didn't love the guy, but if I did, I'd love words like that. Maybe men have forgotten how to woo women. That's what I think. You know what else I think?"

"No June, what else do you think?"

"I think they've gotten lazy."

He rummaged around in the box and pulled out another. "So now you're calling me lazy?"

"I don't know. I've never dated you, have I?"

"No, I guess not."

There was an awkward silence.

James shifted and handed her the letter. "Read this one. More of the same with a lot of Xs. You want a beer?" He jumped up and headed to the kitchen before she answered.

"Sure, but wait, I'm not done talking about this letter." She yelled to him. "Don't you think it's very telling?"

He returned with two Sam Adams and handed her one. "You mean besides the fact that he's totally whipped?" He plopped down again, bouncing the cushions and June.

"It's pretty obvious they had a physical relationship. Don't you think? It sounds more serious than puppy love."

"Hell yeah. He asked her to marry him. What's the big deal?"

"I thought it seemed like a big deal." June lowered her voice. "It sounded like they were sleeping together. I thought girls in the 40s all wore white to their wedding."

"Oh, that's what you're getting at. Of course they were doing it." He rolled his eyes.

June gave James a playful glare. "Never mind. Give me the letter."

Dearest Violet,

Thank you for all your sweet letters and words of praise and encouragement. It really gives me strength. I got the lock of your hair. It still had your curl and smell. I keep it under my pillow.

Thank Paddy and Jeannie for their letters too, but please tell Jeannie not to send any more cookies. By the time they arrive, they're either in crumbs or moldy. I know you guys back home are on rations and I don't want you wasting them on me. Think of me when you're out shoveling the goo and moo. And don't forget my favorite Chop Suey joint. It better be in business when I get back.

I was glad to hear you made Jeannie's Prom dress. She sent a picture of them. They looked swell. I'm sorry I wasn't there to take you. You know I would've if I could.

Oh and thank you for the new pair of Jitterbug socks. They made me smile even if I have nowhere to dance. It wouldn't be the same unless I could dance with you, anyway.

I'm sure you heard things are a little tense and the **XXXXX** are marching through **XXXXX**. Two of my guys didn't come back. Don't worry about me, though, I'm safe. I just needed to tell somebody.

These were fellas I knew. I launched their planes off the deck. I was the last person to see them alive. It eats me up sometimes. Even though I'm on a boat full of people, I feel so alone. I miss you.

Don't read the papers and don't believe everything you hear. This big boat is hard to put down and we're surrounded by the XXXXXX XXXX. They're all out here to protect us.

I hoped we wouldn't be so long and I'd already be on my way back to you, but cleaning up this mess is going to take a lot longer than anyone thought. Keep praying for us and I'll be back twirling you around the floor and winning more Jitterbug contests. We'll grow old dancing together. It'll keep us young.

I miss you, I love you, I want you.

Yours,

Charles

"Whoa, the tone is totally different in this one. Is it my imagination or does he sound scared?" June shifted closer to James.

"I agree with you about the tone. It gets to me."

"What do you mean?"

"Those guys were my age or younger." He took a big swig of his beer.

"How is that different than the Gulf War? Loads of young men shipped-out over there."

"I don't know. I can't see signing up for a war like the Gulf War. I don't even get what that war's about. Those guys in WWII were literally saving the world." James got up and paced around his living room. "Hey, can I get you another beer?"

"Not yet, thanks." June took a sip. "Maybe that's why we

keep going back to WWII."

"What do you mean?"

"We seem enchanted with WWII. Violet said something about us, me and Clara, or maybe she meant our generation, being naïve. Parades, flag waving, and kissing sailors are all people want to remember."

"Seems better than remembering the carnage and desecration." He sat down again.

June had an icky, sick feeling in her stomach. She didn't want to think about young men dying. She looked at James and tried to picture him in battle. The thought of him bleeding on a battlefield almost brought her to tears. *How did Violet get through it?*

"We can't forget, can we?" June ran her finger along the bottle, drawing a line in the condensation. "We can't let war be all happy homecomings and victory parades. Look at how many didn't come home." Now she had to fight the tears. "Never mind. I don't want to talk about this anymore." She looked away.

"Let's change the subject." James scooted closer. "Have we learned anything useful for the story you wanna write?"

June took a long swig of beer then held the cold bottle to her temple. "We know that the letters stopped after about five and half months. We don't know if they broke up. If she found another guy. If he was killed in action or didn't come home. It's been a complete waste of time."

"I wouldn't say a complete waste of time. It's been cool hanging out again. Cheers." James held up his bottle. She clanked it with hers.

"I thought of a plan. I'm gonna get her drunk."

"Who are we going to get drunk?"

"Violet. I'm going to get her drunk and ask her Clara style."

"Do you think it'll work?"

"It'd take a miracle. Let's find out."

Violet ~ 1990s & 1940s
28. Search my Heart
(Chuck Willis)

June arrived at Violet's apartment first, her homemade chocolate chip cookies in a Tupperware bowl. Violet quickly transferred them to a pretty serving plate. Shortly thereafter, the gang seemed to converge at once. One of the kids brought a tray of sushi, of all things. Violet laughed to herself. Chips tumbled into waiting bowls and beers were sunk into an ice bath in one half of the sink.

Once food was done, the boys moved furniture for a makeshift dance floor. Violet smiled at the memory of doing the same thing so many years ago. Clara was thrilled with what she called the vintage glassware. She immediately began polishing and took over Violet's kitchen, helping herself to one of Violet's vintage aprons. Violet couldn't help admire her enthusiasm, chuckling every time Clara used the word vintage.

James carried Rose up the stairs, through the apartment, and set her down in the living room like a princess on a throne. Her foot was apparently too delicate for walking with crutches or a cane.

I don't know why, Rose seems very sweet, but something about that girl bothers me.

It'd been a long since Violet had entertained. Larissa helped Clara with the glassware. James and Marty set up speakers and a portable compact disc player. Samantha and Clara rearranged the snacks, which looked like a small wedding buffet. Kris and Dave had beers open and were already at the balcony, talking. In a small way, Violet felt like these were all her kids, or her grandkids. *Do they realize what a charmed life they lead?*

"Knock, knock." A tall, well-dressed gentleman—whom Violet had not met before—popped his head in the back door.

"Hello, Gary, Come on in." Clara continued to rinse and dry glasses. The young man crossed the room and took Larissa's spot beside Clara. Clara offered her cheek to him and received an intimate peck.

"Violet, this is Gary. Gary this is Violet." Clara gestured with her elbow.

He crossed to Violet and stuck out his hand. "Nice to meet you, Violet." His voice was a deep bass.

"Nice to meet you, and you can call me Vi."

"Gary, I'm almost done here. Go on out and introduce yourself. I'll be right behind you."

"Here, Gary, why don't I introduce you to the ki...to everyone." Gary wasn't quite the kid her jitterbugs were. *It should be interesting to see how he fits in.* Violet made the rounds with Gary, surprised that no one besides June had met him. He didn't quite fit, but he was friendly, polite, and easy on the eyes.

"So tell me, Gary, are you a jitterbug?" Violet asked.

"Excuse me, a what?" He looked around for Clara.

Clara strolled up behind them and locked her arm in his. He startled a little, but smiled wide. It was clear to see he was smitten.

"Nope. Gary doesn't dance. Yet." Clara's eyes twinkled.

He grinned nervously. "I'm willing to give it a go, but I warned you. I've got no rhythm and two left feet."

"Nonsense." Clara and Violet both said at once.

The three laughed and Gary relaxed. *Poor guy.* Violet felt for him walking into this crowd. They were genuinely nice people, but it would take a while for him to be accepted.

Clara, Larissa, and Marty kept everyone's glasses full and handed Violet a Vodka Martini with a twist. She hadn't had one in years and had forgotten how much she like them. Who would've thought Vodka Martinis would've ended up her drink of choice. She remembered the first time she tasted Vodka, right here in this room. The past bent like an accordion, squeezing together snapshots of her life.

The boys fired-up the music. Violet danced with all the fellas several times, but liked dancing with James best. He really knew how to dig the jive. She trusted that he wouldn't fling her out too hard or be too rough on her old bones. And when she watched June and James dance together, it brought tears to her eyes. She knew how they felt and envied them feeling it. She wanted to be a young woman on the dance floor, in love. June didn't realize it, but Violet could see it plain as day. She wondered if Rose and Clara could see it, too.

They danced, laughed, and drank enough that the world softened around the edges. Violet tired, but glowed with happiness. Eventually the night moved in reverse. As the sandwiches, chips, and cookies disappeared, the trays and bowls were washed and put away. The sink emptied of beer and bottles were stacked neatly in paper bags to be taken to blue recycle bins. Violet lazed languidly on the sofa, sipping her tea and watching the rewind. One by one, they gave kisses and hugs, said their goodnights, and drifted out the way they came.

"Hey, Vi, do you mind if I stay the night?" June asked. "I don't think I oughta drive."

"Of course not dear. I was going to suggest it. You know you're always welcome, but I think it would be best if Kris slept on the sofa."

June gave Violet a funny look and whispered in her ear. "I wasn't planning on asking him to stay. Thank you, but, that's not necessary. I'll walk him out and be back up."

June scooted toward the dining room where Kris lingered. *I hope I didn't embarrass them. I was trying to be open-minded.*

The familiar crackle of phone wires against the damp air kept her company, but became too chilly. She started to close the doors and glanced down to where June and Kris stood on the sidewalk below. She didn't mean to spy, but they looked like characters in an old movie. The street light cast a soft circle of light surrounding them like a spotlight. Violet could barely hear the murmur of words, but they both looked awkward. Kris had one hand in his pocket, the other raked through his hair. June held her hands behind her back, rolling her feet, and periodically losing her balance. She wobbled into him. He caught her. Violet thought he would take a cue and kiss her, but he didn't. They went back to talking and fidgeting.

This repeated for several minutes until he finally leaned and kissed her. Her hands flopped to her sides, and she leaned forward. Neither made any move toward a more passionate embrace. Violet shut the doors and sat back down before June bounced back through the living room.

"That was fast." It probably wasn't the best thing to say, but Violet couldn't help herself. She felt grandmotherly toward June and wanted something spectacular for her.

"Yeah, I guess."

"Would you like to join me for a cup of tea?"

"I shouldn't. I probably won't be able to sleep. But what the heck, it looks good and warm. I'm tired but not ready for sleep. Know what I mean?"

"I know just what you mean." Violet started to rise.

"Please don't get up. I've got it."

June helped herself to the cabinet and returned to the couch with a tea cup. Violet poured the hot liquid.

"I'm sorry I didn't put out any cream or sugar."

"No worries. You've taught me to like it black." June took a sip and grimaced. "Maybe a little sugar." She jumped up and darted to the kitchen. "Need anything?" she hollered across the apartment.

"No. Well, on second thought, are there any of those sandwiches left?"

"Sure, I'll bring us a couple."

June rebounded with the sugar bowl and two mini-sandwiches, one on each luncheon plate.

"Mmmmm, tastes even better now. I kind of like it when the bread gets a little stale. Don't you?"

"Sure, especially with tea."

"So, are things going well with Kris?"

"I guess so."

"Is it getting serious?"

June sighed. "I don't know. I thought I'd give it a try. He's a nice guy, not bad looking, dances. I don't know. But hey, feelings can change, and sometimes you learn to like people more, right?"

"I've never known it to be true." *I've loved, been loved, but only truly been in love with one man.*

"What about all those people with arranged marriages? I've read that statistically, those marriages fare the same, if not better, than romantic matches. They grow to love each other."

"Yes, but where's the passion?" Violet argued, but wondered if June may be more right than she.

"I don't know, hiding?" June blew across her tea. "Can I ask you something?"

"Sure honey, what?"

"What happened with your guy in the letters? I'm sorry. I didn't throw them out. I read them. I read them all. I was so curious, and you're so mysterious. I don't understand. All those letters, he sounded devoted to you. Was he killed?"

Violet recoiled and narrowed her eyes.

"I'm sorry." June stared intently into her teacup.

Violet chastised herself. *What right do I have to be angry? I gave the letters away. Told June to toss them.* She rubbed her tired eyes. "I don't know what happened to him."

"Do you want to tell me about him?"

"Yes, I think I do." Violet took a sip of tea. The deep ache slashed across her heart. "One day he quit writing. The letters stopped. I'd had long droughts with nothing, but then I would get a package of six or seven letters all at once. So, I didn't worry at first." Violet's hands shook. *How does this still hurt?* She continued, "Days turned into weeks, weeks into months, and something told me that there would be no more letters."

"That's terrible? Was he wounded or MIA?"

"I don't know."

"Didn't you try to find out?"

Violet shook her head. "Of course I did. I called. I wrote letters. Stood in line at military offices. I couldn't find anyone with answers. Even though I told them I was his fiancée, I was a non-entity to them. They had his mother as next of kin contact and could give out very little information to me. They couldn't even give me his mother's address or telephone exchange. I'd never felt more alone or depressed, except once."

The memory hit her hard as it washed over her. She told it to June...

Violet had asked not to see her. She asked them to take her. She didn't even want to know what it was, but when her baby girl heard her mother's voice, she stopped crying. Violet couldn't keep her eyes from searching the void created by the baby's hushed sobs. Violet locked eyes with the baby's bright sea green eyes — Charles's eyes. It felt like a sharp hooked punctured her insides.

"Please." Violet stretched out her arms. The nurse and doctor exchanged a look then laid the baby in her arms. Her daughter was tiny, pink, and breathtaking. She looked like her father.

The loneliness and sorrow overwhelmed Violet. She began to cry, dripping large drops across the baby's perfect face. One tiny, flawless hand unwound from the tightly wrapped cocoon. She swept it across Violet's face, as if to banish her tears. Violet's body shook with sobs. She kissed the babe's small hand, her tiny fingernails, eyelids, hair, cheeks, lips, ears, her tiny baby brows, sobbing into her wrappings. The nurse grew alarmed and tugged the baby out of Violet's arms. Waves of misery pulled Violet down into a bottomless pit.

The clatter of metal and the smell of alcohol preceded a sharp jab in her arm. The nurse's words turned into meaningless drivel. All she wanted was for Charles to hold her. Charles to be there. Charles to be alive. Charles to be the father he was meant to be, and for her to be his wife. Why couldn't she keep anything in her life that she loved?

Mrs. Peppy knew. Violet didn't know when she knew, but she remembered when Mrs. Peppy finally told her she had to start making bigger clothes. For a while Violet had been ecstatic, scared, and excited. Mrs. Peppy flatly insisted Violet move in with her.

Only after the letters stopped did Mrs. Peppy ever talk to Violet about it. Mrs. Peppy asked her straight out if she wanted to have a bastard. The word slapped Violet in the face, but sobered her to the reality that this was not something she could keep secret for much longer. She couldn't think of the baby growing inside her as a bastard. Surely if Charles were dead, she would've felt it. If he were wounded, he'd come back to her.

The truth skirted her consciousness until she could no longer hide it from herself. If she chose to keep the baby, it would be a bastard. She would be everything they said about her, just as wicked as her mother. All the taunts and whispers behind her back would be vindicated.

What could she give a child? She was a dropout living on the kindness of Mrs. Peppy. How long would that last? If she only knew why the letters stopped. If she had married Charles. If she had a mother who hadn't been so selfish. Violet vowed not to be selfish like her mother.

Mrs. Peppy arranged everything. Violet went to the border to a Catholic birthing house where they took unwed mothers. She couldn't believe she was an unwed mother. It sounded so unseemly. She wasn't a bad girl. She wasn't an able-grable. She was engaged. She was...an unwed mother.

Violet's body ached in places she didn't know existed. She felt stretched thin and filled with lead. When she sat up in bed, stitches tugged in a place she knew she'd never use again. Her entire body felt like it'd been dropped from a three-story building. She gingerly twisted her legs to the side of the bed. The pain blackened her vision for a second, and she had to stifle a loud gasp not to awaken the other sleeping mothers. Her legs wobbled but were steady enough as she dressed and grabbed her few possessions: a worn copy of *The Good Earth* and her pocketbook.

The heavens rained for five days straight, unusual, even for a wet winter. The streets, buildings, and cars washed clean. The sun glowed cheerful and bright, mocking her pain. With each bump in the road, the bus lurched and sent new spasms of pain through Violet's body.

A two-week stay was customary, longer if you wanted to help the others, but she couldn't. She snuck out like a thief unable to stay another second. A deep and searing pain sliced her soul whenever she thought of those tiny little fingers, delicate lips, and sea green eyes.

"June, don't look at me like that. It was different when I was a young girl." *I knew I should've kept my mouth shut.* Violet shifted in her seat and took another sip of tea. The guilt crawled across her heart and deepened the pain.

"No, no it's not that." Tears glistened in June's eyes. "I have no idea what it must've been like for you. I think you're very brave. No, it's something else entirely. It's my mother. She was adopted. From San Diego. I've been looking...and what if...I mean, how cool would it be. Violet, what if you're my grandmother?"

June ~ 1990s
29. Rock This Town
(Brian Setzer Orchestra)

Racks of vintage clothing swayed like colorful hedges. Fully dressed and coiffured models waited nervously, the air thick with hairspray, pressed gabardine, and steamed wool.

"Isn't this exciting? I can't believe the launch party for Swivel Magazine came together so smoothly." June exclaimed to Amy.

"I still wish you and James were doing the contest, but I get why. It would look like nepotismism if you won."

They hustled out of the prep room across long corridors to look for Clara to let her know the models were ready for the fashion show. Communication would've been easier with walky-talkies, but June thought it great fun running through the hotel halls with Amy.

With the launch of the magazine—fashion show, dance contest, and big band dance—Amy had flown out to be distracted from her recent break-up. The magazine had turned out better than everyone expected. James had done an amazing job with the layout, and June was pleased with her first published article. Violet graciously let her write about the 1942 Spring Fling Swing Contest. June had found an archive photo to go with it. She only wished Violet could've been at the event.

"Hi, Clara's sent me to check in." Kris met June and Amy in the hall. "How's it going? You guys ready on your end?"

"Yup, everything looks good. Our girls are all set, but one of the vintage shops forgot their script. Clara's gonna have to wing it for Wear it Again Sam's," June said.

"Oh that's not good." Kris frowned.

"Clara'll be fine. She knows more about vintage clothes than anyone. Go tell her, and I'll get the girls lined up behind the screen like we rehearsed."

She handed him the scripts for the other two vintage stores, and the three of them headed back the way they came.

Amy grabbed June's arm. "Kris is hot."

"You think so?"

"Totally. Too bad you've got your hooks into him." She laughed. "I could go for him."

"I'm not sure it's really going anywhere with us. We feel more like friends."

"Oh really? I mean, ahhh that's too bad." Amy looped her arm in June's. June rolled her eyes, and they burst into giggles.

They watched from the wings as Clara—perched on the edge of the stage—emceed from behind the lectern. The lanky waifs sauntered across the portable parquet floor. Although they were beautiful, most vintage clothing was made for smaller women or at least shorter ones. June took comfort in that.

On their first pass, the models pranced and displayed casual playwear: overalls, jumpers, halters, and shorts outfits. Dapper Dans took the floor next, in an array of beach and sportswear. Their very own James sauntered across the floor with all the panache and confidence of the professional models, a fill-in for a no-show. Although he was a tad shorter than the others, the clothes fit him perfectly. June admired the way the tailored pants flattered his figure, and the Tiki barkcloth shirt fit his broad shoulders. Amy nudged her.

"What?" June raised her brows.

"Nothing. Just that you're practically drooling."

"I am not. He's my friend. He's doing a good job out there. I'm proud of him." June turned back to watch the show.

Femme fatales flounce forward in swishy rayon dresses with puffy sleeves, Kate Hepburn trouser ensembles, and Rosalind

Russell suits. The long sleeve blouses sported whimsical patterns, long collars, and full sleeves—buttoned cuffs bound with Bakelite.

The audience clapped loudly with many finger pointing, oohs and aahs.

The gents trailed the ladies, again. This time in evening wear. June had seen suited men in old movies, but in person—on the young models, they were not only handsome—they were gorgeous.

"I wonder if any of those guys dances?" June whispered to Amy. "Maybe I could teach them."

"I'm trying to pay attention." Amy giggled.

In a dramatic twist, the men froze and turned into vintage mannequins. The women, in luscious ball gowns, slithered back onto the floor, weaving through the posed men. The effect was eerie, but choreographed magic, Clara brilliance.

June lusted over an elegant full length, pink satin gown with matching bolero. It'd be perfect to wear to a wedding, maybe James's and Rose's. *If they ever set a date. If Rose ever told her father.* June liked Rose, but she didn't like the way she treated James. *He deserves better.*

After the fashion show and the dance contest, the night marinated in laughter, dancing, drinking, and more dancing. Bill Elliot's Swing Orchestra ignited the night like a four alarm fire. Trumpeters saluted with white muting cones, blinking to the beat. Singers crooned around an old-timey mic, and the lead vocalist preened like a canary in a yellow full-length gown, a ringer for Helen Forest.

Low lit chandeliers cast soft prisms around the edges of the room. Martini and fat-bottomed Daiquiri glasses littered the tables. The packed floor swirled with well-dressed bodies. Not all vintage, but not a sweat pant or blue-jeaned dancer in sight. June was satisfied.

If I squint my eyes, I could almost believe I'm in a 1940s Dance

Hall. I just wish Violet were here to see it.

"I'm coming, I'm coming." June ran to her phone smashing her toe into the edge of the chair as she grabbed the receiver. "Hello."

"Good morning." Amy greeted her in a sing-song voice. "Wakey, wakey."

"I'm awake. I have to work in an hour. What's up Ame?" They'd been talking more since Amy's visit last month at the Swivel launch party. *Sometimes you have to see someone again to realize how much you missed them.*

"I just called to see how you were doing. I'm having June withdrawals."

"Well, except for almost ripping off my toe, I'm good."

"We can't have that. It's your turn to visit me, and I've found the perfect excuse. Big Sandy is playing the Rhythm Room and Arizona Swing Jam Productions are..."

"The what?" June sat down and inspected her toe.

"That's right you don't know about them. After you moved, the scene really snowballed. Do you remember a guy named Stan? He started beginner classes right after we moved up to intermediate."

"Yeah, I do. He gave me a hell of a dance at my going-away, birthday jam."

"That's him. Anyway, he got really good, really fast. Like us, he did some traveling and took private lessons. He recently started his own beginner class and is bringing in bands and teachers from all over. We, of course, stayed loyal to Saul."

"Ah, how is Saul?"

"Good, but listen. Stan's got the hook up for bringing in music. He's promoting this Big Sandy gig with a dance contest. The winners win fifty bucks, free tickets to his classes for a month, and free admission to the next Arizona Swing Slam Production.

So, I was thinking that this would be the perfect opportunity for you to visit and strut your stuff. You know, shake out your nerves in front of a crowd before the International Jitterbug Contest. Whaddaya say?"

"I'm not sure I'm ready, but I do need the practice. I'll check with the gang and see who can go. When is it?"

"Two weeks from today. I know your family lives here, but if you need a place, you're welcome to flop on my couch."

"Thanks, but my mom would totally kill me if I came home and didn't stay with her."

"The offer's open to Clara, James, or any of your friends. We'll have a party at my place for sure. There's so many new people I want you to meet."

"Is there something you're not telling me?"

Amy giggled. "I'm not sure where this is going. So, I wasn't going to say anything, but, I did meet someone."

"Ah ha, I knew it. Tell me more."

"I met him at a car show. He's a friend of Chad's."

"What?" June yelled. "I thought we hated Chad?"

"Not really. Once I got over myself, I realized he's a good friend, just not a good boyfriend for me. And I adore his new girlfriend. We all hang out together."

"That's so weird."

"I know."

"Call me back soon, so I can start planning. Plus I need to sign you up for the contest ahead of time. I'll get with Stan and put you and James on the list."

"Wait 'till I talk to James at least. I don't know if he'll be into it or not. I'm sure he'll have to check with Rose."

"I almost forgot. How's Kris?"

"Kris?"

"You know, that guy you're dating."

"Okay." June twirled the phone cord in her finger.

"Hmmm."

"Hmmm what?"

"I don't know, but you need to figure that out. If you're single when you get here, I could introduce you to some hot prospects."

"Amy." June smiled to herself. "I'll call you as soon as I have a plan."

"Well?" June asked.

James sat next to Rose on Larissa and Marty's couch, holding hands. June didn't know why, but it struck her as phony. *Maybe because I feel phony, cozied up with Kris.* Larissa wiped cup rings and scooted coasters under glasses, watching Marty's reaction. If he was in, she was in. Dave and Samantha had thoughtful expressions, and Clara looked like the cat that ate the canary.

"I was waiting for the right opportunity to spring this on you all, and this couldn't be more perfect." Clara's lips curved into a smile. Her eyes sparkled. "Some of us will have to go to Phoenix and while we're there, we'll have to take a side trip to Tucson."

"Okay drama queen what gives? What's in Tucson?" James asked.

"It's not what. It's who." She purred.

"Still lost." June took a sip of her drink.

Clara sighed loudly. "Have you people no sense of mystery? Adventure? Romance? I found him."

"Who?" Larissa sat on the arm of the chair next to Marty.

"Charles Mangino."

"Who?" Kris asked.

"Vi's Jitterbug," June whispered.

Violet ~ 1940s & 1990s
30. Walkin' Away with my Heart
(Betty Hutton)

Powdery sand dusted their shoes beige as they shuffled around Mission Beach Amusement Center. Violet, Charles, Jeannie and Paddy came for the roller coaster, but looking up at the towering monstrosity, Violet wasn't so sure. The smell of fresh cotton candy momentarily overpowered the fishy sea breeze, distracting her from the ride. Her mouth watered, and she followed her nose.

"I take it you like cotton candy, Vi?" Charles grinned, amused.

"I can't pass it up. I love to let it melt on my tongue into a pool of sugary goodness." Violet watched the worker catch the edible pink clouds on a paper cone as the wispy webs spun out of the drum.

"Sounds tasty. Does anyone else want any? Pat? Jeannie?" He reached into his pocket for coins.

"Thanks." Jeannie made a face. "But it'd be gruesome to eat all that. You wanna share Vee Vee?"

"Sure Jean. Don't you fella's want any?"

"Negative. I'm saving my stomach for a corn dog and fries," Paddy replied.

Violet looked to Charles. He patted his stomach. "Yeah, me too."

"You fellas better not eat that stuff before we go on the coaster. Come on. Let's get in line. Vee Vee and I can eat our spun sugar before we reach to the front."

Violet frowned at the skeletal crisscrossing beams above her.

The riders raised their hands when the cart tacked to the top and plummeted toward the ground. Violet shivered.

Charles squeezed her shoulder, pulled her to his side, and rubbed her arm. "It'll be fun. I won't let anything bad happen to you." He kissed the top of her head. She trudged toward the line.

"I can't believe you've never been on the Giant Dipper. The entire Glee Club came here. Don't you remember? You were in Glee Club." Jeannie stopped. "Never mind."

Violet had already left school by that time.

The line moved faster than she wanted it to. They made idle small talk, and Charles stole earlobe kisses when no one was watching. Every time her fear started to rise, he breathed softly into her ear or fixed her hair when it stuck to her sugared mouth. She wanted to kiss his hand, each of his fingers, the crook of his elbow, work her way to his mouth, but she behaved.

His distraction worked. By the time it was their turn to board, her fear was almost forgotten. The cart pulled to a stop in front of them. They waited while flushed passengers disembarked. Jeannie and Paddy jumped in, gesturing wildly for them to hurry.

"Miss, miss."

"Me?" Violet asked the man with the snaggle-tooth grin.

"Are you getting on or not?" He grumbled. "You're holding up the line. I haven't got all day here."

"Yeah, what's the hold-up?" someone yelled from behind.

"Move it or lose it toots," someone else shouted.

No. No. No. No. I can't do it. Her stomach hurt. Her head dizzy.

"You guys go on." Charles pulled Violet close. "I need to find an ameche. I promised I'd call Ski and let him know where to meet us. He oughtta be off watch by now. We'll catch the next one. Have fun."

Eager passengers pushed by Violet and Charles and scrambled into the seat behind Jeannie and Paddy. Violet waved at her friends and leaned into Charles. *He saved me.* Jeannie scowled, but traded her scowl for a smile when Paddy wrapped his arm around her shoulder and pulled her close.

"Where should we meet?" Jeannie hollered as the car lurched forward.

"Corndogs?" Violet yelled, uncertain if she'd heard.

Violet threw her arms around Charles's neck and planted a happy kiss on his mouth. She didn't mean to linger, but a pack of marines hooted and whistled at them. Charles smiled under her kiss, broke the spell, and extricated her arms from around his neck.

"We've got a couple minutes until they catch up to us. What should we do?" he asked.

"I don't know. More of what we were doing?"

He rolled his eyes and tugged her ponytail. They walked toward the midway games.

"Hey, how 'bout that?" Violet pointed to the High Striker attraction. "Let's see how strong a man you are." She squished his bicep. He flexed in response, his arm becoming steel. "Think you can ring that bell?"

"Of course I can. They don't send us to boot camp for nothing. I'm an ideal specimen of military trained perfection."

He struck a strong man pose, encouraging her to feel his biceps again. She tingled as she ran her hand across his tight jumper. *He's beautiful.*

They watched and waited as a young bobby-soxer attempted to ring the bell. He swung the mallet high over his head, the awkward weight made him stagger to keep his balance. He grazed the target and only made it one third up the mark.

"Step right up. Step right up. Who's strong and brave? Who can ring the bell? Show the little lady what you're made of."

Charles dug in his pocket and handed the man a dime. Violet stood back to watch. Charles raised his eyebrows and then gave her a wink. His swing was tight and controlled, arcing to the very apex, then boring straight down to hit the target with explosive force. They watched the ball go up, up, up and rejoiced as it rang the bell. Scattered applause sprinkled across the spectators. Violet skipped into his arms and gave him a congratulatory hug.

"You'll always be my strong man."

His smile dissolved into a grimace. "What if...."

"What if what?"

"What if I don't end up being your strong man? What if I come back to you weak or broken?" he whispered.

"Don't be silly. That won't happen to you."

"But, what if?"

Violet woke with a jolt and chastised herself for falling asleep on such a short bus ride. The driver announced they'd crossed the border and needed to exit. He had a return trip to make, and Violet had business on this side.

She tried to shake the sharp images of her dream, but the memory left her swimming in love and regret. *There's no going back. I need to go forward and see what I can find.* She ached at the possibility of June's revelation. *Could I be June's grandmother?* In a short time, she'd grown to love June, love her company, her insight, her energy, her presence. She'd brought so much life back to her. June was a gift she didn't deserve.

But, if June was Violet's granddaughter, that would make June's mother, her baby, now a grown woman. Unexpected tears ran down Violet's cheeks. She thought of what she'd missed, what could've been...

I keep myself from running to catch her as she lets go of the chair, wobbling, standing free on chubby legs, taking her first real steps, padding the short distance into my proud waiting arms.

Her tiny warm hand slips out of mine on her first day of school, both mother and daughter feign brave smiles for each other.

The first time she gets her heart broken, folding her into my arms, stroking her hair telling her over and over again how wonderful she is and that there's nothing wrong with her.

I fix a ringlet that falls teasingly around her nervous face and pull a bobby-pin from my own hair, tucking her hair back in place. Tugging the white satin, fanning it out behind her, my hands held by hers, she whispers, "I love you, mom."

A lifetime of memories lost. A life not hers to claim, but her soul ached for it. The life she abandoned. The baby girl must've grown up to be a fine woman to raise a daughter as wonderful as June. Violet knew she had no part in that and no right to it.

Would June's mother – could June's mother – forgive me?

The original building remained, but under new stucco and added arches. It looked nothing like it did when she was there. Violet's soft shoes padded down the breezeway. She took a right and found the older familiar part, where they now housed the archives. She thought being back would break something in her, but she felt excitement and hope, a chance at redemption.

She pushed open the Records door.

"Hola, como puedo ayudar te?"

She didn't know why she was expecting English. She was, after all in Mexico. All the years living close to the border she'd never learned more than a few phrases, hardly enough to request what she needed.

"Habla Ingles?" Violet asked.

"No, un momento, por favor."

The girl disappeared behind pristine rows of long, gunmetal gray cabinets. Violet was sure she would find her answers in this organized room. Another woman waddled out from the door.

"Hi, how can I help you?"

Violet eyed the small woman's protruding belly. She wanted to reach out to her, give her advice, tell her not to give it up, but she knew nothing of the girl's story. She was here for her own.

Violet smiled into the young woman's face. She didn't know where to start, so she started at the beginning.

June ~ 1990s
31. Let Me In
(Steve Lucky and the Rhumba Bums)

"Could you please pass the mashed potatoes?" James asked as he sat across from June in the Andersen's formal dining room.

"I take it you like my mom's cooking?"

"Uh, yeah. Mrs. Andersen, this is really good. Can you pass the green beans too, please?" He piled mounds of potatoes.

June laughed out loud. "James, you act like you haven't eaten in years."

"I haven't eaten anything homemade in years. This is killer. Thanks again for having me." He continued to shovel huge spoonfuls of gravy-covered mashed potatoes into his mouth.

"I've always said, a way to a man's heart is through his stomach." Junes mother slid the green beans toward James.

"Isn't that a little old-fashioned and counter-productive to the women's movement?" June replied.

"Ack, whatever." Her mom waved her off. "June, June, June. I remember when I was your age, those kind of things were important. You'd be surprised at how that changes." Her dad chuckled and shook his head.

"I don't want to argue, but I will say it's good to have choices."

"Choices are all about trading freedoms." Her mother countered. "Nothing is gained without losing something else."

James looked from June to her mom. Her dad leaned over to James. "Best not to get in the middle of this." June's dad winked and helped himself to more gravy.

"Give me an example? I'm not following," June asked.

"If a woman has the choice to work or not work and she chooses to work, she gives up the choice of staying home with her children and the joys of being a homemaker."

"Hmph, how joyous is it to scrub toilets, Mom, really?"

"No job is perfect. How joyous is working overtime, or on a holiday, or when you're sick or when your boss is an ass?"

June sighed. "It's not the same. You get paid for dealing with mean bosses."

"Well honey, you get paid in other ways that may not be monetary, but are payment all the same."

"In hugs?"

"There's no better currency on earth." Her mom sighed. "Actually, it's very rewarding until you children grow up and become ungrateful teenagers." She suppressed a smile.

"All right, I give. For now."

"James, can I get you another biscuit?" her mom asked.

"No thanks. I think I'm actually getting full."

"Finally." June shook her head and laughed.

"You've been great. Thanks for the dinner and thanks for letting me crash in your guest room."

It used to be Julian's room.

"We're very happy to meet one of June's San Diego friends. So, what are your plans for the weekend?"

"Amy's got a—you remember Amy, right mom?"

"The girl with the pink in her hair?"

"Yup. Well, she's having a little dance party at her apartment tonight, so we're gonna head over there."

"Is there going to be drinking?" her mom asked. "Do you drink, James?"

"Mom!"

"I do like a little beer now and again, but I'm of legal age, twenty-two, and I'd never drink and drive," he replied. "Your daughter is safe with me."

June was mortified. She knew staying with her parents was going to be lame, but this was the limit. They had to get out of there, but James was still eating. At least James was the only one subjected to her parents. No one else could make the trip. She was still surprised Rose didn't pitch a fit and wondered what James told Rose. She didn't ask.

"And tomorrow, we're going to find this old jitterbug guy," June said. "Remember the lady I told you about who made the dress? The one I found in the thrift store?"

"You know honey, we donate to the thrift stores."

June scowled and continued. "Clara found her old dance partner, and we're going to interview him for the magazine."

June didn't mention anything to her Mom about Violet possibly being her grandmother. *It's one thing for Violet to be my grandmother, but something else for Violet to be my mom's mother.*

"That sounds nice," her mom replied.

"And then we're going to see Big Sandy and enter a dance contest," James interjected between mouthfuls.

"Right, June said something about that. Did you get us tickets?" her dad asked.

The heat rushed to June's face, and she shot her dad a look.

"You don't need advance tickets. You guys are welcome to come."

What is he thinking? I don't want my parents there. I'm nervous enough. We're not dancing at the State Fair for Pete's sakes. Time to go.

"Let me do the cleanup." June rose and began collecting plates and silverware.

"No, don't worry about it, sweetheart. I've got it. You kids go to your party. I'll see you in the morning."

"At least let us help clear the table." James sopped the rest of his gravy with his remaining biscuit. His plate was spotless. *Maybe there is something to what my mom said.*

"No arguing. Now you kids get."

"Thanks, Mom." June kissed her. "See ya, Dad." She kissed him, feeling babyish in front of James, but couldn't deny them.

"Thanks again, Mr. and Mrs. Andersen."

"Now James, I told you to call me Charlene. Really, you make me feel ancient."

"Okay thanks, Charlene and Mike."

It'd been a while since June had heard her parents called by their names. Sometime she forgot they were people outside of being Mom and Dad. She grabbed her sweater and headed out the door with James.

"You're parents are totally cool."

"Really?"

"Totally."

Amy's dance party was in full swing when June and James arrived. June greeted familiar faces—introducing James—and danced with old friends. Her Phoenix friends complimented her dancing and commented on how she was one of those vintage dancers now. She glowed. She'd become all the things she wanted to be. Almost.

The most surprising guests were Nancy and Elroy. June had never forgotten them. They were the reason she'd learned to dance in the first place. She didn't know why she was nervous talking to Nancy. When she first saw them dance, she thought they were the epitome of vintage style. They still impressed the crowd with tricks and aerials, but paled in comparison to the L.A. dancers' footwork.

When Nancy said she and Elroy were entering the contest at the Big Sandy show, June became self-conscious. She noticed Nancy watching her as she danced with James. She wasn't dancing her best on the carpeting, but James assured her, it was good since they didn't want to tip their hand, anyway. Let Nancy think she was better. They'd whomp them tomorrow night. June wasn't so sure.

The infamous Stan Conner — promoter extraordinaire — finally made an appearance. He worked the room like a man running for office, making sure to say hi to everyone there. He invited June and James to teach a weekend workshop, maybe Balboa or Shag or both? They didn't have any Bal or Shag teachers in Phoenix. Stan and James exchanged numbers. Then he asked June for a dance.

She didn't know what she was expecting, but it was clear why he'd risen to the top. He was good. Not as good as James, but the best she'd danced with all night. And as far as she could tell, Amy had assembled the elite of the Phoenix swing scene. By the end of the night, they all shed their shoes and reveled in a crazy, Lindy/Bal/Shag sock hop.

The next morning, they drove to Tucson and found Charles Mangino at an old farmhouse nestled in the shadow of Mt. Lemmon. He sat on the wrap-around porch in an old metal glider. When they approached, he stood and wobbled, leaning on his cane before settling into a balanced stance.

A touch shorter than James, with a full head of silver hair, he looked like he hadn't changed his style since 1942. June was a terrible judge of age, but it was hard to believe he'd fought in WWII. Harder still to believe, if Violet could be her grandmother, then this man could be her grandfather. Her stomach fluttered with hope and trepidation.

"Howdy. Well, come on up. You must be the kids from the magazine? I talked with a gal named Clara. She said she'd be sending you. Why you'd want to bother with an old codger like me is a wonder, but here I am. I guess you know my name is Charles, but you can call me Chas."

"Nice to meetcha. I'm James, and this is June." Charles and James shook hands.

Why am I so nervous? Are we going behind Violet's back?

"It's really nice to meet you." Charles shook June's hand. His grip was firm, but felt strange. Then she realized two fingers were missing on his right hand. She'd never met anyone with missing body parts. Sorrow and guilt washed over her. She felt like they were trespassing.

"Um, we, um." She shuffled through her notepad and pulled out a Xerox of an old newspaper clipping. Charles's and Violet's youthful smiles were frozen in time.

"We found this picture and article in an archive. This is you isn't it, winners of the First Annual Spring Fling Swing Jitterbug Contest?" James asked.

She handed the Xerox to him, her hand shaking, slightly.

"I'll be damned. Pardon my French." He nodded to June and sat down with a thud, the glider rocked like a canoe. He ran his hand through his hair. A host of emotions played across his face.

"That's me all right. And looky here…" His face softened. He touched the photograph. "You know who this is?"

James and June exchanged a look. They'd already discussed not bringing up Violet unless he did. June felt like she was walking across a rickety bridge, waiting for a rotten plank to break beneath her feet.

"It says Violet Mangino," James replied, much better at subterfuge than June.

"That is does. But I bet you didn't find her." He rubbed his temples. "She never got to be her," he said, almost to himself. He paused and took a deep breath. "Our battlegroup shipped out before we could say our I Dos. There's not a day that goes by that I don't think about that gal."

"Why didn't you try to find her?" June blurted.

James shot her a look, but Charles didn't see it.

"Well that's a long story. You sure that's something your readers would be interested in?"

"Yes," James answered. June had forgotten about the pretense of the magazine.

Charles gave them a funny look and leaned back. June and James fell into the past as Charles retold and relived a wartime nightmare....

"I heard the Zeroes before I saw them and launched my birds as fast as I could, but not fast enough. A Jap torpedo hit and the ship listed to port. I was knocked off my feet. Couldn't see a damn thing. My head buzzed. I opened my eyes, looked sideways. The Wildcat had been hit, and her fuel tank had blown. Lieutenant Ingraham was trapped in his bird, unconscious. A wall of fire cut him off from me. His canopy offered some protection, but it was only a matter of time before he roasted like a cooked goose, and the bombs loaded on his bird exploded. If those went up, God help us.

"The Crash Crew pumped salt water, changing the black smoke to white. The air was thick with the scent of sulfur and burning rubber. Another Jap bomb rocked the carrier. I was thrown to the deck. When I looked up, flames engulfed the Crash Crew. They burned to a crisp, and there wasn't a damn thing I could do about it. Men ran in different directions unsure which fire to put out first.

"My training took over. I got the other salt hose and put a man on charging, one on the nozzle, the rest to hold the length. As soon as the hose was plump with water, I gave the go-ahead. They blasted a heavy rain of seawater and cleared a path to the bird.

"As much as I wanted Ingraham out, I wanted the ordnance off the plane and off our boat. I grabbed two Ordies, Hale and Shepherd, and told them to follow me. Shepherd shouted that we needed at least one more guy to unload and move the thousand pound bombs. I didn't have another guy.

"The three of us raced across the deck and reached the plane.

The Wildcat's paint blistered. Toxic fumes burned my nose and blurred my eyes. Shepherd banged on the drop release with a hammer. We got one bomb on the cart, braced our boots against the charred deck, and heaved. The cart rolled toward the bomb chutes, and we dropped the first into the ocean.

"The ship rocked again. Hale tumbled over the side, but grabbed the cart handle. I grabbed the other end and threw myself to the deck, twisted away from the edge, and pulled the cart with Hale into reach.

"We regrouped and worked the second ordnance down the chute. We still had to save the Lieutenant. I popped the canopy and pulled Ingraham out of the cockpit. Hale grabbed his feet. I took his shoulders. His head lolled against my arm, his face as young as mine. I thought about the charred guys I couldn't save, their parents getting the telegram. We had to save Ingraham. I began to lift.

"The sound of artillery rang in my ears. Then a searing pain went through my leg. White hot. Then cold. Then nothing. Nothing 'till I woke up in the hospital. My leg gone. My fingers gone. Parts of me gone forever."

Charles stared out at the mountain in silence. Pain, horror, and deep sorrow played across his face. Beads of sweat stood out across his forehead, his cheeks wet with tears. He raked a handkerchief across his face and blew his nose. His hands shook.

"What happened to Ingraham. Did you save him?" James blurted.

Charles nodded. "Yeah. Him I saved. Not a scratch on him. Went on to be a war hero with top honors." He closed his eyes. His whole body shook.

June and James exchanged a look.

"Not all parades and happy homecomings," June whispered.

Charles nodded and regained his composure. The past tucked

back into the past.

James reached out and squeezed June's hand. A picture of her brother's grave flashed in her mind.

"I'm sorry. Thank you." June sat back. "There's something I don't understand. When you were shipped stateside and discharged, why didn't you go back for her?"

Charles rocked on the glider, silent for a few moments. "I was young and foolish and proud." He paused again and exhaled. "I didn't think she'd have me. I didn't think she'd want half a man."

June looked at him confused.

He knocked on his thigh, a low thunk echoed around the porch.

"I not only lost these." He held up his hand with the remaining three fingers. "I lost the whole damn leg."

June started to open her mouth in some kind of misguided protest, but James shot her a look.

"I know what you kids must be thinking. It was different back then. I was a cripple. What chance did I have in the real world? I left whole and came back half a man."

A surge of panic and pity washed over June. She hadn't realized how much she'd counted on seeing Violet and Charles dance together again. *Did James get there before me?*

"I did go back." Charles continued. "After I went through rehab and got my peg leg, as I like to call it." He knocked on it again. "I went back to Mrs. Peppy's tailor shop. Know what I found?"

They shook their heads.

"A sign on the door: Closed — Due to Illness. I went to her old apartment. She wasn't there. Neighbor said her Pop had died. There was a young couple living there in our — her place." Charles wiped his eyes, again.

"Damn dust. Anyway, I looked and searched. I couldn't find her. Biggest regret of my life."

That's it? Anger rose in June's chest. Her hands started to shake. She searched James's face for a clue to proceed. He reached over and held her forearm, giving her a calming squeeze. It worked. She let the silence stretch out before them. She could quiet her tongue even if she couldn't hide her feelings. The rickety plank in her head splintered beneath her.

"Trust me little lady, there's not a day goes by, that I don't wonder what would've happened if I'd not of been wounded. If I hadn't felt so damn sorry for myself. If I'd come back sooner. It's enough what ifs, to drive a man crazy."

June was about to burst. She looked at James. He nodded.

"I have another what if." She took a deep breath. "What if I told you we knew where she was?"

Silence. Charles's shoulders began to shake. He sobbed quietly. June didn't know where to look. He sopped his streaming eyes, cleared his throat, and offered no apologies.

June was trespassing again, this time on a sacred ground.

Charles sat up straight. "Let me get this straight. You kids know where Violet Woe is? How the hell, pardon my French. I tried everything I could think of. I looked up her old friends, but none of them knew where she'd gone. When the interweb came out, I looked there and found nothing but her birth and school records. She'd disappeared." A smile spread across his face. "I want to hear all about her."

June and James took turns telling the story of finding the jitterbug dress, meeting Violet, and becoming friends. They reminisced about the apartment and the shop. He couldn't believe she was back living there after all these years. June told him about Jeannie and Wally's passing. His eyes glossed over, but he smiled and told stories of meeting them and hanging out at the malt shop.

He remembered Paddy and Wally, and Wally working at the malt shop. He told them about a girl who'd flirt with him and tick off Violet. By the time June and James headed out, he had them laughing so hard they were crying. June said nothing of her fantastic suspicion that he and Violet could be her biological grandparents.

The three of them came up with a plan, if Charles could wait that long. He could. June couldn't wait to get home and tell Clara, but first she had a special errand to run and hoped she could trust James.

"Are you sure you want me to come with you?" James asked before they got out of the car at the cemetery.

Her emotions were stretched taut and thin, but she was sure. She nodded.

"James this is Julian. Julian this is James." June stood over the granite marker, a myriad of emotions competed for dominance. Resolve rose to the top.

"He was my brother, my twin, my best friend, and my parents made me act like he never existed. You're staying in his room." She sank down and sat in front of the plaque. James sat down beside her, took her hand, and waited.

"What if I'm going crazy?" She raked her free hand through the grass. "I keep having nightmares of the accident. Weird episodes of feeling like I'm going to die. Like I'm having a heart attack, or aneurysm, or that my brain will never be right again."

"Do you want to talk about it?"

"Yeah." She felt the fear and tears gathering inside her. "It was random. Stupid." She punched the earth. "We were hiking South Mountain. We hiked almost every Saturday morning. We were six." When she said his age, her breath flew out of her. His sweet face appeared crisp in her mind—hair falling over one eye, devilish smirk, inquisitive, teal eyes. He was so handsome. He was going to grow up and be something amazing.

She hitched her breath. "I walked along the path holding

Dad's hand. Mom and Julian were behind us. Dad and I turned a corner. I bent to pick up a pretty rock that looked like petrified wood. I heard a scream. Pain. Fear. My body prickled with charged particles. I knew that voice.

"*Julian,* my mother shouted. Joining his howl. His stopped. Only my mother's high-pitched shriek remained. Dad ran back. Leapt in bounds. I couldn't keep up. Hikers from behind and in front drew toward the edge of the cliff.

"Mom tottered on the precipice. Dad pulled her back before she went over. She pushed him away and threw herself on the hard packed dirt, trying to edge over the ravine.

"*My shoe. My shoe. I was tying my shoe. Oh, God. I have to save him. My baby. My boy.* She flopped like a fish on deck. Dad pulled her back. Several people called 911.

"Julian was gone. Dead. I could feel it in my center. My head ached. My body shook with fear. Snakes crawled through my veins. A big hollow space expanded inside me. I was alone."

June sobbed so hard she couldn't speak.

She cried harder than she ever remembered crying. James held her and rocked her. She laid her head on his chest. He stroked her hair and rubbed her back until her sobs subsided.

After a half hour, June hiccupped and pulled away from James. "Thank you." She laid her head on Julian's grave.

James nodded. "That's a heavy burden to carry alone. Is there anything I can do?"

"You already have. I don't think it will cure all my panicky moments, but I feel lighter and stronger."

"We don't have to do the contest tonight if you don't want to." James laid down beside her, his shoulder touching hers. She liked it.

"I want to. Julian and I used to play we were Fred Astaire and Ginger Rogers after watching their movies. He'd want me to keep dancing. Striving to be the best."

Clad in a vintage western suit and hand-painted horse tie, Big Sandy doubled as a caballero out of an old movie. His moon-pie face glowed beneath his black silk hair while he crooned to the audience. After almost every song, he acknowledged the jitterbugs with a, "Thank ya dancers."

That's why we love you, Big Sandy. June smiled up at the stage. No other bandleader ever made the dancers feel more welcome. The live music filled her up in ways dee-jayed music never could. Big Sandy satiated June's and everyone's euphonious need.

Low cocktail tables edged the dance floor. Rockabillies and hoppers jammed themselves into every space and chair available. An indigo curtain displaying The Rhythm Room's logo hung behind the musicians. The black walls and ceiling created an underground grotto effect in the boxy building.

June and James advanced through the first round of the contest. Her old friends cheered her on, though she felt their expectations pressing her like a weight. She'd screwed up the same lift she'd been having trouble with in practice. James, covered her mistake, but it'd shaken her confidence. Her stomach burbled, and the icky feeling raced through her veins as the finals drew closer.

After the first round, James dashed off to talk to Stan. June wanted to practice. Instead, she approached Big Sandy and thanked him and the band for a great set. Big Sandy grabbed her hand and didn't let go.

June wasn't attracted to Big Sandy, but not un-attracted to him either. She was supposed to be dating Kris and felt the same way about him. Big Sandy made her feel desirable. *Did being desired create desire?* She smiled at his moony face and relaxed. *Holding hands is sweet.*

James and Stan walked over to them. James's eyes flicked down to where Big Sandy held June's hand. James narrowed his eyes. June blushed and had an urge to let go. She didn't.

"Robert, do you have a minute?" Stan asked Big Sandy, using his real name. "June, I was talking to your partner about you two doing a workshop for me. I meant it last night. James'll fill you in the dates I'm looking at for you guys."

"June, mind if we talk over our dance strategy?" James's voice had a strange edge.

"I'm sorry. Is this your gal?" Big Sandy asked.

June scrunched her face and snatched back her hand. "I'm no one's gal but my own." She marched away. *Why did that bother me? Am I still reeling from the meeting with Charles? Talking about Julian? I don't know, but they're all bugging me.*

James caught up with her and grabbed her arm. "June, wait."

She shook him off and continued through the door. Once outside, the glamour of the club, Big Sandy's attention, and the suspended reality fell away. She stood against the club wall and closed her eyes. James leaned next to her. *I won't cry.* She kept her eyes closed until the feeling passed.

When she opened her eyes, James had a pained expression.

"Uh, Robert, Big Sandy, told me to give you this."

He shoved a white card at her. Her hand brushed his—and though she'd held his hand a million times before—this time his touched tingled her skin. He watched her as she turned the card over and read the handwritten scrawl of a phone number.

"So you gonna call him?"

"Should I?"

Their eyes met. The current between them surged. They inched forward. Every pore on his handsome face shone clear and bright. His chest rose and fell with measured breaths. They leaned closer. June took a deep breath and parted her lips.

"Are we gonna try to win this contest or what?" He popped up from the wall and held out his hand in dance position.

June pressed her lips into a thin line. "I don't think so. I can't get that move, and I'm off tonight. I'm not good enough."

"Come on, June. When are you going to start believing in yourself?"

"Maybe when we win."

She took his hand, and they practiced until it was time for the finals. They didn't win.

Violet ~ 1940s & 1990s
32. Sing Song Swing
(Ella Fitzgerald)

The restaurant lounge looked exactly as it had fifty years ago. Dark wood booths decorated in reds and browns surrounded a long bar and small dance floor like a cozy brocade cave. It smelled the same, too. Garlic, steak, and odors associated with manly food, wafted from the restaurant.

"I can't believe my eyes. Letty, is it really you? No, it can't be. How many years has it been?" Felix, the maître de, rolled his Rrrs like a Spanish Prince.

"Too many to count," Violet replied.

"Are you going to sing for us tonight?"

"Perhaps. It's been a long, long time."

She kissed Felix on both cheeks, smiled, and glowed at the warm reception. Peeking over his shoulder, she scanned the room looking for the kids. She found them with Clara holding court in a corner booth. The high red leather seat framed her like a queen. Clara spied Violet and raised her drink in acknowledgement. The gang was all there except for June and James who were in Phoenix. *When Clara invited me here for drinks, I almost fell off my seat, but how could Clara have known I had a history with the place.*

More unbelievable, sitting at the piano was an old friend, Jon LaDuc. *I didn't realize he was still alive, let alone still playing.* He'd played with the best of them, Miller, Goodman, James. A few years Violet's senior, his blonde hair had turned platinum. Deep crevices lined his face. She touched her own hair, fluffing the loose curls, soft brunette—June and Clara had convinced her to dye the gray. She looked and felt ten years younger.

When she was younger, she wondered at what age she'd stop

caring about her appearance. After Wally and Jeannie died, she let herself go a little. *Dignity had nothing to do with age, and everything to do with having people who cared.*

Violet's stage persona possessed her as she sauntered toward the piano.

"Aren't you a sight for sore eyes?" Jon stood from behind the piano. His smile crinkled his face.

"Good to see you, Jon. What in the world are you doing back here?"

"What can I say? History repeats itself. These kids love the old standards. They come to dance, sip martinis, and play at being 1940s guys and dolls. They want to be us in our youth."

"I know. See that handsome crowd over there? I'm with them."

"No kidding? Grandkids?"

"No, but wouldn't that be a lark?" Violet laughed.

"I have to say it's a might bit more fun than weddings and anniversaries."

Violet nodded and winked.

"What are you up to these days?" Jon got a mischievous look in his eye. "Maybe you should come in with me. I could use a good set of pipes."

"Ah, I don't know. These pipes are old and rusty, my friend."

"Come on, let's try one out. How 'bout an Anita O'Day or Betty Hutton song, nice easy range. Make an old friend happy."

"How can I resist?" She set her handbag behind a scruffy piano leg.

"Ladies and gentlemen," Jon dripped into the mic. "Tonight we have a special guest, not only a personal friend, a hell of a canary, but a classic songbird from the golden era. I give you Miss Letty Starr."

Violet's young friends' faces reflected their confusion. She winked at them and leaned back against the piano. The mic smelled of stale whiskey, just the way she remembered. It made her smile. She relaxed and glided into *I'm Beginning to See the Light.*

Jon's agile fingers drifted across the eighty-eights. Violet held her own, feeling better than good. She felt terrific, almost as good as dancing. She played with the phrasing. Jon followed her, giving her extra counts. He complimented her last note with an energetic tink on the keys. The cocktailers jumped to their feet clapping, not thunderous, but sweet and appreciative. She took a bow then gestured to Jon. He stood and took his own bow.

"How 'bout another?" he whispered.

"Later, I promise."

She grabbed her handbag and sashayed to her young friends. Their faces beamed, and they scooted around the booth to make room. Felix brought an extra chair. Before Violet could catch her breath, Felix had set a Cosmopolitan in front of her as well as a dish of bar snacks. *How could he remember after all these years?*

"On the house, my dear."

"Can I get anyone else, anything?" asked the perky waitress at Felix's side.

"I'll take another Bourbon, neat, and she'll have a Lemon Drop. How about you Larissa? Ready for another?" Gary asked.

"Ummmm. Can't decide." She swished the remaining liquid and licked a bit of sugar from the rim.

"She'll take another Lemon Drop. How about you?" He pointed to Kris and Marty.

"I'm good," Kris replied.

Marty picked up his bottle, swirled it, and downed the last of the amber liquid. "I'll take another one of these, thanks."

"You were amazing," Larissa said. "You sound like all my favorite big band singers."

"She dances, she sings, she sews, what don't you do?" Gary asked.

"I hope that's not all we get to hear tonight. Quite the enigma aren't you Vi, or should I call you Letty?" Clara grinned.

Violet wasn't sure how much to tell.

"Let's just say, at one point in my life I no longer wanted to be Violet Woe. I needed another name, something more glamorous for my new line of work. So I became Letty Star."

"It sounds so mysterious." Larissa picked through the bar snacks.

"Not really, but I'm glad you think so."

"I'm confused. How do the piano player and Felix know you as Letty?" Clara asked.

"I met them after I left San Diego. I met Jon in Las Vegas."

"So do you feel more like a Jitterbug or a canary?" Larissa asked.

What an odd question. She'd spent more of her life singing, but there was a lot of jitterbugging in those years, too. Every time she heard a solid beat, something inside her started to roll—and old as she was—she had to dance. Right then, Jon launched into a great version of Benny Goodman's, *Roll 'Em.* Violet's feet started tapping. Earnest faces turned toward her, waiting for an answer.

"Kris, would you do me the honors?" She held out her hand.

He was slow on the uptake, but then was on his feet, guiding her to the dance floor. She smiled at the table, raised an eyebrow, and shrugged. Her heart knew the answer better than her mind. Kris swung her out, and she was lost in the rhythm.

June ~1990s
33. Boogie Woogie on a Saturday Night
(Stompy Jones)

The time for the International Jitterbug Contest had come. June and James made it to the finals. Her hands were damp and sticky, her stomach gurgled. Waves of hot and cold competed with dizziness. She was afraid she'd pass out. Her panic magnified her unease as hard pains twisted in her gut. She balled her hands into fists and shuddered.

"Breathe June," James whispered in her ear. His breath on her neck distracted her for a moment and calmed her nerves. When he pulled away cool air filled the void, and she was back to feeling sick. Yup, she was going to be sick. She dashed past two other finalist and ran for the bathroom. She didn't want to barf on anyone's shoes.

After coming in second at the Big Sandy contest, she and James had come home and worked like never before. James still had an odd vibe around him whenever they weren't working on dance, but they were almost always working on dance. They met on campus at lunchtime, dancing on the grass, throwing aerials on the lawn. Coeds would walk by and glance at them, some amused, some annoyed, but most indifferent.

June was surprised neither of them had been fired at work, either. Their manager caught them twice dancing in the stockroom when they were supposed to be shelving. Not to mention the looks they got when someone would catch them swinging-out behind a shoe display.

Amy videotaped the Phoenix competition, and James spent

hours dissecting every step, everybody angle, every shoulder shrug, line, and smile. James and Rose got into a fight over it. Rose tired of watching videos of June and James dancing. June guessed they'd reached a truce. Rose wouldn't say anything about the practices, and he wouldn't say anything about not telling her folks they were engaged.

The entire gang had planned to stay at Rose's parent's house for the contest weekend—it was big enough—but Rose never mentioned it again. No one knew if she'd even show for the contest. James didn't talk about it. June didn't ask.

◆◈ ◆ ◈◆

"June, are you okay?" James asked through the door.

I can't do it. I can't go through with it. I'm not ready. Her stomach clenched again, though there was nothing left.

"June. We gotta get out there."

She pressed her hands into the hollows of her cheeks, gritting her teeth, willing herself not to cry. Her entire body crawled with spiders and nervous adrenaline coursed through her veins. Hot. Cold. Hot. Cold.

She'd had no idea what a big event the International Jitterbug Contest was. If she had, she might not have agreed to it. She and James were in with the best in the world—New York, L.A., Sweden, Germany, and June and James from San Diego.

James tapped on the door. "June. We got this. We made it this far. It's all fun from here on out."

"Okay. Okay," she whispered, then said louder, "I can do this."

"What? I can't hear you." He rapped on the door again.

I can do this. I'm not going to die. I'm not going to pass out. I won't hurl on the dance floor. I've already thrown up. I owe it to James. I owe it to Julian. I owe it to myself. I can do this.

"Okay. Okay." She opened the door.

"Gum?" He handed her a stick, and she popped it into her

sour mouth, looking for somewhere to put the wrapper. James smiled and extended his hand. She gave him the balled wrapper, and he put the foil pea in his pocket.

"You know we got this, Kid." He put his arm around her shoulder and kissed her forehead. Fire curled through her body, but she couldn't think about that right now. She had to focus. Violet crept into her mind. *Has Violet found out about the secret plan? What if it all goes wrong? What if I pass out? What if I miss a step?*

James gave her hand a squeeze. "Time to go."

They walked hand in hand to the edge of the floor, joining the other contestants. A soft glow from the stage illuminated the dance floor and crowd. Balmy, thick air saturated the room.

Hailey, the pert promoter and organizer, took the stage and re-introduced Dean Mora and his Modern Rhythmist. The band embodied 1930s Hollywood. The musicians sported matching tuxedos, the singer shimmered in a sequined, full-length gown. Dean's band would play live for this last showdown.

Hailey, an accomplished jitterbug in her own right, signaled her stagehand. He ushered out June, James, and the other finalists to the empty floor in front of the stage. A semi-circle of dancers, six rows deep, lined the perimeter in anticipation. June chomped on her gum at a furious pace, never letting go of James's hand. *You can do this, June. You can do this.* She chanted in her head.

"Okay jitterbugs, you know the rules: you have eight eight-counts to do your thing, and then come back in line to do it again. Dean is going to increase the tempo on your second go-round. Then it's everyone on the floor for an all-skate. The band will turn on the gas, and you'll give it all you've got. Don't forget NO aerials during the all-skate."

June eyed the completion, taking in everyone's costume choice. The SoCal dancers rocked the vintage while the Swedes, New Yorkers, and Germans preferred satin outfits reminiscent of

Whitey's Lindy Hoppers. James had pieced together an authentic WWII Navy Uniform, and June wore the dress. *I'm wearing the dress.* She loved the way it swished around her legs and wrapped around her thighs like a morning glory. It was Violet's winning dress, but now hers. She'd become the girl in the jitterbug dress. *I am the girl in the jitterbug dress and I can do this.*

The seated audience started drumming the floor with their bare hands, others stomped and clapped. Hailey's last words were lost in the thunder as Dean struck up the band.

June and James were third in line. The rhythm of a hundred stomping feet miraculously synched with the band. June watched and waited. The floor vibrated under her feet. *I am the girl in the jitterbug dress.* A surge of joy curled up her spine and mixed the anxiety into a perfect tonic. *I'm ready. I can't wait to swing.*

She watched in awe and delight as the first two couples flew around the floor. Dance moves from old movie clips were repeated and enhanced. Those in the know cheered at the homage. As much as everything was derivative, she was proud of the original moves she and James had created. In the weeks leading up to the contest, June would fall into bed exhausted, but dream new combinations and footwork. Other times, she'd have a burst of inspiration while practicing. James was hesitant to try her ideas, but when he saw them work, he began consulting her on everything. They'd become equals.

Vintage-clad and topped with a newsboy cap, Hailey's right-hand-man gave June and James their cue. They entered with jig walks — swinging like saloon doors — and into a quick flip. June tucked backwards, landed, and slid into the splits. The floor under her legs felt good and cool. The crowd clapped wildly. June's feet flicked fast, and they nailed the facing Charleston with original variations. The jitterbug dress swished around her legs, music coursed through her blood. Before she was ready to stop, their first solo time was up.

They joined the queue and waited for their second shine time. The band cranked up the tempo and their competitors pulled out all the stops. June had never seen so many crazy aerials in such a short amount of time, but she liked the fancy footwork best.

Their second turn came quick. She was ready and gave into the joy. James's smile charged her with confidence and security. The music pulsed through her body and into James's, connecting them like never before.

Air rushed by and tickled her skin as she flew around James in Dean Collins swing-outs. Her nemesis of a move was coming up. Her nerves prickled. Then momentum and determination took over. James tugged. Her feet pushed off the floor, toes, arch, heel, calves, thighs, hips, all working in synch to lend her flight. And she flew. Perfectly. Landing with grace and spring, hitting the footwork with hot stepping rhythm.

James gave her a wink. She returned it with a smirk, continuing into shadow Charleston with double drops thrown in. June glowed, starlight shining out of every pore.

They returned to the line and waited for the all-skate. Mora turned up the tempo again, and Hat Boy gave the finalists a last nod. Complete bedlam. The drummer cracked the whip, the horns trumpeted like stampeding elephants. June was on a boat in a roiling sea, James her life jacket. At tempos that fast, they were flying blind, and the dance became all instinct, training, and talent. June did more than keep her head above water. She sailed across the polished wood floor with James, the underdog pirates conquering all. The audience lent their energy, and she gave it back to them ten-fold.

The band began winding up for a big ending. The room took a collective breath. Ten sweating, spinning, swirling bodies left the earth for the briefest of seconds, and when the song clashed to its finish, every competing arm, leg, torso, and head melted to the floor in a puddle of near-lifeless jitterbugs. The tableau looked like an unseen director had ordained a simultaneous *Groovie Movie* re-enactment.

June's chest heaved, rills of perspiration dripped earthbound. She laid motionless for five counts as all the competitors played dead. Then, with applause so loud it swayed the old building, they rose, joined hands, and bowed together in mutual respect, turned and clapped for the band. The room shimmered with community.

The guys shook hands, the women hugged — their faces shiny with sweat and etched with smiles. Each of the competitors wanted to win, but were bound to each other in their final struggle and their collective caper. Hailey re-appeared and shook Dean's hand.

"Now that, my friends," she said to the crowd, "is the spirit of jitterbug. That's why we're here and with your help we can continue this for many years to come. I hope this is the beginning of many years dancing together. Let's hear it for the amazing Dean Mora and his Modern Rhythmist."

The room exploded with applause.

"And how about our finalist? I don't know how they did it, and I wish I would've thought of it, but that ending. That's one of the most amazing, good-spirited contest wrap-ups I've ever seen. Let's hear it again for your Hollywood jitterbugs."

More ear-splitting applause.

"I know you have your favorites and ideas about who you think should walk away with the trophy, but you're gonna have to wait until the end of the night when we announce our winning couple."

A few good-meaning groans and humorous heckles sprinkled across the crowd.

"I know, I know. I can't wait myself, but we've got Dean to keep us company for the next hour. Then, another event you've been waiting for, our Masters Q and A, and one more set from

Dean. So without further ado, Dean, take it away."

"One down and one to go," James said. "Do you need to rest, cuz I'd like to just dance with you? I'm kinda keyed up."

"Me too. Isn't that funny? I should be exhausted, but I'm totally buzzing."

"Wait until we crash and the adrenaline wears off. Remember how tired you were after the Phoenix contest? I almost got lost getting back to your folks' place. I couldn't wake you."

"Oh yeah, I forgot about that."

He smiled. "Never mind the dancing. Let's get out of here. You wanna go get a snack or a drink. I'm all jangly. My nerves are raw."

"Really?" June eyed him curiously. "You? Nervous?"

He laughed and shook his head, guiding her off the dance floor, his arm around her. She liked it.

"How do you think we did?" June couldn't stop talking. "I think we did great. Wasn't that couple from New York amazing? Did you see any moves you might want to pilfer? I can't believe we pulled off that ending. That was so cool. Whose idea was it anyway? I can't believe everyone went for it. I could almost go for popcorn and beer in the hotel room with an old movie. Isn't that funny?"

June took a breath as they walked through the backstage door to outside. "Remember, popcorn and beer when we first started practicing at your place? James, have I thanked you? I mean really thanked you for everything? You're amazing, I'm so lucky to…"

James kissed her. Hard. On her squawking mouth. His hands tightened on her arms and pulled her toward him. It took her two seconds to catch up, and she jumped in with both feet. Her hands wound around his neck. They pressed their churning bodies together. The stress and tension of the past months poured into their limbs. The cool night air was no match for their overheated bodies.

Condensation surrounded them like a shroud. Her body jumped to attention but at the same time melted into his. Rolling tremors started deep within her core and fanned outward. Her body flamed, and she opened her mouth, devouring his. His mouth was warm with salt and a faint hint of mint. She didn't remember when they'd thrown their gum away.

His hands caressed her damp skin. *The jitterbug dress feels paper thin or does it feel too thick?* She wasn't sure, but knew she wanted more. He wanted more, but they were sweaty messes and dared not leave each other's lips. They kissed like the first and last and best kiss in all of time.

"Let's get out of here," June whispered.

"As...you...wish," he replied. "As long as we make it back for the next band break."

She gave him a confused look.

"Violet?"

"Oh yeah. She said she had something important to tell me, but wanted to wait until after the contest. Do you think she found out about our surprise?"

"I honestly don't know, but we better be back in time to find out. Let's run back to that Chinese joint. See if we can get some fried won tons and a beer." He held her hand and started walking toward the restaurant. "Or a Mandarin Special?"

"What's a Mandarin Special?" June asked.

"I don't know, wanna find out?"

"I do."

Violet ~ 1990s
34. The Best Things Happen While You're Dancing
(Danny Kaye)

Dean Mora's band continued to impersonate a 1930s jazz band to the delight of everyone in the room. Vibrant notes bounced off the high ceiling of the WWII era building. Violet spied June in the back of the hall and trod through the throng of dancers, edging her way down one side of the dance floor.

"June, I'm so glad I found you." Violet gave June a big hug. "Where'd you run off to? Clara's been looking all over for you. She told me how sick you were before the contest and then you disappeared right after. We were all worried about you." Violet's eyes were soft with concern.

"I'm sorry, Vi."

"Never you worry. This is your night. June honey, you and James were fantastic. Fluidity, two halves of a whole."

"Thank you. We couldn't have done it without you."

"Yes you could've." June started to open her mouth. "Eh, eh, eh, don't protest. I'm happy to have played a small part. But that's not what I wanted to talk to you about." Violet guided June to a quiet room off the main floor.

June's face brimmed with happiness and excitement. *Maybe now's not the right time to tell her.* Violet didn't want to spoil the night. She pushed on. "June, I know you were really excited about the idea of us being related." June's smile almost undid Violet and shook her resolve. "Remember when I didn't come to the Swivel launch party?"

"Yeah, I was disappointed you missed it."

"Well, that same weekend I took a trip across the border."

Violet wrung her hands, her heart hurt to tell June.

"Oh?" June looked confused and leaned against a set of built-in cupboards.

"You know how you entertained the idea of us being related? Me perhaps being your maternal grandmother?"

"Yeah."

"I'm sorry dear, but I went down to...." *Why am I so nervous?* "I'm disappointed. I had so wanted...."

"Oh, I see." June's face fell. She mashed her lips together with a resigned smile. Violet's heart ached. She wanted to put a claim on June, change the past.

"I wanted to be sure. I wanted to bring you proof. I really, really wanted to be the grandmother you were looking for."

"But you are." June moved off the cupboards and took a step toward Violet. "And, it doesn't matter whether we are blood related. In my heart, we're family."

Buried emotions bubbled through Violet. She closed her eyes for a moment, a grateful smile spread across her face.

"June you came into my life and gave me hope and love and friendship at a time when I thought I was at the jumping off point. You made me want to go a few more miles. Thank you for letting me love you."

June threw her arms around Violet. Violet melted in the hug like the long lost grandmother she wanted to be.

"June dear," Violet continued, "It's not that you are or you aren't, or I am or am not. It's that there was a terrible earthquake which caused a flood of the records building. I've been waiting this last month to hear if my records were salvaged and saved to microfiche, but the truth is, they found nothing. There's no record on their computer files and nothing in their archives. There's no record of me or my baby."

"Well it's settled then. You are. I am. We are."

"June, how'd I get so lucky to find you. And you're right. We feel like family." They hugged again. Violet filled with joy. *I love this girl.*

An event assistant came to fetch Violet for her turn in the spotlight. She and June wiped the tears from their smiling faces. Violet followed the young man to a long table, set up in front of the stage. Evenly spaced microphones sprouted like silver tulips along its length. She took her seat next to a fella named Ray, a fellow contest winner from the 40s.

Violet was still unsure about the Question and Answer session, but June's love and acceptance strengthened her. She didn't know how the gang had talked her into being part of the event. She'd only won the one jitterbug contest and most of the panel was made up of the surviving 1940s and 1950s Hollywood Dancers and some of The Ray Brand Dance Troop.

Even though Violet had never met her fellow old-timers, their faces were familiar beneath their aged mask. James had played the clips so many times that the images were burned into her brain. Clara sent the 1942 Spring Fling Swing article and jitterbug picture of Charles and Violet to Hailey, who insisted Violet attend. She couldn't say no. She'd planned on coming to watch June and James dance, anyway.

Plus, Violet loved Hailey's story of how the event came to be. Hailey and her friend Percy wanted to bring back the heyday of the old Hollywood Jitterbugs and preserve the World War II style of swing dancing.

Percy had already amassed vintage video clips from every old movie featuring all forms of jitterbug. Once he and his fellow dancers gleaned all the dancing they could from the clips, he began tracking down old-timers who were still alive. Not only the movie dancers, but anyone who'd won a contest during the war years. *I qualified.*

I thought June and her gang an anomaly, but seeing the sold-out crowd, I was wrong. The balmy room in West Hollywood filled to the brim with fledgling jitterbugs waiting to pick her brain.

Hailey floated onto the scene in her second outfit of the night, a tailored—*His Girl Friday*, hard-boiled, 1940s journalist—suit. Violet had a feeling it wouldn't be her last. What fun to still play dress-up at her age.

The panelist introduced themselves and more. The man sitting next to Violet listed his dance achievements, his former profession, and his golf stats. *I used to think people grew wiser and improved their character flaws as they aged, but no, some people's flaws became more pronounced. I hope I've improved on mine.* She shook her head.

Behind them, a screen slid down in front of the empty bandstand. A slide show alternated pictures of each of the panelists in their jitterbugging heyday. The old-timers were questioned about what gum they chewed. What kind of car they drove. What it was like to dance to the big guys like Artie Shaw, surprised that Shaw thumbed his nose at jitterbugs, he didn't play swing—he played jazz. Violet winked at her young friends in the audience. James gave her a thumbs-up, Clara a salute, and June a proud smile.

The young dancers continued the questions. Where'd they shopped? Who was their favorite singer? And what was the preferred dance shoe? *Wedgies, of course.*

After the Q and A, it was time for the old-timers to show their stuff. More women than men were still alive so Hailey had arranged a few younger leads to aid in the showcase. James was more than willing to lead Violet. The old-timers transformed into spry jitterbugs on the dancefloor. Gratitude and pride welled up in Violet, honored to be in their company. James swirled her around the floor to the delight and awe of the young crowd.

The pre-recorded song came to an end. The screen rolled back into the ceiling and Hailey took the stage, again, this time in a lovely rayon gown in canary yellow. The spotlight glinted off the antique microphone. Everyone turned to her.

"What time is it?" Hailey cupped her hand around her ear.

"Jitterbug time." The audience yelled back.

"I can't hear you. What time is it?"

"JITTERBUG TIME!" The crowd's voices filled the hall with claps and stomps.

Hailey smiled and nodded. "I know you're all dying to know who won the contest. All of them are exceptional dancers and any one of them could have taken the top spot." She turned to Dean. "Can I get a drum roll?" He cued his drummer.

"I'm proud to announce this year's winners of the International Jitterbug Contest, newcomers James Clark and June Andersen from San Diego!"

Violet clapped and yelled as loud as she could. June and James made their way to the stage—James, handsome in his sailor dress whites, June, with the jitterbug dress dancing around her legs. *Don't they look amazing? Look at my old Jitterbug dress on June. I love that she gave it new life. She gave me new life. They both did.*

Hailey presented the trophy to them. James held June tight around the waist. They smiled at each other. June whispered something in James's ear. He smiled and nodded. June disappeared backstage.

Yes, I think there is something more between them.

"Now before we bring Dean Mora back for his last set." Hailey took the mic. "We've got a little business to take care of. As you know it wasn't all dance halls and soda fountains in the 1940s. There was a war going on. Friends, families, and loved ones were separated. Not everyone came back."

The twittering and soft talk silenced. Hailey relinquished the mic to James.

"Around the world POWs are still unaccounted for. I know it's hard for us to imagine, but these fellas were our age and younger when they took the pledge and joined the armed forces.

It wasn't all big bands, jitterbug, and fun fashions. The world was at war. Our lives today could be very different. We are here today because of them."

Hailey and Dean nodded. James gestured to the old-timers, sitting at the table. "Take a minute tonight to thank those folks in front of you for the sacrifices they and their generation made. Not only the soldiers, but the brave men and women who kept the factories working and kept the home fires burning. Let's have a moment of silence for those who cannot be here, but are not forgotten."

A hundred heads nodded, eyes dropped to the floor. Hope and love coalesced into quiet reverence.

After a full minute of silence James continued. "Thank you. Sometimes things that are lost for a long time are finally found. This is one of those times. With a lotta help, a lotta digging, and a bit of luck, we found a long lost half of a winning team. A jitterbug couple separated by war and lost to time."

Violet looked at her fellow panelist trying to guess who it could be and looked up at James questioningly. James smiled and flicked his eyes toward the audience, then made his way to Violet's side. A spotlight scanned the crowd and stopped.

Violet gasped and forgot to breathe. She swayed on her feet. James steadied her.

June stood next to *him*, her Jitterbug sailor. Arms locked.

Violet saw a ghost, a waking dream. Tiny pins pricked behind her eyes.

She trembled.

Her eyes filled with tears.

My body is too small, too insignificant, too frail to hold these feelings inside me.

Violet took a ragged breath. June chewed the corner of her mouth. June's eyes searched Violet's for acceptance. Violet smiled, and a tear rolled down her cheek.

Afraid she'd break the spell. Violet froze at James's side. Then Charles stepped forward, leaning on a simple cane.

Violet's eyes locked on his, and his on hers, and although someone was talking, she couldn't hear a word of it. Everything around her was in slow motion except the steady even progress of this beautiful man walking up to her, his eyes never leaving her face. The how and whys collided, time folded and folded again. They reached across the years.

Charles's and Violet's names echoed from somewhere far away. He smelled like…pine and fresh baked biscuits. She rested her cheek on his firm chest.

From somewhere underwater soft music played, Charles started to sway. Violet followed. Rhythmic snaps whispered and called. The sublime slipped into reality.

"I'm not the man I used to be." He slid her hand to his prosthetic leg. Hot rhythm pulsed through her awakened body. The band was swinging. Her breath came in shallow gasps. She quivered.

"Hello Gorgeous."

"Hello sailor."

"May I have the next dance?"

Notes From the Author

The chapter titles are songs from Violet's and June's respective eras. They are meant to enhance the mood of each chapter and can be found with links on the website. I've fudged a little on release dates for June, but all her songs fall into the era of neo-swing, featuring a variety of big bands, jump blues, rockabilly, and Western swing bands. I tried to keep Violet's songs grounded in the swing era, but have borrowed from the 30s through the early 50s.

June's experiences are based on my experiences in Phoenix, Arizona, and San Diego, California, during the resurgence of swing and are an amalgamation of different venues, teachers, and dancers. Different parts of the country experienced this era in different ways, but my goal was to capture the excitement and energy of the worlds rekindled passion for swing dancing beginning for some in the 1980s but reaching fad popularity in the 1990s.

The slang used in the novel is derived from hours of watching old movies, particularly teen movies such as *Twice Blessed, Jive Junction, Don't Knock the Rock,* and others. A complete list of slang terms and their meaning can be found on the website.

It is my greatest desire that if you are a dancer, I brought those feelings back for you, and if you're not already a dancer, this book inspires you to go out and learn to Jitterbug.

Since the characters go through various life-changing events and face many moral challenges, there are in-depth Book Club discussion questions for your convenience on the website as well.

For exclusive stories, previews, give-aways, games, how-tos, interviews and more visit my website and sign up to follow at: www.girlinthejitterbugdress.com

Acknowledgements

To my mom, Judy Anderson, for listening and giving straight advice when I needed it. And for dancing around the living room while singing off key, always teaching me to live with zest and love. I wish you were here to see its publication. To my husband, David, and children, Clara and Chas, for letting me check out of the family for hours on end.

A very special thanks to Sarah Hendrix, Brian Reamer, Lynnda Shepherd, and Electra Hale for listening and brainstorming at the very beginning of this journey, another lifetime ago in San Diego.

Special thanks to the wonderful beta-readers who've added their input and time: Jeff Curtiss Welch, Jill Michalski, Sondra Schaible, Carol Januszeski, Mary Ann Fielder, Liza McCarthy, Suzanne Fulton, Marci Froh Willenberg, Ellen Massey (for a bit of un-tingling), and the Amazing Writer's Workshop in San Diego, Ca.

A big nod to Lockhart Area Writers: Janet Christian, Phil McBride, Pagan Jackson, Gretchen Rix, and Wayne Wathers for their work on the sequel which applied to the original, *The Girl in the Jitterbug Dress*.

Karen Phillips, www.phillipscovers.com for an original cover. Lauren Ashley Photography for the amazing cover photos at: www.laurenashleyphotography.net Kathy Anderson, www.andersonbusinesssupportservices.com for her amazing web design and unwavering belief in my writing. Candace Johnson from Change it Up Editing www.changeitupediting.com and Heather Wheat at wanderingbarkbooks.com for their wonderful manuscript evaluation.

And finally to ALL swing dancers I've had the honor of teaching and dancing with. Swing it, brother, swing.

Photo by Brian Tassie

About the Author

Tam Francis has taught swing dancing with her husband (a US Navy veteran of two wars) for fifteen years and is an avid collector of vintage patterns, vintage clothing, and antiques.

She's served as Editor-in-chief for two indie magazines: *From the Ashes* (Arts & Literature 1990-1994) and *Swivel: Vintage Living* (Swing dancing, vintage lifestyle culture 1994-2000).

Tam has been a poet, short story wordsmith, blogger, and novelist. She's currently working on The *Girl in the Jitterbug Dress* trilogy and the paranormal, time-travel, murder mystery romance, *The Flapper Affair*. For 1940's slang, music, fashion, games, freebies, and history, check out her blog at:

www.girlinthejitterbugdress.com

She now lives with her family in Lockhart, Texas in a 1908 home, and can be found on its wide porch with a pen in one hand and a vintage cocktail in the other.

If you enjoyed this story, please take a moment to write a review on Amazon and check out her other books.

Thank you for reading.

Made in United States
North Haven, CT
10 May 2022